RETURN
TO MARS

Other Fiction by Ben Bova

Moonwar
Moonrise
Orion Among the Stars
Death Dream
The Watchmen
To Fear the Light
    (with A. J. Austin)
Orion and the Conqueror
Sam Gunn, Unlimited
Empire Builders
Challenges*
Triumph
To Save the Sun
    (with A. J. Austin)
Mars
The Trikon Deception
    (with Bill Pogue)
Orion in the Dying Time
Future Crime*
Voyagers III: Star Brothers
Cyberbooks
Peacekeepers
Vengeance of Orion
The Kinsman Saga
Battle Station*
Voyagers II: The Alien
Within
Prometheans*
Privateers
The Astral Mirror*

Orion
Escape Plus*
The Winds of Altair
Test of Fire
Voyagers
The Exiles Trilogy
Kinsman
Maxwell's Demons*
Colony
The Multiple Man
Millennium
City of Darkness
The Starcrossed
End of Exile
Gremlins, Go Home!
    (with Gordon R. Dickson)
Forward in Time*
When the Sky Burned
As On a Darkling Plain
Flight of Exiles
THX 1138
    (with George Lucas)
Exiled from Earth
Escape!
The Dueling Machine
Out of the Sun
The Weathermakers
Star Watchman
The Star Conquerors

*collection

BEN BOVA

RETURN TO MARS

AVON · EOS

AVON BOOKS, INC.
1350 Avenue of the Americas
New York, New York 10019

Copyright © 1999 by Ben Bova
Interior design by Kellan Peck
ISBN: 0-380-97640-4
www.avonbooks.com/eos

Library of Congress Cataloging in Publication Data:

Bova, Ben, 1932–
Return to Mars / Ben Bova.—1st ed.
p.   cm.
I. Title.
PS3552.084R47   1999   99-21635
813'.54—dc21   CIP

First Avon Eos Printing: June 1999

AVON EOS TRADEMARK REG. U.S. PAT. OFF. AND IN OTHER COUNTRIES, MARCA REGISTRADA, HECHO EN U.S.A.

Printed in the U.S.A.

FIRST EDITION

QPM   10 9 8 7 6 5 4 3 2 1

To Barbara:

... constant as the northern star,
of whose true-fixed and resting quality
there is no fellow in the firmament.

ACKNOWLEDGMENTS

I owe an enormous debt of gratitude to Lynn Harper and her colleagues at the NASA Ames Research Center, who answered my myriad questions promptly and cheerfully and provided many of the technical details in this story (for example, making glass bricks from *in situ* materials on Mars). I have taken a novelist's liberties with their excellent information, of course, so any faults with the techniques and technologies used by the characters in this tale are my own, not theirs.

The mission plan for the Second Mars Expedition was adapted from the Mars Direct concept originated by Robert Zubrin, as detailed in his book, *The Case for Mars*. Again, I have deviated from the specifics of his concept, but the basic mission plan stems from his innovative and highly creative work.

Ed Carlson, South Florida Area Manager for the National Audubon Society, kindly provided the background information about the Living Machine, an organic technique for using solar energy, bacteria, and green plants to produce potable water from waste water. This served as the basis for my Martian explorers' garden, which provides them not only with the bulk of their food but recycles their water. Living Machines, designed and built by Ocean Arks International, are at work in South Burlington, Vermont; Sonoma, California; Henderson, Nevada; the Corkscrew Swamp Sanctuary in Collier County, Florida; and elsewhere.

Dr. Janet Jeppson Asimov kindly granted permission to quote the late Isaac Asimov's "classic" limerick.

My good friend Philip Brennan patiently detailed the methods used by modern geologists to date rocks.

Alexander Besher graciously answered my questions about the Russian language.

The term *bytelock* was coined by another good friend, Jan Howard Finder, who defines it thusly: "When the Information Superhighway slows to a crawl or stops, you are experiencing BYTELOCK!"

The quotation from Freeman J. Dyson is from "Warm-Blooded Plants and Freeze-Dried Fish," by Freeman J. Dyson, *The Atlantic Monthly*, Vol. 280, No. 5, November 1997, p. 69.

The quotation from Malcolm Smith originally appeared in "Facing Mars Rationally," by Malcolm Smith, in *Spaceflight* magazine, Vol. 40, No. 2, February 1998, p. 45.

We should not be surprised if we find that life, wherever it originated, spread rapidly from one planet to another. Whatever creatures we may find on Mars will probably be either our ancestors or our cousins.

FREEMAN J. DYSON

Certain topics in science are deemed "unsuitable." A form of scientific censorship arises to prevent these ideas getting out into wider circulation and challenging the current orthodoxy's accepted status quo. Yet the history of science is littered with ideas which were initially frowned upon, only to be accepted later, sometimes long after the death of their proponents.

MALCOLM SMITH

Listen to the wisdom of the Old Ones. The red world and the blue world are brothers, born together out of the same cold darkness, nourished by the same Father Sun. Separated at birth, for uncountable ages they remained apart. But now, like true brothers, they are linked once more.

PROLOGUE: THE SKY DANCERS

THE RENTAL MINIVAN JOLTED AND LURCHED ALONG THE RUTS OF THE UN-paved road as Jamie Waterman squinted briefly at the dying red sun touching the ragged skyline of the mountains. Jamie was driving too fast and he knew it. But he wanted to get there before his grandfather died.

Soon it would be dark and he'd have to slow down. The unmarked road twisting through the desert hills would be unlit except for his headlamps—and the stars. Might as well be driving the rover on Mars, he said to himself.

As the sun disappeared behind the distant mountains and the shadows reached across the desert to overtake him, Jamie knew he would have to stop again to ask directions. He had passed a hogan several miles back, but it had looked dark and empty.

Now he saw a mobile home, rusted metal sides and a slanted awning over the screen door. Lights inside. A pair of battered pickup trucks in front. As he pulled to a stop, spraying dust and pebbles, a dog yapped from out of the shadows.

The screen door banged open and a young man appeared in the doorway: jeans, tee shirt, can of beer clutched in one hand, long braided hair.

Jamie slid the driver's side window down and called, "I'm looking for Al Waterman."

With the light from inside the mobile home behind him, the young man's face was impossible to see. Jamie knew what it looked like, just the same: stolid, dark eyes, broad cheeks, emotions hidden behind an impassive mask. Much like his own.

"Who?"

"Al Waterman."

The young Navaho shook his head. "He don't live here."

"I know. He's in a hogan up along this road, I think. That's what they told me down at the post."

"Not here," the young man repeated.

Jamie understood his reticence. "He's my grandfather. He's dying."

The young Navaho stepped down to the dusty ground and slowly walked over to Jamie's minivan, boots crunching on the gritty soil.

He looked closely at Jamie. "You the guy who went to Mars?"

"Right. Al's my grandfather. I want to see him before he dies."

"Al Waterman. The old guy from Santa Fe."

Jamie nodded.

"I'll take you there. You can follow me." Without waiting for a reply he loped to the nearer of the two pickups.

"Don't drive too fast," Jamie called. He had driven across the badlands of Mars, but he didn't want to have to chase a pair of dim taillights at breakneck speed across the dark New Mexico desert.

Sure enough, the youngster took off in a roaring cloud of dust. Jamie shifted into four-wheel drive and followed him grimly, sweating as he wrestled the wheel of the jouncing minivan with both clenched hands.

Al Waterman had been a shopkeeper in Santa Fe all his adult life, with a condo in town and a ski lodge up in the mountains, but now that he was dying he had returned to the reservation where he had been born.

Everyone seemed to know about Al and his famous grandson, the man who had travelled to the red planet. Wherever Jamie stopped to ask directions, they knew exactly where Al's hogan was. Trouble was, Jamie thought as the minivan jolted through the darkness, there aren't any direction signs along these old roads. Nothing but darkness and the clear desert sky. Thousands of stars but not one sign to point his way.

At last the pickup skidded to a stop near the low hump of a hogan. Jamie pulled up beside him, but the young man was already backing his truck, heading home.

"Thanks!" Jamie yelled out his window.

" 'Kay," he heard from the truck as it spit gravel and roared off into the night.

Frightened of death, Jamie thought. The Navaho would not stay in a place where a death had occurred, whether out of respect or fear of evil spirits, Jamie did not know. They would abandon this hogan after Al died. I wonder what they do with mobile homes? Jamie asked himself as he got out of the minivan.

The hogan seemed little more than a rounded hump of dried mud on the desert floor with a single light shining through a curtained window. The night was chilly but still; the dark sky so clear that the sparkling stars seemed close enough almost to touch.

It was even colder, somehow, inside the hogan. Jamie kept his sky-blue windbreaker zippered; the pitiful little blaze in the fireplace cast flickering light, but no heat. An old woman sat on the floor in a corner near the fire, wrapped in a colorful blanket. She nodded once to Jamie but said nothing, silent and sturdy as a rock.

Al was curled fetally on the bed in the far corner, nothing but a shell of the man he had been; a husk whose insides had been devoured by cancers. Yet he opened his eyes and smiled when Jamie bent over him.

"Ya'aa'tey," he whispered. His breath smelled of decay and sun-baked earth.

"Ya'aa'tey," Jamie replied. It is good. That was a lie, in this place at this time, but it was the ancient greeting.

"That's what you said when you got to Mars," Al said, his voice already as faint as a ghost's. "Remember?"

They were the words Jamie spoke to the television camera when the first expedition landed.

"I'm going back there," Jamie said, bending low so his grandfather could hear him.

"Back to Mars? You're going?"

Nodding tightly, Jamie said, "It's official. I'll be mission director."

"Good," breathed Al, with a wan smile. "Mars is your destiny, son. Your path leads to the red world."

"I guess it does."

"Go in beauty, son. Now I can die happy."

Jamie wanted to say no, you're not going to die, Grandfather. You're going to live for many years more. But the words would not come to his lips.

Al heaved a sigh that racked his frail body. "The sky dancers are coming soon. They'll take me with them."

"Sky dancers?"

"You'll see. Wait with me. It won't be long now."

Jamie pulled up the hogan's only chair and sat by his grandfather's bed. His parents had been killed in an auto crash two years earlier. Al was the only close relative he had left. After him there would be nothing, no one. The old man closed his eyes. Jamie could not tell if he were breathing or not. The only sound in the chill little room was the crackling of the fire as the silent woman fed sticks to it.

The wooden chair was hard and stiff, its woven rope seat as unyielding as rock, yet Jamie dozed off despite himself. He stepped off a high cliff, naked in the hot sun, and began to fall, slowly, as in a dream, falling down the face of the blood-red mesa.

He awoke with a start. Al was clutching at his knee.

"The sky dancers!" Al croaked in his feeble voice. "They've come!"

He's delirious, Jamie thought. He turned to the woman, still sitting silently near the fire. She looked up at him with dark, calm eyes but said nothing.

"Look!" Al pointed a quavering finger toward the curtained window. "Go outside and look!"

Confused, Jamie pried himself out of the chair and went to the door. He hesitated, turned back toward his grandfather.

"Go on!" Al urged, excited, trying to lift himself up on one emaciated arm. "You'll see!"

Jamie opened the door and stepped out into the cold dark desert night. His breath frosted in the air. He looked up at the stars.

And saw shimmering curtains of delicate pinkish red, pale green, flickering white, pulsating across the sky, dancing silently, glittering, rippling, covering the sky with their ghostly glow.

The northern lights, Jamie knew. The sun must have erupted a monster flare. Then the Navaho side of his mind said, The sky dancers. They've come for Al.

Jamie stood transfixed, watching the delicate, awesome display in the night sky. He remembered that you could see auroras almost every night on Mars, even through the tinted visor of your spacesuit helmet. But here on Earth the sky dancers were rare. Yet so beautiful that they made even death seem less frightful.

At last he ducked back inside the hogan. His grandfather lay still, a final smile frozen on his face. The woman had come over to his bed and was smoothing Al's blanket over him.

"Good-bye, Grandfather," Jamie said. He felt he should cry, but he had no tears.

He went outside again, walking slowly toward his rental minivan. There's no one left, Jamie said to himself. No one and nothing left to keep me here.

Low on the rugged horizon the unblinking red eye of Mars stared at him, glowing, beckoning. Two weeks later he lifted off from Kennedy Space Center on a Clippership rocket, the first leg of his journey back to Mars.

DATA BANK

THE FIRST MARS EXPEDITION CONFIRMED MUCH OF WHAT EARLIER ROBOT spacecraft had discovered about the red planet.

Mars is a cold world. It orbits roughly one and a half times farther from the Sun than the Earth does. Its atmosphere is far too thin to retain solar heat. On a clear midsummer day along the Martian equator the afternoon ground temperature might climb to seventy degrees Fahrenheit; that same night, however, it will plunge to a hundred below zero or lower.

The atmosphere of Mars is too thin to breathe, even if it were pure oxygen, which it is not. More than ninety-five percent of the Martian air is carbon dioxide; nearly three percent nitrogen. There is a tiny amount of free oxygen and even less water vapor. The rest of the atmosphere consists of inert gases such as argon, neon and such, a whiff of carbon monoxide, and a trace of ozone.

The First Mars Expedition discovered, however, something that all the mechanical landers and orbiters had failed to find: life.

Tucked down at the floor of the mammoth Valles Marineris—the Grand Canyon that stretches some three thousand kilometers across the ruddy face of the planet—sparse colonies of lichenlike organisms eke out a perilous existence, hiding a few millimeters below the surface of the rocks. They soak up sunlight by day and absorb the water they need from the vanishingly tiny trace of water vapor in the air. At night they become dormant, waiting for the sun's warmth to touch them once again. Their cells are bathed in an alcohol-rich liquid that keeps them from freezing even when the temperature falls to a hundred degrees below zero or more.

Fourth planet out from the Sun, Mars never gets closer to the Earth than fifty-six million kilometers, more than a hundred times farther than the Moon. Mars is a small world, roughly half the size of the Earth, with a surface gravity just a bit more than a third of Earth's. A hundred kilograms on Earth weighs only thirty-eight kilos on Mars.

Mars is known as the red planet because its surface is mainly a bone-dry desert of sandy iron oxides: rusty iron dust.

Yet there is water on Mars. The planet has bright polar caps composed at least partially of frozen water—covered over most of the year by frozen carbon dioxide, dry ice. The First Mars Expedition confirmed that vast areas of the planet are underlain by permafrost: an ocean of frozen water lies beneath the red sands.

Mars is the most Earthlike of any world in the solar system. There are seasons on Mars—spring, summer, autumn and winter. Because its orbit is farther from the Sun, the Martian year is nearly twice as long as Earth's (a few minutes short of 689 Earth days) and its seasons are consequently much longer than Earth's. Mars rotates about its axis in almost the same time that Earth does. A day on Earth is 23 hours, 56 minutes, and 4.09 seconds long. A day on Mars is only slightly longer: 24 hours, 37 minutes, and 22.7 seconds.

To prevent confusion between Earth time and Martian, space explorers refer to the Martian day as a *sol*. In one Martian year there are 669 sols, plus an untidy fourteen hours, forty-six minutes and twelve seconds.

The discovery of the rock-dwelling Martian lichen raised new questions among the scientists: Are the lichen the only life form on the planet? Or is there an ecological web of various organisms? If so, why have none been found except the lichen?

Are these lowly organisms the highest achievement that life has attained on Mars?

Or are they the rugged survivors of what was once a much richer and more complex ecology?

If they are the sole survivors, what destroyed all the other life-forms on Mars?

BOOK I:
THE ARRIVAL

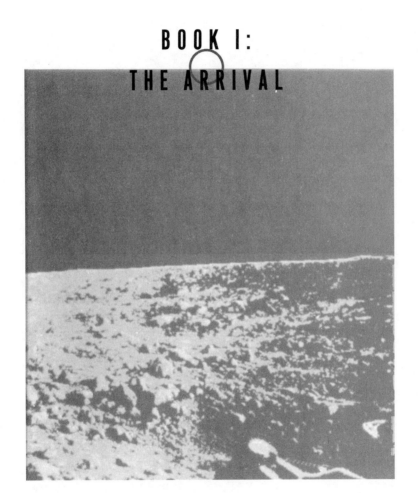

MARS HABITAT: SOL 1

"WE'RE BACK, GRANDFATHER," JAMIE WATERMAN MURMURED. "WE'VE come back to Mars."

Standing by the row of empty equipment racks just inside the domed habitat's airlock, Jamie reached out and picked up the small stone carving from the shelf where it had waited for six years: a tiny piece of jet-black obsidian in the totem shape of a crouching bear. A miniature turquoise arrowhead was tied to its back with a rawhide thong, a wisp of a white eagle's feather tucked atop it. He held the Navaho fetish in the palm of his gloved hand.

"What is that?" asked Stacy Dezhurova.

Jamie heard her strong bright voice in his helmet earphones. None of the eight members of the Second Mars Expedition had removed their spacesuits yet, nor even lifted the visors of their helmets. They stood in a rough semicircle just inside the airlock hatch, eight faceless men and women encased in their bulky white hard suits.

"A Navaho fetish," Jamie replied. "Powerful magic."

Dex Trumball shuffled awkwardly toward Jamie, his thick boots clomping heavily on the habitat's plastic flooring.

"You brought this all the way with you?" Trumball asked, almost accusingly.

"On the first expedition," Jamie said. "I left it here to guard the place while we were gone."

Trumball's face was hidden behind the tinted visor of his helmet, but the tone of his voice left no doubt about his opinion. "Heap big medicine, huh?"

Jamie suppressed a flash of anger. "That's right," he said, forcing his voice to stay calm, even. "The dome's still here, isn't it? Six years, and it's still standing and ready for occupancy."

Possum Craig said in his flat Texas twang, "Let's pump us some breathable oxy in here before we start clappin' ourselves on the back."

"Six years," Trumball muttered. "Left it waiting here all that time."

Six years.

Even the discovery of life clinging precariously to the rocks at the bottom of Mars' Grand Canyon had not made this return to the red planet easy or simple. It had taken six years to put together the people, the equipment—and most important of all, the money—to make this Second Mars Expedition a reality.

To his surprise and anger, Jamie Waterman had been forced to fight for a berth on the second expedition, fight with every molecule of strength and skill he possessed. But his grandfather's fetish must have truly been powerful: he had returned to Mars at last.

After five months in space between the two worlds, after a week in orbit around Mars, after the blazing fury of their descent through the thin Martian atmosphere heated to incandescence by their fiery passage, Jamie Waterman and the other seven members of the expedition had at last stepped out onto the rust-red sandy surface of Mars.

Five men and three women, each encased in bulbous hard-shelled spacesuits that made them look like lumbering tortoises rearing on their hind legs. All the suits were white, with color-coded stripes on their sleeves for easy identification. Jamie's three stripes were fire-engine red.

The habitat that the first expedition had left looked unchanged. The dome was still inflated and appeared unscarred from its six-year wait.

The first thing the explorers did was to troop to the dome's airlock and go inside. After a few moments of just gazing around its empty domed interior, they fell to their assigned tasks and checked out the life-support equipment. If the dome was unusable they would have to live for the entire year and a half of their stay on Mars in the spacecraft module that had carried them to the red planet and landed them on its surface. None of them wanted that. Five months cooped up in that tin can had been more than enough.

The dome was intact, its life-support equipment functioning adequately, its nuclear power generator still providing enough electricity to run the habitat.

I knew it would be, Jamie said to himself. Mars is a gentle world. It doesn't want to harm us.

Possum Craig and Tomas Rodriguez, the NASA-provided astronaut, started the oxygen generator. It was cranky after six years of being idle, but they got it running at last and it began extracting breathable oxygen from the Martian atmosphere to mix with the nitrogen that had kept the dome inflated for the past six years.

The rest of the explorers went outside and fell to their assigned tasks of setting up the video cameras and virtual reality rigs to record their arrival on Mars and transmit the news back to Earth. With his stone fetish tucked into the thigh pocket of his spacesuit, Jamie remembered the political flap he had caused when the first expedition had set foot on Mars and he had spoken a few words of Navaho instead of the stiffly formal speech the NASA public relations people had written for him.

And he remembered one thing more: the ancient cliff dwelling he had seen, built into a high niche in the soaring cliff wall of the Grand Canyon. But he dared not mention that to the others.

Not yet.

HOUSTON: THE FIRST MEETING

JAMIE HAD MET THE EXPEDITION'S SCIENCE TEAM FOR THE FIRST TIME IN A tight little windowless conference room in NASA's Johnson Space Center, near Houston. The two women and three men had been chosen out of thousands of candidates, their names announced weeks earlier. Jamie himself had been selected to be their leader only two days ago.

"I know what you're going through," Jamie said to the five of them.

This was the first time he had met the four scientists and the expedition's physician face-to-face. Over the months of their training and Jamie's own struggle to be included in the Second Mars Expedition, he had communicated with each of them by electronic mail and talked with them by Picturephone, but he had never been in the same room with them before.

Now he stood, a little uneasily, at the head of the narrow conference table, feeling like an instructor facing a very talented quintet of students: younger, more certain of themselves, even more highly qualified than he himself. The four scientists were seated along the rickety oblong table, their eyes on him. The physician/psychologist sat at the table's end, an exotic-looking Hindu woman with dark chocolate skin and midnight-black hair pulled straight back from her face.

They were all in mission coveralls, coral pink, with name tags pinned above the breast pocket. The physician, V. J. Shektar, had tied a colorful scarf around her throat. She was watching Jamie with big, coal-black, almond-shaped eyes.

None of the others had added to their standard uniform, except C. Dexter Trumball, who had sewn patches on both his shoulders: one bore the microscope-and-telescope logo of the International Consortium of Universities, the other the flying T symbol of Trumball Industries.

"We're going to be living together for more than three years," Jamie continued, "counting the rest of your training and the mission itself. I thought it's high time we got to know each other."

Jamie had fought hard to be accepted for the second expedition. He would have been happy to be included as a mission scientist. Instead, the only way he could get aboard was to accept the responsibilities of mission director.

"You said *our* training," the geophysicist, Dexter Trumball, interrupted. "Aren't you training for the mission, too?"

Trumball was handsome, with dashing film-star looks, dark curly hair and lively bright eyes the blue-green color of the ocean. As he sat back comfortably in his padded chair, he wore a crooked little grin that hovered between self-confidence and cockiness. He was no taller than Jamie, but quite a bit slimmer: a nimble, graceful dancer's body compared to Jamie's thicker, more solid build. He was also ten years younger than Jamie, and the son of the man who had spearheaded the funding for the expedition.

"Of course I'm training, too," Jamie answered quickly. "But a good deal of what you're going through—the Antarctic duty, for example—I did for the first expedition."

"Oh," said Trumball. "Been there, done that, eh?"

Jamie nodded tightly. "Something like that."

"But that was more than six years ago," said Mitsuo Fuchida. The biologist was as slim as a sword blade, his face a sculpture of angles and planes.

"If you were a computer," he added, with the slightest of smiles cracking his hatchet-sharp features, "you would be an entire generation behind."

Jamie forced a returning smile. "I'm being upgraded. I'm requalifying on all the physical tests," Jamie assured them, "and putting all the latest programming into my long-term memory. I won't crash or succumb to bytelock, don't worry."

The others laughed politely.

Fuchida dipped his chin in acknowledgment. "Only joking," he said, a bit sheepishly.

"Nothing to it," Jamie said, smiling genuinely now.

"Well, I don't know about the rest of y'all," said the stubby, sad-faced geochemist that Jamie knew as Peter J. Craig, "but I'm damned glad we got an experienced man to come along with us."

Craig had a bulbous nose and heavy jowls dark with stubble.

"Lemme tell you," he went on, pronouncing *you* as *yew*, "I been out in the field a lotta years and there's nothin' that can replace real experience. We're lucky to have Dr. Waterman headin' up this rodeo."

Before anyone could say anything more, Jamie spread his hands and told them, "Look, I didn't come here this afternoon to talk about me. I just wanted to meet you all in person and sort of say hello. We'll be talking to each other individually and in smaller groups over the next few weeks."

They all nodded.

"You people are the best of the best," Jamie went on. "You've been picked over thousands of other applicants. The research proposals you've presented are very impressive; I've studied them all and I like what I've seen, very much.''

"What about the cooperative studies?" Trumball asked.

While on Mars, each of the four scientists would carry out dozens of experiments and measurements under direction from researchers back on Earth. That was the only way to get the full cooperation—and funding help—from the major universities.

Jamie said, "I know they're going to cut into the time you have for your own work, but they're part of the mission plan and we'll all have to pitch in on them."

"You too?"

"Certainly me too. I'm not going to spend all my time on Mars at a desk."

They grinned at that.

"And listen: If you run into problems with scheduling, or the demands from Earthside get to be troublesome, tell me about it. That's what I'm here for. It's my job to iron out conflicts."

"Who gets priority?" Craig asked. "I mean, if it comes down to either doin' my own stuff or doin' what some department head from Cowflop U. wants, which way do we go?"

Jamie looked at him for a silent moment, thinking. This is a test, he realized. They're sizing me up.

"We'll have to take each case on its own merits," he told Craig. "But my personal feeling is that in case of a tie, the guy on Mars gets the priority."

Craig nodded agreement, acceptance.

Jamie looked around the table. Neither of the two women had said a word. Shektar was the medic, so he wasn't surprised that she had nothing to say. But Trudy Hall was a cellular biologist and should contribute to the discussion.

Hall looked to Jamie like a slight little English sparrow. She was tiny, her thick curly brown hair clipped short, her coral coveralls undecorated except for her name tag. Alert gray-blue eyes, Jamie saw. She had the spare, lean figure of a marathon runner and the kind of perfect chiselled nose that other women pay plastic surgeons to obtain.

"Any questions?" Jamie said, looking directly at her.

Hall seemed to draw in a breath, then she said, "Yes, one."

"What is it?" Jamie asked.

She glanced around at the others, then hunched forward slightly as she asked in a soft Yorkshire burr, "What's it like on Mars? I mean, what's it *really* like to be there?"

The others all edged forward in their seats, too, even Trumball, and Jamie knew that they would get along fine together. He spent the next two hours telling them about Mars.

ARRIVAL CEREMONY: SOL 1

THEY HAD LANDED ONLY MINUTES AFTER LOCAL DAWN, TO GIVE THEM-selves as much time in daylight as possible for unloading their landing/ascent vehicle and getting their domed habitat restarted. And they had to allow time to transmit a landing ceremony back to Earth.

It had been agreed that the explorers would check the habitability of the old dome first, and only after that conduct the ritual of presenting themselves to the Earth's waiting, watching billions.

Of course, the instant they had touched down, cosmonaut Anastasia Dezhurova had notified mission control in Tarawa that they had landed safely. Their L/AV's instrumentation automatically telemetered that information back to Earth, but for the first time since Jamie had met Stacy, the Russian's broad, stolid face beamed with delight as she announced the news that was played on every television station on Earth:

"Touchdown! Humankind has returned to Mars!"

The mission controllers, a hundred million kilometers away on the Pacific atoll of Tarawa, had broken into whoops and yowls of joy, hugging each other and dancing in their relief and excitement.

Jamie blinked sweat from his eyes as the eight of them lined up before the vidcams that Trumball and Rodriguez had set up on their Mars-thin tripods. He touched the keypad on his wrist that turned up the suit fans to maximum and heard their insect's buzz whine to a higher pitch. Strange to feel hot and sweaty on a world where the temperature was almost always below freezing. Can't be from exertion, Jamie thought. It must be nervous excitement.

He wished he could open his visor and wipe at his eyes, but he knew that his blood would boil out of his lungs at the pitifully low Martian atmospheric pressure.

Later, Dex Trumball would take the viewers from Earth on a virtual reality tour of their landing site while everyone else worked at bringing out the tractors and unloading the spacecraft. For now, all eight of them would go through the arrival ceremony.

As mission director, it fell to Jamie to make the first statement before the camera. It would take nearly a quarter of an hour for his words to cross the gulf between the two worlds. There were no conversations between Mars and Earth, only monologues travelling in opposite directions.

Six years earlier, when he had been the last member of the expedition to speak, he had said simply the old Navaho greeting, "Ya'aa'tey." It is good.

Now, though, he was mission director and more was expected of him.

At least this second expedition was not as rigidly controlled as the first one had been. Instead of the almost military hierarchy imposed by the governments who sponsored the First Mars Expedition, Jamie had worked out a more relaxed, more collegiate organization of equals. The two astronauts and six scientists lived and worked together as a harmonious team—most of the time.

"You ready?" Trumball's voice buzzed in Jamie's helmet earphones.

Jamie nodded, then realized that no one could see the gesture. "Ready as I'll ever be," he said as he stepped in front of the hand-sized vidcams.

Trumball, standing behind the spindly tripods, jabbed a finger at him. Jamie raised his hand and said, "Greetings from the planet Mars. The Second Mars Expedition has landed as planned at the site of the habitat left by the First Expedition."

Turning slightly, Jamie waved an arm in the general direction of the dome. "As you can see, the habitat is in excellent shape and we're looking forward to spending the next year and a half here.

"Later," he continued, "Dr. Trumball will conduct a virtual reality tour of the area. Right now, I'd like to thank the International Consortium of Universities, the Space Transportation Association, and the taxpayers of the United States, Australia, Japan, the European Community, and the island nation of Kiribati for providing the funds that have made this expedition possible."

They had drawn lots weeks earlier to decide the order of appearances. Vijay Shektar stepped up to the camera next, anonymous in her bulbous hard suit, except for the bright green rings on its arms.

"Hullo to everyone on Earth, and especially to the people of Australia," she said, in her decidedly Aussie accent. Her voice belied her heritage: Shektar was of Hindu descent, dark skin and wide black onyx eyes. But she had been born and raised in Melbourne. She was a first-rate physician and psychologist who would also assist the biology team.

After Shektar's little speech, Mitsuo Fuchida, one of the expedition's two biologists, gave his greetings: first in Japanese, then in English.

Dex Trumball, with his royal blue armbands, followed.

". . . and I want to thank the aerospace companies who donated so much of their equipment and personnel to us," he said after the ritual salutations and compliments, "and the more than forty-five universities around the world who have contributed to this expedition. Without your financial and material and personal support, we wouldn't be standing here on Mars now.''

Jamie felt his nose wrinkling slightly. I should've expected Dex to work a commercial in. He's more interested in making money out of this expedition than doing science.

''And a very special thanks to my father, Darryl C. Trumball, whose energy, vision and generosity has been a primal force in creating this expedition and an inspiration to us all.''

Jamie and Dex had argued about the expedition's goals for the whole five months of their flight to Mars. Politely, at first, like two mannerly academicians. But over the long months of their passage in space their ideological differences inevitably sharpened into shouting matches; real anger had developed between them.

I'm going to have to iron that out, Jamie told himself. We can't go on snarling at each other. We've got to be able to work together, as a team.

Find the balance, the Navaho part of his mind whispered. Find the path that leads to harmony. Only harmony can bring you to beauty.

His rational mind agreed, but still he seethed at Trumball's cavalier assumption that the expedition should be aimed at making a profit.

The last person to appear before the camera was Trudy Hall, the English cellular biologist.

''I've been rehearsing this speech for months,'' she said, her voice high with excitement, ''but now that we're here—well, all I can say is: Crikey! This is a bit of all right! Let's get on with it!''

Jamie laughed to himself inside the privacy of his helmet. So much for English aplomb, he thought.

The brief ceremonies over, Trumball started to move the cameras while most of the others headed for the cargo hatch of their spacecraft and the labor of unloading.

Nobody sees us at work, Jamie thought. The sweat of unloading our equipment and supplies isn't glamorous enough for the media and the folks back home. They want drama and excitement; just hauling supplies from the L/AV to the dome isn't thrilling enough for them.

He turned and gazed out across the Martian landscape. Once we thought it was dead. Dry and cold and barren. But now we know better. He blinked, and thought for a moment he was looking out at the Navaho land in New Mexico where his grandfather had taken him so many times. Many summers ago. A lifetime ago, on another world. That land looked dry and dead, too. Yet the People lived there. Thrived there, in a hard and bitter land.

The Martian landscape held an uncanny beauty. It stirred a chord within Jamie, this red world. It was a soft landscape, barren and empty, yet somehow gentle and beckoning to him. Jamie saw that the shaded sides of the rocks and dunes were coated with a light powdering of white that sparkled and winked and vanished where the new-risen sun touched them.

I'm home, he thought. After six years, I've come back to where I belong.

"What's that white stuff?"

Jamie heard Vijay Shektar's smoky feline voice in his earphones, softly curious. He turned his head, but the helmet blocked his view; he had to turn his whole body to see her standing beside him.

"Frost," Jamie answered.

"Frost?"

"Water vapor in the atmosphere freezes out on the ground and the rocks."

"But this is spring, isn't it?" Her voice sounded slightly puzzled, unsure.

Nodding, Jamie answered, "That's right. It won't be summer for another four months."

"But frosts should come in autumn, not in spring," she said.

Jamie smiled. "On Earth. This is Mars."

"Oh." She seemed to consider that for a moment, then said with a gleeful lilt in her voice, "We can have a snowball fight, then?"

Jamie shook his head. "Afraid not. The ice here won't compact. It's not wet enough; not enough hydrogen bonding."

"I don't understand."

"It's like very dry, very powdery snow. Much drier and more powdery than anything on Earth." Jamie wondered if she had ever gone skiing in Australia. Maybe New Zealand, he thought. They have good ski mountains there.

"Can't make snowballs, then," Shektar said. She sounded disappointed.

Raising his arm to point toward the horizon, Jamie answered, "You could once, long ago. There was an ocean here . . . or at least a sizeable sea. Like the Gulf of Mexico, most likely: fairly shallow, warmed by the sun."

"Really?"

"Sure. See the terracing? The scallop-shaped indentations?"

"That was caused by an ocean?"

Jamie nodded inside his helmet. "It lapped up to the slope of the Tharsis bulge, off to the west there. Where we're standing was probably seashore, once. There might be fossils of seashells beneath our feet."

"And what would Martian seashells look like?" Dex Trumball asked sharply. "How would you recognize a fossil here? The forms would be completely different from Earth."

Jamie turned and saw Dex's hard suit with its royal blue armbands nearly a hundred meters away. He'd been eavesdropping on their suit-to-suit frequency.

"There's always bilateral symmetry," Jamie said, trying to keep the resentment out of his voice.

Trumball laughed.

Vijay added, "Something with legs would help."

Bounding across the iron-red sand toward them, clutching a plastic sample case in one gloved hand, Dex said, "But that stuff about the ocean is good. I could use that in my VR tour. Give me a couple hours with the computer and I could even *show* a visual simulation to the viewers back home!"

Dex was all youthful enthusiasm and vigor. Jamie felt distinctly annoyed.

The geophysicist hustled up the slight rocky incline in two-meter-long strides to where Jamie and Vijay stood.

"It's really frost, all right. Look at it! Come on, I want to get some samples before the sun evaporates all of it." He hoisted the insulated sample case.

Without waiting for Jamie, Trumball started down the slope toward the frost-rimed dunes.

Jamie clicked the keyboard on his left cuff to the suit radio's base frequency. "Waterman to base. Shektar, Trumball and I are going down into the dune field."

Stacy Dezhurova's answering voice sounded slightly nettled. "You will be out of camera range, Jamie."

"Understood," Jamie said. "We should be no longer than thirty minutes and we won't go beyond walk-back range."

Dezhurova made a sound somewhere between a sigh and a snort. "Copy thirty minutes max in walk-back range."

As senior of the two astronauts, Dezhurova was responsible for enforcing the safety regulations. Her primary station was at the dome's communications center, watching everyone working outside through the surveillance cameras spotted around the dome.

I can understand why she's ticked off, Jamie thought. We ought to be at the dome, helping to stow the equipment and consumables instead of wandering off across the landscape. The others had both the small tractors trundling between their L/AV and the dome.

Still, he turned his back to the work and walked slowly beside Vijay, ready to offer his hand if she stumbled on the rocks scattered across the ground. His geologist's eye took in the area. This must be a really old impact crater, he told himself. Weathering on Mars takes eons, and this rim is almost eroded down to the level of the sand floor. Must have been a big hit, from the size of the basin. What's left of it.

Trumball was already down in the shadows, on his knees, carefully scraping the fragile, paper-thin coating of ice into an open sample container.

"It's water ice, all right," he was saying over the suit-to-suit frequency as they approached him. "Same isotopic composition as the ice at the north pole, I bet. Stuff sublimes into vapor up there and the atmosphere transports it down toward the equator."

Vijay pointed with a gloved finger. "It's melting where the sun is hitting it."

"Subliming," Trumball said without looking up from his work. "It doesn't melt, it sublimes."

"Goes from ice to vapor," Jamie explained, "with no liquid phase in between."

"I understand," she replied.

"The atmosphere's so thin, liquid water evaporates immediately."

"Yes, I know," she said, with a slight edge in her voice.

Trumball snapped the container shut and inserted it into his sample case. "This'll help us nail down the global circulation of the atmosphere."

"Will this water be carbonated, too?"

Closing the plastic box and climbing to his feet, Trumball said, "Sure. Just like the water from the permafrost underground. Martian Perrier, loaded with carbon dioxide."

Jamie started them back toward the base, feeling left out of the conversation but not knowing how to jump in without making it seem obvious that he was competing with the younger man.

"Life has the same needs here as on Earth," Vijay was saying.

"Why not?" Trumball replied, waving his free hand. "It's all the same, basically: DNA, proteins—same on both planets."

"But there are differences," Jamie said. "Martian DNA has the same double-helix structure as ours, but the base pairs are different chemicals."

"Yeah, sure. And Martian proteins have a few different amino acids in 'em. But they still need water."

They had reached the crest of the rim rock. Jamie could see the camera atop its high skinny pole peering at them.

Reluctantly, he said, "We'd better get back to the dome and help finish the unloading."

She answered, "Yes, I suppose we should."

Jamie couldn't see Trumball's face behind the heavily tinted visor of his helmet, but he heard the younger man laugh.

Hefting his container box, Trumball said, "Well, some of us have *important* work to do. Have fun playing stevedores."

And he loped across the rock-strewn ground toward the base shelter, leaving Jamie and Shektar standing on the rim of the ancient crater.

VIRTUAL TOUR: SOL 1

LATER THAT AFTERNOON, C. DEXTER TRUMBALL WAS STILL EXCITED AS HE clicked the two miniaturized VR cameras into the slots just above his visor. They were slaved to the movements of his eyes, if the electronics rig worked right. Together with the molecular-thin data gloves he had already wormed over his spacesuit gloves, he would be able to show the millions of viewers on Earth whatever he himself saw or touched.

Briefly he looked back at the rest of the crew, now carrying crates and bulky canisters through the dome's airlock. They would spend the rest of the day setting up equipment and making the dome livable. Trumball's job was to entertain the people back home who were helping to pay for this expedition.

The first expedition to Mars had been run by national governments and had cost nearly a quarter-trillion dollars. This second expedition was financed mostly by private sources and cost less than a tenth as much.

Of course, the six years between the two missions had seen the advent of Clipperships, reusable spacecraft that brought down the cost of flying into orbit from thousands of dollars per pound to hundreds. Masterson Corporation and the other big aerospace firms had donated dozens of flights into Earth orbit to the Mars expedition; it was good public relations for them and their new Clipperships.

And Dex's father had indeed spearheaded the drive that raised the money for the expedition. The elder Trumball had personally donated nearly half a billion dollars of his own wealth, then shivvied, cajoled, or shamed fellow billionaires into contributing to the cause.

But the real reason for the lower cost was that this second expedition was going to live off the land. Instead of carrying every gram of water, oxygen and fuel all the way from Earth, they had sent automated equipment ahead of them to land on Mars and start producing water, oxygen and fuel from the planet's atmosphere and soil. Dex Trumball dubbed the procedure "Plan Z," after the engineer who had pioneered the concept decades earlier, Robert Zubrin.

Still, even with Plan Z, the expedition ran into problems before its first module took off from Earth.

Nuclear rockets would cut the travel time between Earth and Mars almost in half. But there was still so much controversy in the United States and Europe over using nuclear propulsion that the expedition planners moved the main launch site to the island nation of Kiribati, out in the middle of the Pacific. There the nuclear engines were launched into orbit on Clipperships, to be mated with the living and equipment modules launched from the United States and Russia. Anti-nuclear demonstrators were not allowed within two hundred miles of the island launch site.

Kiribati's price for being so obliging was to have the expedition's mission control center established at their capital, Tarawa. Pete Connors, astronaut veteran of the first expedition, and the other controllers did not at all mind moving to the balmy atoll. And Kiribati got global attention for its fine hotels and tourist facilities. And security.

The biggest problem had been selection of the personnel to go to Mars. Two biologists and two geologists would be the entire scientific staff, and the competition among eager, intense young scientists was ferocious. Dex sometimes asked himself if he would have been selected as one of the geologists even if his father had not been so munificent. Doesn't matter, he always answered himself. I'm on the team and the rest of them can torque themselves inside out for all I care.

Trumball grimaced as he checked out the VR electronics with his head-up display. The diagnostic display flickered across his visor. Everything operational except the damned gloves. Their icon blinked red at him.

The first law of engineering: when something doesn't work, kick it. As he jiggered the hair-thin optical fiber wires that connected the gloves to the transmitter on his backpack, Trumball told himself once again that he was the only man on the team who understood the economics of this mission. And the economics determined what could or could not be accomplished.

Waterman and the rest of the scientists always have their heads in the clouds, he thought. They're here to do science. They want to convert their curiosity into Nobel Prizes. Yeah, but unless somebody foots the frigging bills they'd still be back on some campus on Earth spending their nights chatting about Mars over the Internet.

Hell, I want to do good science, too. But the thing is, somebody's got to pay for all this. They look down on me because I'm the only realist in the crowd.

The glove icon at last flicked to green in his HUD. He was ready to start the virtual reality tour.

Trumball cleared the display from his visor, then tapped his wrist keypad for the radio frequency back to mission control at Tarawa. It would be twenty-eight minutes before his signal reached Earth and their confirmation and go-ahead returned to him. He spent the time plotting out the route he would follow through this little travelogue.

"Mission control to Trumball," at last came Connors' rich baritone voice across a hundred million kilometers. "You are go for the VR tour. We have sixteen point nine million subscribers on-line, with more logging in as we announce your start time."

We'll hit twenty million easy, Trumball thought happily. At ten bucks a head, that pays for almost half of our ground equipment. We're going to make a profit out of this expedition!

The Zieman family—father, mother, nine-year-old son and five-year-old daughter—sat in the entertainment room of their suburban Kansas City house in front of the wall-to-wall video screen.

Only one corner of the screen was activated: a serious-looking black man was explaining that the transmission from Mars took fourteen minutes to cover the distance between the two planets, even with the signal travelling at the speed of light, "which is three hundred thousand kilometers per *second*," he emphasized.

The nine-year-old shook his head emphatically. "It's two hundred and ninety-nine point seven nine kilometers per second," he corrected righteously.

His sister hissed, "Ssshh!"

"Put your helmets on," their father said. "They're going to start in a couple of seconds."

All four of them donned plastic helmets that held padded earphones and slide-down visors. They worked their fingers into the wired data gloves—mother helping her daughter, the boy proudly doing it for himself—then pulled the visors down when the man on the screen told them the tour was about to start.

The black man's voice counted down, "Three . . . two . . . one . . ."

And they were on Mars!

They were looking out on a red, rock-strewn plain, a ruddy, dusty desert stretching out as far as the eye could see, rust-colored boulders scattered across the barren gently rolling land like toys left behind by a careless child. The uneven horizon seemed closer than it should be. The sky was a bright butterscotch color. Small wind-shaped dunes heaped in precise rows, and the reddish sand piled against some of the bigger rocks. In the distance was something that looked like a flat-topped mesa jutting up over the horizon.

"This is our landing site," Dexter Trumball's voice was telling them. "We're on the westernmost extension of a region called Lunae Planum—the Plain of the Moon. Astronomers gave Martian geography bizarro names back in the old days."

The view shifted as Trumball turned slowly. They saw the habitat dome.

"That's where we'll be living for the next year and a half. Tomorrow I'll take you on a tour inside. Right now, the other members of the expedition are busy setting things in order; you know, housekeeping stuff. By tomorrow we'll be able to walk through and see what it's like."

Not a word from any of the Ziemans. Across the country, across the world, people sat staring at Mars, fascinated, engrossed.

"Hear that faint, kind of whispering sound?" Trumball asked. "That's the wind. It's blowing at about thirty knots, practically a gale force wind on Earth, but here on Mars the air's so thin that it's not even stirring up the dust from the ground. See?"

They felt their right hands groping into a pouch on the hard suit's leg. "Now watch this," Trumball said.

They pulled out a toy-store horseshoe magnet, red and white.

"The sand here on Mars is rich with iron ores," Trumball explained, "so we can use this magnet . . ."

They crouched down laboriously in the bulky hard suit and wrote out the letters M–A–R–S in the sand with the magnet as Trumball said, "See, we don't have to touch the sand. The magnet pushes against the iron in the grains."

"I want to write my name!" said the Zieman daughter.

"Shut up!" her brother snapped.

Both parents shushed them.

Trumball pocketed the magnet, then bent down and picked up a palm-sized rock. The viewers felt its weight and solidity in their gloved hands.

"The rocks that're scattered all around here were torn out of the ground," Trumball explained, straightening up. "Some of them might be from volcanic eruptions, but most of 'em were blasted out by meteor impacts. Mars is a lot closer to the asteroid belt than Earth is, y'know, and so gets hit by meteors a lot more."

They seemed to be walking away from the dome, out toward a boulder the size of a house. Red sand was piled up on one side of it.

"You can see a field of sand dunes out there," said Trumball, and they saw his gloved hand pointing. "They must be pretty stable, because they were there six years ago, when the first expedition landed."

The pointing hand shifted against the tawny sky. "Over that way you can see the land starts rising. That's the eastern edge of the Tharsis bulge, where the big volcanoes are. Pavonis Mons is roughly six hundred kilometers from us, just about due west."

The view shifted again, fast enough to make some viewers slightly giddy. "To the south is the badlands, Noctis Labyrinthus, and about six hundred kilometers to the southeast is Tithonium Chasma, the western end of the big Grand Canyon. That's where the first expedition found the Martian lichen."

Turning again, Trumball walked toward a small tractor. It looked almost like a dune buggy, but its wheels were thin and springy looking. It was completely open, no cabin; the seats were surrounded by a cage of impossibly slim metal bars.

The viewers saw themselves slide into the driver's seat. The Zieman boy muttered, "Way cool!"

"I want to show you our standby fuel generator," Trumball said as he started up the tractor's engine. It clattered like a diesel, but strangely high-pitched in the thin Martian air. "It's about two klicks—kilometers—from the dome. Been sitting out there for more than two years now, taking carbon dioxide out of the air and water from the permafrost beneath the ground and making methane for us. Methane is natural gas; it's the fuel we'll use for our ground rovers."

Before putting the tractor in motion he turned around and leaned slightly over the vehicle's edge. "Take a look at the bootprints," Trumball said. "Human prints on the red sands of Mars. No one's ever walked here before, not in this precise spot. Maybe you'll put *your* footprints on Mars someday."

"Yah!" the nine-year-old whooped.

Trumball drove twenty-eight million paying viewers (and their friends or families) slowly toward the fuel generator.

"It's not much to look at," he admitted, "but it's a very important piece of equipment for us. So important, in fact, that we carried another one along with us."

Once they reached the squat cylindrical module, Trumball got out of the tractor and rested a gloved hand on the smooth curving metal side of the generator.

"Feel that vibration?" Dozens of millions did. "The generator's chugging away, making fuel for us. It also produces drinkable water for us."

"I'm thirsty," the five-year-old whined.

Trumball walked them around the automated module, found the main water tap and poured a splash of water into a metal cup he had brought with him.

"This water is Martian," he said, holding up the cup. "It comes from the permafrost beneath the surface of the ground. It's laced with carbon dioxide, sort of like fizzy soda water. But it's drinkable—once we filter out the impurities."

As he spoke the water boiled away, leaving the cup utterly dry.

"Martian air's so thin that water boils even though the temperature here is below zero," Trumball explained. "The important thing, though, is that there's an ocean of water beneath our feet, all frozen for millions and millions of years. Enough water to supply millions and millions of people, someday."

Mrs. Zieman murmured, "I didn't know that."

After precisely one full hour, Trumball said, "Well, that's all for today. Got to pack it in now. Tomorrow we'll walk through the dome. In a few days we'll be sending a team in one of the ground rovers out to the Grand Canyon. Later on, we'll fly two people out to the shield volcanoes in the rocketplane. And we'll be flying the unmanned soar-planes over longer distances, too. If all goes well, we'll fly them out to the old Viking 1 landing site and maybe even farther north, to the edge of the ice cap.''

Through all this, the viewers stared out at the Martian vista.

"But that's all for the future," Trumball concluded. "For now, so long from Mars. Thanks for being with us.''

For long moments the Zieman family sat unmoving, unspeaking. At last they reluctantly pulled off their helmets.

"I wanna go to Mars," announced the nine-year-old. "When I grow up I'm gonna be a scientist and go to Mars.''

"Me too!" his sister added.

DINNERTIME: SOL 1

JAMIE FOUND HIS OLD PERSONAL CUBICLE UNCHANGED FROM SIX YEARS earlier. The bunk with its thin Martian-gravity legs was waiting for him. The plastic unit that combined desk and clothes closet stood empty, just as he had left it.

Everything's in good working order, he marvelled. They had filled the dome with inert nitrogen when they'd left, six years earlier. Now the air was an Earth-normal mix of nitrogen and oxygen, so they could live inside the dome in their shirtsleeves. Or less.

During the first expedition they had been hit by a meteor swarm, almost microscopic little pebbles that had punctured the dome in several places and even grazed Jamie's spacesuit helmet. One in a trillion chance, the astronomers from Earth had told them. Jamie nodded, hoping that the odds remained that way.

Someone had gotten the loudspeakers going and was playing a soothing classical piano recording. Beethoven, Jamie thought. He remembered how the cosmonauts played Tchaikovsky and other Russian composers during the first expedition.

Yet the dome felt subtly different. Its new-car smell was gone. The first expedition had occupied it for only forty-five days, but that had been enough to take the shine off it. The dome felt like home, true enough, but not exactly the way Jamie had remembered it.

"Toilets ain't workin'.''

Jamie turned to see Possum Craig standing in his doorway, a gloomy frown on his heavy-jowled face. The accordion-slide door had been left open, so there had been no need to knock.

"Both toilets?" Jamie asked.

Craig nodded glumly. "Must be the water line clogged up. Or froze."

Officially, Craig was a geochemist, recruited from a Texas oil company to run the drilling rig. The biologists theorized that Martian life thrived underground, perhaps miles underground, and the lichen they had found in the surface rocks were merely an extension of this below-ground ecology. "Plutonian biosphere," they called it.

Unofficially, Craig was the expedition's repairman. There wasn't a tool he could not wield expertly. He was plumber, electrician, and general handyman, all wrapped in one package. Trumball had started calling him "Wiley J. Coyote" within a week of their launch toward Mars, when Craig had cleverly repaired a malfunctioning computer display screen with little more than a screwdriver and a pair of tweezers from the medical equipment.

Craig preferred the new name to his usual "Possum," an old oil-field reference to his painfully prominent nose.

"You think it's frozen?" Jamie asked, crossing his compartment in two strides and stepping past Craig, out into the dome's open space.

"Most likely. We shoulda buried it, first thing."

"And the recycling system's not on-line yet."

"I could try overpressurin' the line, but I don't wanta run the risk of splittin' the pipe. You don't want that kinda mess, not the first night."

Stacy Dezhurova came up to them, a troubled pair of furrows between her heavy brows. Her hair was sandy brown; she wore it in a short pageboy that looked as if she'd put a bowl over her head and chopped away herself.

"Possum has told you the news?" she asked gloomily.

Jamie nodded. Across the open area, at the row of lockers next to their airlock, he saw Rodriguez worming his arms through the torso of his hard suit.

"Tomas is going outside?"

"The chemical toilets are in the lander. He's going to bring them in here for tonight."

"It's already dark out." That meant the temperature was plunging.

"We must have toilets," Dezhurova said firmly. She was almost always somber and serious, an impressive and very capable woman whose formidable exterior masked a keen, dry sense of humor. But now she was in her no-nonsense mode. "Toilets are primary."

"Who's going with Tomas?" Jamie asked. Safety regulations forbade anyone from going out alone, even a NASA-trained astronaut.

"I'll go," Craig said, without much enthusiasm.

Dezhurova shook her head. "No, I will do it."

"Not you, Stacy," Jamie countered. "We can't have both our astronauts outside at the same time if we can avoid it."

Craig walked off toward the lockers. After a moment, Stacy said, "I will help them check out their suits."

"Fine," said Jamie.

Left alone in front of his cubicle, Jamie saw that the two other women, Hall and Shektar, were talking quietly together at the galley table. Trumball and Fuchida were not in sight, probably in one of the labs. He went back into his compartment, slid the door shut, and booted up his laptop computer. Time to make my report back to Tarawa, he told himself, debating mentally whether the toilet problem was important enough to mention.

Let the news media find out our toilets aren't working and that's all they'll talk about for the next two weeks, he told himself.

Jamie had insisted, from the very beginning of the expedition's planning, that the whole team should have dinner together whenever possible. Everyone in the dome must come together for the evening meal; only those out on field excursions were excused. There had to be one time during each day when they could all get together, discuss the day's work casually, informally, and relax and socialize.

Once the chemical toilets were carried into the dome and installed in the two lavatories, everyone washed up from the water supply they had brought with them and congregated at the galley tables. Jamie started pushing the tables together to make one large table; Fuchida immediately came over to help.

Then they lined up at the microwave ovens, heating the precooked meals that each person had taken from his or her personal store of supplies.

"It's been an eventful day," Jamie said, once they were all seated.

"Tomorrow will be better," said Trudy Hall. It was a line she had used almost every day of their journey from Earth. She said it with an enforced, almost desperate kind of cheerfulness that made Jamie wonder about her.

"Tomorrow will be better only if the toilets are working," Stacy Dezhurova added. She was sitting next to Hall, thickset big-boned Russian next to the slight little English sparrow.

"They will be," said Trumball confidently. Then he turned to Craig. "Won't they, Wiley?"

"Sure, sure," Craig said, pronouncing it, *Shore, shore.*

Rodriguez looked up from his tamales and refried beans. "They better be," he said.

Jamie wanted to get off the subject. "Dex," he called out, "what about the backup water generator? Will we have to move it?"

Trumball sat exactly opposite Jamie. Deliberately, Jamie had chosen a seat in the middle of the table. He did not want to appear to be placing himself at its head. Trumball had taken the chair on the other side.

The backup water generator had been launched two years earlier, on the same booster as the methane fuel generator. The uncrewed landing vehicle, without direct human guidance, had set itself down more than two kilometers away from the dome.

Before Trumball could reply, Craig said, "It's just th' backup; we brought the primary along with us."

"I know," Jamie said. "But if the primary breaks down, then what? Is it smart to have our backup water supply sitting two klicks away?"

Trumball chewed thoughtfully on a mouthful of roast beef, then answered, "We've got three options. Either we run piping out to the backup, or we jack the module up and tow it closer to home base with one of the tractors."

"The third option?" Dezhurova asked.

With an impish grin, Trumball said, "We take a walk out there every time the primary gunks up on us."

Most of the people around the table laughed politely.

"Do we have enough piping to cover that distance?" Jamie asked.

Trumball nodded. "Plenty."

"I don't think it's such a good idea to run piping all that distance," Craig said. "It'll freeze ever' night, 'less we bury it really deep, below the permafrost line."

Trumball shrugged nonchalantly. "Then we'll have to move the rig."

Craig nodded his agreement.

The one problem they had encountered with Plan Z was that the modules sent ahead of the human team could not be piloted to a sufficient accuracy. The communications lag between Earth and Mars prevented real-time control from Tarawa of the uncrewed modules' landings. A two-kilometer radius was excellent shooting over a distance of a hundred million klicks. But it was not quite good enough for the needs of the explorers.

"All right," Jamie said slowly. "First order of business tomorrow is to bring the backup closer to home."

"And then we head for the Canyon," Trumball said.

"Possum starts drilling core samples," Jamie said.

"I move the garden out of the ship and into its own dome," said Fuchida, with a happy grin.

"While we head for the Canyon," Trumball insisted.

"While we head for the Canyon," Jamie conceded.

Trumball nodded, apparently satisfied.

"We've got a big job ahead of us," Jamie said to them all. "We're going to be living here for a year and a half. We've been able to grow food crops in the ship; now we've got to really start living off the land—growing the foods we need and generating our air and fuel from local resources. We have to make ourselves as self-sufficient as possible.''

They all nodded.

''Mars will test us,'' Fuchida murmured.

''What?''

The Japanese biologist looked surprised that anyone had heard his comment. ''I merely meant that Mars will present challenges to each of us.''

Jamie nodded. ''Challenges . . . and opportunities.''

''Make no mistake about it,'' Fuchida countered. ''Each of us will be tested by Mars. Our strength, our intelligence, our character—all will be tested by this alien world.''

''The eight of us against Mars,'' murmured Stacy Dezhurova.

Dex Trumball said, ''Just like the Seven Against Thebes.''

''The what?'' Rodriguez asked.

''It's an ancient Greek play,'' Trumball replied. ''By Euripides.''

''By Aeschylus,'' corrected Fuchida.

Dex glared at him. ''Euripides.''

''Euripides wrote 'The Phoenician Women,' '' Fuchida said confidently. ''It was Aeschylus who wrote 'The Seven Against Thebes.' ''

Interrupting their dispute, Jamie said, ''It's not the eight of us *against* Mars. We're here to learn how to live *with* Mars. To teach the others who'll follow us how to live here.''

''Damn straight,'' muttered Possum Craig.

Trumball conceded the point with a nod, then probed, ''So when are we going to move our base of operations to the Canyon area?''

It was an argument they had gone over for months during the flight. Life had been found in the bottom of the Grand Canyon, why not establish the expedition's base there?

Suppressing a burst of irritation, Jamie said, ''It makes no sense to move our base. We can traverse out to the Canyon and survey the area for a secondary base when the next team comes.''

''If a next team comes,'' Trumball muttered.

''This isn't going to be the last expedition to Mars,'' Jamie said firmly. ''We're part of an ongoing effort—''

''Not if we just diddle around and don't accomplish anything.''

Jamie felt his temper simmering. ''We're here to accomplish several goals. This base is well situated and working fine.''

''Except for the toilets,'' Dezhurova chipped in. She said it with an unlikely grin, but no one laughed.

''It would take a month or more to move this camp,'' Jamie went on, tightly. ''And by going to the Canyon we move away from the volcanoes.''

"Look," Trumball said, hunching forward eagerly, "I'm just as interested in the volcanoes as you are. I'm a geophysicist, remember?"

Before Jamie could reply, Dex went on, "But the people who've put up the money for this expedition want to see *results*. Everybody's screaming to know what those lichen are all about. The volcanoes are dead! Let's get our priorities straight, for god's sake."

"Who says the volcanoes are dead?" Fuchida snapped. "We don't know that!"

Jamie took a breath. "Our priorities were decided more than two years ago, and the people who are funding us agreed to them. We're not here for show business. We're here to determine how widespread life is on this planet, if we can."

Trumball slouched back in his chair, the grin on his face close to a sneer. "If we can," he mimicked.

Trudy Hall spoke up. "I want to get down into that Canyon and study the lichen, of course," she said, in her soft Yorkshire accent. "But I also want to see if there's life elsewhere: the volcanoes, the cores Possum's going to drill, up at the ice cap—we've got a whole world to explore."

Before Trumball could argue, Jamie said, "Look, Dex . . . everybody: We're going to be here for a year and a half. Moving the base isn't a decision we have to make tonight."

"Especially with the toilets not working," Dezhurova piped.

"You mean you'll consider moving later on?" Trumball probed eagerly.

Feeling tired of the whole matter, Jamie nodded. "I'll consider it, depending on what we find both at the Canyon and elsewhere."

Trumball's expectant grin faded. "That's like a parent telling his kid, 'We'll see.' It means no, but you don't want to argue about it."

"I'm not your daddy, Dex."

Trumball snorted. "That's for damned sure."

"As your faithful physician," Vijay Shektar said, a bright smile on her dark-skinned face, "I have the authority to prescribe a certain amount of celebratory stimulant for this occasion."

Like all the others, she was wearing tan coveralls. But with her lush figure, the strained fabric looked enticing.

"Medicinal alcohol?" said Stacy Dezhurova, her somber face lighting up.

"Australian champagne, actually," Shektar replied. "I brought two bottles."

"I have an excellent Scotch whisky," Fuchida said enthusiastically.

"Hell, all I brought," said Craig, "was a quart of red-eye."

Jamie leaned back in his chair. Vijay's defused the argument, he realized. She's a pretty good psychologist. He remembered the first night on the first expedition. The mission regulations had strictly prohibited alcohol or drugs, so everybody had smuggled a bottle or two in their personal effects—everybody except Jamie, who had been added to the team so late that he never had time even to think about booze.

He hadn't carried any with him this time, either. I should have brought something, he chided himself. That's a mistake.

Sure enough, Trumball asked across the table, "And what has our revered leader brought for the party?"

Jamie made himself grin. He spread his hands. "Nothing, I'm afraid."

"Not even a six-pack of beer?" Craig asked.

"Not even a button or two of peyote?" Trumball added.

Jamie just shook his head. He remembered that even the dour Vosnesensky, so safety-conscious as leader of the ground team that he was almost paranoid, had produced some vodka on that first night.

Jamie got to his feet and all their banter stopped.

"Okay, have a party. You've earned it. But only this one night. Starting tomorrow morning, no liquor until we're safely on our way back home."

"Correct!" Dezhurova said, and they all scrambled to their quarters and their stashes.

Jamie stayed for one sip of Shektar's champagne, then retreated to his quarters. He worked on his daily report and studied the plans for the traverse back to the Canyon, where the first expedition had abandoned a rover vehicle that had sunk into a crater filled with treacherous sand.

It was hard to concentrate on the work, with the others singing limericks at the top of their lungs to the tune of "Cielito Lindo."

"*Ay, ay, ay, ay,*
"*Your mother swims after troopships!*
"*So sing me another verse,*
"*Worse than the other verse,*
"*Waltz me around again, Willy.*"

Stacy Dezhurova's voice rang above all the rest, a rich, clear soprano. She could have been an opera star, Jamie realized. Madam Butterfly. A chunky, dour Madam Butterfly.

The limericks got raunchier and raunchier, including one that Trumball loudly proclaimed had been written by no less than Isaac Asimov:

"*A harlot from South Carolina*
"*Tied fiddle strings 'cross her vagina,*
"*With proper sized cocks*
"*What was sex became Bach's*
"*Toccata and fugue in G minor!*"

Then Shektar's unmistakable Aussie voice rose above the babble: "Do any of you know 'The Jolly Tinker'?"

Silence. Jamie could sense them all shaking their befuddled heads. In a mezzo soprano, Shektar began:

> *"Oh, the tinker was a-strolling,*
> *"A-strolling down the strand,*
> *"With his knapsack on his shoulder*
> *"And his penis in his hand . . ."*

Everyone laughed uproariously. The song went on and on, worse and worse. Jamie wondered if they would be in any shape for work the next morning.

DIARY ENTRY

We've made it down at last, after five months cooped up in that sardine tin. Another day in that metal coffin and I would've started screaming. The dome is bigger, more spacious. But it's strange. It doesn't smell right. I know that something's wrong here. The dome smells bad.

NIGHT: SOL 1

JAMIE WAITED UNTIL THEY AT LAST QUIETED DOWN BEFORE HE STRIPPED off his clothes and pulled a pair of Jockey shorts and a tee shirt from his garment bag.

I ought to unpack the clothes and stow them away properly, he told himself. But he felt too tired, drained physically and emotionally, to do anything but lie back on his bunk. I'll get up early tomorrow and do it.

He had plugged his laptop into the dome's power line and set it up beside the bunk, where he could reach the keyboard easily. He tapped into a news broadcast from Earth, realizing that whatever he saw and heard had been beamed from a satellite a quarter-hour earlier.

Most of the major news and entertainment networks on Earth had gladly agreed to beam their broadcasts to Mars, free of charge. The expedition planners had willingly paid the costs of setting up the transmitters; a link with home was important for the explorers' emotional well-being, even if the link was only electronic.

Jamie saw the eight of them in their blank-faced hard suits, standing on the red sands of Mars, mouthing their little speeches. Then the screen cut to scenes of schoolchildren watching the landing ceremony. The second landing on Mars did not draw the huge throngs of people that the first landing had.

Jamie stretched back on his bunk and locked his fingers behind his head. Well, that's natural enough, I guess. The first time's exciting for the general public. The second landing looks a lot like the first one did. There won't be any excitement back home unless we run into some real trouble.

Or unless we find—

Someone tapped at his door.

Almost annoyed at the interruption, Jamie called, "Who is it?"

"Vijay."

Jamie swung his legs off the bunk and stood up. "Hold on for a second." He grabbed his discarded coveralls and pulled them on. As he sealed the Velcro front seam he stepped to the door and unlatched it.

"Something wrong?" he asked.

She had changed from her standard coveralls to a bulky, loose-fitting nubby turtleneck sweater and a pair of shapeless baggy slacks.

She sure isn't flaunting her body, Jamie thought. But she does like bright colors. The sweater was coral red, the slacks sunshine yellow.

"No, nothing wrong," she said, holding up a sealed plastic bag in one hand. "Just your vitamin delivery service, mate."

"Oh." Jamie took the bag from her hand.

"This week's supply of the supplements you'll need," she said. Shektar had personally delivered the vitamin supplements to every member of the expedition all through the flight from Earth.

"Right."

"Don't want you coming down with scurvy," Shektar said, almost impishly. The whole ground team of the first expedition had done just that when their vitamin supplement supply had been contaminated.

"No," Jamie agreed, "once is enough."

"Do you have time for a nightcap, or are you ready for sleep?"

He almost snorted at her. "After the blast you guys had, you still want a nightcap?"

"Orange juice, Jamie. Blood sugar."

"I thought you'd be needing aspirin."

"No worries," she said, leading the way toward the galley. "I didn't drink enough to hurt."

The dome was dimly lit now; since the partitions of the privacy compartments only rose eight feet high, nighttime illumination was kept low.

"Where'd you learn those songs?" he asked, following her across the shadowy floor.

"The benefits of a college education."

"Some education."

Vijay looked at him curiously. "Din't you ever get drunk at college and sing bawdy songs?"

"No, I guess not," Jamie said, thinking of how many Navahos he had seen reeling from beer.

"You don't have to look so disapproving," she said, with a smile.

"I didn't realize I was."

"You're scowling like a cut snake."

"Like a what?"

"I mean, it's not as if we'd gone completely devo. Nobody jumped me."

She isn't drunk or hung over, Jamie realized. She's the expedition's psychologist as well as our medic. This little visit isn't personal, it's professional. She's testing me.

Is she wearing perfume? he wondered. A faint flowery scent tickled his nostrils. Maybe she's using perfume to cover up body odor. Without the water from the recycler, they had gone without showering after their long sweaty day of physical labor.

"I wish somebody had brought some beer along," Shektar said as she tapped the dispenser for a squirt of orange juice. Once the water line was working properly they would mix powdered concentrate with fresh water and save the precious prepackaged supplies for emergencies.

"Why wish for beer when you've got champagne?" Jamie asked.

She shrugged, and the motion stirred him despite the bulky sweater. "Aussie beer's a lot better than Aussie fizz," she said.

Jamie wished for hot chocolate, settled for a tea bag and a squirt of hot water.

"Rank has its privileges," Shektar murmured as they sat at the table.

Jamie blinked at her, puzzled.

"You're using some of our reserve water supply," she explained.

"Oh, that. We'll bring the generator on-line tomorrow. We won't run short of water."

She leaned back in her chair, as relaxed as if they were in a neighborhood café. "If we do run short, we'll have to return to Earth, won't we?"

"We won't."

"You're very confident."

Jamie made himself smile at her. "Is this a psych test?"

She smiled back. "No, not really. I just wanted a chance to talk to you privately for a few minutes. Hard to do on the ship."

"Easier here."

"Yes. Much roomier here in this dome."

"So?"

Shektar took a sip of juice, then put her plastic cup down on the table. Leaning slightly toward Jamie, she said, "You and Dex are going to have an explosion soon if you're not careful."

So that's it, Jamie thought. Aloud, he replied, "No, we're not. I won't let that happen."

"How can you prevent it?"

Jamie hesitated, then answered, "I'm not going to lose my temper. I can understand how he feels and I'm not going to let it bother me."

"It already bothers you. That's obvious."

"Look," Jamie said, "I know that Dex's father was a major driving force behind getting this expedition funded. But we're a long way from daddy now. Dex is going to have to figure that out for himself. Here on Mars it doesn't count who your father is or what happened back on Earth. Here on Mars the only thing that counts is what you can do, what you can accomplish."

"Nice theory, but—"

"I'm not going to let him get under my skin," Jamie insisted, consciously keeping himself from clenching his fists. "The work we've got to do here is too important to let personalities get in the way."

"Do you really think you can spend a year and a half here without some sort of confrontation?'' Shektar's face was deadly serious, her eyes locked onto Jamie's.

"Yes," he said. He couldn't look away from those eyes: so deep and dark, shining and grave. Her midnight black hair was pulled away from her face, pinned back behind her neck. Jamie wondered what she would do if he reached back there and unpinned it, let it fall loosely around her shoulders. He recalled that it had been nearly a year since he'd made love.

Shektar seemed to sense something. She looked away briefly.

"I can do it," Jamie assured her, trying to keep his voice light and relaxed. "I won't let him get to me."

"The stoic Indian, hey?" she said, without humor. "Let your enemies burn you at the stake without uttering a peep."

Jamie grasped her slender wrist. "Nobody's going to burn me, and nobody's going to die here. We're going to explore as much of this planet as we can and Dex will just have to learn that he's a member of the team, not the mission director."

"He's an alpha male, y'know. Just like you."

"What's that mean?"

Shektar looked into his eyes again. "You're both natural leaders. You both *have to* be top dog. It's a prescription for trouble. Maybe disaster."

Feeling nettled, almost angry, Jamie asked, "How did you psychologists allow the two of us to come on this mission?"

"Because," she answered, "Dex was clever enough to hide it. He *knew* what the psychologists were testing for and he fooled all of them."

"You too?"

"Me too," she admitted. "It wasn't until the two of you started arguing on the way out here that I realized what a mistake we've made."

"You mean I've got the same psychological profile as he does?"

"You're both alpha males, that's clear as sunshine. You're natural-born competitors."

Jamie shook his head, more in wonder than disbelief.

She mistook the gesture. "Look at what you did on the first expedition. You took it over, din't you? You overwhelmed that Russian cosmonaut who was supposed to be the leader of the ground team and you even pushed the mission director into letting you go to the Grand Canyon, din't you?"

"Well . . . yeah . . ."

Very seriously, she said, "That's alpha male behavior, Jamie. Top dog. Ruler of the roost. King of the hill."

"And you're saying Dex is just like me?"

"Same profile. Different personality, in many ways, but he's got the same kind of devils driving him that you have."

Jamie blew out a breath. Then he asked, "Are you having the same talk with him?"

"Not yet. I wanted to speak with you first."

"Do you think talking to him will do any good?"

"No. Frankly, I don't."

"Hmm."

"He can't alter his basic personality any more than you can. You can't change yourself. The only reason I brought this up to you is because you're the mission director and I thought you had to know what you're up against."

"What we're all up against—us," Jamie said.

"That's right," Shektar agreed. "We're all in the same canoe, aren't we?"

Jamie mulled it over in silence for several moments. Shektar watched him, unmoving, leaving her wrist in his grasp.

"Okay," Jamie said at last. "I don't know if it'll do any good to mention this to Dex or not."

"It might heighten his competitive drive. Give him a stimulus to push harder."

"Then leave him alone," Jamie said quickly. "Let me deal with it."

She disengaged her wrist gently. "I'll try to help all I can, Jamie."

He grinned ruefully. "Maybe you could slip a couple of kilos of tranquilizers into his vitamin supply."

She smiled back at him. "Sorry to drop this load on you the first night, but I thought you'd better know about it as soon as possible."

"Right. Thanks."

She gulped down the rest of her orange juice, then said goodnight and headed for her quarters.

Jamie sat alone in the dim nighttime lighting. The dome structure was darkened by an electrical current that polarized the plastic to keep the interior heat from escaping into the frigid night. Everyone else was asleep, or at least in their own quarters.

Watching Shektar walk away from him, Jamie realized again that sex would be a problem sooner or later. She could wear six overcoats and it still wouldn't help, he knew. The other women, too. Month after month, living this close to them—maybe she'll have to start putting suppressants in our food.

There had been no trouble about sex during the five-month flight to Mars; except for one night, if anyone had bedded down with anyone else, they had kept it quiet. That one night had involved Dex, Jamie knew. Had it been Vijay with him? He had never asked, never really wanted to know.

Jamie remembered Dr. Li's fumbling little lecture, from six years earlier:

"We all have healthy sex drive," the first expedition's director had said. "We will be living together for nearly two years. As your expedition commander I expect you to behave in adult manner. Adult human beings, not childish monkeys."

Good advice, Jamie thought. Behave in an adult manner. Great advice.

Vijay with Dex. A one-night stand, he told himself. Doesn't mean anything. Not much it doesn't. Then why is she warning me about him? What game is she playing?

He sat at the galley table for a long time, listening to the chugs and hums of the equipment that was keeping them alive on the surface of Mars, waiting for the familiar sounds to soothe him, reassure him that everything was normal.

It didn't work. Jamie leaned back and peered up into the shadows of the dome overhead, trying to close his mind to it all. Find the balance, he commanded himself. Find the path. He closed his eyes, deliberately slowed his breathing. Then he heard it. The soft keening of the wind outside, stroking gently against the plastic bubble from another world.

Hear it, Grandfather? he asked silently. That's the breath of Mars, the voice of the red world. It's a gentle world, Grandfather. It welcomes us.

There's nothing to fear here on Mars, Jamie thought. We've got the proper equipment, we can protect ourselves and live and work here. Mars doesn't want to harm us. As long as we don't do anything foolish, Mars will be good to us.

The real dangers are those we carry with us: envy, ambition, jealousy, fear and greed and hate. We carry it all with us, locked in our hearts. Even here on Mars, we haven't changed. It's all here with us because we brought it ourselves.

He thought he heard above the sighing of the cold night wind the mad laughter of the trickster Coyote.

DOSSIER: JAMES FOX WATERMAN

JAMIE WAS SHOCKED WHEN HE REALIZED THAT HE WAS NOT BEING considered to go on the second expedition to Mars.

For three years he had been something of a celebrity in the international community of scientists: the man who had insisted on exploring the Valles Marineris. The man whose stubborn determination had led to the discovery of life on Mars.

He married Joanna Brumado, one of the two biologists who actually made the discovery. Joanna and her colleague, Ilona Malater, shared a special Nobel Prize for their find. Jamie went with his Brazilian bride to conferences all around the world, often accompanied by her father, Alberto Brumado, the astronomer-turned-activist who had spent his life cajoling the world's governments and corporations into supporting a human expedition to the red planet.

The marriage had been a mistake from the start. Born of the enforced intimacy of the long years of training and the actual expedition to Mars, it fell apart almost as soon as they took their vows in the magnificent old Candelaria Church in Rio de Janeiro. Jamie was a celebrity among the scientists, but Joanna was an international star, beloved of the media, the woman who discovered life on Mars, an instant target of the paparazzi wherever she went.

They drifted apart even though they travelled together. And Jamie had known from the beginning that Joanna's world really revolved around her father. The kindest, gentlest man in the world, Alberto Brumado was still the one man whom his daughter worshipped. She had gone to Mars despite her inner terrors because he was too old to go himself. She had married despite her inner doubts because he wanted to see her married before he died.

He died much too soon, cut down while he labored as a volunteer during an ebola epidemic that decimated São Paolo despite a multinational task force of medical aid.

With her father gone, but her stardom elevated even more by the tragedy, Joanna for the first time in her life found that she wanted to live to please herself. She enjoyed the limelight; Jamie did not. She wanted her freedom; Jamie numbly agreed.

That was when he discovered that he was being passed over for the return expedition.

"You are three years out of date," said Father DiNardo, his naturally soft voice even gentler than normal. "For three years you have been attending conferences and media interviews instead of doing research."

Jamie had gone to the Jesuit geologist once he realized that the planning for the second expedition was going ahead without him. They sat in a small office in the Vatican, Jamie tensely hunched in an ornately carved wooden chair that dated to the high Renaissance, DiNardo sitting behind a modern desk of gleaming rosewood.

Except for his clerical garb, DiNardo would have looked like the bouncer in a cheap bistro: he was built like a fireplug, short and wide; his scalp was shaved bald, his swarthy jaw stubbled.

"I've kept up with the results coming out of the various studies," Jamie protested.

DiNardo made a sympathetic smile. "Ah, yes, certainly. But you have not produced any of those results yourself. You have allowed others to do the work. Three years is a very long time.''

The priest had originally been selected to be chief geologist for the first expedition; a sudden gall bladder attack had grounded him. Nearly scandalous political maneuverings had put Jamie in his place.

"I've got to go back there," Jamie muttered. "I've got to."

DiNardo said nothing.

Jamie looked into the older man's calm brown eyes. "Nobody's planning to look for the cliff dwelling. That ought to be our first priority."

The priest sighed patiently. "Let me give you a piece of friendly advice," he said, the hint of soft Italian vowels at the end of his English words. "The more you mention the cliff dwelling, the less likely that you will be accepted for the mission."

"But it's there! I saw it!"

"You saw a rock formation that was many kilometers away from you. You believe it might be an artificial construction. No one else believes it is anything but a natural formation."

"I took video footage," Jamie insisted.

"And we have all studied your video very intensely. I myself have had it computer-enhanced. The formation appears to be a wall of some kind, standing in a niche in the cliff face. There is no evidence that it is artificial."

"That's why we've got to go back there, to find out what it really is!"

DiNardo shook his head sadly. "Do you want to be included in the second expedition or not?"

"Of course I want to be."

"Then stop talking about your cliff dwelling. It makes you look ridiculous. It makes you appear to be a fanatic. Be quiet, and I will do whatever I can to find you a berth on the mission."

Jamie stared at the priest for a long while, his mind racing. He can't accept the possibility that there might have been intelligent life on Mars. None of them want to think about that possibility. The lichen surprised them, but the idea of *intelligent* life is too much for them to swallow. They can deal with a simple form of life on Mars, but they won't open their minds to the bigger possibilities.

Why? Jamie asked himself.

The answer came to him: They're afraid.

Li Chengdu was very satisfied with his life now. He had been chosen mission director of the First Mars Expedition as a political compromise. Born in Singapore of Chinese parents, a respected atmospheric physicist, he did not belong in any entrenched political camp.

As mission director, he had remained in orbit above Mars and watched with a mixture of dread and curiosity as Jamie Waterman had wrested actual command of the scientists and astronauts on the ground team and reshaped the expedition to his purposes. Waterman had been extremely fortunate: thanks to his insistence, they found living organisms at the floor of the Grand Canyon.

And Li Chengdu, upon their return from Mars, was invited to join the faculty of the Institute for Advanced Study at Princeton. A fitting reward, he thought, for his leadership and patience—and Waterman's luck.

Now an older, warier James Waterman walked beside him through the woods outside the red-brick campus of the institute.

A scant centimeter short of two meters' height, the lean, sallow-faced Li towered over Jamie, his long legs devouring the forest track at a pace that forced Jamie almost into a jogging gait.

"I agree with Father DiNardo," Li said as they walked through the woods. The trees were blazing with autumn; red and gold and auburn leaves littered the ground like a many-hued carpet that crackled and rustled as they hiked along.

"About not mentioning the cliff dwelling," Jamie said.

"Yes. Why stir up more controversy than necessary? Your goal is to be on second expedition, not to argue the chances of intelligent Martians."

"If they existed they must have died out long ago," Jamie said, puffing slightly as he worked to keep pace with Li. The Navaho part of his mind thought, If they existed they might have migrated to a richer, bluer world.

Li raised one long-fingered hand in a gesture indicating silence. "Be patient. You will be on Mars for a year and a half. There will be ample time to visit the site again—if you can find it."

"Blindfolded," Jamie snapped.

The Chinese looked down on the intent, bronze-faced younger man and smiled slightly.

"Patience is a virtue," he said.

"You'll recommend me for the expedition?" Jamie asked.

"You have little idea of what you ask. There will be only eight berths for this expedition. Only two geologists."

"I know. Anybody would commit murder to get included," said Jamie.

"Worse than that. You have already been to Mars. The younger scientists are clamoring that it would not be fair to allow someone who has already been there to return."

"Fair? This isn't a game!"

"I agree. But by convincing the selection committee to reject anyone who has already gone to Mars, they make it more likely for one of themselves to be picked."

"Christ," Jamie grumbled. "It always boils down to politics."

"Always," said Li.

They walked through the falling leaves in silence for a while. The afternoon sun was warm, but Jamie felt a chill inside him.

At last, Li said, "I will support your inclusion in the expedition, but not as a geologist."

Jamie blinked up at him, puzzled.

"Trying to take one of the geology berths would stir up too much animosity," Li explained.

"Then what?"

"Mission director, of course," said Li. "As mission director, your experience with the first expedition would be an asset, not a liability."

All that Jamie could think to say was, "Oh."

Li smiled again, like a Cheshire cat. "After all, you really were *de facto* mission director the first time, no?"

Jamie was not a politician, but he knew enough to keep his mouth shut. There was no way to answer that loaded question without putting his foot in his mouth.

Li felt delighted. It would be a delicious irony to place Waterman in the same position he himself had struggled with during the first expedition. Let this red man know the stress of responsibility, just as I did. Let him feel the strains of younger men making demands on his judgment and patience, just as he made demands on mine.

This is not worthy of you, Li chided himself silently. This is not the way an enlightened man should behave.

Yet he nodded inwardly, satisfied that the cosmic wheel was going to complete a full turn.

There was one more person Jamie had to see before his post of mission director could be confirmed: Darryl C. Trumball.

Jamie shivered involuntarily as he was ushered into Trumball's spacious office on the top floor of the tallest tower in Boston's financial district. The room was cold, almost painfully so. It wasn't only that the air conditioning was set to a frosty temperature, the entire decor of the office was wintry: bare walls of pallid gray, not a painting or a photograph or even a flower to brighten up the bleakness. Nothing but sweeping windows in one corner, looking out on the city of Boston, far below.

Trumball was lean and hard-eyed as he sat behind an airport-sized desk of hand-polished ebony. He was completely bald, making him look almost like a death's head shining in the glow of a tiny spotlight set into the high ceiling. He was in shirtsleeves with a precisely knotted maroon tie at his throat. A gray vest was buttoned up tight over the silk shirt.

He looked as hard and sharp-edged as flint. Jamie wondered if this was what Dex would be like in thirty years.

"Have a seat, relax," he said, indicating one of the big burgundy leather chairs in front of the desk.

As he sat down, Jamie remembered how his grandfather would sit in silence for several minutes when meeting someone new to him; take the man's measure, size up his persona.

But Trumball was not a patient man. "So you want to be mission director," he said.

Jamie nodded. The truth was, Jamie wanted to go back to Mars and he would accept any position, any job, just to be included.

"That's a lot of responsibility," Trumball said.

"Dr. Li recommended me for the position," Jamie said slowly. "He was mission director for the first expedition."

"I know, I know." Trumball tilted back in his massive desk chair and steepled his long, manicured fingers.

He waited for Jamie to say something. When he didn't, Trumball said, "This is going to be a very different kind of trip, Dr. Waterman. Very different. We're not going just for the sake of sweet science, no sir. We're going to make *money* out of Mars!"

"I hope so," said Jamie.

Trumball went silent for a moment, his hard gray eyes studying Jamie. "You're not against turning an honest dollar, are you?"

"Not if it helps us to explore Mars."

"That it will, that it will."

"Then I'm for it."

"Hasn't been easy raising the funding for this trip. I've had to work like hell."

Jamie realized the man was waiting for a compliment. "You've done a fine job," he said.

Trumball drummed his fingers on the desktop for a moment. "My son's going to be one of the scientists, you know."

"Yes, I've met him. He's a geophysicist."

"Right. But he's got a good business head. Do you have a good business head, Dr. Waterman?"

Jamie was taken aback by the question. "I don't really know," he answered honestly.

Trumball looked displeased, almost angry. But he said, "Doesn't matter. Dex will look out for the business end of this job, don't you worry."

Jamie thought the man was really talking to himself.

"Well, I suppose you've got the best qualifications for the job," Trumball said, grudgingly.

"I'll take good care of your son," he said.

Trumball looked genuinely surprised. "Take good care . . . ! Hah! Dex'll take care of himself, by damn. He'd better! You just make sure that everything goes right. That's your job."

Jamie thought, No one can guarantee that everything will go right. Not when we're a hundred million kilometers away.

But he said nothing. He got up from his chair when Trumball rose from his, reached across the massive desk and shook Trumball's cold, dry hand.

And left Boston with his appointment as mission director assured.

GREENHOUSE GARDEN: SOL 6

TRUDY HALL WAS SAYING, "THE IMPORTANT THING, OF COURSE, IS TO avoid contamination."

"Yes," Mitsuo Fuchida agreed, "we don't want to accidentally introduce Earth microbes on Mars."

Jamie nodded. He was walking with the two biologists between long trays of barely leafed plants. The greenhouse garden was finally set up in its own dome, connected to their habitat dome by a double-hatched airlock. The two domes were exactly the same size, even though much of the garden's floor space was not yet used. Room to grow, Jamie told himself. For the people who follow us.

The atmosphere in the garden was just the same Earth-normal as that in the main dome, but kept at a slightly higher pressure so that air from outside its dome would not leak into the garden.

"Then there's back-contamination to consider, as well," Hall said, her brows knitting slightly. "We can't have Martian organisms infecting us."

"Or our food supply," Fuchida added.

The greenhouse garden served two purposes. The long rows of hydroponic plants were intended to supply the expedition's food: soybeans, potatoes, leafy vegetables, green beans, onions, peas, eggplant, melon and strawberries. All fed by nutrient-rich waste water that the plants themselves recycled—with the aid of specially cultivated scavenging bacteria.

Fuchida intended to raise wheat eventually, using high-intensity full-spectrum lamps instead of natural sunlight.

"It looks good," Jamie said.

"It *is* good," replied Hall, very seriously. Fuchida looked equally proud of the garden.

Hall went on, "We're thinking, Mitsuo and I, of increasing the carbon dioxide partial pressure in this dome."

"To accelerate the growth of the plants," Fuchida said.

Looking across the rows of seedlings, Jamie asked, "Will that mean that we can't breathe in here?"

"You won't need a space suit, just an oxygen mask," Hall said.

"But we don't have masks."

Fuchida allowed a tiny smile to crack his serious facade. "There are four oxygen masks in the medical stores. We could use those."

Before he could reply, Jamie heard the airlock hatch sighing open. Turning, Jamie saw Dex Trumball step through.

"There you are," Trumball said. Striding along the aisle between rows of plants, he said to Jamie, "I just heard you're going to go with us on the first traverse. Is that true?"

As mission director, Jamie's place should have been at the base camp. But the expedition's first overland traverse was heading for Tithonium Chasma, where the lichen had been found, and Jamie had no intention of remaining in the dome while the others were in the field.

"You really want to come out with us?" Trumball asked, looking somewhere between amused and annoyed.

Through the open hatch Jamie could hear a country and western tune that someone was playing, plaintive guitars and nasal yearning.

Jamie nodded solemnly. "You bet I do."

Trumball swept an arm through the air, grinning. "And give up all this luxury?"

"I'm part Navaho," Jamie countered, making himself grin back at Dex. "I'm rugged."

Their base was at last in order. All systems were functioning adequately, even the toilets. Possum Craig was outside with the drilling rig, digging deeper every day, seeking samples of bacteria from the "Plutonian biosphere" that Earthbound biologists had conjectured.

The backup water generator now stood less than fifty meters from the dome; the plumbing lines from both the primary and backup machines were buried underground and heavily insulated. Now that Fuchida and Trudy Hall had transferred the hydroponic garden from the ship to its own transparent dome they could eat a completely "home grown" vegetarian diet again, as they had during the long flight from Earth.

There were two fuel generators, as well. The first one, sent ahead of the explorers, still sat slightly more than two kilometers away. After discussing the situation with the two astronauts and Craig, Jamie had decided to let that one continue to serve as their backup and use the one that had landed with them as their primary fuel source.

Standing in front of Jamie, close enough almost to touch noses, Trumball planted his fists and his hips and cocked his head slightly to one side. "So it's going to be you, me and Trudy: two geoscientists and one biologist."

"And Stacy."

"Our driver."

Safety regulations required that every field mission had to include one of the team's astronauts until each of the scientists qualified as an experienced driver.

Jamie said, "I'll double as her backup; I've had experience driving on Mars."

"Learned how to do it back on the reservation, I'll bet."

With a curt nod, Jamie answered, "It's a lot like Mars back there, yes. Where'd you learn to drive?"

"Boston," said Trumball. "If you can drive in Boston you can drive anywhere."

Mars was bracketed by three communications satellites now, hovering above the equator in synchronous orbit, so they stayed fixed over one spot on the ground.

One of Mars' two tiny moons, Deimos—no bigger than Manhattan island—orbited almost at the synchronous altitude. Its slight gravitational pull would eventually warp the commsats out of their precise orbits, but calculations had shown that the satellites should remain stable for at least the length of the explorers' stay on the ground.

So Jamie was not concerned that he, as mission director, would be away from the base for a week. He could remain in touch with the camp, and with Earth, through the hovering commsats.

As he suited up for the ten-meter walk to the waiting rover, he saw Vijay Shektar step through the airlock's inner hatch and lift off her helmet. She shook her hair free, noticed Jamie, and smiled at him.

"I've double-checked all the supplies," she said. "Everything's in place."

"Then we're go for the excursion," said Jamie.

"Yes."

She sat beside him on the bench that ran the length of the hard-suit lockers and with a sigh began to pull off her gloves.

"Blasted suit is chafing my right elbow raw," she complained.

"Put a sponge pad on the spot," Jamie suggested. No matter how well the suits fit, there was always some discomfort. His own suit felt inordinately stiff. It would be impossible to run in it.

Jamie had already gotten into the leggings and boots, the hardest part of suiting up. Now he stood and stepped over to the waiting torso.

"It's like getting into a knight's armor, isn't it?" Shektar said.

"Going out to joust with the dragons," said Jamie.

"Dragons? That would be news!"

"Real dragons," he said. "Ignorance, the unknown."

"Ah. Yes, real dragons, all right."

"And fear."

"Fear? D'you feel fear?"

"Not fear of going outside," Jamie explained hastily. "Not fear of Mars. This world might be dangerous, but it's not malign."

She sat there encased in the hard suit like a woman being devoured by a metallic monster, and smiled curiously at Jamie.

"Then what are you afraid of?"

"I'm not afraid—but others are. Afraid of finding things that upset them."

"Such as life?"

"Such as intelligent life," said Jamie.

Understanding lit her face. "That's why you insisted on going out on this traverse. Your cliff dwelling."

Jamie nodded solemnly.

"Do you really think you can find it?"

"I could walk to it, if I had to."

"And you really believe it's an artifact, built by intelligent Martians?"

Dex Trumball came through the airlock hatch and slid up his visor. "We're all set to go, soon as the mission director climbs aboard."

"Two minutes," Jamie said. Then, looking back at Vijay's questioning eyes, he added, "We'll find out pretty soon, won't we?"

FIRST TRAVERSE: SOL 6

THE EXPEDITION INCLUDED TWO LARGE SEGMENTED ROVER VEHICLES FOR overland traverses. The rovers were exactly the same as those used in the first expedition: each was a trio of cylindrical aluminum modules, mounted on springy, loose-jointed wheels that could crawl over fair-sized rocks without upsetting the vehicle. They represented a considerable financial saving for the expedition: the cost of developing and testing them had already been absorbed by the first expedition. The second expedition merely had to order two more of them to be built.

One of the cylindrical modules was the fuel tank, big enough to keep the vehicle out in the field for two weeks or more. The middle segment usually held equipment and supplies, although it could be modified to serve as a small mobile laboratory if necessary. The front segment, largest of the three, was about the size of a city bus. It was pressurized like a spacecraft so people could live in it in their shirt-sleeves. There was an airlock at its rear, where it linked with the second module. Its front end was a bulbous transparent canopy, which made the entire assembly look something like a giant metallic caterpillar.

Each rover was designed to carry four in reasonable comfort, although the entire complement of eight explorers could be squeezed into one in an emergency.

Even bundled inside the cumbersome hard suit and sitting uncomfortably in the right-hand seat of the rover's cockpit, Jamie felt free.

He watched the Martian landscape rolling past in a sort of double vision: his trained geologist's eye cataloguing the landforms, the boulders and craters and wind-sculpted sand dunes; his deeper Navaho mind recognizing territory that might have once been home to the People.

How like the desert homeland of the People, he thought. Rusty sand and red rocks, steep-walled mesas off by the horizon. He almost expected to see footprints out there, the trail of his ancestors.

Nonsense! his Anglo mind scoffed. There's not a blade of grass within a hundred million kilometers of here. The temperature out there is below zero and tonight it'll drop to a hundred-and-more below. You can't breathe the air.

Still, Jamie felt as if he had returned home.

And farther along out there, built into a cleft in the mighty cliff wall of the Grand Canyon, there waited the ruins of an ancient city. Jamie felt certain of that. No matter what the others said, no matter what the rational side of his own mind insisted, he knew in his heart that what he had seen on the first expedition had been built by intelligent creatures.

"Thirty klicks," said Stacy Dezhurova. Sitting in the driver's seat beside Jamie, she too was encased in a bulky hard suit, although she had not put on her helmet. With her dirty-blond pageboy she looked like a chunky Dutch woman being swallowed alive by a robot.

Jamie nodded and pushed himself awkwardly out of the seat. He had to bend slightly to get out of the bulbous glassed cockpit without scraping his helmet on the overhead.

He clomped past Trudy Hall, sitting in her tan coveralls in the midsection of the rover's module. She smiled up at him.

The rover slowed to a smooth stop. Jamie hardly felt it; Dezhurova was an excellent pilot.

Trumball was standing by the airlock hatch with one of the beacon rods already in his hand. Jamie took it from him silently. Later on, Dex would suit up and do the outside work, but Jamie wanted to be the first to go outside.

"Checklist," Trumball said as he handed the beacon to Jamie.

Jamie nodded and slid down the visor of his helmet. Trumball riffled through the safety checklist quickly but thoroughly, making certain Jamie's suit was correctly sealed and all its equipment functioning properly.

"Okay, pal," he said, tapping Jamie on the back of his helmet. His voice was muffled by the helmet's insulation.

"I'm going into the airlock." Jamie spoke into the microphone built into the helmet between the bottom of the visor and the neck ring.

"Copy," he heard Dezhurova's voice acknowledge. "Wait one. I have an amber on the UV."

The airlock ceiling held a battery of ultraviolet lamps which turned on automatically as the airlock was pumped down to vacuum. The UV light was supposed to sterilize the outside of the hard suits, killing any microbes clinging to their surfaces, so the explorers could not contaminate the world outside with microscopic life from Earth. The UV was also supposed to kill any possible back-contamination on the suits when the explorers came back into the rover.

"Backup is in the green," Dezhurova's voice said crisply in Jamie's earphones. "I'll check out the primary circuit while you are outside."

"Okay. Entering the airlock now."

The airlock was no bigger than a telephone booth, barely large enough to fit a suited man. Clutching the stubby rod of the geology/meteorology beacon in one gloved hand, Jamie pressed the control stud beside the outer hatch with his other. He heard the pump chug to life as the telltale light on the panel went from green to amber.

The sound of the pump and the slight hissing of air dwindled to nothing, although Jamie could still feel the pump's vibration through the thick soles of his boots. In a minute even that ceased, and the panel light went to red. The airlock was now in vacuum.

The ultraviolet light was invisible to his eyes, of course, although he thought it made the red stripes on his sleeves fluoresce slightly.

Jamie leaned on the control stud and the outer hatch slid open. He stepped carefully down the metal rung and out onto the red sand of Mars.

He knew it was nonsense, but Jamie felt free and happy outside by himself. The barren red sands of Mars stretched all around him, out to a rugged, undulating horizon that seemed almost too close for comfort. The edge of the world. The beginning of infinity. The sky was a yellowish tan along that horizon, shading slowly toward blue as he looked up toward the small, strangely weak sun.

"Good-sized crater off to the left," he spoke into the helmet mike. "Looks recent, fresh rock along its rim."

They were following the route he had taken during the improvised jaunt to the Grand Canyon six years earlier. The excursion that had nearly killed them all. The excursion that had discovered living Martian lichen at the bottom of Tithonium Chasma.

Jamie had half-expected to see traces of the wheel tracks from that trip, but the wind-driven sand had covered them over completely. They had not bothered to plant beacons along the way, six years ago; they had been in too much of a hurry for that. Now Jamie corrected that oversight.

He pulled on the rod, extending it out to its full two meters, then planted it firmly in the red, dusty soil. Not soil, he reminded himself. Regolith. Soil is honeycombed with living things: worms, bugs, bacteria. This rusty iron sand of Mars was devoid of any trace of life. The stuff was loaded with superoxides, like powdered bleach. When the earliest automated landing vehicles first sampled the surface and could not find even traces of organic molecules in it, hopes for discovering life on Mars plummeted.

Jamie smiled to himself inside his helmet as he worked the pointed end of the beacon deeper into the ground. Mars surprised them all, he thought. We found life. What new surprises will we find this time?

Below the superoxide level there might be colonies of bacteria that never saw sunlight, bacteria that digested rock with water from the permafrost. Geologists had been stunned to find such bacteria deep underground on Earth. Possum Craig was drilling for similar Martian organisms.

Jamie was sweating by the time he got the pole set firmly enough into the ground to satisfy himself. Reaching up, he unfolded the solar panels, then clicked on the beacon's radio transmitter.

Sing your song, Jamie said silently to the beacon. A totem for the scientists, he realized. The instrumentation built into the slim pole would continuously measure ground tremors, heat flow from the planet's interior, air temperature, wind velocity and humidity. Of the hundred-some beacons they had planted during the first expedition, more than thirty were still functioning after six years. Jamie wanted to find those that had failed and see what had happened to them.

But not now, he told himself. Not today. He went back to the rover and stepped up to the open airlock hatch.

He turned around and gazed out at the rock-strewn landscape once more before closing the hatch. That fresh-looking crater beckoned to him, but he knew they had no time for it. Not yet.

Jamie gazed out at Mars. Barren, almost airless, colder than Siberia or Greenland or even the South Pole. Yet it still looked like home to him.

DIARY ENTRY

   None of the others seem to understand what danger we are in.
This is an alien world, and all we have to protect us is a thin
shell of plastic or metal. If that shell is ruptured, even a
tiny pinprick, we will all die in agony. I was a fool to come
here, but the rest of them are even bigger fools. They are a
fingernail's width away from death, and they act as if they
don't know it. Or don't care. The fools!

OVERNIGHT: SOL 6/7

"ACTUALLY," SAID TRUDY HALL, "MOST SCIENTIFIC WORK IS CRUSHingly boring."

The four of them were sitting on the lower bunks in the module's midsection, with the narrow foldout table between them and the remains of their dinners on the plastic trays before them. The two women sat on one side of the table, Trumball and Jamie on the other.

"Most of any kind of work is a bore," said Trumball, reaching for his glass of water. "I worked in my old man's office when I was a kid. Talk about boring!"

"That's what they say about flying for the air force," Stacy Dezhurova added, straight-faced. "Long hours of boredom punctuated by moments of sheer terror."

They all laughed.

"I know we could move a lot faster if we didn't have to plant the beacons," Jamie said, "but they're important to—"

"Oh, don't be so serious!" Hall said, looking surprised. "I wasn't complaining. I was merely making a philosophical point."

"The English are very deep," Trumball said, grinning across the table at her. "Really into philosophy and all that."

"Rather," agreed Hall.

Jamie made a smile for them.

"We have made good progress," Dezhurova said. "We will get to within striking distance of the Canyon's edge by sundown tomorrow."

"We could make it to the edge itself if we spaced out the beacons a little more," Trumball suggested. "Say, fifty klicks instead of thirty."

Jamie felt his brows knit slightly. "Thirty klicks means we stop once every hour, more or less."

Trumball turned on the cot to face Jamie, his grin knowing, certain. "Yeah, but if we spread 'em out to every hour and a half we could save six-seven stops tomorrow. I checked it out on the computer. We'll make a helluva lot better time."

Hall's expression turned thoughtful. "How would that affect the data stream?"

Trumball shrugged. "Not much. We picked thirty klicks pretty much arbitrarily, right? Stop once an hour, and the rover's top speed isn't much more than thirty kilometers per hour, right?"

"So if we space the beacons out every fifty klicks—will you still get the data you want?" Hall asked.

Jamie studied her face across the narrow table from him. Her gray-blue eyes were focused on Trumball. Her chin was slightly pointed, her facial bones sculpted almost like a fashion model's. She had been a runner back on Earth; even on the long flight to Mars she had jogged around the spacecraft's outer passageway for hours on end during her free time.

Trumball waved a hand in the air. "Sure. Thirty klicks, fifty klicks, what's the difference?" He was facing Hall, but he glanced sideways toward Jamie.

Taking in a breath to give himself a moment to consider, Jamie said, "Maybe you're right, Dex. Spacing out the beacons a bit more won't hurt all that much."

Trumball's eyes widened momentarily. Quickly, he added, "And we could make better time getting to the Canyon."

Jamie nodded. "Why not? Good suggestion."

Trumball's grin seemed more triumphant than grateful.

While the others took turns using the lavatory and getting into their sleep coveralls, Jamie went forward to the cockpit and called the base dome.

Tomas Rodriguez's chunky, dark-eyed face filled the dashboard screen. As Jamie went through his evening report, which Rodriguez would relay back to Tarawa, an inner part of his mind mused about the colors of the expedition's members. There had been no deliberate attempt to achieve racial or national or even gender balance, yet the skin tones among their members ranged from Trudy Hall's ivory to Rodriguez's olive brown to Vijay Shektar's near-ebony. I guess I'm somewhere between Tomas and Vijay, he realized.

Jamie had tried to plan out the assignments for field missions so that there would always be two women in each team. He knew he was being overly cautious, prudish even, but he thought the women would feel better with another female aboard, rather than alone with several men.

That left Vijay alone at the dome with Fuchida, Craig and Rodriguez, he knew, but he thought Vijay could take care of herself. Fuchida would be no problem and Craig would most likely behave like a benevolent uncle. Rodriguez had his store of testosterone, but he did not seem aggressive enough to worry Jamie.

Still, he wanted to see Vijay, talk with her.

Once he finished his report he asked, "Is Vijay still awake?"

"I think so," Rodriguez said. "Hang two and I'll get her."

There was no intercom system in the base dome, only a public-address network of loudspeakers, reserved strictly for emergencies. Rodriguez simply got up from the comm console and walked to Shektar's cubicle. Jamie waited, staring at an empty screen. Rodriguez came back in a few moments.

"She's on her computer, talking to Dex, from the looks of it."

Jamie turned in the cockpit seat and, sure enough, Dex was squatting on his upper bunk hunched over his laptop, its screen glowing on his grinning, young, handsome face.

OVERNIGHT: SOL 7/8

"THIS IS THE TRICKY PART," JAMIE WARNED DEZHUROVA.

After a whole day of driving, she was edging the rover up the steadily rising ground, skirting boulders the size of automobiles, gearing down as the grade steepened.

Off to their right the setting sun was almost touching the jagged horizon, its pale pinkish light slanting into the cockpit, throwing long shadows across the rocky ground. They were both in their tan coveralls. The last geology/meteorology beacon for the day had been planted almost two hours earlier. Now they were reaching the lip of the greatest canyon in the solar system.

"The edge comes up all of a sudden," Jamie warned, in a near-whisper.

"I have flown the simulations," Dezhurova said flatly, never taking her eyes off the ground trundling slowly by.

"Sorry," Jamie muttered.

She flicked a quick glance at him. "Copilots are always backseat drivers," she said, deadpan.

Jamie half rose in his seat. "I think . . ."

"Yes."

"There it is!"

Dezhurova pressed the brake so gently that Jamie barely rocked forward. He sat there staring out at the immensity of the Grand Canyon. The breath gushed out of him.

There it was.

Stacy muttered, "Oora . . ." stretching out the word, her voice hollow with awe.

They were looking over the edge of the Grand Canyon, a gash in the world that spread the distance from New York to San Francisco, more than five kilometers deep, so wide that they could not see the other side.

The land just dropped away, abruptly, without warning. Far, far below, deeper than most ocean bottoms on Earth, was the Canyon floor, stretching out and beyond the horizon. Not a wisp of mist obscured their view; they could see it all in crisp detail, marred only by the incredible distances they gazed through.

"Come see this!" Dezhurova called back over her shoulder.

"We're there?" Trudy Hall asked as she and Trumball pushed into the cockpit and crouched behind the seats to look out through the windshield.

"Marvelous," Hall whispered.

Jamie glanced up at Trumball. For once in his life, Dex was speechless, staring, overwhelmed with wonder at the majesty of Tithonium Chasma.

Guide me to the right path, Grandfather, Jamie prayed silently. Lead me to the harmony that alone can bring peace to my heart. Let me find the truth of it all, and let me go in beauty.

Trumball found his voice at last. "I don't see the landslide that you guys went down."

"It's off to the right a few klicks," Jamie said, as certain as he was of his own name.

Kneeling behind Jamie's seat, Trumball grunted. "Injun scout know-um territory, huh?"

Jamie looked up sharply at him. "You bet your ass I do."

Dezhurova tapped a finger on the control panel's electronic map display. "Jamie is right. Here is where we are, and here . . ." her fingertip edged to a blinking green spot on the map, ". . . is where we want to be."

"Can we get there before dark?" Hall asked.

"No," said Dezhurova, shaking her head. "The sun is on the horizon already."

"We'll still have a half-hour or so before it gets dark," Trumball pointed out.

Dezhurova half-turned in her seat to face him. "Do *you* want to go feeling your way along this cliff edge in the dark? I do not."

"It won't be that dark, not right away. And you've got the headlights, for god's sake."

Dezhurova's broad chin was set stubbornly. "This is not the Batmobile, and I am no shroomer."

Trumball frowned with puzzlement. Jamie grinned inwardly. He'd been around the astronauts enough to know that "shroomer" was short for "mushroomer," someone with the intellectual capacity of a fungus.

"I still think—"

Jamie cut Trumball short. "In any argument that concerns safety, Dex, the astronaut has the final say. That's the rule."

"And we always play by the rules, don't we?" Trumball grumbled.

Hall tried to defuse the situation. "If we're only a half-hour or so away, why not wait until morning? It won't make that much difference, will it?"

Trumball grinned at her, but it looked half-hearted. "Yeah, I suppose you're right. What the hell."

Trumball got up and headed back toward the midget galley in the module's rear. Reluctantly, Jamie thought. "Might's well start dinner," he called over his shoulder.

Hall went back to join him in pulling packages of their prepared meals out of the freezer and sliding them into the microwave oven.

"I'm going to set up one of the beacons," Jamie told Dezhurova, getting up from his seat.

"That means I will have to suit up, too," she said, with a sigh.

"We can bend the rules a little. I'll just be outside for a couple minutes."

Her sapphire blue eyes flicked toward Trumball. "Bend the rules? How do you think he will feel about that?"

Before Jamie could answer, Dezhurova added, "Besides, I would like to get out of here for a little bit."

So the two of them went back to the hard suits stored by the airlock and suited up while Trumball and Hall unfolded the table and started in on their meals.

"Wait for us before you begin dessert," Dezhurova called cheerfully.

"Fine," said Hall.

They checked each other's suits, then Jamie took one of the beacons and entered the airlock. Once outside, by the time he had slid the rod to its full length and dug its pointed end into the ground, Dezhurova came through the outer hatch to join him.

"That damned UV circuit is still balky," she complained.

Struggling with the pole, Jamie said, "Maybe we should trace it all the way from the console. Find the fault."

"Yes, I suppose we will have to," Dezhurova said. Then she added, "They should have put a motorized auger on the poles."

Bending over, grunting with the effort of worming the pole into the ground, Jamie answered, "Muscle power's cheaper."

He straightened up and turned his suit fans higher. He felt sweat trickling down his ribs.

"I think that'll do it," he said.

Dezhurova replied, "You haven't turned the light on."

"Wait a minute. I want to see if . . ."

"The sun is down. We must get back inside."

"In a minute."

"What is it?"

Jamie turned his back to the faint pink glow where the sun had dropped behind the jagged horizon. The sky out to the east was black, empty.

"Let your eyes adjust to the darkness, Stacy," he told Dezhurova.

"If you are trying to see Earth, it's not—"

"No," he whispered. "Wait."

"For what?"

Jamie saw them. Shimmering bands of light, faint as ghosts, flickering across the sky in spectral pale pinks and whites.

"An aurora!" Dezhurova gasped.

"The sky dancers," Jamie murmured, more to himself than her.

"There must be a solar flare . . . some kind of disturbance . . ."

"No," Jamie heard himself say. "Mars' magnetosphere is so weak that the solar wind hits the upper atmosphere all over the planet. We get the lights almost every night, right after sunset. They fade away pretty quickly, though."

The Navaho side of his mind was saying, The sky dancers are here, Grandfather. I see them. I understand them. They bring your spirit to me, Grandfather. It's good that you are here with me. It brings strength and beauty.

The Old Ones taught that the People once lived in a red world, long before coming to the desert where they now dwell. Coyote, ever the trickster, caused a huge flood that would have killed all the People if they had not been able to reach the blue world safely.

IN TRANSIT

NO MATTER HOW HARD HE TRIED, JAMIE FOUND THE LIVING QUARTERS ON the Mars-bound spacecraft small, cramped and stifling.

He knew his compartment was actually a bit larger than the quarters he had occupied in the first expedition's craft. But that space vehicle had been equipped with a wardroom spacious enough to accommodate all twelve of the scientists and astronauts aboard. And there had been an observation center as well, a place where Jamie could get away from everyone else, at least for a little while.

The second expedition's craft was laid out in a circular plan. Each of the eight compartments was a pie-shaped cubicle; each precisely the same size as all the others. A passageway ran along the outer perimeter, giving access to each cubicle. It also served as Trudy Hall's running track. Every morning, for the entire five months of the flight to Mars, Jamie was awakened by her remorseless thumping, round and round, for at least a full hour.

In each compartment the door at the wide end of the pie wedge opened onto the passageway. The door at the narrow end opened onto one of the ship's two lavatories; the three women shared one lav, the five men shared the other.

There were no observation ports. The ship's designers had placed a flat display screen on one wall of each living compartment, an electronic "window" that could show outside views or videos, at the whim of the occupant. It could also be used as a computer display.

Their cylindrical spacecraft swung at the end of a five-kilometer-long tether composed of microscopic-sized tubules of Buckyballs, man-made molecules of carbon atoms shaped like geodesic spheres. Tough, light and pliable, the Buckyball tethers had a greater tensile strength than the strongest metal alloys. On the other end of the tether was the nuclear rocket system and its radiation shield. The two modules swung around their common center to give a feeling of gravity to the explorers: a full terrestrial g when they left Earth orbit, slowly winding down to the one-third g of Mars as they crossed the gulf between the planets. Thus the explorers would be adapted to Martian gravity when they landed.

Despite the electronic window, Jamie felt like a penned animal, a convict in jail. The spacecraft was never quiet; pumps chugged, air fans buzzed, computers beeped. He could hear people talking from three or four compartments away. Every day Trudy Hall's endless jogging around the outer passageway sounded like a Chinese water torture, padding incessantly at her precise trotting pace.

Jamie spent as little time in his quarters as possible, preferring the galley on the level above. At least it was large enough to hold all eight of them at once, although it was something of a squeeze. They were always bumping shoulders up there, literally. "Good morning" was inevitably followed by, "Oops, sorry."

The galley doubled as a conference room. There was no other room available. Their spacecraft had been designed to minimize cost, not maximize crew comforts.

Despite the crowding, or perhaps because of it, everyone was extremely polite. Most of the time. No one complained about body odors or stale jokes. No one played disks or videos without using an earplug, unless everyone agreed to listen or watch. If any of them paired off for sex, they kept quiet about it, both during the lovemaking and afterward. Most of the time.

But there were tensions. Possum Craig took some teasing about his nose, but to Jamie's eye he was sensitive about his status as the team's repairman. He's a professional scientist, Jamie knew, but he's spent his career working for petroleum companies rather than universities. The other scientists unconsciously looked down at him.

Vijay Shektar seemed constantly on guard against sexual advances. She had seemed like an attractive young woman when Jamie had first met her, but after the months of being confined in the spacecraft she began to look to him like one of the voluptuous dancing girls carved on the face of a Hindu temple. And the other men obviously felt the same way. But with her Aussie caustic wit she shrivelled any man who tried to come on to her. It took several weeks before Tomas Rodriguez finally admitted defeat to himself.

Fuchida was more difficult for Jamie to fathom. He was exquisitely polite at all times and seemed totally at ease in the crowded living spaces. Yet his eyes seemed sad, melancholy, as if he longed for an Eden that was forever lost. Jamie wondered what preoccupied the Japanese biologist: was it something in his past that was bothering him, or something in the future he was worried about?

The other biologist, Trudy Hall, seemed to be quite self-contained: pleasant almost all the time, intelligent, but certainly not outgoing. She went her own way and spent most of her time working with Fuchida.

Anastasia Dezhurova was just the opposite: Stacy looked gloomy, scowling, forbidding, but once you began talking with her she opened up into a friendly, likeable, utterly competent woman. She was big-boned, thick in the middle, slow in movement, but her reflexes were lightning-fast. During a mandatory training session out in the badlands of Dakota, Jamie had seen her snatch a field mouse in her bare hand when it came sniffing into her tent. Then she tenderly carried the terrified rodent out to the brush and set it free.

Dezhurova was the senior of the team's two astronauts, with more than a dozen flights into space for the Russians; she was second in command to Jamie. She worked with Rodriguez and, as the weeks went by, more and more with Craig on maintaining the equipment and running the astronomical experiments at the behest of astronomers back on Earth.

If being subordinate to her threatened Rodriguez's machismo, he gave no outward sign of it. Tomas seemed to be an amiable, easygoing sort, although Jamie wondered how long he could remain cooped up with the three women without causing a problem.

It was Dex Trumball who gave Jamie the most irritation. Dex with his cocky, handsome smile and smooth manners. A young man born to money, who'd never had to struggle for anything in his life. His father had been a major force in funding this expedition, yet Dex would have been chosen to go anyway, he was that good a geophysicist. Degrees from Yale and a doctorate from Berkeley, no less, plus brilliant work on the lunar mascons.

The long months of the journey to Mars went smoothly enough, except for a communications breakdown when the main comm antenna responded to a faulty computer command and pointed itself away from Earth. For a whole day Dezhurova and Rodriguez tried every programming trick they knew to unlock the antenna, to no avail. At last the Russian and Craig had to suit up and go EVA to physically remove the antenna's steering system and reprogram it inside the spacecraft, then go out and reinstall it. No damage done, and no one got hurt, although everyone was jittery until they reestablished contact with mission control on Tarawa.

Jamie noticed, though, that Trudy Hall was ashen-faced with tension. When he asked Vijay about her, Shektar told him she had given the biologist tranquilizers to calm her down.

The only other incident came when a solar flare erupted and they had to spend fifty-three hours in the spacecraft's shielded storm cellar. Hall hyperventilated from anxiety, but otherwise everyone was all right. Trudy took a good deal of teasing about having to clap a retch bag over her face and breathe into it for almost twenty minutes.

Then late one night, when they were halfway to Mars, as he prepared for bed, Jamie heard muffled laughter from the next compartment: Dex's quarters.

"What's he ever done?" Through the thin partition between their compartments, Trumball's voice sounded accusing, almost angry. "I mean, what's he ever contributed to the field of geology?"

The answering voice was too low, too muffled for Jamie to make out either the words or the speaker. It sounded like a woman's voice, he thought.

"I'll tell you what scientific contributions our big Injun chief has made," Trumball went on, loud and clear. "Nothing. Zip. Nada. Zero."

He's talking about me! Jamie realized.

The woman said something; the tone sounded as if it might have been a protest.

"Oh, yeah, sure, he drove the first expedition to go to the Grand Canyon and they found the lichen there. But he didn't make the discovery, the biologists did. He might have married one of 'em, but he couldn't even make that work."

The woman spoke again, lower still.

"If he weren't a redskin he wouldn't be the mission director, I can tell you that," Trumball insisted. "His scientific accomplishments have been zero. He's a political choice, nothing more."

Trumball went on for a while, in a lower tone, his words too muffled now for Jamie to make out.

Jamie sank down on his bunk, feeling empty inside, drained, defeated. He's right, Jamie realized. I haven't contributed much to the field. I got onto the first expedition by a fluke and I'm here as mission director because I campaigned for it.

He tried to sleep. But he could not. Is this what the rest of them think of me? Are they just tolerating me because I was on the first expedition? Or because I'm older than any of them?

Then he heard the woman giggle. Dex shushed her. Jamie tried not to listen, turned on his bunk and covered his head with the slim plastic pillow. Silence for a while. Then a soft moan, almost a sob. Jamie squeezed his eyes shut, tried to will himself to deafness. She moaned again, louder. It went on for what seemed like an hour.

Jamie could not tell for certain who was in there with Dex, but the woman sounded to him like Vijay.

It took several days before he could look her in the eye again. Before he could look at any of them without wondering what was going through their minds.

And he could not look at Trumball at all. Until the evening when he and Dex flared into open conflict.

Fuchida and Hall were giving a seminar to the rest of the scientists about the latest findings from Earth. Everyone was crowded on the benches that lined the one long table of the galley. The display screens along the curving bulkhead showed photomicrographs of the Martian lichen samples that had been returned to Earth by the first expedition.

"We knew before we took off," Trudy Hall was saying, standing at the head of the table, "that the Martian lichen are remarkably like terrestrial lichen in several ways, but decidedly unlike in others.

"Like terrestrial lichen, they are colonies of algoids and fungoids living together in a symbiotic relationship that—"

"Without benefit of marriage?" Trumball cracked.

Unfazed, Hall replied, "They reproduce asexually."

"That's no fun."

"How do you know if you haven't tried it?"

Jamie leaned his forearms on the table and said softly, "Let's get back on the subject, please."

Hall nodded and resumed, "The most interesting thing is that their nuclear material contains double-stranded molecules that are remarkably like our own DNA."

"Their genetic programming," Fuchida took over, getting to his feet to stand beside Hall, "appears to be very similar to our genetic code."

Pointing to a computer-graphic representation of a twining double helix, Fuchida said, "Their genes are composed of four base units, just as our own are."

Jamie thought Fuchida's voice was trembling slightly. Excitement that he was trying to suppress?

"You mean we're related to them?" Shektar asked, wide-eyed awe in her tone.

"Not necessarily," answered Fuchida, raising one hand slightly. "Their base units are not the same composition as ours. We have adenine, cytosine, guanine and thymine. The Martian base units are remarkably similar in function, but of different composition chemically. No formal names have been assigned to them as yet. They are known simply as Mars One, Mars Two, Mars Three, and—"

"Let me guess," Trumball interrupted. "Mars Four?"

Fuchida made a miniaturized bow. "Yes, Mars Four."

"Well now, that's almost poetic," muttered Possum Craig.

As Fuchida and Hall took turns showing how the Martian DNA worked, Jamie's mind began to wander. Same system for passing genetic information from one generation to another, but different chemical structure. Are we related? Could Earth's life have originated on Mars? Or vice versa?

The others were already arguing the same point, he realized.

"Had to be Mars-to-Earth," Craig was insisting stubbornly. "Couldn't be the other way 'round."

"Why not?" Shektar demanded.

"Gravity," Trumball answered. "It's a lot easier to blast a chunk of Mars rock loose and have it meander to Earth than it is to blast off a hunk of Earth and get it to Mars."

"And Mars is much closer to the asteroid belt," piped up Rodriguez, from the foot of the table. "It gets hit by meteoroids a lot more often than Earth does."

"Yes, of course," Hall said.

"Meteoroid strikes blast chunks of Martian rock into space," Rodriguez went on doggedly. "Some of the rocks drift close enough to Earth for our gravity well to capture them and pull them down to the ground."

They delved into a free-for-all about the chances that Mars life and Earth life were somehow related. Jamie listened with only half his attention, wondering about the links between Earth's life and Mars. He forgot about Dex and his snide wisecracks, forgot about his worries of what the others thought of him. In his mind's eye he saw the cliff dwelling in Mars' Grand Canyon and others like it scattered throughout the southwestern desert.

He felt in his heart that there was a relationship, there had to be; two worlds close enough to be brothers and both of them bearing life. They had to be related. At some time, in some way, life seeded both the red world and the blue. How long ago? How did it come to pass?

That's what we're here to discover, his rational mind answered.

"We'd have to protect all the natural species, of course," Trumball was saying. "Assuming there's more than one species to be protected."

Jamie snapped his full attention to their discussion.

"That's rather far-fetched," Hall said, "don't you think?"

"No more far-fetched than finding life on the planet," said Trumball, leaning back on the bench until his shoulders rested against the curving bulkhead.

Shektar was staring at him. "Do you really believe that we could alter the environment of the entire planet?"

"Make it so earthlike that people could walk out on the surface without suits?" Rodriguez looked clearly disbelieving.

"Why not?" Trumball replied easily. "There's plenty of water in the permafrost. Heat it up, pump it out, and we can warm up the atmosphere. Use siderophile bacteria. Sow the atmosphere with blue-green algae and they'll soak up the carbon dioxide in the air and give us a breathable oxygen/nitrogen atmosphere."

"In a hundred thousand years or so," Hall said.

"Don't be a flathead," Trumball snapped. "We've done studies that show you can do it in a century or two."

Jamie saw the crooked, self-confident grin on Trumball's face and remembered his sneering, *What's he ever contributed to the field of geology?*

"And what happens to the native life-forms?" he asked quietly.

"They'll have to be protected, like I said."

"Assumin' you can do all that," Craig asked, "how're you gonna pay for it?"

Trumball's cocky grin widened. "That's the beauty of it. The project pays for itself."

"How?"

"Colonization."

"Colonization?" several voices echoed.

"Sure, why not? They've got tourists taking flights to that orbital hotel, don't they? And Moonbase is setting up facilities for retirees. Why not colonize Mars?"

"Very expensive, don't you think?" said Dezhurova.

Jamie felt something like red-hot lava beginning to churn in his guts.

Trumball nonchalantly laced his fingers behind his head as he replied, "Look, you guys ought to get with the program. There are plenty of people right now who'd pay for a trip to Mars. So it costs ten million per person, what's that to the CEO of Masterson Aerospace or the head of Yamagata Heavy Industries? Or to some video star? And the price'll come down as we establish facilities here on Mars for refueling and growing food."

"So you can build permanent colonies on Mars," Rodriguez muttered.

"Sure," Dex repeated. "Why the hell not?"

"Good lord," Hall murmured.

"The big corporations will lead the way," Trumball went on, "and the tourism industry will jump in with both feet. Vacation on Mars! See the Grand Canyon! Climb the tallest mountain in the solar system!"

"Why not ski down it?" Dezhurova muttered.

"We could make snow, sure!"

"But tourists don't stay—"

"Yeah, but that'll be just the beginning," Dex replied, with growing enthusiasm. "We'll have to build facilities for the tourists, right? That'll be the start of permanent colonies, lemme tell you."

"No," said Jamie.

Trumball turned slowly to face him, the crooked grin still on his handsome face. "I didn't think you'd go for it."

"Mars is not going to be turned into a tourist site or a colony."

"Wanna bet?"

"I think it's utter nonsense," Hall said with a huff.

"So'd your grandfather think about going into orbit for a honeymoon," Trumball shot back, "but people are doing it now, aren't they."

"What you are talking about," said Dezhurova, "transforming the entire planet—that is called terraforming, correct?"

"Terraforming, right." Trumball nodded.

Trying to control the anger seething within him, Jamie said, "You want to change the entire planet, make it just like Earth."

"That's the basic idea. Then it'll be a lot safer for visitors. Then we can build permanent settlements on Mars. Build cities, colonies."

"Just like the Europeans did to the Americas," Jamie said.

Trumball laughed out loud. "I knew it'd torque you. Cultural bias and all that."

"And you'll put the lichen on a reservation, where the visitors can come and stare at them."

Trumball's grin did not fade a centimeter. "Hey, don't get so stoked. It's the wave of the future, pal. And the thing is, you've done more than anybody here to make it possible."

"I have?"

"Sure," said Trumball. "You're the guy who pushed the first expedition to the Grand Canyon, aren't you? Without you they never would've found the lichen."

Jamie felt suddenly off balance. Praise from Trumball was totally unexpected.

"And you even made a fuss about some cliff dwelling, didn't you?" Dex continued. "Now that'd make a helluva tourist attraction! A native Martian village. People would pay a flippin' fortune to see that, lemme tell you."

"Not while I live," Jamie said, with all the iron in his soul.

"You can't stop it, chief," Trumball said, with just as much steel. "It's inevitable. We come, we see, we conquer."

"Not while I live," Jamie repeated. Then he added, "Nor in your lifetime, either."

"Oh no? How much you want to bet that the next expedition to Mars carries tourists? Only a couple very rich old farts who don't mind spending a few million bucks to prove their machismo. But they'll come."

"Perhaps media reporters," Fuchida muttered.

"And ruin Mars the way the Europeans ruined everyplace they touched," Jamie said.

"What ruin?" Trumball countered. "You wouldn't be going to Mars if your precious Native Americans had their way. You'd still be hunting buffalo and weaving blankets."

Jamie pushed himself to his feet, too furious to trust himself much further.

He pointed a finger at Trumball like a pistol. "No one's going to fuck up Mars, Dex. Not you or anyone else. That, I promise you."

Dex grinned lazily. "How're you going to stop us, chief?"

Jamie had no answer.

MORNING: SOL 8

JAMIE STOOD ALONE IN THE ANCIENT CITY, THE HOT SUN SO BRIGHT IN THE clear golden sky that its glare against the alabaster buildings made his eyes hurt. The heat of the sun felt good against his naked skin. The city was abandoned, still, silent, yet as beautiful as the day its builders had finished their work.

Where are the people who made this wonderful place? Jamie wondered as he walked barefoot through the central plaza. The fluted columns of magnificent temples stood on either side of him. Before him rose a palace, its steps reaching to the sky.

Where have they all gone? he wondered.

Suddenly the peaceful silence was shattered by the roar of thousands of people who poured into the plaza from all sides, streaming in unending hordes, men and women and children in shorts and tee shirts and baseball caps pointing cameras and munching burgers and fries and slopping sodas from plastic mugs.

He knew some of the people. He saw a beautiful dark-skinned woman in an emerald green thong bikini stretched out on one of the high temple ledges, sunning herself, alone and aloof from the crowds that jostled him.

The noise of hammering and power saws rattled the air; construction cranes rose into the sky as more and always more people crowded into the ancient, doomed city.

A lean, hard-eyed man with a shaved skull was directing everyone, sending people scurrying each time he pointed his outstretched hands.

"You people go up to the temple there, take a good look at the artwork on the walls before we tear it down and bring it back home. The rest of you can eat at the new fast-food franchise we're building."

The man looked toward Jamie and seemed to recognize him. "You can't stay here!" he shouted angrily. "What're you doing off your reservation?"

Jamie recognized the man. It was Darryl C. Trumball. And standing just behind him was his son, Dex, grinning smugly.

Jamie's eyes popped open. He was sweating and his bedsheet was tangled around his legs. Inches above him was the rover's upper bunk, sagging slightly under Dex Trumball's weight. Across the way the two women slept.

He blinked and rubbed his eyes. He had been dreaming, but he could not remember all of his dream. Something about hordes of people swarming across the barren face of Mars in loud sports shirts and bathing suits, leaving tons of emptied beer cans and wadded fast-food wrappers across the rust-red landscape. A disturbing dream, its essence retreating into nothingness as Jamie tried to remember its details.

Trumball had been in the dream. And Vijay Shektar, wearing a skimpy bikini rather than expedition-issue coveralls.

Jamie shook his head, trying to clear away the remnants of his dream, then slid quietly out of his bottom bunk without disturbing Dex. He stole a glance at the younger man; Trumball's face was peaceful, relaxed. No bad dreams for him.

Across the narrow aisle, Stacy Dezhurova was turned to the bulkhead, curled slightly with her knees drawn up. Trudy Hall, on the top bunk, lay on her back with a tiny knot of a frown creasing her brows.

Jamie felt almost guilty, looking at them in their sleep. Soul-stealer, he thought. Let them have their dreams to themselves.

He took his wrinkled coveralls and padded to the lavatory. By the time he came out, all three of the others were up, sitting on the edges of their bunks, yawning and rubbing the sleep out of their eyes.

Jamie went up forward to the cockpit and slid the thermal screen back from the windshield.

And gasped.

The mist. He had forgotten about the mists that sometimes rose from the valley floor. Now, with the sun barely over the eastern horizon, the valley was filled with pearl-gray vapor, undulating slowly in the morning breeze, like the soft lapping waves of a gentle sea, like the easy rhythmic breathing of a world.

"Come and see this!" he called back to the others.

Trumball was in the lav, but the two women padded barefoot to the cockpit.

"Oooh," breathed Trudy Hall. "It's *beautiful*!"

Stacy Dezhurova nodded and ran a hand through her lank blonde hair. "Beautiful, all right. But how will we drive through it?"

The rising sun burned the mist away, as Jamie recalled it did when he had first seen the Canyon. By the time they had breakfasted and started the rover's engines, Dezhurova was no longer worried about driving into fog.

"Sun is burning it off faster than we're travelling," she said, driving along the Canyon's rim.

"There it is," said Jamie, pointing. His outstretched finger nearly bumped the rover's bulbous windshield.

"I see it," Dezhurova said.

The landslide was still there. Jamie knew it would be. Several thousand million tons of slumped dirt do not disappear over six years, but still he felt an inner thrill of relief and excitement that it was still there, like a ramp prepared by the gods for them to ride down to the floor of the Canyon.

A shadow flickered overhead and they both looked up. One of the soarplanes, remotely piloted by Rodriguez back at the base camp, its cameras and radar serving to scout the territory ahead.

Jamie punched up the soarplane's camera view on the rover's control panel display screen. The ramp is just the way we left it, he saw. He squinted hard, trying to make out the tracks their vehicles had left the first time. But the tireless winds of Mars had erased them, filled them in with fine iron-rich dust.

"Give me the radar view," Dezhurova ordered. Jamie knew the radar data could tell them about the ground's consistency. They had lost one of the rovers on the first expedition, stuck in an ancient crater filled in with treacherous fine dust that swallowed up half the vehicle like quicksand.

It's still there, he knew, stuck half in the dust pool. If we could pull it out we'd have an extra vehicle to work with.

Jamie shook his head at the idea. We're here to study the lichen down at the Canyon floor, not to salvage old equipment.

"Steady now," Jamie muttered as Dezhurova nosed the rover over the lip of the canyon rim. Her gaze was riveted straight ahead, down the steeply angled slope, although her eyes flicked every few seconds to the radar display, like a novice pianist glancing back and forth from her music sheet to the keyboard.

"Easy does it," Dezhurova whispered, half to herself.

Jamie felt the bump as each set of wheels crossed the rimrock. Staring out the windshield, he almost felt as if he were in a diving airplane. Dezhurova was bent over the steering wheel, both hands locked tightly on it. Her knuckles weren't white, Jamie noticed, but her grip on the wheel was far from relaxed.

"Will you look at that!" Trumball's voice sounded excited, almost frightened, from behind Jamie's chair. "Like crash-diving a submarine."

"Rather an unfortunate term, crash-dive," said Trudy Hall. Jamie glanced over his shoulder at the two of them. Trumball looked excited, like a kid about to bungee jump off a high bridge. Hall seemed cool, although she kept licking her lips.

After a few tense, silent moments, Dezhurova eased up from her cramped posture and grinned. "Piece of cake."

All three of the others relaxed. Jamie hadn't realized he'd been holding his breath until he let it out in a big, relieved gust.

"The only bad spot we found was that dust-filled crater," he said, as if Dezhurova hadn't gone through this a thousand times already. "Although there might be other bad patches we just happened to miss," he added.

"That's the stuff," said Trumball, "look on the bright side."

"Oh hush, Dex," Hall said crossly.

Trudy pulled down the jumpseat behind Jamie and settled in to watch their slow descent toward the valley floor, several kilometers ahead. Trumball went back toward the rear of the module.

"Don't you want to see this?" Hall called back to him.

"Not just see it," he yelled back. "I want to make certain it's getting onto the VR database. People back home will flip their toggles over this!"

"It's all being recorded," Dezhurova said.

"Just checking," Trumball called back. "Yep. Every little pixel is coming through in living color. All we need is Tars Tarkas standing out there to greet us."

"Tars Tarkas?" Jamie asked.

"A sixteen-foot-tall, green, four-armed Martian," Hall explained, with seeming distaste. "From some lurid skiffy novel Dex must have read in his misspent youth."

"Sounds like you read it too, kiddo," Trumball said, as he made his way back up to the cockpit.

Hall replied, "You're not the only one to have had a misspent youth, Dex."

Trumball took the other jumpseat and they all fell silent for a while. Jamie offered to spell Dezhurova at the wheel, but she shook her head.

"I don't want to stop. Besides, this isn't as bad as I thought it would be."

Jamie nodded, then realized that he'd been at the wheel when the rover ploughed into the sand trap, six years earlier. Of course, they had all been miserably sick with scurvy, but still he was the driver and he had gotten them all stuck.

"Look!" Trumball shouted. "I see it!"

"The old rover," Jamie said.

It looked like a giant metal caterpillar trying to burrow into the ground, its forward module half buried in the sand. Wind-blown dust had piled up on its left side; the right side was bright bare aluminum, perhaps even scoured clean.

"It's still there," said Hall.

Trumball laughed. "What, you think somebody would repo it?"

"Hardly."

"Maybe we should," he said.

"Should what?"

"Repo the old rover."

Jamie glanced back at him.

"What do you think, big chief?" Trumball asked. "If we can drag it out of that sand trap, we'd have an extra rover to play with."

"We don't need an extra rover," Jamie said.

Dezhurova had slowed down as she maneuvered carefully around the area, staying well clear of the treacherous sand-filled crater. They could all see the faint outline of the crater and the little ridges of sand in it, like ripples on a pond. Jamie had been too ill and exhausted to notice them when he had piloted the rover into the sand trap.

"Sure we could use an extra rover," Trumball said, enthusiasm warming his tone.

"We've only got eight people here, Dex," Jamie said. "Only three qualified drivers. We—"

"If you can drive a rover," Trumball interrupted, "I sure can. We've all practiced in the simulators."

Trudy Hall asked, "All the excursions have been planned out, Dex. What do we need another rover for?"

Trumball's grin was dazzling. "To go out and get the Pathfinder."

"Pathfinder?" Jamie and Dezhurova blurted in unison.

"Sure! It's sitting at the Sagan site, over at Ares Vallis. With that little Sojourner buggy, too!"

"That is more than a thousand kilometers away, Dex," said Dezhurova.

"More like four thousand," Trumball admitted, "from our base camp."

They were slowly passing the old rover, crawling over the firmer ground where Jamie had walked, staggered, crawled to carry a safety line to the Russians who had come to rescue them.

"Let's at least stop and see if the old clunker is still usable," Trumball urged.

With a glance at Dezhurova, who slowed the rover even more, Jamie asked, "Why? How will salvaging the rover get you to Ares Vallis?"

Grinning even wider, Trumball said, "Now here's my plan. *If* the old rover is usable, we drive it back to the base. Or tow it, most likely."

"Tow it?" Trudy Hall muttered.

Ignoring her, Trumball went on, "Then Wiley and I repair whatever needs repairing and get her in good working order."

Stacy Dezhurova asked laconically, "Would you buy a used car from this man?"

"Then I drive her out to the Sagan site and pick up the Pathfinder and Sojourner."

"But why?" Hall demanded.

Trumball turned a pitying gaze on her. "Do you have any idea how much a museum would pay for that hardware? The Air and Space Museum in Washington, for example?"

"Not much," Dezhurova said. "That is a government operation, remember."

"Okay, what about Disney? Or one of the Las Vegas casinos? Or some of the big amusement complexes in Japan or Europe?"

"How much would you expect?" Hall asked.

Instead of answering directly, Trumball replied, "Lemme tell you, it'll be plenty. How much did that Picasso painting go for last year? Fifty mil? And that was just a piece of canvas with some colors smeared on it. We're talking about hardware that's been to freaking *Mars,* for chrissake!"

"Do you really think—"

"You start a feeding frenzy," Trumball explained eagerly. "Get all the big players heated up about it. The Disney execs. The Trumps and Yamagatas and whatnot. They'll bid it up to a billion in no time."

"But the thing doesn't belong to you," Hall objected. "It belongs to NASA, doesn't it? Or the U.S. government."

Trumball wagged his head back and forth. "Nah! I looked that up. There's the law of salvage—"

"That's for sunken ships," Hall said.

"Or treasure," added Dezhurova.

"It's for hardware that's been lost or abandoned," Trumball retorted firmly. "Works the same in space as it does on Earth. That guy—what's his name? Gunn, wasn't it? He recovered the original Vanguard satellite, I think. Something like that. It's salvage."

"Then if you can grab it, it's yours?" Hall asked.

"Yep," Trumball replied smugly.

Jamie saw that they had passed the half-buried rover. The floor of the Canyon was only a couple of klicks away now, still shrouded in thinning tendrils of mist. The idea of taking the old Pathfinder hardware away from its landing spot bothered Jamie, deep down below the rational level of his mind. It smacked of sacrilege, of desecrating a holy place.

But he said nothing, knowing that if he spoke it would be with anger.

Stacy Dezhurova did not stay silent, though. "Dex, even assuming you are right, none of these rovers has the range to go out four thousand klicks and back again."

"I know that," Trumball said condescendingly. "I'm not completely braindead. We fly the backup fuel generator to Ares Vallis so it'll be there to fill up the rover when it gets there."

"Fly the . . . that's crazy!"

"We'll have to put the backup water recycler back on the fuel generator, too," Dex added.

"Even crazier."

"The fuel generator's just sitting two klicks from the base, standing by for an emergency, isn't it? And we don't need the spare water recycler now that the garden's working. So why not put 'em to use?''

"How can you fly it?'' Stacy demanded.

"The descent engines have enough thrust to lob it on a ballistic trajectory. I've checked out the numbers seventeen ways from Friday. It'll work.''

"Fly our backup fuel generator to Ares Vallis,'' Dezhurova muttered. "Insane.''

"I can show you the computer evaluation,'' Trumball said, unperturbed.

"Those descent engines were not built for repeated use,'' Dezhurova pointed out. "They don't have enough thrust—''

Trumball wagged a finger in the air. "I checked it all out with the manufacturer months ago, Stacy baby. You can get a half-dozen burns out of those engines, no sweat. And if they can soft-land the bird, they can lift it again. We're not talking orbit now, just a little hop across the desert.''

"If it doesn't work—''

"Worst case, we lose the backup fuel generator. Best case, we pick up a billion dollars worth of hardware for auction back at Sotheby's.''

Jamie sat there and let Stacy and Dex argue it out. I don't want to be in the middle of this, he told himself. Yet he knew that, ultimately, inescapably, he would be the one to make the real decision.

Trudy Hall made a sardonic face. "Why not pick up one of the original Viking landers while you're at it?''

"Too big,'' Trumball answered, matter-of-factly. "Pathfinder's small enough for us to carry back with us. The Vikings are big clunkers.''

"There are a half-dozen other landers scattered around the planet,'' Dezhurova said.

Trumball made a wry face. "Yeah, but most of 'em are too big or too far away to reach. Besides, if we take *too* much of the old hardware back, their value starts to go down. Got to play this game smart, kiddo.''

He's been thinking about this for a long time, Jamie realized. Doing computer evaluations. Dex doesn't do anything without planning it all out first.

They were leaving the old rover behind. The mist was clearing from the Canyon floor.

Trumball tapped Jamie on the shoulder. "Well, big chief, what do you have to say about it?''

Jamie grimaced at Trumball's ethnic wisecrack, but he said only, "I think your idea will have to wait until the next expedition, Dex.''

"That's about what I thought you'd say,'' Trumball replied.

Jamie had expected him to be sullen, piqued at being rebuffed.

Instead, Trumball looked like a young man who held a trump card up his sleeve.

"Suppose we make a trade," he suggested, his smile turning crafty. "I go for the Pathfinder and you can go look for your cliff dwellings."

DOSSIER: C. DEXTER TRUMBALL

NO MATTER HOW WELL HE DID, NO MATTER WHAT HE ACCOMPLISHED, Dex Trumball could never satisfy his coldly indifferent father.

Darryl C. Trumball was a self-made man, he firmly proclaimed to anyone and everyone. One of Dex's earliest memories was his father cornering a U.S. senator at a house party and tapping him on the shoulder with each and every word as he declared with quiet insistence, "I started with nothing but my bare hands and my brain, and I built a fortune for myself."

In truth, the old man had started with a meager inheritance: a decrepit auto body shop that was on the verge of bankruptcy when Dex's grandfather died of a massive stroke in the middle of his fourth beer at the neighborhood bar.

Dex had been just a baby then, an only child. His mother was pretty, frail, and ineffectual; totally unable to stand up to her implacably driven husband. Dex's father, blade-slim, fast and agile, had attended Holy Cross on a track scholarship. He never graduated; he had to take over the family business instead. His dream of going to the Boston College Law School, as he had been promised, was shattered, leaving him bitter and resentful.

And filled with an icy, relentless energy.

Darryl C. Trumball quickly learned that business depends on politics. Although the body shop was practically worthless, the land on which it stood could become extremely valuable if it could be converted to upscale condominiums for the white-collar types who worked in Boston's financial district. He pushed feverishly to get the old neighborhood rezoned, then sold the shop and his mother's house for a sizable sum.

By the time Dex was ready for college, his father was very wealthy, and known in the financial community for his cold-blooded ruthlessness. Money was important to him, and he spent every waking hour striving to increase his net worth. When Dex expressed an interest in science, the elder Trumball snorted disdainfully:

"You'll never be able to support yourself that way! Why, when I was your age I was taking care of your grandmother, your two aunts, your mother and *you*."

Dex listened obediently and registered anyway for physics at Yale. His high-school grades (and his father's money) were good enough to be acceptable to Harvard and half a dozen other Ivy League schools, but Dex decided on Yale. New Haven was close enough to Boston for him to get home easily, yet far away enough for him to be free of his father's chilling presence.

Dex had always found school to be ridiculously easy. Where others pored over textbooks and sweated out exams, Dex breezed through with a near-photographic memory and a clever ability to tell his teachers exactly what they wanted to hear. His relationships with his peers were much the same: they did what he wanted, almost always. Dex got the brilliant ideas and his friends got into trouble carrying them out. Yet they never complained; they admired his dash and felt grateful when he noticed them at all.

Sex was equally easy for him, even on campuses electrified by charges of harassment. Dex had his pick of the women: the more intelligent they were, the more they seemed to bask in the temporary sunshine of his affection. And they never complained afterward.

Physics was not for Dex, but he found himself drawn to geophysics: the study of the Earth, its interior and its atmosphere. His grades were well-nigh perfect. He was a campus leader in everything from the school television station to the tennis team. Yet his father was never pleased.

"An educated bum, that's what you are," his father taunted. "I'll have to support you all my life and keep on supporting you even after I'm gone."

Which suited Dex just fine. But deep within, he longed to hear one approving word from his father. He ached to have the callous old man smile at him.

His life changed forever at a planetarium show. Dex liked to take his dates to the planetarium. It was cheap, it impressed young women with his seriousness and intelligence, and it was the darkest place in town. Very romantic, really, sitting in the back row with the splendors of the heavens spangled above.

One particular show was about the planet Mars. After several failures, an automated spacecraft had successfully returned actual samples of Martian rocks and soil to a laboratory in orbit around the Earth. Now there was talk of sending human explorers there. Suddenly Dex stopped fondling the young woman who had accompanied him and sat up straight in his chair.

"There's more than one planet to study!" he said aloud, eliciting a chorus of shushing hisses from around him, and the utter humiliation of his date.

Dex spent that summer at the University of Nevada, taking a special course in geology. The next summer he went to a seminar on planetary geology in Berkeley.

By the time the first expedition had returned from Mars, triumphantly bearing samples of living Martian organisms, Dex had degrees from Yale and Berkeley. He went to the struggling Moonbase settlement for six months to do field work on the massive meteorites that lay buried deep beneath Mare Nubium and Mare Imbrium.

Much to his father's dismay.

"I give the government fortunes of tax money for this space stuff," the old man complained bitterly. "What damned good is it?"

Dex's father was a real-estate tycoon now, with long fingers in several New England-based banks and business interests in Europe, Asia and Latin America. He kept in touch with his far-flung associates through satellite-relayed electronic links and even leased space in an orbital factory that manufactured ultrapure pharmaceuticals.

Dex smiled brightly for his father. "Don't be a flathead, Dad. I want to be on the next expedition to Mars."

His father stared at him coldly. "When are you going to start bringing some money *in* to this family, instead of spending it like it's water?"

Challenged, wanting to please his father and win his approval for once, Dex blurted, "We could make money from Mars."

His father fixed Dex with an icy, disbelieving expression in his flinty eyes.

"We could, really," Dex said, groping for something that would convince the old man. "Besides, it'd make your name in history, Dad. The man who led the way back to Mars. It'd be your monument."

Darryl C. Trumball seemed unmoved by thoughts of a monument. Yet he asked, "You think we could make money out of an expedition to Mars?"

Dex nodded vigorously. "That's right."

"How?"

That was when Dex began planning an expedition to Mars that would be funded by private donors. To be sure, a good deal of taxpayers' money went into the pot. But once Dex enlisted the interest and drive of his profit-oriented father, funding for the Second Martian Expedition came mainly from private sources.

Dex was determined to make the expedition profitable. He wanted his father's praise, just once. Then he could tell the old man to go bust a blood vessel and drop dead.

MORNING: SOL 8

"THE CLIFF DWELLING," JAMIE ECHOED.

With a knowing grin, Trumball said easily, "Sure. You want to go chase down the cliff dwelling you think you saw and I want to get the Pathfinder hardware. You scratch my itch and I'll scratch yours."

Jamie glanced at Stacy Dezhurova, sitting beside him in the pilot's seat. The rover was almost to the bottom of the landslide now. Morning sunlight had reached the floor of the Canyon, driving the mist away.

"I've heard about your cliff dwellings," Trudy Hall said from behind Jamie, very softly, as if it was a dangerous topic.

"It's only one," Jamie corrected, "and it's not *my* cliff dwelling."

"But you're the only one who believes it *is* an artifact," Trumball pointed out.

"It's not on the mission schedule," Hall said, still in a hushed, almost scared voice.

"There's plenty of flexibility built into the schedule," Jamie pointed out.

"Enough for us to salvage the old rover and go after the Pathfinder," said Trumball brightly.

"Maybe."

"Why not? We could tow the old clunker out of the sand on our way back from here."

Jamie nodded slowly, his mind racing. I'm the mission director, he told himself. I can set an excursion to the cliff site when I see fit. I don't need his permission or even his cooperation. I don't have to let him go off on this crazy jaunt after the Pathfinder. I don't have to offer him a bribe to do what I want to do.

Yet he heard himself say, "We'll stop and inspect the old rover on our way back to base, Dex."

"Great!"

"That doesn't mean that we'll do anything more," Jamie warned. "I agree with you to this extent: we ought to see if the old rover is still usable."

"It will be."

"Because you want it to be?"

"Because it will be," said Dex, as convinced of the notion as a little boy who still believes in Santa Claus.

*   *   *

For three days Trudy Hall studied the lichen living just beneath the surface of the rocks at the base of the Canyon cliffs. Three days and three nights.

Hall's purpose was to study the organisms in their natural habitat, especially their diurnal cycles. To do so, she had to leave the lichen undisturbed, so her instruments were mainly remote sensors. She took photographs, set up thermometers that recorded the exterior and interior temperatures of the rocks continuously, sampled the Martian air micrometers from the lichen and monitored with infrared cameras the heat flow from rocks that bore lichen and others that did not.

On the second day she began making more direct measurements of some of the lichen: with Jamie's help she inserted probes into several of the rocks to measure chemical balances.

Trumball, meanwhile, collected rock samples, dug shallow cores (finding no permafrost at all), and began the detailed geological mapping of the area. And, of course, he planted a half-dozen geology/meteorology beacons along a carefully paced path that parallelled the cliff face. Jamie helped him. Dex made a few cracks about the mission director serving as his assistant. Jamie let them slide past without comment.

"We need to get samples from the cliff itself," he told Jamie the second evening of their stay in the Canyon. "And implant beacons in the cliffs."

Jamie nodded agreement. The two of them were just inside the airlock hatch, vacuuming off the dust from their hard suits with hand-held cordless Dustbusters. The Martian dust smelled pungent with ozone, enough to make eyes water if it wasn't cleaned off immediately.

"Still no permafrost?" Jamie asked, over the whine of the vacuums.

"Not a bit. Must be deeper below the surface. It's a couple of degrees warmer down here, y'know."

"But the heat flow measurements—"

"Yeah, I know," Trumball interrupted, bending over to clean his boots. "Less heat flow from the interior here than up topside."

"But no permafrost."

"It's got to be deeper down."

Jamie shook his head. "Doesn't make sense. How can the lichen live here if there's not as much heat coming up from the interior and water is farther away?"

Trudy Hall, sitting on her bunk with her laptop computer on her outstretched legs, called to them, "Listen to my seminar after dinner and all your questions will be answered." Then she made a thoughtful face and added, "Well, some of them, at least."

Hall's impromptu seminar started after the remains of their dinners had been slid into the recycling bin and the folding table mopped clean of crumbs. Jamie drew his second cup of hot coffee, then sat on his bunk. Dex sat next to him, nursing a mug of fruit juice. The upper bunks were still folded back against the curving shell. Stacy Dezhurova was up in the cockpit, checking the rover's diagnostic systems, a chore she did every evening.

Sitting her laptop on the table and using its screen to display photos and graphs, Hall showed the two men that the lichen draw their heat energy from the sunlight that warms the rocks during the day—"as high as twelve degrees Celsius in direct sunlight," she reported.

"So they don't depend on heat flow from the interior," said Jamie.

"Not at all."

"That's why—"

"More than that," she went on. "They actually maintain a higher temperature than ambient!"

"What?"

Her eyes alight with excitement, Hall told the two men, "The rocks that hold lichen in them are six to twelve degrees warmer than rocks without lichen."

"How do they do that?" Trumball asked.

"The lichen store heat, as if they're warm-blooded!"

"But they're plants, not animals," Jamie protested.

Hall waved a hand in the air. "I don't mean that they're actually warm-blooded, of course. But somehow they maintain a higher temperature than the unoccupied rocks. They actually store heat! It's unprecedented!"

"Are you sure?"

"How much cold can they take?" Trumball asked.

Hall shrugged her slim shoulders. "They've survived for goodness knows how long. Overnight lows get far below minus one hundred."

"What about dust storms?" Jamie wondered.

"What about them?" she countered.

"Well, the rocks can be covered with dust for days at a time, maybe more. . . ."

"Ah, I see," Hall said, bobbing her head up and down briefly. "The lichen must be able to survive such blanketing." Her brow knit with thought. "I don't know how a layer of dust would affect the temperature of the rock. Is the dust a thermal insulator or would solar infrared get through it without much absorption?"

Jamie and Trumball both shook their heads. Hall tapped out a note on her laptop keyboard. "That's something we'll have to look into, isn't it?"

"If the lichen get their water from the humidity in the atmosphere," Trumball pointed out, "several days of being covered with dust would desiccate them, wouldn't it?"

"Obviously not," Hall said. "Otherwise they would have died out long ago, don't you see?"

Jamie said, "Then they can go for some time with no water input at all."

"Apparently. Unless they can obtain water from another source."

"Such as?"

She ran a hand through her mousey brown hair. "I haven't the faintest notion. Dex, you say you haven't found permafrost below the surface, is that correct?"

"Not yet," Trumball replied. "It may lie deeper than my probe can reach."

"Have you tested the humidity of the soil?"

Slouched back against the rover's curving shell as he sat on the bunk beside Jamie, Trumball said, "It's part of the automatic analysis program. Not enough H_2O to register, so far."

"The lichen must be able to hibernate, sort of," Jamie suggested. "Slow down their metabolic processes when they can't get water and wait it out."

"That's what they do on Earth," Hall agreed.

Trumball's eyes lit up. "Y'know, there's probably hydrates in the rocks. Maybe the lichen can separate them out, chemically, and use their water!"

"Has anyone—"

Jamie cut Hall's question short. "There *are* hydrates in the rocks," he said, more to Trumball than Trudy. "We found that out on the way back during the first expedition. Not the rocks up on Lunae Planum, but the rocks we picked up down here in the Canyon definitely bore hydrates."

"Water molecules locked up in the rock's silicates," Trumball said. "Yeah."

Across the table from them, Trudy Hall sat up straighter. "We've got to see if the lichen can extract water from the hydrates!" she said, her voice trembling slightly with eagerness.

She and Trumball launched into an animated dialogue on how to test the lichen. Jamie watched the excitement on their faces, the fervor in their voices.

"We'll have to take samples and bring them back to the base," Hall said. "I don't have the facilities to do the work here."

"Take whole rocks and keep 'em in sample boxes outside the rover," Trumball recommended. "Don't take any chances on contaminating 'em."

"Right. But where can we store them?"

Trumball got up from the bunk and went around the table to sit beside her. They bent over her laptop screen, heads practically touching.

Stacy Dezhurova came back from the cockpit and cast an eye at the two of them, chattering and tapping away at the laptop keyboard.

"What is going on?" she asked Jamie.

"They're trying to figure out where they can hang a few sample boxes outside the rover for the trip back."

"Outside? Take your pick. We have attachment points every few meters on the outside skin."

With that problem solved, Dezhurova slid past Jamie and headed for the lavatory. Jamie sat alone on his bunk, feeling left out. They're so excited about this that they're oblivious to everything else, he told himself.

Then Hall looked up from the screen and said, "But don't you understand what this means? About the lichen's heat capacity, I mean."

Trumball looked puzzled for a moment.

Jamie started to think: If the rocks with lichen in them are warmer than rocks without lichen, then—

"We can map them from the satellites!" Trumball snapped.

"Right-o," exclaimed Trudy. "The infrared sensors in the satellites can detect temperature anomalies on the ground . . ."

"And the warmer patches will be where the lichen are living," Jamie finished for her.

"Hey, we could get a complete map of the whole planet in a few hours that way," Trumball said. "Tell us exactly where colonies of lichen are living!"

"It'll take more than a few hours," Jamie cautioned. "We'll need to make several passes, make certain the data's firm, cover the same territory several times to nail down the temperature differences."

"Can the satellite sensors measure a difference of six degrees or so?" Hall asked.

"Sure," said Trumball. "Easy."

"Ground temperatures, I mean," she said.

Jamie said, "I'm pretty sure that won't be a problem, Trudy. There isn't much absorption from the atmosphere; it's so thin that ground heat escapes right into space. That's why it gets so cold every night, no matter what the daytime temperature is."

She nodded thoughtfully. "Five or six degrees, then. If the satellites can measure that small a difference we can map the whole planet and see where the lichen colonies are."

"Or other forms of life," Trumball suggested.

"We haven't found any other forms, as yet," she said.

"We will," Trumball answered confidently.

"I hope so."

"Let's pull up the specs on the satellites' sensors," Trumball said. "That oughtta tell us whether the IR scanners can measure your temperature differences."

Hall nodded eagerly, and Trumball pulled the laptop toward him and began tapping on its keyboard. Jamie got up and made his way up to the cockpit. Time to check in with the base and make the nightly report, he thought.

NIGHT: SOL 10

VIJAY SHEKTAR WAS ON DUTY AT THE COMM CONSOLE. SHE SMILED AT Jamie. "How's it going, mate?"

"Really well," Jamie said. He related their hypothesis about the lichen leaching water from their host rocks' interiors and the possibility of scanning the whole planet for colonies of lichen.

"That's wonderful, Jamie," Shektar said, smiling happily.

"Trudy's a really sharp one," he said. "She's on her way to a Nobel."

"Good for her," Vijay said, a bit abstractly, Jamie thought.

Then her smile faded and she asked in a lower voice, "How are you and Dex working out?"

Jamie thought of two nights ago, when he wanted to talk to her, but she was locked in chat with Trumball.

Keeping his face impassive, Jamie replied, "Not bad. He wants to salvage the old rover."

"Yes, I saw that in your report from last night."

"And he's offered me a bribe to do it."

"A bribe?"

Jamie explained about the cliff dwelling.

Shektar said, "But you were going to do that anyway, weren't you?"

He had to admit it. "I certainly intended to. But now that Dex has brought it out in the open, I'm kind of glad about it."

"That's good."

"Uh . . . you were talking with him a couple of nights ago, weren't you?"

Her dark-skinned face showed no trace of surprise. Her onyx eyes did not waver. "Jamie, I try to talk to each team member every few days. It's part of my job."

"I understand," he said.

With a smile, she said, "Sure you do."

Suddenly Jamie felt uncomfortable. He wanted to talk with Vijay for hours, talk about everything and anything, not just the business of the expedition. Yet he sensed that she knew more about what was stirring inside him than he himself did.

"Are you okay?" he heard himself ask. "Everything going well back there?"

"We're all fine," Vijay said. "Possum's drill has reached the two-hundred-meter level and he's starting to pull up bacterial samples. He and Mitsuo are burning up the lab equipment, examining them."

"Living bacteria?"

"Yes. The biologists back on Earth are dancing in the streets, to hear the two of them talk."

"Why the hell didn't they tell me about it?"

She looked startled. "I thought they did. They just pulled up the first sample this morning. I thought they sent you a quick report."

Jamie took a deep breath. "Maybe it's in my incoming mail. I haven't checked it this evening."

"I'm sure it must be."

Without breaking his connection with Shektar, he pulled up the list of incoming messages. Yes, there were two of them from Fuchida, sent within minutes of each other, less than three hours earlier.

I ought to check my mail before I call the base, Jamie reminded himself. He realized he had been foolish, wanting to talk to Vijay so much that he neglected to go through his incoming messages first.

She was saying, "Mitsuo thinks the volcanoes might be even better sites for an underground ecology. He can't wait to get started on his excursion."

Jamie sighed. "I know the feeling."

"You're well?" she asked.

Almost startled by her simple question, Jamie answered, "Sure, I'm fine."

"Not feeling tired or perhaps a little irritable, especially in the evening?"

Jamie shook his head. "No, nothing like that."

"How about when you wake up in the morning? Any signs of depression?"

"What are you talking about?" He remembered how he had felt during the first expedition when vitamin deficiency had brought on scurvy. Is Vijay worried about that? he wondered.

But she answered, "Jet lag."

"Jet lag?"

Shektar nodded, quite serious. "The Martian sol is more than half an hour longer than an Earth day. Several of the people here at the base have shown some difficulty in adjusting their internal clocks."

Jamie was instantly alarmed. "Who? How serious is it?"

"It's not serious," Shektar replied. "Nothing to be worried about. And I'm not going to break doctor-patient confidentiality over it."

"But if it affects people's performance—"

"It hasn't and I doubt that it will. They're adjusting; just a bit slowly, that's all."

Jamie tried to keep himself from frowning at her. We should have thought of that, he scolded himself. We made the adjustment for the gravity, but nobody thought of adjusting for the different length of day.

"Cheer up, Jamie," Vijay said, smiling again. "It's nothing for you to worry about."

"You're sure?"

"Yes, I'm absolutely, positively certain." Then her smile turned impish. "Pretty much."

They bantered back and forth about internal biorhythms and natural cycles. Jamie enjoyed chatting with her; he could feel the tensions of the day relaxing their hold on him. He noticed how white her teeth gleamed against her dark complexion. Her skin looked smooth and soft. Jamie thought how he'd like to stroke her face, her shoulders . . .

"Talking about biorhythms," Vijay was saying, "I've been keeping an eye on the harem effect."

That put an end to his fantasizing. "On what?"

"The harem effect," she said. "The tendency of women who live together to have their menstrual cycles synchronize."

Jamie said to himself, I don't want to hear about this. But he heard himself ask, "Is that happening here?"

Shektar nodded, her eyes teasing. "Indeed it is, mate. I talked with Stacy a little while ago. We're all within three days of each other."

"The harem effect," he muttered.

"Part of the general cussedness of nature," she said.

"Is it?"

"We don't do it on purpose, Jamie. We can't control our cycles, not unless we take hormone therapy, and as far as I know none of us is on birth control pills."

Jamie thought maybe they should be, then wondered why they weren't. Because they don't want to be sexually active?

"We agreed to keep off the pill before we left Earth," Shektar explained. "The three of us are volunteers in a medical experiment on the harem effect."

"You're going to write a paper about this?"

"When we get back, yes. Publish or perish, you know."

Jamie could not tell if she were serious or baiting him.

"Of course," she went on, "if any of us thinks she has cause to, she can take a 'morning after' pill. I've got a good supply of those on hand."

Jamie heard himself ask, "Has anybody . . . ?"

Her smile became dazzling. "Patient-doctor confidentiality, Jamie. My lips are sealed."

He sighed with exasperation. It sounded more like a growl.

Suddenly changing the subject, Shektar said, "You haven't done a medical diagnostic since you left base, you know."

"I don't need—"

"You okayed the regulations, Dr. Waterman. We all agreed to abide by them."

"Yes, I know."

"It's my responsibility to look after your physical and mental health." She was totally serious now. "But I can't do that if you don't cooperate."

"Have the others . . . ?"

"Dex and Trudy have been very cooperative. Stacy has an astronaut's aversion to medics, but she went through a diagnostic last night. I've got the data here."

"I'd rather have you examine me personally than that dumb machine," he blurted.

Her brows rose. "Really?"

Jamie cursed himself for an idiot. "What I meant to say is—"

But Vijay was smiling again. "I'll be happy to examine you when you return. But for now, I'm afraid the diagnostic machine is as romantic as we can get."

"Romantic?"

She laughed. "I'm sorry. I didn't mean to fluster you. It's my evil sense of humor."

He forced a smile back at her. A weak one. "I'm not flustered. It's all right."

"Yes, I can see that."

Trying to regain command of the conversation, Jamie said, "I've got to talk with Tomas."

"Now?"

"Before I sign off."

"Do you want to make your formal report?"

"I want him to program one of the soarplanes to do a reconnaissance run past the cliff dwelling."

MORNING: SOL 11

DESPITE ALL THE VACUUMING, JAMIE SAW, THE SUITS WERE STARTING TO look soiled, used. The once-gleaming white boots and leggings now had a faintly reddish tinge. The hand vacs don't take off all the dust, he realized. He remembered how stained and used the suits had looked on the first expedition, after only a couple of weeks.

"Here's the rig," Dex Trumball said, handing Jamie his helmet. Its visor was already closed; the VR cameras attached just above eye level. Stacy Dezhurova had plugged the virtual reality electronics module into Jamie's suit backpack.

"Okay," Jamie said, sliding the helmet carefully over his head. As he sealed the neck ring, he said, "Once I get the VR gloves on I'm ready for my big chance at show biz."

Trumball was all business. "Just take it slow and easy. No sudden moves. You don't want to make the viewers back home dizzy."

Dezhurova was in her suit, visor raised, ready to check out Jamie before he went through the airlock. Jamie heard their voices muffled through his padded helmet. Then Dezhurova came through his earphones: "Radio check."

"Loud and clear, Stacy."

"Then you are go for the excursion."

Jamie trudged awkwardly into the airlock and started its pump-down cycle. We could bring a couple of samples inside, he thought. As long as they're sealed in sample cases they'll be okay. The cases are insulated and the UV lights can't get through them. But then he thought, Why take a chance? Leave them outside; they'll be better off in their natural environment.

The light on the indicator panel flicked to red. Jamie touched a gloved thumb on the stud that opened the outer hatch. Then he stepped out onto the red sand of Mars once again.

The ground was covered with bootprints. Jamie walked a dozen paces away from the rover, then looked up the face of the gigantic cliff that ran out to the horizon in either direction. His vision blocked by the hard suit's helmet, he could not see the top of the cliff even when he bent back as far as he could.

His breath caught in his chest as he realized all over again that he was on another world, a magnificent, bold, fresh planet that held an entire world of surprises and mysteries for them to discover and decipher. He could feel the warmth of the morning sun soaking into the rocks strewn across the ground and the massive cliff that rose beyond his vision.

A river ran through here, Jamie told himself. A tremendous torrent that carried boulders as big as houses along with it. But when? How long ago? What happened to it?

The cliff dwelling's less than fifty klicks from here, Jamie told himself. We could drive out there for a quick look at it and be back before sunset.

Turning, he stared out across the Canyon floor. The cliffs on its other side were over the horizon, out of sight. The horizon itself seemed too close, disturbingly close, and as sharp as a razor cut across the edge of the world. A whole planet to explore. A whole world. If there really is one cliff dwelling out there, how many others will we find?

But the voice of his responsibilities answered, Not today. You can't go searching for your cliff dwelling. Not on this mission. You'd be cutting into the rover's fuel reserve, taking an unnecessary risk.

Be patient, he counselled himself. Get the soarplane to make a recon of the area. Then you can plan a specific excursion out there.

If the soarplane's cameras show anything worth looking at.

"Are you ready for your fifteen minutes of fame?" Stacy Dezhurova's voice in his earphones startled Jamie out of his musings.

Turning back toward the rover, Jamie saw her standing by the airlock hatch, the boots and legs of her hard suit stained faintly pink, the yellow stripes on her sleeves still as bright and pristine as buttercups.

"I guess," he said.

"Tarawa is ready for your transmission," she said. "Pete Connors is running the comm console."

"Which frequency is he on?"

"Two."

Jamie took a deep breath as he tapped the keyboard on the wrist of his suit. It'd be good to talk with Pete, he thought. Have a nice, long, friendly chat. But Jamie knew that distance defeated that hope. It would take almost fifteen minutes for his words to reach Earth, an equal span of time for Connors' reply. We could spend the whole morning just saying hello, how are you, Jamie knew.

Reluctantly, Jamie spoke into his microphone, "Welcome again to Mars, from the floor of the Grand Canyon. Today we're going to show you real Martians . . ."

Fulvio A. DiNardo, S.J., sat in his one-room apartment on the top floor of what had once been a Renaissance *palazzo*. The stately old building overlooked the ornate fountain in the center of the Piazza Navona. Centuries ago it served as the Roman home for the boisterous family of a prosperous dealer in precious metals; for the past two centuries it housed a dozen marble-lined apartments that generated lucrative rents for that family's distant descendants.

Fr. DiNardo had been born to considerable wealth, although to his credit he took his Jesuit vows seriously enough to live modestly. Geology was his passion, his one vice. He burned to understand how God had built this Earth and the other worlds He had been pleased to create.

A brilliant student, marked early for success, he had become a world-class geologist, the obvious choice for a berth on the first mission to Mars. He tried to be as humble as possible about it, but inwardly he glowed with pride at the thought of leading the way to another world.

The sin of pride brought him a punishment: a gall bladder attack that required surgery and removed him from the First Mars Expedition.

Now he sat in his small but well-appointed apartment, a virtual reality helmet over his head and data gloves on his thick-fingered hands, experiencing Mars through an electronic illusion.

He saw the rocks that Jamie Waterman saw, hefted them and inspected their pitted, coarse surfaces closely. He examined the yellowish patches where the Martian lichen lived a few millimeters below the surface of some of those rocks. He felt the solidity of the compact electronically boosted microscope Waterman gripped in one hand as he knelt to peer closely at the alien lichen.

"Those dark patches along the lichen's surface," he heard Waterman's voice explaining, "are actually windows that allow light to penetrate through the outer skin of the organism."

DiNardo nodded with understanding.

"At night, they close, like eyes," Waterman continued, "so that the organism's internal heat doesn't leak through the windows back into the atmosphere."

Of course, thought DiNardo. A wonderful adaptation.

Through the senses of Jamie Waterman the Jesuit walked along the cliff face, examined rocks, scuffed boot marks in the rusty sand.

To his surprise, Jamie found himself enjoying his stint as a tour conductor. Maybe I was cut out to be a teacher, after all, he thought as he walked slowly along the cliff face, pointing out the layers of different colored stone: iron-dark red, ocher, bleached tan, even a few extrusions of pale yellowish rock.

"These layers give every indication of being laid down over a long period of time, billions of years, most likely. They're probably telling us that there was an ocean here, or at least a very large sea, that deposited this material, layer by layer."

He came to a house-sized boulder that had obviously tumbled to the Canyon floor from some height.

"Problem: What are the ages of these rocks?" Jamie asked rhetorically as he ran his gloved fingers over the boulder's strangely smooth surface. "Before we learned how to date rocks by radioactive decay, geologists determined age by how deep a stratum was from the surface. Now . . ."

As he explained how radioactive dating works, how geologists estimate the age of a rock from the ratio of radioactive elements in it, Jamie climbed up to the boulder's top, scrambling up clefts in its side until he was standing atop the big rock.

"As you can see . . ." he said, panting. Then stopped. His visor had erupted into a cascade of blinking red lights. The data gloves, the eye-slaved cameras, the entire VR rig was down, no longer functioning.

Jamie muttered a string of curses.

Across the world, people raptly exploring Tithonium Chasma with Jamie suddenly were cut off. Their visual displays went dark.

Before they could remove their helmets, the somber dark face of former astronaut Pete Connors appeared before them.

"We've lost VR contact with Dr. Waterman," Connors said, his voice serious but not anxious. "All our data links here tell us that Dr. Waterman's life-support equipment is still functioning; he's in no danger. But the virtual reality link is down because of some technical malfunction."

Fr. DiNardo slowly removed his helmet.

I was on Mars, DiNardo told himself. God granted me that much, at least. I should be thankful.

I hope Waterman is all right and that he is in no danger. I will offer a prayer for his safety.

Still, as he ran a tired hand over his shaved head, Fr. DiNardo's eyes were filled with sad, bitter tears. It should have been me on Mars. It should have been me.

My God, my God, why did you abandon me?

NEW YORK CITY

"SO WHERE DO WE STAND ON THIS?" ASKED ROGER NEWELL.

Two other men and three women sat around the conference table in the headquarters offices of Allied News. Dress was strictly informal: sweaters, chinos and Levis, not a tie or jacket in sight.

Newell prided himself on keeping the office relaxed. Gathering and broadcasting the news was a high-pressure profession; no sense adding to the strain with silly dress code requirements.

"They're okay," said the lean, languid young man sitting on his left. "No physical danger. Just the VR equipment crapped out on them."

Newell suppressed a smirk.

One of the women—roundly overweight and pasty-faced—said in a crisp, biting tone, "This morning's poll results show the Mars expedition ranks behind the animal rights conference and the fruit picker's strike in Florida."

"It's the old story," said the woman beside her, who was considerably younger. She radiated ambition, from her modish blonde buzz cut to her stiletto heels. "Nobody gives a rat's fart about what they're doing on Mars unless they get into some trouble."

"And a breakdown of their VR equipment isn't trouble?"

"Not enough, anyway."

"The tabloids don't think so," said the man on Newell's right. "Did you see 'em last night? Three straight shows about how Martians living underground are using psychic powers to destroy the expedition's equipment."

The pasty-faced woman laughed. "Last week the tabloids were saying that the Martians would show themselves to our people and give them the cure for cancer."

They all snickered, even Newell.

But then he said, "So their equipment breakdown doesn't mesmerize our viewers, eh?"

"Naw. People want a real disaster."

"Lives at stake."

"Burning and bleeding."

"All right," Newell said, raising his hands. Their banter shut off immediately.

He smiled at them. "So they can't beam their virtual reality broadcasts to their subscribers, is that it?"

"Not until they patch up the equipment."

"So their subscribers have to tune in to us to get their news about Mars, right?"

"Or the competition."

"So what do we do? We can't take ten-fifteen seconds every night to tell our audience that nothing's happened on Mars."

"We could do a quickie science report," said the overweight woman.

Everyone groaned. Science reports lost viewers, they all believed that firmly. Science was dull. Doing science reports was like *handing* the audience to your competition.

"Do we just ignore Mars altogether?"

The oldest woman at the table—she must have been approaching forty, at least—tapped a forefinger against her chin. "I remember . . ."

"What?" asked Newell.

"Something they showed us in school . . . when I was—no! It was in the media history class I took a couple of years ago."

"What?" Newell repeated, with some exasperation.

"Cronkite did it! Yeah, that's right."

"What?" the others chorused.

"There was some kind of crisis. Hostages or something. Dragged on for more than a year. At the end of every broadcast, Cronkite would say, 'This is the fifty-fourth day' of whatever it was."

"Like a countdown?"

"More like a reminder. A calendar, sort of."

Newell cocked his head to one side, a sign that he was thinking. The others stayed silent.

"I like it," he said at last. "At the end of the evening news we have the anchor say, 'This is the fifty-fourth day that our explorers are on Mars.' "

"Whatever the right number is."

"Of course."

"The phrasing needs work, I think."

"That's what we've got writers for," said Newell, somewhat crossly.

"This way, we remind the audience that those people are still on Mars."

"But we don't waste air time doing a science story."

"Unless something happens to them."

"Oh, if they get into trouble we'll hop on it with both feet," Newell promised. "Nothing like real danger to boost the ratings."

BOSTON

DARRYL C. TRUMBALL HAD BEEN MUCH TOO BUSY TO PLUG INTO THE LATEST virtual reality transmission from Mars. He had watched the first two of them, which his son had conducted on the first two days of their arrival on the planet. That was enough.

He kept tabs on the income from the VR transmissions, of course. The first two broadcasts had an audience of slightly more than twenty million. Twenty million paying viewers, at ten dollars each, had watched the explorers on the day they landed on Mars and the next day, when Dex took them on a tour through the dome in which they were going to live for the next year and a half.

And then the audience had quickly dwindled to about three million. If you've seen Mars rocks once, who wants to see them again, except school kids and space nuts? But three million was respectable: it meant thirty million dollars for the expedition with every transmission.

Of course, not everybody paid their ten bucks, Trumball knew. It was ten dollars per receiver, not ten bucks per head. A school class of thirty kids paid only ten dollars. A family could pay their ten dollars and plug in all their relatives. Bars full of drunks paid their ten bucks and that was that. Trumball fumed at the thought, but there was no practical way to stop the freeloaders.

Now the VR equipment had broken down. That damned Indian broke something while he was out frolicking over some damned rocks.

They'd better get it repaired P.D.Q., Trumball groused. We're losing thirty million dollars a shot.

AFTERNOON: SOL 15

"THERE SHE IS!" DEX TRUMBALL EXCLAIMED.

He was sitting in the copilot's chair as Stacy Dezhurova piloted the rover up the gentle grade of the ancient landslide.

"Did you expect it'd moved off?" Trudy Hall asked lightly. She was sitting in the jumpseat behind Jamie; Trumball sat in the fold-down behind Dezhurova.

Jamie tapped at the comm console and got Mitsuo Fuchida's face on the control panel's small screen.

"We're approaching the old rover," Jamie reported. "We're going to stop and inspect it."

"I understand," Fuchida said.

"How's everything there?"

With the barest dip of his head, the biologist answered, "Rodriguez and Craig are repairing the drill rig. Vijay is—"

"Repairing the drill?" Jamie interrupted. "What happened?"

Fuchida blinked twice, rapidly. "The hydraulic line to the auger head froze overnight. Possum believes the electrical heating system failed."

"How serious is it?"

With a slight shrug of his slim shoulders, Fuchida said, "I don't know. Possum didn't seem very upset about it."

Jamie settled back in his seat. "Ask him to call me when he gets a chance, please."

"Yes, I will. It probably won't be until nightfall, though."

"That's okay. I think we'll be outside checking out the old rover until then, anyway."

Fuchida nodded, then said, "We've received half a dozen more messages from Boston inquiring about the VR system."

"Whatever's wrong with it," Dex said from behind Jamie, "it's more than I can handle. It'll have to wait until we get back to the dome."

"Perhaps Possum could work with you on it from here," Fuchida suggested.

"The scientific tasks have priority," Jamie said. "We don't have much time to work on the entertainment system."

Fuchida's brows rose. "Mr. Trumball in Boston is very insistent."

"I'll send him a message tonight," Dex said. "I'll calm him down."

Jamie turned to look at Dex. "Thanks," he said.

Dex shrugged.

Turning back to the display screen, Jamie waited for Fuchida to say something more, but when the biologist stayed silent, he realized he had to ask, "What about Shektar? What's she doing?" He also realized he felt somewhere between nettled and embarrassed about asking.

Fuchida replied as if it were a routine question, "She's been running the comm link with Tarawa most of the day. I believe she's been reviewing our medical records."

"Any problems?"

"Not that I'm aware of. We all seem to be healthy enough, even though several of us have lost a kilo or two."

Trumball piped up, "With this vegetarian diet from the garden, what can you expect?"

Fuchida smiled. "What's the matter, you don't like soy derivatives? The garden crops produce a completely balanced diet. "

"Yeah, sure," said Dex. "Microwaved soyburgers and eggplant."

The biologist's smile widened. "No steaks on Mars, my friend."

Trumball leaned closer between Jamie's seat and Dezhurova's. "No sushi, either, pal."

"Ah, but we could cultivate fish," Fuchida retorted. "I am writing a prospectus on adding fish tanks to the garden."

"Just what we need," Trumball said breezily, "fish crap in our water supply."

Jamie glanced at him, over his shoulder, then turned back to the screen. "All right, we'll be at the old rover until nightfall, at least. Might spend the night there."

"Understood," Fuchida said, all business again. "I will have Possum call you when he comes in."

"I'd like to see the imagery from the soarplane as soon as Tomas can send it," Jamie said.

Fuchida's eyes widened for the barest flash of a moment. "He sent it last night. It should be in your incoming data."

Surprised, Jamie said, "I'll check it out . . . wait a minute."

He switched from the biologist's image to a list of his incoming messages. Sure enough, there was one from Rodriguez marked "imagery": several dozen gigabytes.

Putting Fuchida back on the screen, Jamie said, "Yep, it's here, all right. I'll review it tonight. Thank Tomas for me, please."

"I will," said Fuchida.

After Jamie ended the transmission, Trumball said softly, "Missed your mail, huh? Maybe you oughtta tell Rodriguez to send up smoke signals."

Jamie did not turn around to look at Dex. He knew the smug grin that would be on his face. And he didn't want Dex to see the annoyance on his own.

That was dumb, he raged to himself. Stupid. You should have checked your incoming messages last night. That's the second time you've made that mistake. Jamie knew that what nettled him most was not that he had neglected to check his mail, but that he had let Trumball and everyone else see his oversight.

"How close do you want to get?" Dezhurova asked.

Jamie looked up and saw through the windshield that they were less than a hundred meters from the old, abandoned rover.

"Close enough to attach a tow line," he said, then added, "But be careful of the footing."

"Don't worry," she replied. "I don't want to get *us* stuck in the dust."

"You can see the edge of the old crater," Trumball said, pointing his extended arm between Dezhurova and Jamie. "Shouldn't be a problem."

True enough, Jamie saw. The phantom outline of the old crater was easy enough to see, if you knew what you were looking for. The oval of the crater was rimmed with dark rock, raised a few centimeters above the rest of the sloping ground. Within the crater, the dust formed tiny dunes, like wavelets lapping across a pond.

I should have seen them when I was driving the rover, Jamie said to himself. I should have spotted it and driven around it. Even sick and exhausted, a geologist shouldn't have missed something so god-damned obvious.

He glanced over his shoulder at Trumball. The look on the younger man's face seemed almost gloating, he thought.

As Stacy Dezhurova carefully edged the rover up to the rear end of the old vehicle, she reached down with her right hand and activated the laser rangefinder.

"Read it out for me, will you, Jamie?"

"Thirty meters," he said, watching the green glowing digital numbers. "Twenty-eight . . . twenty-five . . ."

"Ten meters okay?"

"Fine," Trumball answered.

"Jamie?"

"Fine," he echoed.

She slowed the rover still more as Jamie called out, "Nineteen meters . . . seventeen . . ."

At precisely ten meters Dezhurova stopped the rover. The old vehicle's rounded rear was dead ahead, scoured to glistening metal by six years of wind-driven iron-rich dust particles.

"Piece of cake," Dezhurova said, shutting down the drive motors. Then she added, "So far."

Jamie, Trumball and Dezhurova suited up and, one by one, went through the airlock and outside. They left Trudy Hall in the rover. She could call the base for help if an emergency arose. As if help could come in time to do any good, Jamie thought. Still, the safety regulations required that at least one person remain inside the rover at all times. If worst came to worst, Trudy would have to drive back to the base by herself.

They walked around the back end of the rover.

"Sand has piled up high on this side," Dezhurova said, her voice sounding calm, almost clinical, in Jamie's earphones.

"It's pretty soft stuff," Jamie said. "Like fluff. Connors and I were able to shovel it away after we got caught in a sandstorm down on the Canyon floor."

Trumball dug a gloved hand into the sand bank. "Fluff is right. Look!" He tossed his handful of sand into the air; it drifted like powder, falling slowly in the light Martian gravity.

"We could ski on this," Trumball said. "Hey, that'd be something for the tourists! Ski Mars!"

He laughed while Jamie gritted his teeth. Is he serious, Jamie wondered, or is he just trying to get a rise out of me?

"The solar panels are caked with the dust," Dezhurova pointed out.

Looking up toward the top of the rover's segments, Jamie saw that she was right. "Wind blew the sand onto the panels, but didn't blow it off again."

Trumball said, "This stuff is pretty damned gritty, too. Probably gouged up the panels."

"Come this way," Dezhurova said. "The hatch is on the lee side."

Jamie followed her, watching the prints her boots made on the ground. It was firm here, but a few meters away was the lip of the crater.

Dezhurova pressed the hatch's control stud. "No joy."

"With the solar panels out, the batteries must've died years ago," Trumball said.

"We must go to manual," Dezhurova muttered, pulling a slim cordless power screwdriver from the tool set nestled in her suit's thigh patch.

Jamie watched her unfasten the panel that covered the manual control. The screws resisted, frozen by time and gritty dust. Dezhurova began swearing softly in Russian as the power screwdriver whined away. Jamie heard her mumbling in his earphones and worried that a slip of the screwdriver could tear her gloves. A rip in the space suit's gloves would be far worse than a skinned knuckle.

The power driver finally got the first screw moving, and Dezhurova's muttered curses stopped. The other screws went much more easily.

"Always the way," she said, without looking up from her work. "The first one you pick is always the bitch."

The wheel that opened the hatch manually was even tougher. Dezhurova could not budge it. Trumball eagerly grabbed at it, and together the two of them grunted and heaved until the airlock hatch cracked open. Then the turning became easier and the door slid all the way open.

"Okay, Jamie," Dezhurova said, panting. "After you."

"You stay outside, Stacy," he reminded her, "until we check out the interior."

"Right, chief," she said.

Wondering if she were using Trumball's nickname for him unconsciously or deliberately, Jamie wedged one boot on the middle rung of the short ladder and gripped the edges of the open hatch with both hands. Then he pulled himself up inside the airlock, noting in the back of his mind that being accustomed to Mars' one-third gravity had its drawbacks: in the suit and backpack it took a real effort to lift himself.

The manual override for the inner hatch was just beneath the electrical control panel. It too was hard to turn at first, but Jamie got the wheel turning by himself and the inner hatch cranked slowly open.

"Okay, I'm going in," he said.

"Me too," said Trumball. Hearing him grunt as he pulled himself into the airlock, Jamie grinned inwardly that Dex had to exert himself to climb up, too.

The interior was a mess. The four of them had been sick with scurvy when the Russians had come to rescue them. They had left the rover without a thought to tidying up. The sheets on the bunks were roiled and wrinkled, just as they had left them. Jamie thought they still looked sweaty, though he knew that any moisture would have evaporated years ago.

He heard Trumball, behind him. "So this is where it happened." The younger man's voice was softer than usual.

Turning to look at him, Jamie saw that Dex was peering through the hatch that connected to the rover's middle segment, which had been converted into a mobile biology lab.

"This is where Brumado and Malater discovered the lichen," Trumball said, almost as if he were gazing upon a holy shrine.

"That's right," Jamie said. The memory that came to his mind was of Joanna, frightened and lovely Joanna, with her big dark eyes and her lonely, vulnerable waif's face. The child-woman he had fallen in love with. The daughter of Alberto Brumado whom he had married. The woman who became an adult at last and walked away from him.

She never loved me, Jamie realized for the millionth time. Maybe she thought she did, at first, but she never loved me. Was I really in love with her? Shaking his head inside the helmet, he thought, Whatever it was, you certainly made a mess of the whole thing.

"Boy, what some museum would pay to have this chunk of hardware in their hands," Trumball said, the awe in his voice giving way to excitement.

Jamie started to snap out a reply, but caught himself in time. This hardware's much too heavy for us to carry back to Earth, he told himself. The ascent section of the L/AV couldn't possibly lift it.

As if reading Jamie's thoughts, Trumball went on, "We'll make this into an exhibit for the visitors. Maybe park it back down on the Canyon floor, where the discovery was originally made, and bus the tourists out there."

Jamie got a vision of the Navaho women who spread their blankets on the sidewalks along Santa Fe's central plaza to sell trinkets to the tourists.

"Are you all right?" Stacy Dezhurova's voice demanded in their earphones.

"We're inside," Jamie reported. "No problems."

"I'm coming in," she said. "We must check out the electrical systems."

"Right."

Nearly an hour later, Dezhurova announced what they had already known. "Dead as a dinosaur," she said, sitting in the pilot's chair.

Standing behind her, gazing at the blank screens and lifeless gauges of the control panel, Jamie nodded inside his helmet. What did you expect? he asked himself. She's been sitting out here for six years, a hundred below zero every night, dust covering the solar panels. The batteries must've died within a few days, a week, at best. The fuel cells are gone, hydrogen leaked away.

"We'll have to tow it," Trumball said.

"If we can," said Jamie.

"Why not?"

Jamie wanted to shrug, but the hard suit defeated it. "We'll have to try it and see."

"Okay," said Dezhurova. "Let's get to it before the sun goes down."

SUNDOWN: SOL 15

JAMIE STILL FELT A SLIGHT SHUDDER OF UNEASE WHEN HE LOOKED AT THE sun; it was eerily small, shrunken, a visible reminder of how far they were from home.

Now the distant sun was almost touching the uneven horizon, an unblinking warning red eye set in a glowing coppery sky. Jamie had to turn his entire body inside his cumbersome hard suit to see the other way. The sky was dark there, with a few stars already glistening brightly. Earth was an evening star now, he knew, but he had no time to search it out or to wait for the aurora.

As the shadows of twilight reached across the cliffs toward them, they hitched a Buckyball cable from the winch drum sticking out from the nose of their rover to an attachment hook on the tail of the old vehicle, then went inside their vehicle, one by one. It took another half-hour to vacuum off the dust, although none of them got out of their suits.

Dezhurova slid her visor up and clomped to the cockpit. Trudy Hall was sitting in the right-hand seat, looking small, almost elfin, in only her coveralls.

Stacy checked out the control panel and began to power up the wheel motors. Jamie and Dex stood behind the two women. Both men had slid up their visors and taken off their gloves.

"You're sure its wheels are in neutral?" Trumball asked.

Jamie nodded inside his helmet. "All drive wheels go to neutral once the power's off, unless they're actively set in gear."

"Or locked in parking mode," Dex added.

"They're not locked," Jamie insisted. "I was there; we didn't lock the wheels when we fell into the dust. Just the opposite, we tried to back out of the crater.''

"Then they might be set in reverse.''

"They're in neutral,'' Jamie insisted.

Trumball's glance slid from Jamie to Dezhurova, sitting in the pilot's seat with her back to them. "I sure wish we could've checked the wheel settings,'' he muttered.

"Not possible,'' Stacy said, from her chair. "Not unless we run a power line to the old rover and boot up her electrical systems.''

"Maybe we ought to do that,'' Trumball said.

"Let's see if we can tow her without getting into that kind of work,'' Jamie said.

"Spooling up,'' Dezhurova muttered, engaging the drive motors. Jamie could not see her head, only the top of her gleaming white helmet.

"Take it easy, now,'' said Trumball.

"Be quiet, Dex,'' she snapped. "I know what I'm doing.''

Dex went silent. Jamie, beside him, stared straight ahead at the curved rear end of the old rover looming ten meters in front of the windshield.

The motors whined as Dezhurova began to slowly back the rover. The tether cable stretched taut.

"Come, come, my sweet one,'' Dezhurova coaxed gently, in a whisper Jamie could barely hear. Then she lapsed into Russian, cooing softly, tenderly.

Standing behind Trudy's seat, Jamie marvelled at the cool, gentle, almost motherly softness of Stacy's whispered urgings. Is this the same woman who was swearing like a biker at a screwdriver just a couple of hours ago?

The rover rocked slightly, and Jamie grabbed the back of Hall's chair for support. The drive motors whined louder. Jamie thought he smelled something burning.

"Come, baby,'' Dezhurova cooed.

Trumball muttered, "It's not going . . .''

The rover lurched again, and Jamie reached out with his free hand to hold onto Trumball. Dex grappled for Jamie's arm clumsily, rocking backwards in his hard suit and nearly tumbling over.

"Here she comes!'' Dezhurova shouted.

The rounded end of the old rover trundled toward them in slow motion, bigger, bigger.

"Hang on!''

The tail of the old vehicle thumped against the projecting winch drum on the nose of their rover hard enough to rock Jamie against the cockpit's rear bulkhead. Both vehicles stopped.

For a long moment none of them said anything. Then Trudy Hall giggled and declared, "Whiplash! Where's the nearest lawyer?"

They all laughed, shakily.

"I guess the old bird's wheels are in neutral," Trumball admitted.

"I guess they are," said Dezhurova.

Jamie noticed that she locked their rover's wheels in park before she pushed herself up from the pilot's chair.

"I have to pee," she announced cheerfully.

Over dinner they planned how they would tow the old rover up to the Canyon rim. As usual, the two women sat on one of the lower bunks while Jamie and Trumball sat side-by-side on the other.

"Why not bring it all the way back to the base?" Trumball urged.

"Cuts into our fuel reserves," Dezhurova said, looking across the foldout table to Jamie.

"Not by that much," Trumball countered.

Jamie said, "Stacy, you'll have to make the call as far as safety is concerned. I need to know exactly how much of our fuel the tow job would eat up."

"I can give you an estimate, but I don't know *exactly* how much fuel we'll consume towing the beast."

"Your best estimate, then," Jamie said.

"We'll want the rover at the base sooner or later," Trumball went on. "Might's well bring it along with us."

"If we can," said Jamie.

"Right. But I'm willing to bet that we can do it with no strain."

"We'll see."

"Yes, Daddy," Dex kidded.

After dinner they put away the table and folded down the upper bunks. Trumball took his turn in the lav while the two women went up to the cockpit together. Jamie squatted on his bunk, opened his laptop and checked in with the base. Rodriguez was at the comm desk.

"Did you get the imagery I sent last night?" he asked, his beefy face frowning with concern.

"Yes, I just haven't had a chance to go over it."

"Doesn't show much. The soarplane's not such a good platform for the kind of data you want."

Sitting cross-legged on his bunk, Jamie shrugged. "It's all we've got, for now."

"Yeah, right."

He went through the day's report with Rodriguez. Possum Craig had the drill rig running again. Fuchida was plotting out his excursion to Olympus Mons. Rodriguez himself was beginning to assemble the manned rocketplane that would carry him and the biologist to the top of the tallest mountain in the solar system.

Jamie listened, watched inventory lists flicker down his screen, waited patiently until he heard himself ask, "What's Shektar been doing?"

"Vijay? She's tending Fuchida's garden and looking after the bugs that Possum's drill is bringing up. Want to talk with her?"

"Sure. Yes."

Trumball came back from the lavatory and ducked low enough to grin at Jamie. "Don't stay up too late now, chief. Big day tomorrow."

"Right," Jamie said. He reached for the earplug attachment to his laptop and pressed it into his ear, then pulled its microphone arm down until the pin mike was almost touching his lips.

As Trumball swung up on the top bunk, Rodriguez's face on the screen was replaced by Vijay Shektar's. She seemed to glisten, as if her skin had been oiled. Jamie thought again how much fun it would be to massage her with pungent balms.

She smiled and talked easily enough, answered Jamie's questions about the iron-eating bacteria that Craig's drill rig was now pulling up from several kilometers below the surface.

"They're magnetically active," she reported. "They align themselves with magnetic fields."

"Must be from the iron they ingest," Jamie guessed.

"Yes, but what advantage does that give them? Mars' magnetic field is so weak that I can't see how it helps them to survive."

"Maybe it doesn't," Jamie said. "Maybe it's just incidental."

She looked doubtful.

"Or maybe Mars had a much stronger field once," he suggested, "and the field has dissipated over time."

"That could be," Vijay said thoughtfully. Then she brightened. "They're reproducing quite nicely in culture. They fission every hour, on average."

"In ambient conditions?"

"Mitsuo's rigged a special high-pressure box for them," she answered. "They've got to be kept in total darkness. Light kills them."

"What about heat?"

Her eyes flashed. "Oh, they're thermophiles, all right. At eighty degrees they switch from fissioning to conjugation. You ought to see them, Jamie. The busy little buggers mate like rabbits!"

"Just what we need," Jamie murmured. "Sex-crazed bacteria."

"They're just like most men," Vijay said, smiling brightly. "They only do it in the dark—and under great pressure."

"Australian men, you mean," he said.

"Some Yanks, too."

He had no reply for that one.

Still smiling, Vijay asked, "And how are you getting along?"

Jamie felt grateful for the change in subject. He returned to the safety of the work they were doing. As he told her about pulling the old rover out of the sand, he reminded himself that this very desirable woman could destroy this expedition if she had a mind to.

He remembered Ilona Malater, who decided that she would be the resident sex therapist for the first expedition. She caused tensions that became almost unbearable, particularly among the Russians.

Vijay was different. Younger, for one thing. And she seemed to be laughing at some private, inner joke. She admitted to having a wicked sense of humor, but Jamie felt that she was professional enough to keep it—and her other passions—under control.

She'd better, he said to himself.

Then a voice in his mind asked, What if she doesn't? What are you going to do about it?

IMAGERY

TOMAS RODRIGUEZ DRUMMED HIS FINGERS ABSENTLY AGAINST THE DESKTOP in rhythm to the trumpets and strings of the mariachi CD he was listening to while he squinted hard at the computer's display screen. He was trying to force some sense out of what the soarplane's cameras showed.

It was well past midnight. He was sitting alone in the dome's geology lab, surrounded by shelves laden with red, pitted rocks and plastic containers of rusty red soil. The dome was dark and quiet; he kept the music low, just enough to keep him company while everyone else slept.

Rodriguez desperately wanted to see what Jamie Waterman thought he had seen: an artificial structure built into a niche two-thirds of the way up the steep rugged cliff of Tithonium Chasma's northern face. He tried his best to see it.

The image on the screen showed the niche, a dark cleft in the massive cliff face with a bulging rock overhang above it. The overhang kept the niche in shadow, despite the fact that the sun was shining on the cliff wall.

The plane's not a good platform for this, Rodriguez thought as he watched the niche get bigger and bigger, then slide out of view as the soarplane banked away and climbed out of the Canyon.

With a patient sigh he went back to the beginning of the sequence, slowed it down, and watched even more intently. The plane was flying almost straight into the cliff, its forward cameras aimed at the niche.

Rodriguez's fingers flicked across the computer keyboard, calling up the best level of brightness the machine could produce. The cliff face washed out almost entirely, but the interior of the niche remained maddeningly unresolved.

He froze the image with a bang of a thick forefinger on a key. Yes, there was something in there, a formation of rock that was lighter than the rest. And it looked like it ran roughly parallel to the lip of the niche. Pretty straight.

A wall? Rodriguez puffed out a pent-up breath. Quién sabe?

"Is that Jamie's village?"

Her voice startled him. Rodriguez spun around in his little wheeled chair and saw Vijay Shektar standing at the doorway to the lab cubicle, each hand holding a plastic mug. She was wearing coveralls, as everyone did. But the Velcro seal down the front was open a few inches, enough for him to notice. Jesus, but she's a sexy one, Tomas thought.

"I couldn't sleep," she explained. "Thought some hot tea would help."

Tomas noticed that both mugs were steaming slightly. And he realized that, when she spoke quietly like this, Vijay's voice was a throaty, sultry purr.

"I heard the music. Mexican, isn't it?" she said, stepping into the lab. "Thought you might like a cuppa."

He took the cup and started to say thanks, but found that his voice stuck in his throat. Like a goddam kid, he thought. He took a breath, then said carefully, "Mexican, right. Mariachi. Their equivalent of country and western."

"Really?"

He nodded. "Yeah. Same old stuff: I loved you but you left me. My heart's broken because you were unfaithful."

"And you took my pickup truck," she added.

"And my dog."

Vijay laughed. Then she said, "Somebody told me once that it's music for losers."

Rodriguez shrugged. "I like it."

"Is that Jamie's village?" she asked again. She remained standing, her eyes focused on the display screen, looking past him.

The mug of tea was hot in his hand. He sighed. "It's no village."

"Are you certain?"

"Pretty much."

The tea felt too hot to drink, he thought, but she put it to her lips and drank with no qualms. He took a cautious sip. It was scalding. Suppressing a yowl of pain, Tomas put the cup down on the desk beside him.

"Pull up a chair," he said, wondering if his tongue would blister, "and I'll show you what we've got."

As she sat in the lab's other little wheeled chair, Vijay commented, "You're up awfully late."

"So are you."

She shrugged, and the movement excited him. "I'm not much of a sleeper. Never have been."

"Uh-huh."

"What about you, though? Shouldn't you be getting your rest? You ought to be taking tip-top care of yourself. We need you to be bright and shiny in the morning."

According to the expedition's regulations, Rodriguez was in charge at the dome while Jamie and Stacy Dezhurova were both away. He was the second-ranking astronaut, and that put him in command when the first astronaut and the mission director were absent. Not that the scientists paid any attention to such protocol. The only time they would obey his commands, Rodriguez was certain, would be if some emergency came up. Maybe not even then.

"I'm okay," he said, thinking that he'd be more than willing to march off to bed this instant if she would come with him.

She turned her attention to the screen again. "So you don't think it's a village or anything artificial?"

She was wearing perfume, he was certain of it. Faint, but a scent of something feminine. It took an effort to keep from reaching out and taking her in his arms. Turning reluctantly back to the screen, Tomas found the strength to say, "See for yourself."

They spent the next half-hour studying the imagery from the soarplane: visual, infrared, radar, false color, even the brief burst of data from the gas chromatograph that gave them nothing but the composition of the air in the Canyon.

She sat next to him, so close they were almost touching shoulders. Tomas felt a thin sheen of perspiration beading his upper lip.

Vijay sighed stirringly. "There's certainly no signs saying, 'Welcome Earthlings,' are there?"

Is she doing that deliberately? Tomas wondered. Does she know how it affects a man?

"If it was anybody but Jamie, I'd say we're wasting our time," he told her.

"But Jamie's different?"

"He's the expedition's director," Rodriguez said. "And he's been here before."

"Does that make him right?"

He thought about that for a moment. "No. But it means we go out of our way to follow up his hunch."

Vijay looked directly into his eyes. "How far out of your way would you go for Jamie?"

"For Jamie? What do you mean?"

"Suppose Jamie asked you to go with him to this area, to poke about in that niche and see what's really there. Would you go?"

"Yeah. Sure."

"Because he's the expedition director?"

Rodriguez hesitated. "I guess so. Also . . . I guess I'd want to go with him even if he wasn't the boss."

"Why?"

He could feel his brows knitting. This is a psych test, he realized. That's all she's after. She's just doing this to fill out her goddamned psych report on me.

"I like Jamie," he said. "I trust him. I guess if he asked me to go with him to the Canyon I'd be kinda flattered."

Vijay nodded. "He is likable, isn't he?"

"Yeah."

"But he's wrong about the village." She said it softly, with real sadness in her voice.

"You like him, too, don't you?"

Staring at the display screen image of the shadowed niche high up on the cliff wall, Vijay Shektar answered very softly, "Yes, I like him too."

Abruptly, Rodriguez turned to the computer and began to shut it down. The image of the rock niche winked off. The screen went dark.

"You're right," he said, almost angrily. "It's late. I better get some sleep."

Dr. Shektar got up from her chair. "Yes, I suppose I should, too."

Rodriguez stood up and noticed for the first time how small she really was. Tiny. Like a little doll. With curves. I could pick her up off her feet with one hand.

She looked up at him and said, "I'm sorry I disturbed you, Tom. Have a good sleep."

She turned and headed for the doorway, leaving Rodriguez standing alone in the geology lab.

She likes Jamie, he told himself. She likes him, not me. I'm just one of her patients, one of her goddamn study subjects. Sorry she disturbed me. Like hell she is. She knows goddamn well the effect she has on me. She's getting her kicks watching me sweat.

He fell asleep fantasizing about her.

NOON: SOL 18

AS THE DOME OF THEIR BASE CAMP APPEARED ABOVE THE RUST-RED HORI-
zon at last, Jamie heard in his mind the strains of *Peter and the Wolf*:
the climactic march, with Peter leading the captured wolf back to his
grandfather's house.

They were dragging the old rover behind them, a triumphant return
to their base camp with an extra piece of equipment to add to their
inventory.

If Possum Craig and the two astronauts could get it to work.

Jamie was driving the rover, with Trumball in the right-hand seat.
Stacy Dezhurova was taking a well-earned break after driving nearly
every kilometer of the way back from the Canyon. Trudy Hall was
already back by the airlock, struggling into her hard suit, ready to carry
her samples of the lichen into the dome's laboratory.

We ought to be able to construct an access tunnel, Jamie thought,
so we can go from the rover's hatch to the dome's interior without
needing to bundle into the damned hard suits.

"Y'know what we need?" Trumball asked, one foot planted jauntily
on the control panel. Without waiting for Jamie to reply, he went on,
"A flexible tunnel. You know, like the access ramps at airports. That
way . . ."

The strains of the triumphal march disappeared. Jamie remembered
that in science it doesn't matter who gets the original idea; what matters
is who publishes the idea first.

With a slow smile, Jamie said, "That's a good idea, Dex. An access
tunnel makes a lot of sense."

Trumball's eyes flashed with pleased surprise, but he quickly suppressed it.

Jamie spent the afternoon going over the old rover with Possum
Craig. It was cramped inside, with both of them in their hard suits.
Through his helmet earphones Jamie could hear Craig sighing and
moaning like a neighborhood repairman trying to figure out just how
high an estimate he could get away with and still be awarded the job.

"Fuel cells completely gone," Craig muttered. Some time later,
"Batteries ain't worth shit now."

When they went out again and clambered up the ladder built into the front module's flank to inspect the solar panels, Craig's voice went from somber to dismal. "Y'all ain't gonna get diddley-squat from these guys."

By the time they had come back inside the dome and gotten out of their suits, Jamie was ready to write off the rover completely.

But Craig rubbed a hand across his stubbly chin and said, "Well, boss honcho, if the drill rig keeps on behavin' itself and the creek don't rise, I can get her runnin' in about a week, I imagine."

Surprised, Jamie blurted, "A week?"

"Give or take a coupla days."

"Really?" Jamie sat on the bench that ran the length of the hard-suit lockers.

Craig nodded sagely and planted one foot on the bench beside Jamie. "Her structural integrity's okay. We got replacement batteries and solar panel spares in th' supplies."

"Enough . . . ?"

"Gotta check out the inventory on the computer and then *find* the sumbitches in the cargo bay. But we oughtta be okay."

"Great!"

"Her fuel cells are a pain in th' butt," Craig complained. "Old style, run on hydrogen and oxy. We'll have to electrolyze some of the water from the backup recycler, I expect."

The fuel cells in the newer rovers used methane and oxygen, Jamie knew.

"Funny thing," Craig went on. "I was more worried about damage to th' windshield . . . you know, pitting or even crazing from the sandstorms. But you had her front end buried nice and cozy in the sand, so the windshield's okay."

Jamie got to his feet, a little shakily. "I never thought—"

"Electrical stuff we got backups for," Craig went on. "But if that windshield had gone, that'd be all she wrote."

When he checked the comm center, Jamie saw Rodriguez sitting at the communications console with a glum look on his swarthy face. And he noticed that the young astronaut seemed to be trying to grow a mustache; his upper lip sported a sprinkling of short, dark hairs.

"Què tal, Tomas?"

Rodriguez looked up at him with an almost guilty expression. "Troubles, man."

"What's the matter?" Jamie asked, pulling up the other wheeled chair to sit next to him.

"I lost contact with number two."

"The soarplane?" Jamie felt a twinge of apprehension in his guts.

Rodriguez nodded unhappily. "Been trying to reestablish contact. No go."

"Where was the plane?"

"Recce flight over Olympus Mons."

The unmanned soarplane was mapping out the huge volcano for Fuchida's upcoming mission to its peak.

"What happened?"

The astronaut shook his head. "I been going over the flight record. Hit some turbulence while she was climbing through twenty thousand meters, but then it cleared up."

Olympus Mons was nearly thirty thousand meters tall, more than three times taller than Mt. Everest.

"Might've been wind shear," Rodriguez guessed, "but up at that altitude the air's so thin it shouldn't be a problem."

"How long has the plane been out of contact?" Jamie asked.

Rodriguez glanced at the digital clock set into the comm console. "Fifty-three minutes, fifty-four."

Jamie let out his breath. "Well, we've got number one, and a backup in storage, at least."

"Only the one backup."

"We'll have to use it if number two is down."

"Yeah, I know. But I don't want to send the backup out to the mountain until I figure out what went wrong with number two."

Jamie pushed himself to his feet. Looking down at Rodriguez's somber face once more, he grasped the younger man's sturdy shoulder.

"Don't blame yourself for this, Tomas. It isn't your fault."

The astronaut shook his head sadly. "How do you know?"

For the first time in almost two weeks, all eight of the explorers sat together for dinner. Trumball monopolized that conversation with his plans for recovering the Pathfinder/Sojourner hardware at Ares Vallis. He and Rodriguez got into a heated discussion on how reliable the backup fuel generator's landing engines were.

"I don't care what the computer simulations say," Rodriguez said, with unaccustomed fervor. "You're gonna be putting your necks on the line based on what some engineer assumed and put into the simulation program."

Jamie knew that the astronaut was feeling the shock of losing the unmanned soarplane.

"You mean," Trudy Hall corrected, "what some programmer assumed out of the engineer's assumptions."

"And they both worked for the company that built the rocket engines," Stacy Dezhurova pointed out.

"Aw, come on," Trumball disagreed. "We've got test data, for chrissakes. They fired those engines dozens of times."

Jamie let them argue. Let Tomas work off some steam about the plane. He's blaming himself for losing it, or at least for not being able to figure out what happened to it. Let him argue and make some points for safety and caution. It'll do us all some good.

Jamie had decided to buck the decision on flying the backup generator to Pete Connors and the rocket experts back on Earth. Trumball wasn't going to go traipsing off to Ares Vallis unless the top experts in the field agreed that the generator could be flown reliably and be positioned where they needed it for the excursion.

But Dex seemed to have every angle figured out. He's been working on this plan for a long time, Jamie thought, probably from before we took off from Earth. He's shrewd, all right. A very clever guy.

Across the table from Jamie sat Vijay Shektar, as silent as he was. Her eyes were on Trumball, who was putting on an animated defense of his idea against the combined doubts of both the astronauts and Possum Craig.

Craig's attitude amused Jamie. He muttered darkly, "Murphy's Law, Dex: if anything can go wrong, it will. And you'll be a helluva long way from help when it does."

Trumball was utterly undeterred by such cautions. Jamie realized, though, that Craig had hit the sensitive point squarely. Expedition regulations required that no excursion be made so far from base that a backup team could not reach a stranded rover. If Trumball got into difficulties all the way out at Ares Vallis, there would be no way to rescue him.

Unless Stacy or Rodriguez could fly the rocketplane out to them. Even at that, the plane could only carry two people at a time. We'd need two rescue flights. Dicey, Jamie thought. Very dicey, but just good enough to squeeze through the safety regs. Nodding to himself, Jamie realized again that Dex had worked out every angle of this trek to Ares Vallis.

Jamie turned his gaze back to Vijay, who was still watching Trumball with an amused half-smile on her lips.

If Dex wants to risk his ass, so what? Jamie thought. Then he remembered that Dex would not go alone. Too bad, he thought. And immediately felt guilty about it.

NIGHT: SOL 18

". . . AND THAT'S THE PLAN, DAD," DEX TRUMBALL SAID INTO THE PIN mike hanging a few millimeters before his lips. "You can start soliciting bids for hardware that's been sitting on Mars for more than a quarter of a century! Oughtta bring in a few megabucks, huh?"

Trumball was sitting on the bunk in his quarters, laptop resting on his knees, earplug and microphone connected to the machine. Not that he was afraid of anyone overhearing him, although the privacy walls of these cubicles did not extend to the dome's ceiling, of course. Nor did he expect a quick reply from his father; the distance to Earth defeated that. Besides, he knew his dad; the old man would want to think this over for a while before answering his son.

Dex felt quite confident that his father would be impressed with his idea. Retrieving the Pathfinder and its little Sojourner rover would be a masterstroke. He could picture the frenzied bidding by museums and entertainment moguls all around the world. Dad's *got* to like it, he told himself. It's money in the bank.

Darryl C. Trumball was in his office, talking on the phone with the head of his London office. Real estate values in eastern Europe were nosediving again, and the elder Trumball saw opportunity smiling upon him once more. Buy cheap, sell dear: that had been his guiding principle all his life. It had never failed him.

One wall of Trumball's office was a huge window with a sweeping view of Boston harbor. He could make out the masts of Old Ironsides at its pier in Charleston. Trumball tested his eyesight that way, every clear day. The opposite wall was a smart screen that could show panoramic views of anything he chose to look at. He had shown his staff the videos of Mars his son had sent to him personally. They had all been dutifully impressed.

At the moment most of the smart wall was blank; only the sleekly handsome face of the head of the London office was showing, in one corner.

"I'm afraid the French are doing their best to make things sticky for us," said his London office chief, dolefully.

"In what way?" Trumball asked.

The man was the picture of a dapper English upper-class type: silver hair, trim mustache, Savile Row suit jacket.

He replied, "They've dug up some rather antique European Union requirements about tax rates on property . . ."

As the Londoner spoke, the message light on Trumball's desktop phone console began to blink. He touched it with the elegant pen he had been twirling nervously in his fingers. The console's little display screen spelled out: PERSONAL MESSAGE FROM YOUR SON.

". . . so I'm afraid that we'll either have to deflect the Froggies in some manner or face the prospect of adding a tax surcharge to every—"

"I'll have to get back to you on that," Trumball said abruptly.

The Englishman looked surprised.

"Something personal has come up. My son. He's with the Mars expedition, you know."

"It's not trouble, I hope."

"I doubt it. I'll get back to you. In the meantime, see if there's a way to sweet-talk the French into seeing things our way." *Sweet talk* was Trumball's term for a bribe.

The Englishman looked skeptical, but he said, "I'll look into it."

"Good."

Trumball cleared the wall screen, then pulled up his son's message. Dex's face loomed over him, enormous. Trumball quickly adjusted the size of the image to normal.

"Dad, I've got the deal of the century for you," Dex began, with a canary-eating grin on his face.

Trumball listened to his son's scheme for retrieving the old hardware, thinking that the boy looked thinner than normal. If his mother saw this she'd go into hysterics and want to tell him to eat more and watch his vitamin supplements.

But he soon forgot about Dex's physical appearance as his son excitedly unreeled the details of his plan. By god, Trumball thought, the boy's got a good idea there. I could get a dozen bidders going for that old junk with a few phone calls. That's all it'd take. Maybe not even that many. By the end of the day there'd be hundreds of bidders, from every corner of the globe.

Then a new thought struck him. What if we offered the hardware to the French? They must have some science museum that'd want it. Or the Paris Disneyland!

He laughed out loud. Sweet-talk the French with this old heap of space junk and get them to ease up on the Eastern Europe deal. That'd work! Wait till I tell the London office about it. Show them who's the man who can solve their problems for them. Tell them their year-end bonuses ought to go to *me*!

He replayed Dex's message through from the beginning, then called his resident science advisor, a physicist from MIT whom he kept on retainer. He made two more calls after that, one to the CEO of the firm that made the landing engines for the fuel generator's rocket vehicle, the other to the mission control people at Tarawa.

It was dusk by the time Trumball had enough information to make his decision. Only then did he send a message to his son on Mars.

The next morning Dex had plenty of work to do, cataloguing the rocks and soil samples he had brought back from Tithonium Chasma and testing selected rocks to see if they bore hydrates inside them. Like a surgeon dissecting a tumor, he cut open several rocks with a diamond-bladed saw, then sliced out sections so thin he could see through them.

Like a surgeon, he had an assistant working with him: Trudy Hall, whose interest in the water content of the rocks was equal to his own. All day they spent in the geology lab, examining the rocks in the scanning gas chromatograph/mass spectrometer. Its miniature laser flashed a microscopic amount of the rock sample into vapor, which the GCMS resolved into its constituent molecules.

By the end of their day, the two of them were tired and aching from bending over lab equipment for long hours without a break. Yet Trudy was practically prancing as they left the geology lab and headed for the galley. Dex was grinning from ear to ear, too.

"You guys look happier than honeymooners," said Possum Craig, looking up from the workbench where he was repairing a balky valve from one of the air pumps.

"You betcha, Wiley," Trumball said, with a wink. "If she could cook, I'd marry her."

"I can cook," Hall shot back, "but I'm much too young to consider marriage."

Jamie Waterman came across the dome floor to them, his stolid face showing a hint of curiosity.

"Anything?" he asked, falling in with Trumball and Hall as they headed for the hot water urn.

"Quite a bit," Trudy said. "Quite a bloody bit, actually."

Jamie broke into a puzzled smile. "Well, are you going to tell us about it?"

"I thought we'd wait until dinner," Trumball said, still grinning broadly, "when everybody's gathered around the campfire."

"How about a little preview?" Jamie asked.

Trumball looked at Trudy Hall. "Should we tell him?"

She glanced at Jamie, then turned back to Dex. "Well, he is the director, actually."

"Yeah, but . . ."

Jamie folded his arms across his chest. "Come on, you two. What have you found?"

"Simply this," Trudy replied, almost bubbling with excitement.

"The rocks that contain hydrates also contain lichen. The arid rocks have no lichen in them."

"The lichen must be able to sense the hydrates," Trumball said. "They can smell the presence of water, somehow, even when it's not liquid."

"Even when it's chemically locked up inside the molecular structure of the rock!" Hall added.

They had reached the hot water dispenser, but none of them reached for a cup.

Jamie asked slowly, "Are you sure about that?"

"Every sample we tested," Dex replied. "Hydrates and lichen together; no hydrates, no lichen."

Shaking his head, Jamie said, "No, I mean about the lichen sensing water."

"How else would you explain it?" Hall asked.

"Well, maybe lichen that try to establish themselves in rocks that don't bear hydrates just die out, from lack of water."

Trudy's face fell. "Oh."

"Now wait," Trumball said. "That's one possibility, okay, but that doesn't mean—"

"Occam's razor, Dex," said Hall glumly.

"What?"

"Occam's razor," she repeated. "When you have two possible explanations for a phenomenon, the simpler one is usually correct."

"That doesn't mean he's right," Trumball said, almost belligerently.

"Yes, I'm afraid it does," Trudy said, her voice down almost to a whisper. "We were so excited about finding the hydrates that we overlooked the obvious explanation."

Trumball frowned at her, then turned to Jamie. "I still think we ought to look deeper. Maybe the lichen really can sense hydrates in the rocks."

"Maybe," Jamie admitted. "But wouldn't your time be better spent figuring out how they crack the water molecules out of the rock? That's a real problem."

Hall's face brightened again. "Yes, that *is* the problem, isn't it? That's an incredible adaptation!"

Jamie nodded and started to walk away. He kept himself from smiling about bursting Dex's balloon until he was safely behind the closed door of his own quarters.

Trudy and Dex gave the full account of their day's work to the whole team over the dinner table. Everyone agreed that Jamie's explanation for the absence of lichen in the non–water-bearing rocks was more likely: lichen that tried to establish themselves in the arid rocks died from lack of water. Trumball held out grudgingly for the idea that the lichen could somehow sense the hydrates, but it was half-hearted and soon drowned out in the excitement of trying to figure out how the organisms extracted usable water from the hydrates.

Fifteen different theories were proposed in as many minutes, with everyone throwing in ideas as fast as they could think of them. Everyone, Jamie noticed, except Rodriguez, who sat in moody silence. He's still blaming himself for losing the soarplane, Jamie thought. What can I do to snap him out of it?

Possum Craig came up with a theory about the lichen: "I think the li'l buggers all got degrees in chemistry and they build tiny li'l chem labs inside the rocks."

The others hooted and yowled.

"Now wait," Trudy Hall said, as the laughter died down. She was sitting across the table from Craig, and looked him squarely in the eye as she said, "Dr. Craig is completely correct, actually."

The table fell silent.

"If the lichen actually are extracting usable water from the hydrates, then they must be excellent chemists and they must have extraordinary chemical equipment built into them."

Mitsuo Fuchida, down at the end of the table, spoke up. "A thought has just occurred to me: What happens to the lichenoids when they use up all the water inside a particular rock?"

They all turned toward him.

Fuchida went on, "An individual rock has only so much water in it, right? What do the lichenoids do when they have consumed all the water in the rock?"

"They must die of desiccation," Hall said, reluctantly.

"They must reproduce before that and spread their seed to other rocks," suggested Vijay Shektar.

"Maybe they go into a spore state," Trumball suggested, "and wait until another source of water becomes available."

"We haven't seen any spores."

"You haven't looked for any."

"That's true," Hall admitted.

"Wait a minute," Jamie said. "This brings up a major question, doesn't it? There's only a finite number of hydrate-bearing rocks. What happens when the lichen have drained all of them?"

"Maybe the rocks without hydrates have been cleaned out by the lichen in earlier years," Trumball said.

Hall shook her head. "That's a process that would take millennia . . . eons, for goodness' sake."

"That's the time scale for planetary development," Craig said. "Jus' like ol' Carl Sagan used to say: billions and billions of years."

"It's also the time scale for evolutionary development of life-forms," Fuchida added.

"Jesus and all his saints," muttered Trumball. "It's just like Lowell said—this planet is dying."

"Lowell was the one who saw canals?" Stacy Dezhurova asked.

With a nod, Trumball replied, "He thought he saw canals and proposed that Mars was inhabited by intelligent creatures who were struggling to stay alive."

"Aren't we all?" Trudy quipped.

"All what?"

"Struggling to stay alive."

"No, seriously," Trumball said. "Lowell's canals were mostly eyestrain and optical illusion. But his basic idea was that Mars was losing its air and water, the whole planet was dying . . ."

Trudy Hall said in a hushed voice, "And that's exactly what we're finding."

"The lichen are struggling to stay alive," Jamie said, "but they're running out of the resources they need."

"Using up the hydrates in the rocks."

"Dying off, slowly."

"But dying."

"Or going into a spore state," Trumball reminded them. "Suspended animation, waiting for better conditions to arise, so they can swing back into life again."

"How long can they stay that way?" Craig asked.

Fuchida said, "Spores from the age of dinosaurs have been revived on Earth."

"Millions of years, then."

"Tens of millions."

"Spores survived on the Moon's surface," Dezhurova pointed out. "Despite vacuum and hard radiation."

"Lunar spores?" Trumball asked.

"Spores we brought with us, without knowing it," the cosmonaut answered. "They were waiting on the old Apollo hardware when we got back there, more than forty years later."

"Didn't they decontaminate the Apollo hardware before they took off for the Moon?"

"Yes, certainly, but that didn't kill all the bugs. They're very tough."

Craig snorted disdainfully. "Makes you wonder what we're carryin' around with us, don't it?"

"The important point is," Jamie said, "that the lichen seem to be indicating that life was once much more abundant on Mars, and now it's dying out."

They all nodded in agreement, all around the table. Jamie thought, Mars is dying. Once life was thriving here. Once there were intelligent

Martians who built cities for themselves up in the cliffs. I know it! I've got to get out there and prove it.

Dex Trumball watched the expression on Jamie's face and knew exactly what was going through the Navaho's mind. He's building a theoretical house of cards to prove to himself that the mirage he saw in that niche in the Canyon was a structure built by intelligent Martians.

Keeping his opinion about that to himself, Dex sat out the rest of the dinner-table discussion as it rambled on, people repeating themselves, thinking out loud, taking wild stabs of guesses just for the joy of hearing themselves talk.

He stayed for it all, not wanting to be the first to walk away from the gab fest. At last, though, Jamie tapped his wristwatch and suggested they clean the table and go to sleep.

Dex smiled inwardly. He always says "go to sleep." Never "go to bed." Wonder how long it's been since he's gotten himself laid? Hell, it's been too damned long for me, and he tries to carry himself like some kind of Navaho holy man. A saint, that's our noble leader: Saint Jamie of Mars.

Still laughing to himself, Dex went to his quarters and booted up his laptop. Dad should have answered my last message by now.

Sure enough, there was a communication from his father. And one from Mom, too. A lot longer than Dad's.

Dex ignored his mother's message and called up his father's gaunt, austere image on the laptop's screen.

He looks like an ice sculpture, Dex thought: cold and hard, inhuman. Dad was in his office, obviously. Dex could see the Boston skyline through the window behind his desk.

"Dex, I think this idea of recovering the old Pathfinder hardware is all right. I've already contacted a few select individuals and started their glands salivating. We could clear a very tidy little bundle on this deal."

Say, Good work, Dex, he thought. Or, I'm proud of you, son.

But the elder Trumball went on, "Now, I know this scheme of yours is not without its risks. I've checked with the people who know about these things, and they tell me it's technically feasible, but on the risky side. If anything goes wrong, there'll be very little chance of getting help."

That's right, Dad, he answered silently. You're always saying I've never risked my butt at anything, I've always had it easy. So now I'm going to show you how wrong you are about me.

"For that reason, I want to make certain that the people picked for this mission are the least needed for the success and safety of the expedition. Get Dr. Waterman to send that Mexican astronaut, Rodriguez. And the Texan, what's his name. Craig, isn't it? They'll get along well together and they won't be that big a loss if anything happens to them.''

Dex stared at the little screen, wide-eyed. ''You don't know shit, Dad,'' he muttered. ''You just don't know anything about anything.''

But his father was saying, ''Under no circumstances are you to go on this mission. Do you hear me, Dex? I absolutely forbid it. You stay where it's safe. Let the others do the work; you take the glory.''

MORNING: SOL 21

''THREE WEEKS ON MARS,'' SAID VIJAY SHEKTAR. ''WE SHOULD HAVE A celebration tonight.''

Jamie was sitting on a spindly-legged stool in Shektar's infirmary, the top of his coveralls pulled down, a blood pressure cuff wrapped around his left forearm and half a dozen medical sensor patches adhering to the skin of his chest and back.

''The first expedition stayed forty-five sols,'' he said. ''Let's wait until we've broken their record.''

''You're not much fun, Jamie.'' Vijay made a face somewhere between a pout and a grin.

''Or better yet, wait until we've got something more to celebrate than a date on a calendar.''

Vijay glanced at the monitor screens that were reading Jamie's pressure, pulse, temperature and skin pH. When she looked back at Jamie, her eyes were dancing.

''Well,'' she said, ''Christmas is coming—on Earth.''

''Fine. We can celebrate Christmas.''

''No tree.''

''We'll make one out of aluminum. Or plastic.''

She began peeling off the sensor disks. ''You're boringly healthy, mate. Skin pallor's not so good, though. You ought to spend more time under the sun lamps.''

''I could go into the airlock without a suit,'' he suggested, grinning as he pulled up his coveralls and wormed an arm into a sleeve.

''The UV's a bit intense for suntan in there,'' she said.

''Never thought a guy with my complexion would need a sunlamp,'' Jamie said.

''What about me?''

''You've got a permanent tan.''

"Yes, I found that out the first time I went to a chemist's shop and tried to buy flesh-colored Band-aids."

Jamie looked at her closely. There was no trace of rancor in her expression. Just the opposite.

"You're all smiles this morning," Jamie said, sealing up the Velcro front of the coveralls.

"And you're all business, as usual."

"That's my job."

"You could use some relaxation," she said. "All work and no play, you know."

Jamie thought it over swiftly. "Want to take a walk?"

"Outside?"

"Where else?"

"Trudy jogs through the dome every day. She's got a regular route all pegged out."

"No," Jamie said. "I mean outside."

"Do you think we should?"

"I've got some free time late this afternoon, just before dinner. Want to take a stroll with me?"

"I'd love to."

"I'll bet you haven't been outside since the day we landed," Jamie said lightly.

"Oh no, that's not so. Dex and I went out a couple of times. Not since he's gotten so busy planning this Ares Vallis excursion, of course."

"Of course," Jamie replied, feeling deflated.

Vijay giggled. "Dex was trying to convince me that we could both fit into one hard suit."

"Was he?" Jamie growled.

She was grinning broadly at him. "What do you think, Jamie? You're a bit heftier than Dex. D'you think we two might snuggle into one suit?"

Jamie was at a loss for words until he remembered an old line that one of his university classmates had told him about. "Vijay, don't let your mouth write a check that your body can't cash."

For once, she was speechless.

Grinning now, Jamie said, "Sixteen hundred hours. I'll meet you at the lockers. Okay?"

She made a military salute. "Aye-aye, sir."

Dex Trumball was still seething over his father's command. The planning for this excursion out to Ares Vallis was eating up more and more time, especially now that they were testing the guidance system for the fuel generator's rocket booster. Jamie had okayed a serious change in Dex's personal schedule, and Craig's, as well. It allowed them to spend most of their time preparing for the excursion, at the cost of postponing much of their regular work, including the stratigraphy workups that were so important to understanding the time scales of Martian geological forces.

Jamie himself took up some of that slack, since he was a geologist. He could try to make sense out of the different layers of rock and determine when each had been laid down. But Dex knew that he should be doing that himself; his own work was slipping—and Jamie was allowing it.

Sure, he thought. If anybody complains about the geology work slipping he can tell them it's my fault.

Dex had told no one about his father's determination that he should not go on the excursion. He had even erased his father's hateful message and hacked into the expedition's main computer to make certain there was no copy of it in its files.

He doesn't want me to go, Dex grumbled to himself as he stared at the readout display from the guidance computer. Possum Craig was outside, fitting a set of sensors to the rocket vehicle, so that they could make some scientific use of its upcoming flight to the Xanthe Terrra region, east of Lunae Planum. Stacy Dezhurova was going to run the flight remotely from the base dome. Dex was working with her to get all the flight parameters squared away.

He doesn't want me to go because he thinks I'll fuck things up. He doesn't trust me. I'm on fucking *Mars* and he still doesn't trust me! Even if everything goes exactly right and we bring the hardware back here without a hitch he'd still be able to say that I didn't do it, I didn't have the smarts or the guts to go out and do it.

Well, the hell with you, Pop! I'm going. And there's not a damned thing you can do about it. I'm going out there myself and show you I can get the job done. By the time you find out about it I'll be on my way. Stuff that up your nose, Daddy old pal. I'm free of you. No matter what you say or do, I'm on my own out here.

"I thought you said this was free time for you." Vijay's voice sounded slightly amused in Jamie's helmet earphones.

The two of them were walking toward the manned rocketplane that Rodriguez had been assembling over the past week. Like the remotely piloted soarplanes, it was built of gossamer-thin plastic skin stretched over a framework of ceramic-plastic *cerplast*. To Jamie it looked like an oversized model airplane made of some kind of kitchen wrap, complete with a weirdly curved six-bladed propeller on its nose.

But it was big enough to carry two people. Huge, compared to the unmanned soarplanes. Rodriguez said it was nothing more than a fuel tank with wings. The wings stretched wide, drooping to the ground at their tips. The cockpit looked tiny, nothing more than a glass bubble up front. The rocket engines, tucked in where the wing roots joined the fuselage, looked too small to lift the thing off the ground.

The plane was designed to use its rocket engines for takeoffs, then once at altitude, it would run on the prop. Solar panels painted onto the wing's upper surface would provide the electricity to run the electrical engine. There was too little oxygen in the Martian air to run a jet engine; the rockets were the plane's main muscle, the solar cells its secondary energy source.

"This is free time for me," Jamie told Shektar. "Might as well say hello to Tomas while we're strolling by, don't you think?"

"And with all of Mars around us you just happen to walk in this direction," she countered.

He could hear the puckish teasing in her voice. Instead of trying to keep up with her, Jamie called to Rodriguez, "Hola, Tomás! Què pasa?"

The astronaut's spacesuited figure was kneeling beneath one of the plane's wing roots, both gloved hands inside an open access panel on the engine nacelle. It was impossible to see if he turned his head inside the helmet, but Rodriguez's troubled voice came through their earphones:

"Tengo un problema con este maldito . . . uh, fuel injector."

"What did he say?" Shektar asked.

"What's the problem?" Jamie asked in English.

He heard Rodriguez chuckle. "Glad you switched to English, man. I don't think my Spanish is good enough to explain about gas lubrication joints and low-temperature ignition systems."

Rodriguez seemed to have gotten over his blues about losing the unmanned soarplane. Jamie had been watching him closely, knowing that Tomas was slated to pilot Fuchida in the manned plane to the same area where the soarplane went down. The astronaut had tried hard to determine why the unmanned plane had crashed, but the closer they came to his own flight the less he seemed to care about the cause of the crash.

For several minutes Jamie and Rodriguez chatted in tech-speak English that was all but incomprehensible to Shektar.

Finally, Jamie asked, "Well, will she fly, Orville?"

Rodriguez laughed. "She'll fly, Wilbur. Even if I have to use my own blood to lubricate the damned stubborn propellant pumps."

Jamie realized that Rodriguez was totally serious, despite his light tone. He would be piloting this bird, with Fuchida as his passenger. If anything went wrong, it was his butt on the line.

And mine, Jamie realized. I've got to give the final okay for their flight. It doesn't matter how many technical people back on Earth review his work and okay it. The final responsibility is mine. Is Tomas

emotionally prepared for this mission? Maybe I should talk it over
with Vijay.

He remembered something Connors had told him back during his
training days, even before the first expedition.

"Behold the lowly turtle," the astronaut had quoted. "He only
makes progress when he sticks his neck out."

Pilots' wisdom. Astronaut humor. But it was true, Jamie knew. If
we wanted to be totally safe, we'd still be in our homes back on Earth.
Hell, we'd still be in caves, too scared to try to use fire.

"I was promised a stroll out in the countryside," Shektar reminded him.

"Right," he said quickly. "Stay with it, Tomas."

"What else do I have to do?"

Jamie and Vijay walked around the plane's high sweeping tail and
headed out toward the setting sun. They switched their suit radios from
the general communications frequency to another freak that would allow
them to converse without bothering Rodriguez or anyone back in the
dome who might be monitoring the general frequency.

Without preamble, Vijay said, "Tommy seems to be okay now."

Surprised, Jamie replied, "Did he tell you about his problem?"

"Him? No way, mate."

"Then how did you know . . . ?"

"I'd be some psychologist if I couldn't see his bedraggled looks,
wouldn't I?" Shektar's voice sounded slightly amused in his earphones.
"I mean, the poor lad was staggering around like a stunned mullet."

Jamie said, "He felt responsible for the soarplane crash."

"He's worked his way through it."

"With your help?"

She did not answer for a heartbeat or two. Then, "Oh, I gave him
a couple of big smiles and a pat on the back. Seemed to cheer him
a bit."

"Will he be all right to fly?"

"Best thing for him, actually," she replied. "If you tried to take
him off the mission now he'd be totally crushed."

Jamie nodded inside his helmet, wondering how much of this
morale-boosting Vijay wrote into her official records.

They walked slowly away from the dome, across the rock-strewn
red sand.

"God, it's even bleaker than the outback," Vijay murmured.

Jamie said, "But beautiful."

"You think this is beautiful?" Her voice was filled with disbelief.

"You're comparing it with Earth, with someplace that you know,
maybe someplace you love."

"It makes Coober Pedy look like the bloody Garden of Eden."

Jamie shook his head. "Don't make comparisons. This is a different world, Vijay. Look at it for what it is. Look at it with fresh eyes."

Even as he said it, Jamie realized that he himself instinctively compared the Martian landscape to the rugged desert of the Navaho reservation. Take your own advice, he thought. Look at it with fresh eyes.

And he saw beauty. The world lying before their eyes was a symphony of reds: rocks the color of rust scattered everywhere, gentle dunes of ocher and maroon stretching out to the hilly uneven horizon, the sky a delicate pinkish tan deepening to blue overhead. A soft breeze thrummed past; he could hear its friendly murmur through his helmet. It was *right,* harmonious, a balanced world without pressure, without noisy crowds or massive buildings or busy streets.

Without people, he realized. Maybe we weren't meant to live in crowded cities. Maybe we're meant to live in small families, little groups with plenty of open space around us.

"You know," Vijay said slowly, "it really is kind of lovely, in a way. Peaceful."

Yes, Jamie thought. Peaceful. But let Dex have his way and there'll be tourists tramping through here and contractors building cities and an army of engineers swarming everywhere trying to change all this and make it just like Phoenix or Tokyo or New York.

"Of course," Vijay went on, "it's peaceful because we've got to stay inside these suits. It's lovely because we can't really live here, we can only visit."

"Mars tolerates us," said Jamie. "As long as we respect its world."

"We're not really on Mars, are we? I mean, we can't feel the wind or run barefoot through the sand."

"No. We're visitors. Guests."

She moved closer to him and Jamie tried to put his arm around her shoulders. In the oversized hard suits with their bulging backpacks it was impossible.

Instead, he took her by the arm and wordlessly walked her to the crest of a low curving rocky ridge, the late afternoon sun throwing their long shadows ahead of them across the barren sand dunes that marched in symmetric order out to the disturbingly close horizon. There was no warmth in the sunlight; if they had not been encased in the protective hard suits, they would have quickly frozen to death. Without the air from the tanks on their backpacks they would have asphyxiated even sooner.

Yet the uncanny beauty of the Martian landscape stirred a chord within Jamie, this red world. It was a soft landscape, barren and empty, yet somehow gentle and beckoning to him. What's over the next hill? he wondered. What's beyond the horizon?

Yet he stopped.

"Why have you stopped?" she asked. "Let's go over to those dunes."

Jamie tapped her shoulder with one gloved hand and pointed back behind them with the other. "We'd be out of camera range."

One of the pole-mounted surveillance cameras poked just clear of the horizon behind them. Their bootprints were clearly visible in the iron-rich sand, side by side. They'll stay there until the next big storm, Jamie told himself. This soft wind wafting by doesn't have enough strength to push the rusty sand grains.

He said to Vijay, "We can walk along the crest a while. It's still early, we've got time."

"I'd like that."

"We can't stay out very long," Jamie said. "It'll get dark as soon as the sun sets."

"Stacy told me you showed her the aurora," she replied.

"That's right," he said. "I did."

After a few minutes of walking in silence, Jamie stopped and turned completely around. The sky off in the east was already darkening, even though the sun had not quite touched the undulating western horizon.

There ought to be, Jamie thought . . . yes! There it is!

Clutching Vijay's shoulder and pointing with his other hand, Jamie said, "Look up there."

"Where? What is—an airplane!"

"No," Jamie corrected. "It's Phobos, the nearer moon."

A bright spark was moving purposefully across the sky, unblinking, unhurried, travelling across the darkening sky as if on a mission of its own.

"It's too small to make a disk," Jamie explained, "and so close to the planet that it moves like an artificial satellite in low orbit, from east to west."

"I can see a star," she said, pointing.

"Probably Deimos, the bigger moon." Jamie looked to where she was pointing and realized he was wrong. He felt the breath gush out of him.

"That's Earth," he said. Whispered, really.

"Earth?"

Jamie nodded inside his helmet. "Big and blue. That's Earth. It's the evening star here, for the next several months."

"Earth." Vijay's voice was hollow with wonder.

Stacy Dezhurova's voice shattered the moment. "Base to Waterman. Sun is on the horizon. Start back home."

He turned and saw that the sun had indeed touched the distant hills. "Okay," he said reluctantly. "We're heading in."

Safety regulations. Even with the helmet lamps they were not permitted to walk around outside at night. Not a smart thing to do unless there was some overriding reason for it. Still, Jamie would have enjoyed at least a few minutes alone with Vijay and the glittering night sky of Mars.

"No aurora, I'm afraid," he said ruefully.

"Stacy's jealous."

"No, she's just following the regulations."

"Well . . . thanks for the walk," she said as they started back.

"I'm glad you enjoyed it," he said.

"I should get out more often. I've been cooped up in that dome too long."

"You don't mind being cooped up in a suit?"

"Not really. Do you?"

"Not really," he echoed. "I feel kind of free out here, almost like I could take off the suit and run off to the horizon."

"Do you?"

The sudden change in the tone of her voice alarmed Jamie. "Oh-oh. I shouldn't have admitted that to the team psychologist, should I?"

She laughed. "No worries. It's off the record."

Jamie knew better. He tried to make light of it. "I'm not really delusional, you know."

"Not yet," she bantered back at him.

"I've wondered why we needed a psychologist on this mission," he said. "We got along fine on the first expedition without one."

Vijay replied, "You need a psychologist because you're all borderline crazy."

"Crazy?"

"Who else but a madman would journey millions of kilometers to this frozen desert? I could write a research paper on each and every individual on the mission. Every one of them."

"The women too?"

"Yes," she answered easily. "Myself also. Sometimes I think I must be the maddest one of us all."

"You?" He was genuinely surprised.

"Me."

"But you're so level-headed. Always full of good spirits and all that."

She sighed. "I must tell you the story of my life someday."

"Anytime."

"In the meanwhile," she said, quite serious now, "it seems to me that you and Dex are managing to get along rather smoothly."

"Dex isn't that bad . . . as long as he gets what he wants."

"He's a very ambitious young man, and quite accustomed to getting his own way. The more you give in to him the more demands he'll make on you."

And what demands is he making on you? Jamie wanted to ask. But he buried that and said instead, "As mission director, it's my job to make certain that we don't have any personal conflicts that will interfere with the expedition's work."

"That is ridiculous, Jamie. Neither you nor anyone else can avoid personal conflicts. You have four very intelligent, highly motivated and thoroughly individualistic scientists under your leadership. Not to mention the two astronauts, who also have their quirks."

"Plus the expedition's physician/psychologist."

"Her too," Vijay admitted.

"And we're all borderline lunatics, according to you."

"We're living under extremely stressful conditions," she countered. "We're millions of kilometers from home, Jamie."

"We've all been trained to deal with that," he said.

"Perhaps so, but there will be conflicts," she continued, deadly serious. "You won't be able to smooth everyone's feelings all the time."

They walked in silence for several uneasy minutes, passing the plane that Rodriguez had been working on. No sign of him; he must already be inside, Jamie thought.

"Well," he said lamely, "we've survived the first three weeks okay."

The sun was dipping behind the hills now. They were in shadow now. Twilight lasted only a little while, unless a recent dust storm filled the air with particles that scattered the dying sunlight. The curve of the dome was just visible over the rim of the hill before them. Jamie turned as he walked toward the airlock, took a final look at the red world.

"I love it here." The words surprised him. He didn't realize he was going to say them until they tumbled from his lips.

Vijay followed his gaze across the broken rocks scattered across the rusty landscape and the wind-sculpted dunes that waited for the next big sandstorm to rearrange them.

"It's so barren," she said. "So cold and bleak."

"It's like home to me," he said.

"It's not home, Jamie. It's an alien world that could kill you in the flash of a second."

He stared for a moment at her spacesuited figure. "Mars is a gentle world, Vijay. It means us no harm."

"Not until the air in your suit runs out."

He tried to shrug. "Yes, there is that."

"There's always the urge to live," she said. "The impact of reality. It limits our dreams."

"Maybe."

They trudged back toward the shelter. Jamie saw the rounded hump of the dome rising slowly above the horizon with each step. He felt reluctant; he knew he really would prefer to walk out past the dune field, out into the unknown, across the face of this red world.

"You were married to Joanna Brumado, weren't you?"

Startled by her question, Jamie answered, "It didn't work out."

"Do you blame yourself for that?" Vijay asked.

He stopped walking, forcing her to stop and turn to face him.

"Is this part of your psych profiling?" Jamie asked coldly.

"I suppose so," she said.

"In that case, no, I don't blame myself for the divorce. I don't blame anybody. It just didn't work out, that's all."

"I see."

"No-fault divorce. Nobody's to blame."

"Yes."

Wondering why he felt so angry, Jamie said, "I don't see what my marriage has to do with my job performance here. Hell, the marriage didn't even last three years."

"I'm sorry I asked," Vijay said. "I din't realize it would upset you so."

"I'm not upset!"

"No, I can see that you're not."

DIARY ENTRY

What really hurts is that they don't respect me. They toler-
ate my presence among them, but behind my back they laugh at
me. I'm as good as any of them, but they all think of me as
second-class or worse. All of them. Each and every one of them.

NIGHT: SOL 21

JAMIE LINGERED OVER A CUP OF WEAK COFFEE, FEELING ALMOST SATISFIED.

"Four thousand kilometers," said Vijay. "No one's gone even half that distance before."

She was the only other one sitting at the galley table with Jamie. Dinner was over, the table cleared except for their dishes. Rodriguez and Fuchida had trooped off to the bio lab, while Trumball, Craig and Stacy Dezhurova had gone to the geology lab. They were planning two excursions: a trek across nearly four thousand kilometers to Ares Vallis and a flight to the tallest mountain in the solar system. Trudy Hall had pulled the final comm center shift before they all went to sleep.

"I think the trip to Olympus Mons will get more attention from the media," Jamie said.

"Dex is so excited about retrieving the Pathfinder spacecraft, though. Don't you think the media will get excited, too?"

He shrugged. "I suppose so, once they get there. But Dex and Possum are going to be driving across the landscape for several weeks. Pretty boring."

"Unless they run into trouble."

"Yeah," said Jamie. "There is that."

He had been mildly surprised when the technical directors at Tarawa had agreed to the long-distance run. God knows what kind of pressure Trumball and the other financial backers put on them, Jamie thought. Must have been pretty fierce.

"D'you really think the flight to the volcano will draw more attention from the media?" Vijay asked.

"It won't be exactly the same as climbing Mt. Everest," he replied, "but it should draw a lot of interest."

She seemed to think it over before agreeing. "If the virtual reality rig works, millions of people can share in the moment."

The VR equipment had been cranky for more than a week.

"I shouldn't have gone up on that boulder," Jamie admitted. "I shook something loose, I guess."

"That's the technical term for it," Vijay said, with a grin.

Possum Craig had gone over the VR rig briefly and found no identifiable fault. Yet the equipment worked only in sputters now; it would function well enough for a while, then cut off unpredictably.

"I wish Possum had more time to spare," Jamie said. "I'm getting pressure from Tarawa about the lack of VR sessions."

"Dex says we're losing money," said Vijay. "He means, we're not making the money we could make if the VR sessions were going smoothly."

Jamie nodded gloomily. "I've got half a dozen messages from Dex's father. He's not an easy guy."

"Could I see them?" she asked.

Jamie felt his eyebrows rise. "Trumball's messages to me?"

"They might help me understand Dex," she explained. "See what kind of father he's got."

Jamie thought it over briefly, then said, "Okay, come on."

He got up and went to the comm center, Vijay alongside him. As they approached the geology lab they heard the passionate voices of Dex and Stacy, heatedly arguing.

Then Craig's calm, flat Texas twang broke in. "You two are just engagin' in a spittin' contest. Doesn't matter what particular spot y'all pick for landin' the fuel generator, it ain't gonna be the spot y'all actually land it, I can guarantee that."

Jamie glanced in as they passed the lab's open door. Dex was glowering at Craig, but Stacy's strong, heavy features seemed stolid, unemotional.

"He is right, Dex," the cosmonaut said. "I can put the bird down exactly where you want it, but I will bet there will be a field of big, stupid boulders right at that spot and we will have to jink the bird over to a smoother area."

"But we've got the satellite imagery of the territory," Dex insisted as Vijay and Jamie passed the lab.

"Yeah, with a resolution of one meter," Craig grumbled. "Got any idea what a one-meter rock'll do to the landing struts of yore fuel percolator?"

Vijay laughed softly. "It's hard to argue with Possum. He doesn't open his mouth unless he's got the facts."

"I wish he could find out what's wrong with the VR rig," Jamie said.

"What about the backup?"

"Mitsuo's taking it on the Olympus Mons excursion."

"Oh. Of course."

They stepped through the open doorway of the comm center. Even though its partitions were only two and a half meters high, the room felt warmer to Jamie than anywhere else in the dome. Maybe it's the equipment always running, giving off heat, he thought. But the life-support equipment was always running, too, and that section of the dome didn't feel as warm. With an inward shrug he told himself, It's your imagination. It's all in your mind.

Trudy was sitting at the main console, twitching in rhythm to the primal rock music playing in the earphones she had clamped to her boyishly styled dark brown hair. Jamie could hear its heavy thump even through the earphones.

She turned and pulled the headset off. A blast of shrill noise filled the comm center; Trudy quickly clicked it off.

"How did you hear us come in?" Jamie asked, incredulous.

"Didn't, actually," Hall said, "but you're not vampires, are you?"

"Huh?"

She hiked a thumb toward the monitor screen. "I saw your reflection in the display."

"Oh."

"I'm all finished here." She got up from her chair. "Everything's tucked in for the night."

"You really shouldn't play that stuff so loud," Vijay said, quite seriously. "It can damage your hearing."

"What?" Trudy cupped an ear, pretending deafness. Both women laughed and Trudy headed for the doorway with a lighthearted, "Ta."

As Trudy pranced out of the comm center she passed the square, boxy form of the immersion table. I ought to be spending more time planning my own trip out to the cliff dwelling, Jamie told himself. I ought to spend as much time on that as Dex is spending on this damned silly excursion to Ares Vallis. But I'm stuck doing the stratigraphy work that he should be doing instead of planning my own excursion.

Feeling almost weary, he sat in one of the wheeled swivel chairs and pulled up the elder Trumball's messages on one of the display screens. Vijay sat beside him and stared in silence at the icily demanding old man. There were six messages so far, the shortest of them running more than twelve minutes.

". . . this is a totally unacceptable situation, Waterman," Darryl C. Trumball was saying. "Totally unacceptable! Each VR transmission is worth upwards of thirty million dollars to us. Thirty million dollars! That's how much money you're pissing down the drain because you and your pack of brilliant scientists can't get some simple electronics equipment to function properly!"

Vijay sat through all six of Trumball's increasingly vitriolic tirades without speaking. When the last of them was finished she said, "Wow!"

Jamie blanked the display screen. "I'm glad there's a hundred million kilometers between us."

"That's what Dex has had to deal with all his life," she murmured. "No wonder he's so driven."

Jamie said nothing. She's not worried about what I have to put up with; she's thinking about Dex.

"What are you doing to placate him?" Vijay asked.

Jamie said, "Nothing will placate him unless we get the VR transmissions going again. I've thought about using the backup equipment, but Mitsuo's going to use it at Olympus Mons and I don't want to take the chance of messing it up before then."

"I suppose that's right," Vijay said, nodding slowly. "And Possum can't fix this rig?"

"He's looked at it and he can't find what's wrong. He calls it engineer's hell: everything checks but nothing works."

A pair of tiny furrows took form between Vijay's brows. She looked as if she were trying to fix the situation by thinking hard on it.

"The fault must be in the VR system's computer," Jamie said. "The cameras and data gloves look okay."

"Can we switch another computer . . . ?"

"No, it's built into the system."

She leaned back in the chair. "You've got a problem, mate."

"It's an annoyance," Jamie said. "Not a problem. I can't get too worked up about it, even if it's giving Dex's dad a stroke."

She looked at him curiously. "Well, I'd certainly be worked up about it if somebody was coming down on me like he's leaning on you."

Jamie smiled. "What's he going to do, fire me?"

"There is that." She smiled back.

"Some things are important and others aren't. You've got to find the path that lets you deal with the important things."

"And ignore the rest?"

He shook his head. "Not ignore them. Just keep them in their proper balance."

Vijay's gaze took on a slightly different air. "You know, Jamie, you just might be the sanest man I know."

"I thought we were all crazy."

"Oh, we are," she said, standing up. "Certainly we are. But for a madman, you're quite level-headed."

He got up beside her and noticed again that she barely reached his shoulder. "Do you like level-headed men?"

She cocked her head, as if thinking. "Actually, I think the crazy ones are more interesting."

"Is that a personal reaction or a professional one?"

"A little of both, I imagine."

Without thinking, without even knowing he was going to do it, Jamie put his arms around her waist, pulled her to him, and kissed her.

Vijay lingered in his arms for a few breathless moments, then gently disengaged.

"I don't think we should . . ."

"I'm not crazy enough to interest you?"

She took a step back from him. "It's not that, Jamie. It's not you, not who you are or what you are. It's . . . it's *here,* this place. We're a hundred million bloody kilometers from home. What we're doing here, what we feel . . . it's not really us. It's loneliness and fear."

"I don't feel lonely or fearful," Jamie said softly. "I like it here."

"Then you really are the maddest one of us all," Vijay whispered. She turned and fled from the comm center.

Jamie stood there alone, thinking: Beneath her kidding and joking she's scared. She's scared of Mars. She's scared that what she feels isn't real, it's just a reaction to being here.

Would she feel the same way about Dex? he asked himself. Does she feel the same way about Dex?

BOOK II:
THE FIRST EXCURSIONS

The People came up through three worlds and settled in the fourth world, the blue world. They had
been driven from each successive world because
they quarrelled with each other and committed
adultery. In the earlier worlds they found no people
like themselves, but in the blue world they found
others.

The People forgot their earlier worlds, except
for the legends they told of the Old Ones. But the
others, the strangers, they looked to the other
worlds with wonder. They wanted to see them, walk
on them. They did not know that Coyote would go
with them and work to destroy them all.

EVENING: SOL 45

IT'S A DULL PARTY, JAMIE THOUGHT. BUT WHAT CAN YOU EXPECT WHEN you're being watching by ten or twenty million strangers?

They had broken the record of the first expedition at noon, local time, but delayed the celebration until after dinner. Dex had worked out the time for their "party" with the public relations people in Tarawa and New York—as if he didn't have enough to do, Jamie groused silently.

So, with Dex wearing the backup virtual reality cameras clamped to his head like an extra pair of eyes, and the nubby data gloves on his hands, the eight explorers solemnly toasted the new Martian endurance record with fruit juices, coffee and tea.

It was early afternoon in New York. Roger Newell sat behind his broad-sweeping utterly clear desk and participated in the staid little festivity on Mars. It was being broadcast to some ten million VR sets, according to his information, but his network would show snippets of it on the evening news broadcast for all the others who could not afford a virtual reality rig.

"No more than a minute," Newell muttered to himself from inside the VR helmet. "Thirty seconds, tops." Christ, what a bunch of amateurs, he thought. These scientists can make even a party look dull.

"And here," Dex Trumball was saying, "is Dr. James Waterman, our mission director. He was on the first expedition, too."

Jamie felt suddenly tongue-tied, with Dex standing before him staring at him with that extra pair of electronic eyes perched atop his head. He hadn't paid attention to the routine that Dex and the PR people had scripted. But he knew he had to say something.

"We're very happy to be here on Mars, learning more about this planet," he dithered, stalling for time to think. Unconsciously, he raised the cup he'd been drinking from and explained, "Of course, we don't use alcoholic beverages here, but the fruit juices we're drinking come from our own garden. Dex, you should show them the garden."

"I will, later," Dex replied, trying to hide his exasperation. "But first tell us about what we have planned for the next stages of the expedition."

"Oh, you mean the flight out to Olympus Mons."

"Yes, that . . . and the long-distance excursion to the Sagan Station."

"Oh, sure," Jamie said, relieved that he had something concrete to talk about.

Darryl C. Trumball watched the broadcast on the flat wall screen of his office. He had no time or inclination to don a VR helmet and those sticky gloves.

Dex is trying to get that damned redskin to pump up the audience about retrieving the Pathfinder hardware and all the Indian's talking about is that stupid volcano!

Robert Sonnenfeld had begged, borrowed, and even paid with his own money to get a total of eighteen virtual reality helmets and glove sets, so his entire class could experience the broadcasts from Mars.

Now he and his seventeen enthralled middle school students felt as if they were actually walking through the domed garden that the explorers had built on the rust-red sands of Mars.

An English woman was guiding them through the garden, explaining what they were seeing.

"This is actually a very specialized version of a system called the Living Machine. It was first developed in the United States as a way of purifying waste water and making it safe enough to drink."

Trudy Hall stopped by a large vat filled with thick, sludge-brown water. "The process begins with bacteria, of course," she explained. "They begin the job of breaking down the wastes and pollutants in the water . . ."

Fifteen minutes later she was standing amid rows of plastic trays that held a variety of green, leafy plants.

"We can't grow plants in the local soil, of course, because the ground is heavily saturated with superoxides," Trudy was explaining. "Rather like a very strong bleach. However, by using hydroponics— growing our crops in trays through which we flow nutrient-rich water . . ."

Li Chengdu was fascinated by the tour. As mission director of the first expedition, he had remained in orbit about Mars. He had never set foot on the red planet's surface. Now he was walking through a man-made hydroponic garden set up beneath a plastic dome, a garden that recycled the expedition's water and provided not only clean drinking water but fresh food, as well. Remarkable.

He was walking virtually beside Trudy Hall as she paced slowly along an aisle between hydroponics trays, pointing left and right as she spoke.

"And by this point the water is used to nourish our garden vegetables. Soybeans, of course. Lettuce, quinoa, eggplant . . . and over there, in those larger trays, are the melons and strawberries."

Hall reached out and touched a bright green leaf. Li felt it in his gloved fingers.

I am on Mars at last, he marvelled to himself.

Jamie and the others had drifted to the galley tables when Dex and Trudy had gone out to the garden. They sat around and talked shop, now that the cameras were off them.

"It's a good thing the VR rig is working tonight," said Stacy Dezhurova. "Tarawa has been sending up complaints every day about its breaking down."

Tarawa, Jamie thought, was merely relaying the yowls from the elder Trumball, in Boston.

"Well, I'm takin' her with us on the ride out to Ares Vallis," Possum Craig said, both his big hands clutching his mug of cooling coffee. "I'll work on her until she starts behavin' right."

"Good luck," Rodriguez muttered.

The airlock hatch sighed open and Trudy and Dex came sauntering in. Dex had removed the VR cameras from his head, Jamie saw.

"Okay," he proclaimed, "we wowed 'em in Peoria. Trudy's a natural VR performer. You should've seen her."

Hall smiled politely and made a tiny curtsey. "My new career: show business."

Vijay excused herself as Trumball went to the dispenser and filled a cup with coffee. Jamie noticed that he didn't offer to get anything for Trudy, who merely sat at the galley table and took a deep breath, as if she had just finished a footrace.

Looking at Jamie as he returned to the table, Dex said, "You guys have no idea how important these VR transmissions are. We get tens of millions of people watching us, *experiencing* what we show them."

"Mucho dinero," Rodriguez said.

"It's more than the money," Trumball shot back. "It's the support. Those viewers feel like they've really been on Mars with us. They'll support us when it comes to future expeditions. They'll even want to come themselves."

Before Jamie could reply, Vijay returned to the table with a brilliant smile and a half-liter-sized plastic container.

"I have here in my hand," she said, holding the container high so everyone could see, "a certain amount of medicinal alcohol. Now that the cameras are off and we're safe from prying eyes, let the *real* party begin!"

MORNING: SOL 48

A BIG MORNING, JAMIE THOUGHT. THE BIGGEST THAT MARS HAS EVER SEEN since we first landed here.

"It will be lonesome around here," Stacy Dezhurova said morosely over breakfast.

"We won't be gone that long," said Mitsuo Fuchida. "Less than a week."

"Four weeks, tops, for us," Dex Trumball said.

The Russian cosmonaut seemed almost melancholy, which surprised Jamie. Usually Stacy was impassive, businesslike. "The dome will be quiet," she said, turning her glance from Trumball to Fuchida.

Dex grinned at her. "Yeah, but when we come back we'll have the old Pathfinder hardware with us. And the little Sojourner wagon, too."

Jamie noted that the Japanese biologist had finished every bit of his breakfast of fruit and cereal. Despite his bravado, Dex's bowl was still almost full when he pushed it away.

He had decided to let them go off on their separate excursions on the same day, if Stacy could land the fuel generator roughly in the area of Xanthe Terra that it had to be for Dex's trip to succeed.

So the morning's work would be: First, launch the generator and land it safely in Xanthe. Second, get Dex and Possum off on their jaunt. Third, see Fuchida and Rodriguez take off for Olympus Mons.

A big morning. A big day. Inwardly, Jamie worried that they were biting off more than they could chew.

It's not good planning, Jamie told himself. There's no margin for error. It's not smart, not safe. And it certainly isn't good science. Dex is stealing four weeks from his work and Craig's . . . for what? To make money. To get glory for himself.

Everyone crowded into the comm center as Dezhurova made the final preparations to launch the generator. Everyone except Jamie, who suited up and went through the airlock to watch the launch with his own eyes.

He knew he was bending the safety regulations to the breaking point, yet he walked alone to the crest of the little ridge formed by the rim of an ancient crater. The safety regs are too restrictive, he admitted to himself. We'll have to rewrite them, sooner or later.

From his vantage point he could see the rocket booster standing on the horizon, the fuel generator still sitting at its top, as always. He, Craig and Dex had labored hard to install the backup water recycler back into the equipment bay where it had originally been.

The booster's main tanks were filled with liquified methane and oxygen. Jamie could see a wisp of white vapor wafting from a vent halfway up the rocket's cylindrical body. But there was no condensation frost on the tankage skin; there simply was not enough moisture in the Martian air for that.

In his helmet earphones Jamie heard the automated countdown ticking off, "Four . . . three . . . two . . . one . . ."

A flash of light burst from the rocket's base and the booster was immediately lost in a dirty pink-gray cloud of vapor and dust. For a heartbeat Jamie thought it had exploded, but then the booster rose up through the cloud and he heard—even through his helmet—the whining roar of its rocket engines.

Higher and higher the rocket rose, swifter and swifter into the bright cloudless sky. Jamie bent back as far as his hard suit would allow, saw the rocket dwindle to a speck in the sky, and then it was lost to sight.

By the time he had come back through the airlock and taken off his suit, there were whoops and cheers coming from the comm center. Leaving the suit to be vacuumed later, Jamie hurried to join the crowd.

"Down . . . the . . . pipe," Dezhurova was saying. She sat hunched before a display screen, her thick-fingered hands poised over the keyboard like a concert pianist's ready to play.

But she did not touch the keys. She did not have to. The screen showed a plot of the rocket's planned descent trajectory in red, next to a plot in green of its actual course. The two lines overlapped almost completely.

"The wind is stiffer than we expected," Dezhurova said. "But neh problemeh."

Rodriguez, sitting beside her, had an eager kid's look on his face. The others were clustered behind them, huddled together like a short-handed football team.

"Fifteen seconds to touchdown," Rodriguez called out.

"Looking good," Dezhurova said tightly.

"Lookin' *great,*" shouted Possum Craig.

"Ten . . . nine . . ."

"I told you the spot was clear of boulders," Dex Trumball said, to no one in particular.

Jamie saw that Vijay was standing beside Dex; his hand was on the small of her back. Jamie felt his nostrils flare with barely suppressed anger.

"Four . . . three . . . two . . . touchdown!" Rodriguez announced.

"She is down, safe and sound," said Dezhurova. She swivelled her chair around and swept her headset off with a flourish.

"We're set for the run out to the Sagan site," Dex crowed, beaming with satisfaction.

"Not till we check out the fuel generator, partner," Craig warned. "That contraption's gotta be perking right before we go traipsin' all the way out there."

"Yeah, sure," Dex replied, his triumphant grin shrinking only a little.

Within an hour they had all the data they needed. The water recycler's drill had hit permafrost and the fuel generator was working just as if it had never been moved, already replenishing the booster's propellant tanks.

Trumball and Craig were suiting up; Jamie and Vijay were checking them out: Jamie with Possum, Vijay with Dex.

"Hope we can get the VR rig working right," Dex said as he lifted his helmet from its shelf. Even encased in the bulky suit he radiated excitement, practically quivering, like a kid on Christmas morning.

"Well, I'll finally get enough time to really tear her innards apart and see what th' hell's wrong with her," Craig said.

Their plan was for Possum to work on the faulty VR rig during the long hours of the trek when he was not driving the rover.

Jamie was helping him put on his suit's backpack. Craig backed into it and Jamie clicked the connecting latches shut. Then Possum stepped away from the rack on which the backpack had rested.

"Electrical connects okay?" Jamie asked.

Craig peered at the display panel on his right wrist. "All green," he reported.

"Good." Jamie plugged the air hose into Craig's neck ring.

"You're ready for your radio check," Vijay said to Trumball.

Dex slid his visor down and sealed it. Jamie could hear his muffled voice calling to Stacy Dezhurova, who was manning the communications center, as usual. After a moment he slid the visor up again and made a thumb's-up signal.

"Radio okay."

It took Craig another few minutes to get his suit sealed up and check out its radio. Trumball paced up and down restlessly. In the suit and thick-soled boots he reminded Jamie of Frankenstein's monster waiting impatiently for a bus.

"We're all set," Dex said once Craig's radio check was done. He turned toward the airlock hatch.

"Hold on a second," Jamie said.

Trumball stopped but did not turn back to face Jamie. Craig did.

"I know you've checked out the rover from here to hell and back,"

Jamie said, "but I want you to remember that it's an old piece of hardware and it's been sitting out in the cold for six years."

"We know that," Trumball said to the airlock hatch.

"The first sign of trouble, I want you to turn back," Jamie instructed. "Do you understand me? The hardware you're setting out to retrieve isn't worth a man's life, no matter how much money it might bring in on Earth."

"Sure," Dex said impatiently.

"Don't worry, I ain't no hero," Craig added.

Jamie took in a deep breath. "Possum, I'm putting you in charge of this excursion. You're the boss. Dex, you follow his orders at all times. Understand?"

Now Trumball turned toward Jamie, slowly, ponderously in the cumbersome hard suit.

"What kind of bullshit is this?" he asked, his voice low and even.

"It's chain-of-command, Dex. Possum's older and he's had a lot more experience living out in the field than either one of us has. He's in charge. Any time you two don't agree on something, Possum is the winner."

Trumball's face went through a whole skein of emotions within the flash of a moment. Jamie waited for an explosion.

But then Dex broke into a boyish grin. "Okay, chief. Possum's the medicine man and I'm just a lowly brave. I can live with that."

"Good," Jamie said, refusing to let Trumball see how much he hated Dex's sneering at his Navaho heritage.

Gesturing toward the hatch with a gloved hand, Trumball said to Craig, "Okay, boss, I guess you should go through the airlock first."

Craig glanced at Jamie, then pulled down his visor and clomped to the hatch.

Vijay said, "Good luck."

"Yeah, right," answered Trumball. Craig waved silently as he stepped over the sill of the open hatch.

The three of them stood in uncomfortable silence while the airlock cycled. When its panel light turned green again, Trumball opened the hatch and stepped in.

Before closing it, though, he turned back to Jamie and Vijay.

"By the way, Jamie, I didn't get a chance to say so long to my father. Would you give him a buzz and tell him I'm on my way?"

"Certainly," Jamie said, surprised at the sweet reasonableness in Trumball's voice.

The hatch slid shut. Jamie started toward the comm center, Shektar walking alongside him.

Vijay asked, "Did you have to do that?"

"What?" Jamie asked.

"Humiliate him."

"Humiliate?" Jamie felt a pang, but it wasn't surprise. It was disappointment that Vijay saw his decision this way.

"Making him officially subordinate to Possum," she went on. "That's belittling him."

Striding along the partitions that marked off the team's sleeping cubicles, Jamie said, "I didn't do it *to* Dex, I did it *for* Possum."

"Really?"

"Dex would try to steamroller Possum whenever they had a difference of opinion. This way, Possum's got the clout to make the final decisions. That might save both their lives."

"Really?" she said again.

"Yes, really."

He looked down at her. Her expression showed a great deal of disbelief.

By the time they reached the comm center, Craig and Trumball had climbed into the rover and started up its electrical generator.

"The boss is going to let me drive," Dex exclaimed, his radio voice brimming with mock delight. "Goodie, goodie."

With Rodriguez sitting beside her, Stacy Dezhurova went down the rover checklist with him, then cleared them for departure.

"We're off to see the Wizard," Dex said. "Be back in a month or so."

"Sooner," Craig's voice added.

"Better be sooner," Rodriguez said into his lip mike. "Thanksgiving's in four weeks."

"Save me a drumstick," said Dex.

In Dezhurova's display screen Jamie saw the rover shudder to life, then lurch into motion. It rolled forward slowly at first, then turned in a quarter-circle and headed off toward the east.

"Oh, Jamie," Trumball called as they trundled toward the horizon, "please don't forget to call my dad, okay?"

"You can call him yourself, right now," Jamie responded.

"No, I want to concentrate on my driving. You do it for me, huh? Please?"

Jamie said, "Sure. I'll send him a message right away."

"Thanks a lot, chief."

AFTERNOON: SOL 48

JAMIE WENT TO HIS QUARTERS AND SENT A BRIEF MESSAGE EARTHWARD, telling Darryl C. Trumball that his son was on his way to Ares Vallis and wanted him to know that everything was going well.

As he looked up from his laptop screen, he saw Stacy Dezhurova at his open doorway. She looked even moodier than she had at breakfast, almost worried.

"What's the matter, Stacy?"

The cosmonaut stepped into Jamie's cubicle but didn't take the empty desk chair. She remained standing.

With a shake of her head that made her pageboy flutter, she answered, "I can't help thinking that I should be out in that rover with them."

Jamie shut down his computer and closed its lid. "Stacy, we went over that a couple of hundred times. You can't be everyplace."

"The safety regulations say an astronaut must be on every excursion."

"I know, but this trek of Dex's is an extra task that we didn't plan on."

"Still . . ."

"Sit down," Jamie said, pointing to the desk chair. He immediately felt silly; there was no other chair in the cubicle.

She sat heavily, like a tired old woman, and Jamie leaned toward her from the edge of his bunk. "We just don't have enough people to send you along with them. You know that."

"Yes."

"And Possum's about as good as they come—for a guy who's not an astronaut."

"Yes," she said again.

"They'll be okay."

"But if something happens," she said, "I will feel responsible. It is my job to go out with the scientists and make certain they don't get themselves killed."

Jamie sat up straighter. "If something happens, it's my responsibility, not yours. I made the decision, Stacy."

"I know, but . . ." Her voice trailed off.

"Look: Tomas has got to go with Mitsuo, there's no way around that. We need you here at the base. We don't have any other astronauts! What do you expect me to do, clone you?''

She let a weak grin break her dour expression. ''I understand. But I don't like it.''

''They'll be okay. Possum's no daredevil.''

''I suppose so.''

''How's Tomas coming along?''

The grin faded. ''He ate a big lunch. He is not worried about the flight.''

Jamie realized he had skipped lunch. ''I imagine he's excited about it.''

''I would be.''

Is that it? Jamie wondered. Is she sore because Tomas is flying the plane to Olympus instead of her? But she knew that's how it would be. God, we made that decision before we moved to Tarawa.

For the past three weeks Rodriguez had been test-flying the rock-etplane, taking it out on jaunts that started with a simple circle around their base camp and gradually extended as far as Olympus Mons and back again. Never once did Stacy ask to fly the plane. Never once did she show that she was unhappy that Tomas would be the pilot while she ''flew'' the comm console here at the base.

Now she was showing how unhappy it made her. Astronauts are fliers, Jamie realized. She's a pilot and she's not being allowed to fly. He remembered how he had felt when it looked as if he would not be selected for the expedition to Mars.

Leaning closer to her, Jamie said, ''Stacy, the Navaho teach that each person has to find the right path for his life. Or hers. I'm sorry that your path is keeping you on the ground while Tomas gets to fly. But there'll be other flights, other missions. You'll get into the air before we leave Mars, I promise you.''

She brightened only slightly. ''I know. I am being selfish. But still . . . damn! I wish it was me.''

''You're too important to us right now to risk on an excursion. We need you here, Stacy. I need you here.''

Dezhurova blinked with surprise. ''You do?''

''I do,'' Jamie said.

''I didn't think of it that way.''

''Find the right path, Stacy. Find the balance that brings beauty to your life.''

''That is the Navaho way, eh?''

''It's the way that works.''

She pulled her gaze away from Jamie's eyes.

''Well,'' he said, getting to his feet. ''Dex and Possum are on their way, and Tomas and Mitsuo ought to be suiting up by now, right?''

''Right,'' she said, standing also.

Jamie looked into her sky-blue eyes and made a grin for her. "It's not like you don't have anything to do around here," he said.

She forced a grin back at him. "Yes. Right."

She went to the doorway, then turned back and said, "I just wish I was out where the action is."

"What you're doing here is extremely important," Jamie said. "Just about everything depends on you, Stacy."

"Yes. Of course."

She turned and left his cubicle. Jamie stood there for a moment, thinking that her eyes were sky blue only on Earth. Martian skies were shades of orange-brown, almost always.

DOSSIER: ANASTASIA DEZHUROVA

IT WAS THE AMERICANS WHO CALLED HER STACY. HER FATHER'S PET NAME for her was Nastasia.

Her father was a rocket engineer, a hard-working, sober, humorless man whose job took him away from their Moscow apartment for long months at a time. He travelled mostly to the mammoth launch facility in the dreary dust-brown desert of Kazakhstan and returned home tired and sour, but always with a doll or some other present for his baby daughter. Nastasia was his one joy in life.

Anastasia's mother was a concert cellist who played in the Moscow symphony, a bright and intelligent woman who learned very early in her marriage that life was more enjoyable when her husband was a thousand kilometers away. She could give parties in their apartment then; people would laugh and play music. Often one of the men would remain the night.

As Nastasia grew into awareness and understanding, her mother swore her to secrecy. "We don't want to hurt your father's feelings," she would tell her ten-year-old daughter. Later, when Nastasia was a teenager, her mother would say, "And do you think he remains faithful during all those months he's away? Men are not like that."

Nastasia discovered what men are like while she was in secondary school. One of the male students invited her to a party. On the way home, he stopped the car (his father's) and began to maul her. When Nastasia resisted, he tore her clothing and raped her.

Her mother cried with her and then called the police. The investigators made Nastasia feel as if she had committed the crime, not the boy.

Her attacker was not punished and she was stigmatized. Even her father turned against her, saying that she must have given the boy the impression she was available.

When she was selected for the technical university in Novosibersk she left Moscow willingly, gladly, and buried herself in her studies. She avoided all socializing with men, and found that love and warmth and safety could be had with other women.

She also found that she was very bright and very capable. She began to delight in beating men in areas where they thought they were supreme. She learned to fly and went on to become a cosmonaut, not merely a cosmonaut but the first woman cosmonaut to command an orbital team of twelve men; the first woman cosmonaut to set a new endurance record for time spent aboard a space station; the first woman cosmonaut to go to Mars.

AFTERNOON: SOL 48

IT HAD COST THE EXPEDITION AN EXTRA ROCKET BOOSTER TO CARRY THE plane and its spare parts to Mars. The unmanned soarplanes were small, light, little more than gliders with solar-powered motors to get them off the ground and up to an altitude where they could ride the Martian air currents.

The manned plane had to be bigger. It had to accommodate two fragile human beings and their life-support systems. It had to carry supplies enough to last them several days. It had to be able to take off and land on rough ground.

And it had to carry enough fuel and oxygen to take them to Olympus Mons and back again without refueling.

"This bird's a flying fuel truck," Rodriguez quipped more than once as he tested the plane, checked out its performance, its quirks. "She flies like a fuel truck, too."

It had taken several days to clear and smooth a runway area for the plane. The expedition's two little tractors, programmed to run by themselves while monitored from inside the dome, pushed rocks and levelled minor sand dunes until the engineers from Earth were satisfied with the makeshift runway.

Their landing site, atop Olympus Mons, would not be so smooth, although close-up video and still photos from a dozen soarplane reconnaissance flights showed broad areas up at the top of the solar system's tallest mountain that looked smooth and clear enough to serve as a landing area.

The unexplained crash of one of the unmanned planes had delayed Fuchida's excursion. Dezhurova, Rodriguez and the mission controllers back at Tarawa spent a week trying to determine why the soarplane disappeared. For the next three weeks they sent the remaining two unmanned planes out to Olympus Mons every day, retracing the missing plane's route, searching for wreckage, clues, explanations.

Finally Jamie decided they were not going to be able to find out why the plane had crashed. It was either scrub Fuchida's mission altogether or go despite the mishap. Jamie decided on going. After several days of fevered communications back and forth to Tarawa and Boston, his decision was confirmed.

The final decision about landing on the volcano would be Rodriguez's, and no one else's. If he were nervous or anxious about the responsibility, he did not show it one bit.

He looked as happy as a puppy with an old sock to chew on as he and Fuchida got into their hard suits.

"I'm gonna be in the Guinness Book of Records," he proclaimed happily to Jamie, who was helping him get suited up. Trudy Hall was assisting Fuchida while Stacy Dezhurova sat in the comm center, monitoring the dome's systems and the equipment outside. Jamie had no idea where Vijay was, probably in her infirmary.

"Highest aircraft landing and takeoff," Rodriguez chattered cheerfully as he wormed his fingers into the suit's gloves. "Longest flight of a manned solar-powered aircraft. Highest altitude for a manned solar-powered aircraft."

"Crewed," Hall murmured, "not manned."

Unperturbed by her correction, Rodriguez continued, "I might even bust the record for unmanned solar-powered flight."

"Isn't it cheating to compare a flight on Mars to flights on Earth?" Trudy asked as she helped Fuchida latch his life-support pack onto the back of his suit.

Rodriguez shook his head vigorously. "All that counts in the record book is the numbers, *chica*. Just the numbers."

"Won't they put an asterisk next to the numbers and a footnote that says, 'This was done on Mars.'?"

Rodriguez tried to shrug, but not even he could manage that inside the hard suit. "Who cares, as long as they spell my name right?"

Jamie noticed that Fuchida was utterly silent through the suit-up procedure. Tomas is doing enough talking for them both, he thought. But he wondered, Is Mitsuo worried, nervous? He looks calm enough, but that might just be a mask. Come to think of it, the way Tomas is blathering, he must be wired tighter than a drum.

He was jabbering away like a fast-pitch salesman. Jamie wondered if it was nerves or relief to be out on his own, in charge. Or maybe, Jamie thought, the guy was simply overjoyed at the prospect of flying.

Both men were suited up at last, helmet visors down, life-support systems functioning, radio checks completed. Jamie and Trudy walked with them to the airlock hatch: two Earthlings accompanying a pair of ponderous robots.

Jamie shook hands with Rodriguez. His bare hand hardly made it around the astronaut's glove, with its servo-driven exoskeleton "bones" on its back.

"Good luck, Tomas," he said. "Don't take any unnecessary risks out there."

Rodriguez grinned from behind his visor. "Hey, you know what they say: There are old pilots and bold pilots, but there are no old, bold pilots."

Jamie chuckled politely. "Remember that when you're out there," he said.

"I will, boss. Don't worry."

Fuchida stepped up to the hatch once Rodriguez went through. Even in the bulky suit, even with sparrowlike Trudy Hall standing behind him, he looked small, somehow vulnerable.

"Good luck, Mitsuo," said Jamie.

Through the sealed helmet, Fuchida's voice sounded muffled, but unafraid. "I think my biggest problem is going to be listening to Tommy's yakking all the way to the mountain."

Jamie laughed.

"And back, most likely," Fuchida added.

The indicator light turned green and Trudy pressed the stud that opened the inner hatch. Fuchida stepped through, carrying his portable life-support satchel in one hand.

"Tell Vijay to take good care of the garden," he called as the hatch was sliding shut. "The beets need a lot of care."

He's all right, Jamie told himself. He's not scared or even worried.

Once they had clambered into the plane's side-by-side seats and connected to its internal electrical power and life-support systems, both men changed.

Rodriguez became all business. No more chattering. He checked out the plane's systems with only a few clipped words of jargon to Stacy Dezhurova, who was serving as flight controller.

Fuchida, for his part, felt his pulse thundering in his ears so loudly he wondered if the suit radio was picking it up. Certainly the medical monitors must be close to the redline, his heart was racing so hard.

Jamie, Vijay and Trudy Hall crowded over Dezhurova's shoulders to watch the takeoff on the comm center's desktop display screen.

As an airport, the base left much to be desired. The makeshift runway ran just short of two kilometers in length. There was no taxi-way; Rodriguez and a helper—often Jamie—simply turned the plane around after a landing so it was pointed up the runway again. There was no windsock. The atmosphere was so rare that it made scant difference which way the wind was blowing when the plane took off. The rocket engines did the work of powering the plane off the ground and providing the speed it needed for the wings to generate enough lift for flight.

Jamie felt a dull throbbing in his jaw as he bent over Dezhurova, watching the final moments before takeoff. With a conscious effort he unclenched his teeth.

You're more worried about this than you were about the generator launch, he said to himself. And immediately knew the reason why. There were two men in the plane. If anything went wrong, if they crashed, they would both be killed.

"Clear for takeoff," Dezhurova said mechanically into her lip mike.

"Copy clear," Rodriguez's voice came through the speakers.

Stacy scanned the screens around her one final time, then said, "Clear for ignition."

"Ignition."

Suddenly the twin rocket engines beneath the wing roots shot out a bellowing blowtorch of flame and the plane jerked into motion. As the camera followed it jouncing down the runway, gathering speed, the long, drooping wings seemed to stiffen and stretch out.

"Come on, baby," Dezhurova muttered.

Jamie saw it all as if it was happening in slow motion: the plane trundling down the runway, the rockets' exhaust turning so hot the flame became invisible, clouds of dust and grit billowing behind the plane as it sped faster, faster along the runway, nose lifting now.

"Looking good," Dezhurova whispered.

The plane hurtled up off the ground and arrowed into the pristine sky, leaving a roiling cloud of dust and vapor slowly dissipating along the length of the runway. To Jamie it looked as if the cloud was trying to reach for the plane and pull it back to the ground.

But the plane was little more than a speck in the light orange sky now.

Rodriguez's voice crackled through the speakers, "Next stop, Mount Olympus."

OLYMPUS MONS

THE TALLEST MOUNTAIN IN THE SOLAR SYSTEM IS A MASSIVE SHIELD VOL-
cano that has been dormant for tens, perhaps hundreds of millions of
years.

Once, though, its mighty outpourings of lava dwarfed everything
else on the planet. Over time, they built a mountain three times taller
than Everest, with a base the size of the state of Iowa.

The edges of that base are rugged cliffs of basalt more than a
kilometer high. The summit of the mountain, where huge calderas mark
the vents that once spewed molten rock, stands some twenty-seven
kilometers above the supporting plain: 27,000 meters, more than 88,000
feet. For comparison, Mt. Everest is 8848 meters high, 29,028 feet.

Olympus Mons is so tall that, on Earth, its summit would poke high
above the troposphere—the lowest layer of air, where weather phenom-
ena take place—and rise almost clear of the entire stratosphere. On
Mars, however, the atmosphere is so thin that the atmospheric pressure
at Olympus Mons' summit is only about one-tenth lower than the pressure at ground level.

At that altitude, the carbon dioxide that forms the major constituent
of Mars' atmosphere can freeze out, condense on the cold, bare rock,
covering it with a thin, invisible layer of dry ice.

AFTERNOON: SOL 48

"SO HOW DOES IT FEEL TO HAVE ALL THREE OF US TO YOURSELF?" VIJAY
asked.

Jamie and the three women had just sat down for a late lunch.
Rodriguez and Fuchida would be landing at Olympus Mons in less than
an hour. Trumball and Possum Craig had reported a few minutes earlier
that they were trundling along toward Xanthe with no problems.

Vijay grinned devilishly as she said it. Jamie felt his brows knit slightly in a frown.

"Yes," added Trudy Hall. "You've very cleverly removed all the other men, haven't you?"

To cover his embarrassment, Jamie turned to Dezhurova. "Don't you have anything to add to this, Stacy?"

She was already munching on a hastily-built sandwich. Stacy chewed thoughtfully, swallowed, then said, "What is the American word for it? Kinky?"

All three of the women laughed; Jamie forced a smile, then turned his attention to his plate of microwaved pasta and tofu herb salad.

He was thankful when the women began to talk among themselves about the food, the taste of the recycled water, the way the washer/dryer was fading their clothes. They all wore the standard-issue coveralls, but Jamie noticed that they each had individualized their clothing: Dezhurova had stylish Russian logos from her days as a government astronaut sewn above her breast pockets; Hall always clipped bits of glittery costume jewelry to hers; Shektar added a bright scarf at her throat or a colorful sash around her waist.

"We should try the clothes-cleaning system they use at Moonbase," Dezhurova said. "It is much easier on the fabric."

"I've heard about that," Trudy said. "They just put the clothes out in the open, do they?"

Stacy nodded vigorously. "Yes. In vacuum on the lunar surface the dirt flakes completely off the fabric. And the unfiltered ultraviolet light from the sun sterilizes everything."

Vijay pointed out, "We don't have a vacuum outside."

"Very damned close," Dezhurova countered.

"Plenty of UV," said Trudy.

"What do you think, Vijay?" Dezhurova prompted. "Worth a try, no?"

"We'll need some sort of container, won't we? You don't just hang the clothes on a line."

"I suppose we could," said Trudy.

"At Moonbase they put clothes in a big mesh basket and run it up and down a track set into the ground," Stacy explained. "The basket rotates, like the tumbling action in a washing machine."

"We don't have anything like that here."

"I could rig one up," Dezhurova said confidently. "It should be simple enough."

"Do you think you could?"

She nodded solemnly. "Possum is not the only one here who is good with his hands."

"What do you think, Jamie?" Shektar asked.

Grateful that they were no longer teasing him, he replied, "What about the dust? It would get onto the clothes, wouldn't it?"

"There's dust on the Moon, too," Trudy said.

"But no wind."

"Oh. Yes."

Dezhurova said, "We could put the basket track on poles, off the ground."

"I suppose," said Jamie.

"Otherwise our clothes will keep on fading and fraying."

"They'll fall apart completely, sooner or later," said Trudy.

Vijay's evil grin returned. "Jamie wouldn't mind that, would you, Jamie?"

He tried to stare her down, but instead pushed himself away from the table. "Tomas should be calling in in five minutes or so."

As he got to his feet and fled to the comm center, Jamie was certain he heard them giggling behind him.

Rodriguez was a happy man. The plane was responding to his touch like a beautiful woman, gentle and sweet.

They were purring along at—he glanced at the altimeter—twenty-eight thousand and six meters. Let's see, he mused. Something like three point two feet in a meter, that makes it eighty-nine, almost ninety thousand feet. Not bad. Not bad at all.

He knew the world altitude record for a solar-powered plane was above one hundred thousand feet. But that was a UAV, an unmanned aerial vehicle. No pilot's flown this high in a solar-powered plane, he knew. Behind his helmet visor he smiled at the big six-bladed propeller as it spun lazily before his eyes.

Beside him, Fuchida was absolutely silent and unmoving. He might as well be dead inside his suit, I'd never know the difference, Rodriguez thought. He's scared, just plain scared. He doesn't trust me. He's scared of flying with me. Probably wanted Stacy to fly him, not me.

Well, my silent Japanese buddy, I'm the guy you're stuck with, whether you like it or not. So go ahead and sit there like a fuckin' statue, I don't give a damn.

Mitsuo Fuchida felt an unaccustomed tendril of fear worming its way through his innards. This puzzled him, since he had known for almost two years now that he would be flying to the top of Olympus Mons. He had flown simulations hundreds of times. This whole excursion had been his idea; he had worked hard to get the plan incorporated into the expedition schedule.

He had first learned to fly while an undergraduate biology student, and had been elected president of the university's flying club. With the single-minded intensity of a competitor who knew he had to beat the best of the best to win a berth on the Second Mars Expedition, Fuchida had taken the time to qualify as a pilot of ultralight aircraft over the inland mountains of his native Kyushu and then went on to pilot soar-planes across the jagged peaks of Sinkiang.

He had never felt any fear of flying. Just the opposite: he had always felt relaxed and happy in the air, free of all the pressures and cares of life.

Yet now, as the sun sank toward the rocky horizon, casting eerie red light across the barren landscape, Fuchida knew that he was afraid. What if the engine fails? What if Rodriguez cracks up the plane when we land on the mountain? One of the unmanned soarplanes had crashed while it was flying over the mountain on a reconnaissance flight; what if the same thing happens to us?

Even in rugged Sinkiang there was a reasonable chance of surviving an emergency landing. You could breathe the air and walk to a village, even if the trek took many days. Not so here on Mars.

What if Rodriguez gets hurt while we're out there? I have only flown this plane in the simulator; I don't know if I could fly it in reality.

Rodriguez seemed perfectly at ease, happily excited to be flying. He shames me, Fuchida thought. Yet . . . is he truly capable? How will he react in an emergency? Fuchida hoped he would not have to find out.

They passed Pavonis Mons on their left, one of the three giant shield volcanoes that lined up in a row on the eastern side of the Tharsis bulge. It was so big that it stretched out to the horizon and beyond, a massive hump of solid stone that had once oozed red-hot lava across an area the size of Japan. Quiet now. Cold and dead. For how long?

There was a whole line of smaller volcanoes stretching off to the horizon and, beyond them, the hugely massive Olympus Mons. What happened here to create a thousand-kilometer-long chain of volcanoes? Fuchida tried to meditate on that question, but his mind kept coming back to the risks he was undertaking.

And to Elizabeth.

DOSSIER: MITSUO FUCHIDA

THEIR WEDDING HAD TO BE A SECRET. MARRIED PERSONS WOULD NOT BE allowed on the Mars expedition. Worse yet, Mitsuo Fuchida had fallen in love with a foreigner, a young Irish biologist with flame-red hair and skin like white porcelain.

"Sleep with her," Fuchida's father advised him, "enjoy her all you want to. But father no children with her! Under no circumstances may you marry her."

Elizabeth Vernon seemed content with that. She loved Mitsuo.

They had met at Tokyo University. Like him, she was a biologist. Unlike him, she had neither the talent nor the drive to get very far in the competition for tenure and a professorship.

"I'll be fine," she told Mitsuo. "Don't ruin your chance for Mars. I'll wait for you."

That was neither good nor fair, in Fuchida's eyes. How could he go to Mars, spend years away from her, expect her to store her emotions in suspended animation for so long?

His father made other demands on him, as well.

"The only man to die on the First Mars Expedition was your cousin, Konoye. He disgraced us all."

Isoruku Konoye suffered a fatal stroke while attempting to explore the smaller moon of Mars, Deimos. His Russian teammate, cosmonaut Leonid Tolbukhin, said that Konoye had panicked, frightened to be outside their spacecraft in nothing more than a spacesuit, disoriented by the looming menace of Deimos' rocky bulk.

"You must redeem the family's honor," Fuchida's father insisted. "You must make the world respect Japan. Your namesake was a great warrior. You must add new honors to his name."

So Mitsuo knew that he could not marry Elizabeth openly, honestly, as he wanted to. Instead, he took her to a monastery in the remote mountains of Kyushu, where he had perfected his climbing skills.

"It's not necessary, Mitsuo," Elizabeth protested, once she understood what he wanted to do. "I love you. A ceremony won't change that."

"Would you prefer a Catholic rite?" he asked.

She threw her arms around his neck. He felt tears on her cheek.

When the day came that he had to leave, Mitsuo promised Elizabeth that he would come back to her. "And when I do, we will be married again, openly, for all the world to see."

"Including your father?" she asked wryly.

Mitsuo smiled. "Yes, including even my noble father."

Then he left for Mars, intent on honoring his family's name and returning to the woman he loved.

SUNSET: SOL 48

FUCHIDA'S EXCURSION PLAN CALLED FOR THEM TO LAND LATE IN THE AFTER-noon, almost at sunset, when the low sun cast its longest shadows. That allowed them to make the flight in full daylight, while giving them the best view of their landing area once they arrived at Olympus Mons. Every boulder and rock would show in bold relief, allowing them to find the smoothest spot for their landing.

It also meant, Fuchida knew, that they would have to endure the dark frigid hours of night immediately after they landed. What if the batteries failed? The lithium-polymer batteries had been tested for years, Fuchida knew. They stored electricity generated in sunlight by the solar panels and powered the plane's equipment through the long, cold hours of darkness. But what if they break down when the temperature drops to a hundred and thirty below zero?

Rodriguez was making a strange, moaning sound. Turning sharply to look at the astronaut sitting beside him, Fuchida saw only the inside of his own helmet. He had to turn from the shoulders to see the space-suited pilot—who was humming tunelessly.

"Are you all right?" Fuchida asked nervously.

"Sure."

"Was that a Mexican song you were humming?"

"Naw. The Beatles. 'Lucy in the Sky with Diamonds.' "

"Oh."

Rodriguez sighed happily. "There she is," he said.

"What?"

"Mount Olympus." He pointed straight ahead.

Fuchida did not see a mountain, merely the horizon. It seemed rounded, now that he paid attention to it: a large gently rising hump.

It grew as they approached it. And grew. And grew. Olympus Mons was an immense island unto itself, a continent rising up above the bleak red plain like some gigantic mythical beast. Its slopes were gentle, above the steep scarps of its base. A man could climb that grade easily, Fuchida thought. Then he realized that the mountain was so huge it would take a man weeks to walk from its base to its summit.

Rodriguez was humming again, calm and relaxed as a man sitting in his favorite chair at home.

"You enjoy flying, don't you?" Fuchida commented.

"You know what they say," Rodriguez replied, a serene smile in his voice. "Flying is the second most exciting thing a man can do."

Fuchida nodded inside his helmet. "And the most exciting must be sex, right?"

"Nope. The first most exciting thing a man can do is landing."

Fuchida sank into gloomy silence.

Jamie was in the comm center, staring fixedly at the immersion table, trying not to look at his wristwatch.

Tomas will call when they land. There's no point in his calling until they're down safely. He's probably reached the mountain by now and is scouting around, making sure the area is okay for an actual landing.

Behind him, he heard Stacy Dezhurova say tersely, "They are over the mountain now. Beacon is strong and clear, telemetry coming through. No problems."

Jamie nodded without turning around. The immersion table showed a three-dimensional map of Tithonium Chasma, but if you pulled your head away you lost the depth sense and it took several moments of blinking and head movements to see the map in three-d again.

He had marked the electronic display so that the niche in the cliff face where he had seen the—artifact, Jamie called it—was clearly noted in white. Not that far from the landslide we went down to get to the Canyon floor, he saw. But it would save a day's trip if we went straight to the spot and then I lowered myself down on a cable. No sense going to the floor of the Canyon; the niche is more than three-quarters of the way up to the top.

There are other niches along the Canyon wall, he knew. Are there buildings in them, too? And we haven't even looked at the south face of the Canyon yet. There could be dozens of villages strung along the cliffs. Hundreds.

Behind him, he heard someone step into the comm center, then Vijay's low, throaty voice asked, "Have you heard from them?"

"Not yet," Stacy said.

Then Trudy Hall asked, "Anything?"

"Not yet," Dezhurova repeated.

Jamie gave up his attempt to plan his excursion. He closed down the three-dimensional display and it turned into an ordinary-looking glass-topped table. Then he turned toward Dezhurova, sitting at the communications console. Its main screen showed a relief map of Olympus Mons and a tiny glowing red dot crawling slowly across it: the plane with Rodriguez and Fuchida in it.

"Rodriguez to base," the astronaut's voice suddenly crackled in the speaker. "I'm making a dry run over the landing area. Sending my camera view."

"Base to Rodriguez," Dezhurova snapped, all business. "Copy dry run.'' Her fingers raced over the keyboard and the main display suddenly showed a pockmarked, boulder-strewn stretch of bare rock. ''We have your imagery.''

Jamie felt his mouth go dry. If that's the landing area, they're never going to get down safely.

Rodriguez banked the plane slightly so he could see the ground better. To Fuchida it seemed as if the plane was standing on its left wingtip while the hard, bare rock below turned in a slow circle.

''Well,'' Rodriguez said, ''we've got a choice: boulders or craters.''

''Where's the clear area the soarplanes showed?'' Fuchida asked.

'' 'Clear' is a relative term,'' Rodriguez muttered.

Fuchida swallowed bile. It burned in his throat.

''Rodriguez to base. I'm going to circle the landing area one more time. Tell me if you see anything I miss.''

''Copy another circle.'' Stacy Dezhurova's tone was terse, professional.

Rodriguez peered hard at the ground below. The setting sun cast long shadows that emphasized every pebble and dimple down there. Between a fresh-looking crater and a scattering of rocks was a relatively clean area, more than a kilometer long. Room enough to land if the retros fired on command.

''Looks okay to me,'' he said into his helmet mike.

''Barely,'' came Dezhurova's voice.

''The wheels can handle small rocks.''

''Shock absorbers are no substitute for level ground, Tomas.''

Rodriguez laughed. He and Dezhurova had gone through this discussion a few dozen times, ever since the first recon photos had come back from the UAVs.

''Turning into final approach,'' he reported.

Dezhurova did not reply. As the flight controller she had the authority to forbid him to land.

''Lining up for final.''

''Your imagery is breaking up a little.''

''Light level's sinking fast.''

''Yes.''

Fuchida saw the ground rushing up toward him. It was covered with boulders and pitted with craters and looked as hard as concrete, harder. They were coming in too fast, he thought. He wanted to grab the control T-stick in front of him and pull up, cut in the rocket engines and get the hell away while they had a chance. Instead, he squeezed his eyes shut.

Something hit the plane so hard that Fuchida thought he'd be driven through the canopy. His safety harness held, though, and within an eyeblink he heard the howling screech of the tiny retro rocket motors.

The front of the plane seemed to be on fire. They were bouncing, jolting, rattling along like a tin can kicked across a field of rubble.

Then a final lurch and all the noise and motion stopped.

"We're down," Rodriguez sang out. "Piece of cake."

"Good," came Dezhurova's stolid voice.

Fuchida urgently needed to urinate.

"Okay," Rodriguez said to his partner. "Now we just sit tight until sunrise."

Like a pair of tinned sardines, thought Fuchida as he let go into the relief tube built into his suit. He did not relish the idea of trying to sleep in the cockpit seats, sealed in their suits. But that was the price to be paid for the honor of being the first humans to set foot on the tallest mountain in the solar system.

He almost smiled. I too will be in the Guinness Book of Records, he thought.

"You okay?" Rodriguez asked.

"Yes, certainly."

"Kinda quiet, Mitsuo."

"I'm admiring the view," said Fuchida.

Nothing but a barren expanse of bare rock in every direction. The sky overhead was darkening swiftly. Already Fuchida could see a few stars staring down at them.

"Top of the world, Ma!" Rodriguez quipped. He chuckled happily, as if he hadn't a care in the world. In two worlds.

DOSSIER: TOMAS RODRIGUEZ

"NEVER SHOW FEAR." TOMAS RODRIGUEZ LEARNED THAT AS A SCRAWNY asthmatic child, growing up amidst the crime and violence of an inner-city San Diego barrio.

"Never let them see you're scared," his older brother Luis told him. "Never back down from a fight."

Tomas was not physically strong, but he had his big brother to protect him. Most of the time. Then he found a refuge of sorts in the dilapidated neighborhood gym, where he traded hours of sweeping and cleaning for free use of the weight machines. As he gained muscle mass, he learned the rudiments of alley fighting from Luis. In middle school he was spotted and recruited by an elderly Korean who taught martial arts as a school volunteer.

In high school he discovered that he was bright, smart enough not merely to understand algebra but to *want to* understand it and the other mysteries of mathematics and science. He made friends among the nerds as well as the jocks, often protecting the former against the hazing and casual cruelty of the latter.

He grew into a solid, broad-shouldered youth with quick reflexes and the brains to talk his way out of most confrontations. He did not look for fights, but handled himself well enough when a fight became unavoidable. He worked, he learned, he had the kind of sunny disposition—and firm physical courage—that made even the nastiest punks in the school leave him alone. He never went out for any of the school teams and he never did drugs. He didn't even smoke. He couldn't afford such luxuries.

He even avoided the trap that caught most of his buddies: father-hood. Whether they got married or not, most of the guys quickly got tied down with a woman. Tomas had plenty of girls, and learned the pleasures of sex even before high school. But he never formed a lasting relationship. He didn't want to. The neighborhood girls were attractive, yes, until they started talking. Tomas couldn't stand even to imagine listening to one of them for more than a few hours. They had nothing to say. Their lives were empty. He ached for something more.

Most of the high school teachers were zeroes, but one—the weary old man who taught math—encouraged him to apply for a scholarship to college. To Tomas' enormous surprise, he won one: full tuition to UCSD. Even so, he could not afford the other expenses, so he again listened to his mentor's advice and joined the Air Force. Uncle Sam paid his way through school, and once he graduated he became a jet fighter pilot. "More fun than sex," he would maintain, always add-ing, "Almost."

Never show fear. That meant that he could never back away from a challenge. Never. Whether in a cockpit or a barroom, the stocky Hispanic kid with the big smile took every confrontation as it arose. He got a reputation for it.

The fear was always there, constantly, but he never let it show. And always there was that inner doubt. That feeling that somehow he didn't really belong here. They were allowing the chicano kid to pretend he was as smart as the white guys, allowing him to get through college on his little scholarship, allowing him to wear a flyboy uniform and play with the hotshot jet planes.

But he really wasn't one of them. That was made abundantly clear to him in a thousand little ways, every day. He was a greaser, tolerated only as long as he stayed in the place they expected him to be. Don't try to climb too far; don't show off too much; above all, don't try to date anyone except "your own."

Flying was different, though. Alone in a plane nine or ten miles up in the sky it was just him and God, the rest of the world far away, out of sight and out of mind.

Then came the chance to win an astronaut's wings. He couldn't back away from the challenge. Again, the others made it clear that he was not welcome to the competition. But Tomas entered anyway and won a slot in the astronaut training corps. "The benefits of affirmative action," one of the other pilots jeered.

Whatever he achieved, they always tried to take the joy out of it. Tomas paid no outward attention, as usual; he kept his wounds hidden, his bleeding internal.

Two years after he had won his astronaut's wings came the call for the Second Mars Expedition. Smiling his broadest, Tomas applied. No fear. He kept his gritted teeth hidden from all the others, and won the position.

"Big fuckin' deal," said his buddies. "You'll be second fiddle to some Russian broad."

Tomas shrugged and nodded. "Yeah," he admitted. "I guess I'll have to take orders from everybody."

To himself he added, But I'll be on Mars, shitheads, while you're still down here.

NIGHT: SOL 48

IT WAS ALREADY NIGHT ON THE BROAD ROLLING PLAIN OF LUNAE PLANUM, yet Possum Craig was still driving the old rover—cautiously, at a mere ten kilometers per hour. He and Dex Trumball had agreed that they could mooch out a little extra mileage after sunset, before they stopped for the night.

Trumball had the radio set to the general comm frequency, so they heard Rodriguez and Fuchida's landing at the same time the four in the base camp did.

"Those two poor bastards gotta live in their suits until they get back to th' dome," Craig said.

"Look on the bright side, Wiley. They get to test the F.E.S."

The hard suits had a special fitting that was supposed to make an airtight connection to the chemical toilet seat. The engineers called it the Fecal Elimination System.

"The ol' trapdoor," Craig muttered. "I bet they wind up usin' Kaopectate."

Sitting beside him in the cockpit, Dex replied with a grin, "While we've got all the comforts of home."

Craig made a thoughtful face. "For an old clunker, this travelin' machine is doin' purty well. No complaints."

"Not yet."

Dex had spent most of the day in his hard suit. They had stopped the rover every hundred klicks for him to go outside and plant geology/meteorology beacons. Now he sat relaxed in his coveralls, watching the scant slice of ground illuminated by the rover's headlights.

"You could goose her up to twenty," Dex prodded.

"Yeah, and I could slide 'er into a crater before we had time to stop or turn away," Craig shot back. He tapped a forefinger on the digital clock display. "Time to call it a day, anyway."

"You tired already?"

"Nope, and I don't want to drive when I am tired."

"I could drive for a while," said Dex.

Pressing gently on the brake pedals, Craig said, "Let's just call it a day, buddy. We've made good time. Enough is enough."

Trumball seemed to think it over for a moment, then pulled himself out of the cockpit chair. "Okay. You're the boss."

Craig laughed. "Shore I am."

"Now, what's that supposed to mean?" Trumball asked over his shoulder as he headed back to the minuscule galley.

Craig slid the plastic heat-retaining screen across the windshield, then got up and stretched so hard that Dex could hear his tendons pop.

"It means that I'm th' boss long's you want to be agreeable."

"I'm agreeable," Dex said.

"Then ever'thing's fine and dandy."

Sliding one of the prepackaged meals from its freezer tray, Trumball said to the older man, "No, seriously, Wiley. Jamie put you in charge. I've got no bitch with that."

Still stretching, his hands scraping the curved overhead, Craig said, "Okay. Fine."

"Something bugging you?"

"Naw. Forget it."

As he put the meal tray into the microwave cooker, Dex said, "Hey, come on, Wiley. It's just you and me out here. If something's wrong, tell me about it."

Craig made a face somewhere between annoyed and sheepish. "Well, it's kinda silly, I guess."

"What is it, for chrissakes?"

With a tired puff of breath, Craig sank onto his bunk.

"Well, I'm kinda pissed about bein' a second-class citizen around here."

Trumball stared at him in amazement. "Second-class citizen?"

"Yeah, you know—they all think I'm nothin' more'n a repairman, for shit's sake."

"Well—"

"I'm a scientist, just like you and the rest of y'all," Craig grumbled. "Maybe I didn't get my degree from a big-name school, and maybe I've spent most of my time workin' for oil companies . . ." he pronounced *oil* as *awl* ". . . but I was smart enough to get picked over a lotta guys with fancier pedigrees."

"Sure you are."

"That Fuchida. Damned Jap's so uptight I think if he sneezed he'd come apart. Looks at me like I'm a servant or something."

"That's just his way."

"And the women! They act like I'm a grandfather or somethin'. Hell, I'm younger'n Jamie. I'm younger than Stacy is, did you know that?"

For the first time, Dex Trumball understood that Craig was hurting. And vulnerable. This jowly, shaggy, good-natured bear of a man with the prominent snoot and permanent five-o'clock shadow wants to be treated with some respect. That makes him usable, Dex realized.

"Listen, Wiley," Dex began, "I didn't know that we were hurting your feelings."

"Not you, so much. It's the rest of 'em. They think I'm just here to be their bleepin' repairman. 'Least you call me Wiley. Never did like bein' called Possum. My name's Peter J. Craig."

The microwave oven chimed. Dex ignored it and sat on his own bunk, opposite Craig's. "I'll get them to call you Wiley, then. Or Peter, if you prefer."

"Wiley is fine."

A smile crept across Trumball's face. "Okay. Then it's going to be Wiley from now on. I'll make certain that Jamie and the others get the word."

Looking embarrassed, Craig mumbled, "Kinda silly, ain't it."

"No, no," Dex said. "If Jamie and the others are bothering you, you've got a right to complain about it."

To himself Trumball thought, If and when we get to a place where I've got to outgun Jamie, I'll need Wiley on my side. Wiley, and as many of the others as I can round up.

Jamie spent nearly an hour after dinner talking with Rodriguez and Fuchida atop Olympus Mons. They were spending the night in their seats in the plane's cockpit. Like trying to sleep in an airliner, Jamie thought. Tourist class. In hard suits. He did not envy them their creature comforts.

Still in the comm center, he scrolled through the messages that had accumulated through the long, eventful, draining day. It took more than another hour to deal with them: everything from a request for more VR sessions from the International Council of Science Teachers to a reminder that his mission status report for the week was due in the morning.

One message was from Darryl C. Trumball. Since it was marked PERSONAL AND CONFIDENTIAL, Jamie saved it, planning to go to his own quarters before he looked at it.

But when he finished all the other messages, he glanced up from the comm screen and saw that the dome was darkened for the night. Suddenly it seemed chilly, as if the frigid cold of the Martian night were seeping through the dome's plastic walls.

No one seemed to be about. No voices, only the background sounds of the machinery and, if he listened carefully enough, the soft sighing of the night wind outside.

So he opened Trumball's personal message.

Darryl C. Trumball's eyes were blazing, his skull-like face grim as death.

"Who in the hell gave you the authority to send my son out on this excursion to the Sagan site?" he began, furious, with no preamble.

"Goddammit to hell and back, Waterman, I specifically gave orders *not* to allow Dex out on that excursion!"

And so it went, for nearly fifteen blistering minutes. Jamie watched Trumball's angry face, flabbergasted at first, then growing angry himself.

But as the older man blathered on, Jamie's anger slowly dissolved. Behind Trumball's bluster, he saw a man worried about his son's safety, a man accustomed to power and authority, but totally frustrated now because there was no way he could control the men and women on Mars. No way he could control his own son.

He can't even talk to us face-to-face, Jamie knew. All he can do is rant and rave and wait to see if we respond to him.

Trumball finally wound down and finished with, "I want you to know, Waterman, that you cannot countermand my orders and get away with it. You'll pay for this! And if anything happens to my son, you'll pay with your goddamned blood!"

The screen went blank. Jamie reran the whole message, then froze Trumball's angry, snarling image at its end.

Leaning back in the squeaking little wheeled chair, Jamie wondered if he should be firm or conciliatory. A soft answer turneth away wrath, he thought, but Trumball won't be diverted that easily.

There's more involved here than a squabble between Trumball and me, he told himself. That old man is a primary force behind the funding for this expedition—and the next. If you want a smooth road for the next expedition, Jamie told himself, you've got to keep Trumball on the team.

Yet as he stared at the coldly furious image on the screen, anger simmered anew within Jamie. Trumball has no right to scream at me or anybody else like that. If he's sore at his son, he should take it out on Dex, not me. And if I give him the impression that he can push me around, he'll start making more demands. He's a bully; the more I give in to him the more he'll take.

What's the best path, Grandfather? How can I do this without causing more pain?

He took a deep breath, then pressed the key that activated the computer's tiny camera. Jamie saw its red eye come on, just atop Trumball's stilled image on the screen.

"Mr. Trumball," he began slowly, "I can understand your concern for your son's safety. I had no idea you sent a message that Dex was not to go on the excursion to pick up the Pathfinder hardware. There was no such message addressed to me. And with all due respect, sir, you are not in command of this expedition. I am. You are not in a position to give orders."

Jamie looked directly into the camera's unblinking red eye and continued, "Neither Dex nor anyone else here will receive any special privileges. The idea for picking up Pathfinder was his, and he certainly wanted to go out on the excursion. Even had I known of your wishes, I'm afraid I would have had to go against them. This is Dex's job, and I'm sure he'll do it without trouble.

"He's got the best man we have along with him: Dr. Craig. If they run into any difficulties, they will return to base. I had—I have, no intention of taking foolish risks with anyone's life."

Unconsciously hunching closer to the camera, Jamie concluded, "I know that you helped to raise most of the money for this expedition, and we're all very grateful for that. But that doesn't give you the authority to make decisions about our work here. You can go to the ICU and complain to them if you want to. But frankly, I don't see what even they could do for you. We're here, more than a hundred million kilometers from Earth, and we have to make our own decisions.

"I'm sorry this particular decision has you so upset and worried. Maybe when Dex comes back with the Pathfinder and Sojourner you'll feel differently. Good night."

He tapped the keyboard twice: once to turn off the camera, the other to transmit his message to Trumball. Only then did he blank the old man's image from the screen.

"I would've told him to stick it up his arse."

Jamie wheeled around and saw Vijay leaning against the partition doorway, holding a steaming mug in both hands, as if she were trying to warm herself with it.

"How long have you been there?"

She came in and sat down beside him. "I was getting myself a cuppa when I heard Dex's dad ranting."

She was in her bulky coral-red turtleneck sweater and loose-fitting jeans instead of the usual coveralls, sitting so close to him that Jamie caught the delicate scent of the herbal tea she was drinking, sensed its warmth.

He said, "The old man must've told Dex he didn't want him going out on this excursion and Dex never informed me about it."

Vijay took a sip from the steaming mug. "Should he have?"

"It would've helped."

"Maybe he was afraid you'd nix the excursion if you knew."

Jamie shook his head. "I couldn't do that. Let somebody like Trumball think he can boss you around and you'll never hear the last of him."

She dipped her chin in agreement. "There is that."

"I just hope nothing happens while he's out there," Jamie said.

"Din't you hope that anyway? Before Trumball's blast, I mean."

"Yeah, sure, but . . . you know what I mean."

"Yes, I suppose I do."

Jamie blurted, "You slept with him, didn't you?"

"With Dex?"

"During the flight." Jamie was shocked that he mentioned it. The words had come out before he realized what he was going to say.

Vijay nodded, her expression fathomless. "Yes. Once."

"Once," he repeated.

With an odd little smile, Vijay said, "You get to know a lot about a man when he's got his pants down."

Jamie ran out of words.

"I told you he was an alpha male," she said. "Same as you are."

He nodded glumly.

"I'm attracted to alpha males."

"So you're attracted to him."

"I was. Now I'm attracted to you."

"Me?"

She broke into a smile. "Do you see anybody else around here?"

Jamie felt off balance. She's teasing me. She must be teasing.

Placing her mug on the corner of the console desk, Vijay said, "You're attracted to me, aren't you?"

"Um, sure."

She got to her feet and put her hand out to him. "So the only question remaining is, your place or mine?"

Jamie stood up slowly, not certain his legs would support him. "It's not that simple, Vijay. You said that yourself."

"That was then. This is now."

"But . . ."

She planted her hands on her hips. "My god, Jamie, you're as bad as most Aussie blokes!"

"I didn't mean—"

She stepped up to him and slid her arms around his neck. "Don't you ever feel lonely?" she whispered. "Or scared? We're so alone out here. So far from home. Doesn't it ever get to you?"

Her voice wasn't teasing now. He held her tightly and could feel her trembling. Beneath all the flip talk she was shivering with anxiety.

"I don't want to be alone tonight, Jamie."

"Neither do I," he admitted at last. "Neither do I."

DOSSIER: VARUNA JARITA SHEKTAR

IT WAS BAD ENOUGH BEING YET ANOTHER DAUGHTER IN A FAMILY OF FOUR girls and only one boy. Being bright and physically attractive only made things worse. Being a dark-skinned Hindu young woman growing up in Melbourne among fair-haired Aussie males who were either tongue-tied around women or aggressively machismo did not help matters, either.

In grammar school the teachers called out her name as it was written in their records: V. J. Shektar. The other children immediately dubbed her Vijay and she happily adopted the name, more comfortable with it than Varuna Jarita, the names her parents had given her.

Her mother had dedicated her as a baby to the powerful goddess Sakti, whose name means "energy." In the teeming Hindu pantheon, Sakti embodies both virginal innocence and bloodthirsty destruction: both an eternal virgin and the goddess of illicit pleasures.

Her father largely ignored her except to worry about where he could find the money for still another dowry on his slender salary as a CPA in a small accounting agency whose clientele was almost exclusively local Indian business firms.

The family's youngest daughter, she was born with spirit. Her mother tried to instill maidenly virtues in Vijay while her older sisters started dating and then, one by one, dropped out of secondary school to get married and start having babies of their own. Her one brother went on to college, his father's pride.

Vijay refused to quit her classes and find a husband. When her father threatened to beat some obedience into her, she left home and lived on her own with several friends, working nights in restaurants or video stores or anyplace that would hire an earnest, honest high school senior who had no intention of letting any man seduce her.

She went on to Melbourne University on the Higher Education Contribution Scheme, promising to repay the state most of her college expenses out of her income after she graduated. Still living on her own, she easily qualified for a medical school scholarship. Her mother despaired of her ever getting married and starting a proper family. Her father succumbed to cancer in her final school year, admitting only on his death bed that he was proud of what she had accomplished.

By the time Vijay was doing her internship in the university hospital she had learned that sex can be used not merely for fun, but for power. Usually, she chose fun, although often enough she enjoyed wielding the power that sex lent her. While most of her female friends complained that Australian men were "either boors or boobs," Vijay found that there were plenty of intelligent and thoughtful men in her world. Most of them were shy, at first, but that merely added to their charm, as far as she was concerned. For Vijay, sex was a way of learning rather than an all-consuming passion. She enjoyed the power it gave her, and she kept her freedom to choose who, and when, and what she wanted.

She got hurt, of course; more than once. But by the time she began practicing emergency medicine in the rundown hospital of the St. Kilda neighborhood where she had grown up, she considered herself an experienced woman of the world.

Unfortunately, she fell deeply in love with an older man, a physician who was already married. Vijay found that even a woman of the world can be tripped up by an urbane, well-to-do scoundrel who tells lies convincingly. By the time she finally faced the truth, she knew she had to get away from this man, away from Melbourne, away from Australia entirely. And she knew she would never again allow love to overwhelm her.

Her trip to California started as a vacation, a time to heal her emotional wounds and get some fresh air into her lungs. She stayed five years, starting a new career in space medicine. First with the American NASA and then with Masterson Aerospace Corporation, Vijay became a specialist in the effects of low gravity on the human body and mind.

She spent three ninety-day tours on space stations and was thinking about signing up for a year at Moonbase when she heard about the Second Mars Expedition.

Vijay Shektar won the position of physician/psychologist for the expedition. It was not easy. She had to prove herself in surgery, radiation medicine and even emergency dentistry. The competition was very exacting. But she won. Even though she promised herself she would not sleep with any of the decision-makers, she won the appointment anyway.

For Vijay had learned how to go after what she wanted. And she knew that if she worked hard enough, used all her strength and skills, she could usually get what she wanted.

The trick was to know what she wanted. That was the difficult part.

She thought of her patron goddess often. Love and destruction, the twin and inseparable attributes of Sakti. She did not believe in the ancient religion, but she was certain that love carried with it a terrible destructive power, a power that she was determined to keep from hurting her again.

MORNING: SOL 49

FOLLOWING HIS ASTRONAUT TEAMMATE, MITSUO FUCHIDA CLAMBERED stiffly down the ladder from the plane's cockpit and set foot on the top of the tallest mountain in the solar system.

In the pale light of the rising sun, it did not look like the top of a mountain to him. He had done a considerable amount of climbing in Japan and Canada and this was nothing like the jagged, snow-capped slabs of granite where the wind whistled like a hurled knife and the clouds scudded by below you.

Here he seemed to be on nothing more dramatic than a wide, fairly flat plain of bare basalt. Pebbles and larger rocks were scattered here and there, but not as thickly as they were back at the base dome. The craters that they had seen from the air were not visible here; at least, he saw nothing that looked like a crater.

But when he looked up he realized how high they were. The sky was a deep blue, instead of its usual butterscotch hue. The dust particles that reddened the sky of Mars were far below them. At this altitude on Earth they would be high up in the stratosphere.

Fuchida wondered if he could see any stars through his visor, maybe find Earth. He turned, trying to orient himself with the rising sun.

"Watch your step," Rodriguez's voice warned in his earphones. "It's—"

Fuchida's boot slid out from under him and he thumped painfully on his rear.

". . . slippery," Rodriguez finished lamely.

The astronaut shuffled carefully to Fuchida's side, moving like a man crossing an ice rink in street shoes. He extended a hand to help the biologist up to his feet.

Stiff and aching from a night of sitting in the cockpit, Fuchida now felt a throbbing pain in his backside. I'll have a nasty bruise there, he told himself. Lucky I didn't land on the backpack and break the life-support rig.

"Feels like ice underfoot," Rodriguez said.

"It couldn't be frost, we're up too high for water ice to form."

"Dry ice?"

"Ah." Fuchida nodded inside his helmet. "Dry ice. Carbon dioxide from the atmosphere condenses out on the cold rock."

"Yep."

"But dry ice isn't slippery . . ."

"This stuff is."

Fuchida thought quickly. "Perhaps the pressure of our boots on the dry ice causes a thin layer to vaporize."

"So we get a layer of carbon dioxide gas under our boots." Rodriguez immediately grasped the situation.

"Exactly. We skid along on a film of gas, like gas-lubricated ball bearings."

"That's gonna make it damned difficult to move around."

Fuchida wanted to rub his butt, although he knew it was impossible inside the hard suit. "The sun will get rid of the ice."

"I don't think it'll get warm enough up here to vaporize it."

"It sublimes at seventy-eight point five degrees below zero, Celsius," Fuchida said.

"At normal pressure," Rodriguez pointed out.

Fuchida looked at the thermometer on his right cuff. "It's already up to forty-two below," he said, feeling cheerful for the first time. "Besides, the lower the pressure, the lower the boiling point."

"Yeah. That's right."

"That patch must have been shaded by the plane's wing," Fuchida pointed out. "The rest of the ground seems clear."

"Then let's go to the beach and get a suntan," Rodriguez said humorlessly.

"No, let's go to the caldera, as planned."

"You think it's safe to walk around?"

Nodding inside his helmet, Fuchida took a tentative step. The ground felt smooth, but not slick. Another step, then another.

"Maybe we should've brought football cleats."

"Not necessary. The ground's okay now."

Rodriguez grunted. "Be careful, anyway."

"Yes, I will."

While Rodriguez relayed his morning report from his suit radio through the more powerful transmitter in the plane, Fuchida unlatched the cargo bay hatch and slid their equipment skid to the ground. Again he marvelled that this plane of plastic and gossamer could carry them and their gear. It seemed quite impossible, yet it was true.

"Are you ready?" he asked Rodriguez, feeling eager now to get going.

"Yep. Lemme check the gyrocompass . . ."

Fuchida did not wait for the astronaut's check. He knew the direction to the caldera as if its coordinates were printed on his heart.

Jamie woke up and found that he was alone. His eyes felt gummy, and he wanted nothing more than another hour or two of sleep. But the clock's red digital display said 6:58, and seven A.M. was the official start of the working day.

He sat up and smiled. The bunk smelled of sex. It had been great: rushed and eager at first, demanding, and then more languid, gentler, more loving. They had talked, whispered to each other, between the risings of passion. Jamie learned a little of what a dark-skinned woman had to overcome in a male-dominated world: family, school, even in her profession Vijay had not had an easy time of it. Being so damned attractive worked against her as much as for her.

He blinked, then rubbed at his eyes, trying to remember how much he had told her about himself. He recalled mentioning Al and the hidden streak of Navaho mysticism that his grandfather revealed now and then. He told her about the sky dancers, and promised to show them to her tonight.

Tonight. Jamie's smile faded into a troubled uncertainty. Was last night a one-time fling, or is this the start of something serious? He did not know. The last time he got involved with a woman, it had started on Mars and ended in divorce.

With a troubled sigh he got to his feet and began to face the day.

Pale morning sun slanted through the rover's curved windshield as Dex drove steadily across the rolling, rock-strewn plain. Each pebble and gully cast long early morning shadows. The sunlight looks different here, Dex thought. Weaker, pinker . . . something.

He and Craig had been underway for nearly an hour when Dex saw a red light suddenly glare up from the control panel.

"Hey, Wiley," he called over his shoulder. "We've got a problem here."

Craig shuffled into the cockpit and sat in the right seat, muttering, "What's this 'we,' white man?"

Dex jabbed a finger at the telltale.

"Uh-oh," said Craig.

"That doesn't sound so good, Wiley."

"Fuel cells're discharging. They shouldn't oughtta do that."

"We don't have to stop, do we?"

"Naw," said Craig. "I'll take a look."

He headed for the rear of the rover module. The fuel cells were the backup electrical system, to be used if the solar panels outside were unable to charge up the batteries that ran the rover's systems at night. The fuel cells on this old rover were powered by hydrogen and oxygen, which meant that their "waste" product was drinkable water. The fuel cells on the newer rovers ran on methane and oxygen generated from permafrost water and the Martian atmosphere.

Trumball drove on across the monotonous landscape. "Miles and miles of nothing but miles and miles," he murmured to himself. He knew he should be studying the land with a geologist's curious eye, categorizing the rock formations, watching how the sand dunes built up, checking the density of the rocks scattered everywhere, looking for craters. Instead he simply felt bored.

Precisely at the one-hour mark the timer on the panel chimed.

Dex called back to Craig, "Time to stop and plant a beacon, Wiley."

"Keep goin'," Craig said. "I'll suit up; gotta go outside anyway to check out the damned fuel cells."

Dex kept the rover trundling along while Craig struggled into his hard suit on his own. Once Craig announced he was ready, Dex stopped the vehicle and went back to check the older man's suit and backpack.

"Looks good, Wiley," he said.

"Okay," came Craig's voice, muffled by the sealed helmet. "Gimme one of the beacons."

Dex did that, and then started to tug on his own suit. Stupid flathead safety regs, he said to himself as Craig cycled through the airlock and went outside. I've gotta stand here in this tin can like some deadhead just because Wiley's outside. If anything goes wrong, he'll pop back into the airlock; he won't need me to come out and rescue him.

While Dex grumbled to himself he thought briefly about the safety regulation that required a second person to check out his suit. How the hell can you do that when the second man is already outside? he complained silently. He had no intention of going outside anyway, not unless Craig got into some unimaginable difficulty. The morphs who wrote these regulations must be the kind of guys who wear suspenders and a belt, he told himself. Old farts like Jamie.

Dex clomped back to the cockpit and sat awkwardly in the left seat. All the lights on the board were green, except the one for the fuel cells.

"How's it going, Wiley?" he called on the intercom.

"Checkin' these drat-damn fuel cells. Gimme a few minutes."

"Take your time," said Dex.

Sitting there idly, Dex scanned the horizon. Nothing. Dead as Beethoven. Deader. Nothing but rocks and sand and every shade of red the human eye could register. Not a thing moving out there—

He snapped bolt upright, not an easy thing to do in the hard suit.

Something *was* moving out there! Just a flicker, off on the horizon, and then it was gone.

Dex went back to the equipment lockers beneath the bunks in the module's midsection. Bending over in the suit was awkward, he had to lower himself to his knees to reach the latches that opened the lockers. Cursing the suit and its gloves, he fumbled through the neatly ordered sets of tools until he found the electronically boosted binoculars. Then he hurried back to the cockpit, like some old movie monster trying to gallop.

His helmet visor was up, so Dex could put the binoculars against his eyes to scan the horizon. Nothing. Whatever it was had disappeared, gone away.

Wait! A flicker . . .

Dex adjusted the focus and it came into crisp view. A dust devil. A swirling little eddy of dust, red as a real devil. It would have been called a pillar of fire in the Old Testament, Dex thought, except that this one is on Mars, not Israel or Egypt. It occurred to him that there was a region on Mars called Sinai, south of the Grand Canyon.

"You ought to be down there, pal," he murmured while he watched the minicyclone twist and dance across the distant horizon.

As he put the binoculars down Dex remembered that giant dust storms sometimes blanketed Mars almost from pole to pole. Usually during the spring season. He shook his head inside his helmet. It's too late in the season now; we timed the landing so the storms would be over. Besides, there weren't any this year.

Not yet, warned a tiny voice in his head. Spring lasts six months on Mars.

Jamie felt decidedly awkward at breakfast. Usually the team members took their morning meal when they chose to; there was no set time when everyone gathered at the galley each morning. It just happened that when Jamie came out of his quarters, the three women were already sitting at the table, heads together, chatting busily.

When they saw Jamie approaching their chat stopped. He said "Good morning" to them and got a chorus of the same in return. Then watchful silence as he picked a breakfast package from the freezer. He could feel their eyes on him.

"The strawberries ought to be ready for picking in another few days," he announced to no one in particular.

"Yes, and the tomatoes, too," answered Trudy Hall.

Jamie sat at the head of the table, with Trudy and Stacy on his left and Vijay at the other end, facing him. She smiled at him and he made a self-conscious smile back at her.

"Sleep well?" Trudy asked, her face the picture of innocent curiosity.

Jamie nodded and turned his attention to the bowl of instant cereal in front of him.

Conversation was a strain. No matter what Hall or Dezhurova said, it sounded to Jamie like arch references to sex. Vijay seemed perfectly relaxed, though. She's *enjoying* this banter, Jamie thought.

He went through his meal as quickly as he could and then headed for the comm center.

"I've got to check in with the others," he said to them.

"I already talked with both teams," Stacy called to his retreating back. "Possum has a cranky fuel cell, but otherwise everything is okay."

Jamie stopped and turned back toward her. "And Tomas?"

"They are heading off for the big caldera, on schedule."

"Good," said Jamie. Then he kept on walking toward the comm center.

A few minutes after he had spoken with Fuchida, Vijay slipped into the cubicle and sat beside him.

"It isn't a crime, you know," she said, a slight smile curving her lips.

"I know."

"Consenting adults and all that."

"I know," he repeated.

"Did you think the others'd be jealous?"

"Aw, come on, Vijay . . ."

She laughed lightly. "That's better. Lord, you were uptight back there!"

"Do they know?"

"I didn't say anything, but the way you were behaving they must have guessed it."

"Damn."

"It's nothing to be ashamed of."

"I know, but—"

"It happened, Jamie. Now forget about it. Get on with the program. I'm not trying to force a commitment out of you. I don't want that."

He felt relieved and disappointed at the same time. "Vijay, I . . . look, this kind of complicates everything."

She shook her head. "No worries, mate. No complications. It happened and it was very nice. Maybe it'll happen again, when the moon is right. Maybe not. Don't give it another thought."

"How the hell can I not give it another thought?"

Her smile returned. "That's what I wanted to hear from you, Jamie. That's all I wanted to hear."

AFTERNOON: SOL 49

RODRIGUEZ FELT A CHILL OF APPREHENSION TINGLING THROUGH HIM AS they stared down into the caldera. It was like being on the edge of an enormous hole in the world, a hole that went all the way down into hell.

"Nietzsche was right," Fuchida said, his voice sounding awed, almost frightened, in Rodriguez's earphones.

Rodriguez had to turn his entire torso from the hips to see the Japanese biologist standing beside him, anonymous in his bulky hard suit except for the blue stripes on his arms.

"You mean about when you stare into the abyss the abyss stares back."

"You've read Nietzsche?"

Rodriguez grunted. "In Spanish."

"That must have been interesting. I read him in Japanese."

Breaking into a chuckle, Rodriguez said, "So neither one of us can read German, huh?"

It was as good a way as any to break the tension. The caldera was huge, a mammoth pit that stretched from horizon to horizon. Standing there on its lip, looking down into the dark, shadowy depths that dropped away for who knew how far, was distinctly unnerving.

"That's a helluva hole," Rodriguez muttered.

"It's big enough to swallow Mt. Everest," said Fuchida, his voice slightly hollow with awe.

"How long's this beast been dead?" Rodriguez asked.

"Tens of millions of years, at least. Possibly much longer. That's one of the things we want to establish while we're here."

"Think it's due for another blow?"

Fuchida laughed shakily. "We'll get plenty of warning, don't worry."

"What, me worry?"

They began to unload the equipment they had dragged on the skid. Its two runners were lined with small Teflon-coated wheels so it could ride along rough ground without needing more than the muscle power of the two men. Much of the equipment was mountaineering gear: chocks and pitons and long coiled lengths of Buckyball cable.

"You really want to go down there?" Rodriguez asked while he drilled holes in the hard basalt for Fuchida to implant geo/met beacons.

"I spent a lot of time exploring caves," Fuchida answered, gripping one of the beacons in his gloved hands. "I've been preparing for this for a long time."

"Spelunking? You?"

"They call it caving. Spelunking is a term used by non-cavers."

"So you're all set to go down there, huh?"

Fuchida realized that he did not truly *want* to go. Every time he had entered a cave on Earth he had felt an irrational sense of dread. But he had forced himself to explore the caverns because he knew it would be an important point in his favor in the competition for a berth on the Mars expedition.

"I'm all set," the biologist answered, grunting as he worked the first beacon into its hole.

"It's a dirty job," Rodriguez joked, over the whine of the auger's electric motor, "but somebody's got to do it."

"A man's got to do what a man's got to do," Fuchida replied, matching his teammate's bravado.

Rodriguez laughed. "That ain't Nietzsche."

"No. John Wayne."

They finished planting the beacons and headed back to the lip of the caldera. Slowly. Reluctantly, Rodriguez thought. Well, he told himself, even if we break our asses poking around down there, at least we've got the beacons up and running.

Fuchida stopped to check the readouts coming from the beacons.

"They all transmitting okay?" Rodriguez asked.

"Yes," came the reply in his earphones. "Interesting . . ."

"What?"

"Heat flow from below ground is much higher here than at the dome or even down in the Canyon."

Rodriguez felt his eyebrows crawl upward. "You mean she's still active?"

"No, no, no. That can't be. But there is still some thermal energy down there."

"We should've brought marshmallows."

"Perhaps. Or maybe there'll be something to picnic on down there waiting for us!" The biologist's voice sounded excited.

"Whattaya mean?"

"Heat energy! Energy for life, perhaps."

A vision of bad videos flashed through Rodriguez's mind: slimy alien monsters with tentacles and bulging eyes. He forced himself not to laugh aloud. Don't worry, they're only interested in blondes with big boobs.

Fuchida called, "Help me get the lines attached and make certain the anchors are firmly imbedded."

He's not reluctant anymore, Rodriguez saw. He's itching to go down into that huge hole and see what kind of alien creatures he can find.

"Hydrogen is the cussedest damned stuff in the universe," Craig was muttering as he drove the rover. That red warning light still glared from the control panel.

Sitting beside him, Dex said, "But the Lord must've loved hydrogen—"

"Because He made so much of it," Craig finished for him. "Yeah, I know."

"Ninety percent of the universe is hydrogen, Wiley. More."

"That's why the universe is so damned cantankerous."

"What've you got against hydrogen—beside the fact that it's leaked out of the fuel cells?"

"Stuff always leaks. It's sneaky-pete stuff, leaks through seals and gaskets that'd hold anything else."

"The seals on that fuel cell should've held the hydrogen," Trumball said, more seriously. "The manufacturer's going to pay a forfeiture fee because they didn't make the seals hydrogen-tight."

"Helluva lot of good that'll do us if we get ourselves killed out here."

"Hey, lighten up, Wiley! It's not that serious. We're okay."

"I don't like headin' away from the base with our backup power system dead."

"We can take on more hydrogen when we get to the fuel generator," Trumball said.

"Uh-uh. The generator produces methane and oxy. Not hydrogen."

"There's the water recycler on board, remember?"

"Yeah."

"So," Trumball waved a hand in the air, "we take on extra water and electrolyze it into oxygen and hydrogen. Voila!"

Craig cast him a sour look. "Electrolyze the water."

"Right. With electricity from the solar panels."

"And what do we drink, amigo?"

"Water from the fuel cells."

"Now wait a minute . . ."

"Naw, you listen to me, Wiley. Here's the thing of it: We take on the water, electrolyze it and use the hydrogen to run the fuel cells."

"What about the oxygen?"

"Store it, dump it, whatever. We've got plenty oxy anyway. You with me so far?"

"We pump the hydrogen into the goddamned leaky fuel cells, big deal."

"Yeah, but we run the fuel cells to provide our electricity at night, instead of the lithium batteries."

"Now, why the hell—"

"So it doesn't matter if the fuel cells leak; we'll work 'em and get power out of 'em before the hydrogen leaks away."

Both hands on the rover's steering wheel, his eyes fixed on the land ahead, Craig looked like a man waiting for a card shark to deal him a deuce.

"Now what else do the fuel cells produce besides electricity?" Trumball asked, grinning with all his teeth.

"Water."

"Which we drink a little of and electrolyze the rest into fresh hydrogen and oxygen to run the fuel cells!"

Craig shook his head. "Great. You've invented the perpetual motion machine."

"Yeah, sure. I'm not that dufo, Wiley. We'll lose hydrogen all the time, I know that. But the loss'll be slow enough so we can use the fuel cells for overnight power all the way out to Ares Vallis and back to the generator! Save the batteries for backup."

"You done the math?"

"I did some rough numbers. I'll put it through the computer as soon as you give me an accurate fix for the fuel cells' normal efficiency rating."

Scratching his stubbly jaw, Craig said, "That data oughtta be in the computer files."

"Okay, go get it."

The older man hesitated. "We'll need approval. I'll have to tell Jamie what we're plannin' to do and he'll prob'ly buck it up to Tarawa."

Trumball grinned his widest. "Ask for all the approvals you want, Wiley, as long as we do it anyway."

"Now wait a minute—"

"What're they going to say?" Trumball interrupted. "If they say no, they're effectively cancelling the excursion. And we won't let them do that to us, will we?"

"You mean, even if they say no we go ahead anyway?"

"Sure! Why not? How're they going to stop us?"

"Use the fuel cells for overnight power?" Jamie asked, not certain he had heard Craig correctly.

"It's sorta like turnin' a lemon into lemonade," Possum replied.

Jamie stared at the display screen. Craig's unshaven face was dead serious. He appeared to be sitting in the cockpit, in his coveralls. Dex must be right beside him, driving. A glance at the data readouts on the displays beside the main screen showed that the rover was plowing ahead at a steady thirty kilometers per hour.

"It sounds risky to me," Jamie said, stalling for time to think.

"We been through the numbers," Craig replied. "It oughtta work."

"And if it doesn't?"

"Then we'll be ridin' along without a backup power system, the way we are now."

"I don't like it."

"The alternative," Trumball's voice interjected, "is to scrub this excursion and come home with our tails between our legs."

"That's what your father wants," Jamie said. He had intended to wait until evening and speak to Dex privately about the elder Trumball's ire. Dex's father had sent three replies to Jamie's last message within the past twelve hours, each one more furious than the one preceding it.

A hand engulfed the view of the rover's cockpit and swivelled the camera to focus on Dex.

"Dear old Dad's prone to displays of temper," he said easily, grinning. "Just relay his messages to me. I'll handle him."

"You just might be shooting down the funding for the next expedition, Dex," Jamie said.

Trumball shook his head vigorously. "No way. Once we bring back this Pathfinder hardware, investors will be running after us with money in their hands."

So that you can come back to Mars and loot it of anything else you can lay your hands on, Jamie thought. He pictured Trumball in a conquistador's steel cuirass and helmet.

A hand swivelled the camera again. "I ain't worried 'bout the next expedition," Craig said somberly. "I just want to get through with this excursion in one piece."

"I'll have to talk to Tarawa," Jamie said, hating himself for bucking the decision upstairs.

"Okay, fine," came Trumball's voice. "It'll take us at least another week to reach the generator."

Damn! thought Jamie as he went through the motions of continuing their discussion. Dex knows damned well that the farther out they are, the less chance of calling them back.

Once he signed off and cut the connection to the rover, though, a different thought wormed into his consciousness: The longer they're out on their excursion, the longer Dex is away from here. Away from Vijay.

He hated himself even more for that.

"You all set?" Rodriguez asked.

Fuchida had the climbing harness buckled over his hard suit, the tether firmly clipped to the yoke that ran under his arms.

"Ready to go," the biologist replied, with an assurance he did not truly feel. That dark, yawning abyss stirred a primal fear in both men, but Fuchida did not want to admit it to himself, much less to his teammate.

Rodriguez had spent the morning setting up the climbing rig while Fuchida collected rock samples and then did a half-hour VR show for viewers back on Earth. The rocks were sparser here atop Olympus Mons than they were down on the plains below, and none of them showed the intrusions of color that marked colonies of Martian lichen.

Still, sample collection was the biologist's first order of business. He thought of it as his gift to the geologists, since he felt a dreary certainty that there was no biology going on here on the roof of this world. But down below, inside the caldera . . . that might be a different matter.

Fuchida still had the virtual reality rig clamped to his helmet. They would not do a real-time transmission, but the recording of the first descent into Olympus Mons' main caldera would be very useful both for science and entertainment.

"Okay," Rodriguez said, letting his reluctance show in his voice. "I'm ready whenever you are."

Nodding inside his helmet, Fuchida said, "Then let's get started."

"Be careful now," said Rodriguez as the biologist backed slowly away from him.

Fuchida did not reply. He turned and started over the softly rounded lip of the giant hole in the ground. The caldera was so big that it would take half an hour to sink below the level where Rodriguez could still see him without moving from his station beside the tether winch.

I should have read Dante's *Inferno* in preparation for this task, Fuchida thought to himself.

The road to hell begins with a gradual slope, he knew. It will get steep enough soon.

Then both his booted feet slipped out from under him.

DIARY ENTRY

Sometimes I think I'm invisible. They just don't see me. I'm in among them, doing my work, but to them I'm not there. I speak and they don't hear me. At least, they don't listen. I'm as good as any of them but they all look right through me almost all the time. Invisible. I'm nothing to them.

AFTERNOON: SOL 49

"YOU OKAY?" RODRIGUEZ'S VOICE SOUNDED ANXIOUS IN FUCHIDA'S earphones.

"I hit a slick spot. There must be patches of dry ice coating the rock here in the shadows."

The biologist was lying on his side, his hip throbbing painfully from his fall. At this rate, he thought, I'll be black-and-blue from the waist down.

"Can you get up?"

"Yes. Certainly." Fuchida felt more embarrassed than hurt. He grabbed angrily at the tether and pulled himself to his feet. Even in the one-third gravity of Mars it took an effort, with the suit and backpack weighing him down. And all the equipment that dangled from his belt and harness.

Once on his feet he stared down once more into the darkness of the caldera's yawning maw. It's like the mouth of a great beast, a voice in his mind said. Like the gateway to the eternal pit.

He took a deep breath, then said into his helmet microphone, "Okay. I'm starting down again."

"Be careful, man."

"Thanks for the advice," Fuchida snapped.

Rodriguez seemed untroubled by his irritation. "Maybe I oughtta keep the line tighter," he suggested. "Not so much slack."

Regretting his temper, Fuchida agreed, "Yes, that might help to keep me on my feet." The hip really hurt, and his rump was still sore from his first fall.

I'm lucky I didn't rupture the suit, he thought. Or damage the backpack.

"Okay, I've adjusted the tension. Take it easy, now."

A journey of a thousand miles must begin with a single step. Mitsuo Fuchida quoted Lao-tzu's ancient dictum as he planted one booted foot on the ground ahead of him. The bare rock seemed to offer good traction.

You can't see the ice, he told himself. It's too thin a coating to be visible. Several dozen meters to his right, sunlight slanted down into the gradually sloping side of the caldera. There'll be no ice there, Fuchida thought. He moved off in that direction, slowly, testing his footing every step of the way.

The tether connected to his harness at his chest, so he could easily disconnect it if necessary. The increased tension of the line made walking all the more difficult. Fuchida felt almost like a marionette on a string.

"Slack off a little," he called to Rodriguez.

"You sure?"

He turned back to look up at his teammate, and was startled to see that the astronaut was nothing more than a tiny blob of a figure up on the rim, standing in bright sunlight with the deep blue sky behind him.

"Yes, I'm certain," he said, with deliberate patience.

A few moments later Rodriguez asked, "How's that?"

The difference was imperceptible, but Fuchida replied, "Better."

He saw a ledge in the sunlight some twenty meters below him and decided to head for it. Slowly, carefully he descended.

"I can't see you." Rodriguez's voice in his earphones sounded only slightly concerned.

Looking up, Fuchida saw the expanse of deep blue sky and nothing else except the gentle slope of the bare rock. And the tether, his lifeline, holding strong.

"It's all right," he said. "I'm using the VR cameras to record my descent. I'm going to stop at a ledge and chip out some rock samples there."

"Y'know, we shoulda flown out to the Pathfinder site," Wiley Craig mused as he drove the rover through the dry, cold afternoon across the Plains of the Moon.

"Tired of driving?" Dex Trumball asked, sitting in the cockpit's right seat.

"Kinda boring right now."

"I checked out the idea," Dex said. "The rocketplane doesn't have the range to make it out to Ares Vallis."

"Coulda hopped the fuel generator and gassed 'er up, just like we're doin' for this wagon."

"I suppose so. But we'd need a couple of fillups and that would mean flying the generator at least two different hops. And landing the plane twice more, too."

"Too risky, huh?"

"Oh, I wouldn't mind the risk," Dex said quickly. "But the rocketplane couldn't carry the hardware once we got there. Not with a full fuel load, at least."

Craig let out a long sigh that was almost a moan. "So we drive."

"We're getting there, Wiley."

"Awful slow."

"We're setting a record for a land traverse of an alien world. We'll be covering close to ten thousand klicks before we're back at the base."

"More'n those guys who circumnavigated Mare Imbrium back on th' Moon?"

"Oh, hell yes. They only covered twenty-five hundred kilometers."

"Huh."

"Pikers."

"Small-time stuff."

Trumball grinned at his partner. They were both unshaven, their chins and cheeks bristly with the beginnings of beards they had agreed not to cut off until they returned to the domed base.

"We're driving across what used to be the bottom of an ancient sea," Trumball said, gesturing at the undulating ground outside. "I bet if we stopped to do some digging we'd find plenty of fossils."

Craig cocked a brow at him. "And how'd you recognize what's a fossil and what's just a plain ol' rock? Think you'll find trilobites or a chambered nautilus that looks just like fossils on Earth?"

Dex took a deep breath, almost a sigh. "I know that, Wiley. I told Jamie about that the day we landed."

Craig grunted.

After a few moments of silence, Dex said, "Let me ask you something, Wiley."

"What?"

"About this matter of moving the base into the Canyon: Whose side are you on? Mine or Jamie's?"

Jamie stared at the three-dimensional image of the cliff face, bending over the immersion table display and concentrating as if he could force the ancient village to appear before his eyes by sheer willpower.

Stacy Dezhurova was at the comm console, as usual. Trudy and Vijay were tending the hydroponic garden. And Jamie was growing impatient.

I should never have let Dex go out on this crazy excursion of his, he told himself. Not only is it getting me in hot water with his father, it's screwing up the mission to the ancient village.

Jamie knew that he could not head out for the Canyon while four of the expedition's people were in the field. He had to wait for them to come back to the dome. Fuchida and Rodriguez would return in a few days, unless they ran into trouble. But Dex and Possum won't be back for another four weeks, minimum.

Don't let yourself get so worked up about it, he said silently. Be patient. If it's really an ancient village tucked in those cliffs, it's been there a long, long time. Another few weeks isn't going to make much difference.

Still he burned to get going, to get out of this dome, out in the field, away from the others.

Away from Vijay, he realized.

She's got me wound up like a spring. First no and then yes and now maybe. Is she doing it on purpose? Trying to drive me crazy? Is it her sense of humor?

Strangely, he found himself grinning at the thought. We're already crazy. We wouldn't be here otherwise. This just adds another dimension to the craziness.

Be calm, the Navaho side of his mind advised. Seek the balanced path. Only when you're in balance can you find beauty.

Sex. We tie ourselves into knots over it. Why? She won't get pregnant. Not here. Not unless she really wants to and she's too smart to want that. So what difference does a little roll in the hay make?

Then he thought of her admission that she had slept with Trumball, and Jamie knew that sex could be a fuse that kindles an explosion.

Take it one step at a time, he thought. One day at a time. Then he grinned again. One night at a time.

Dezhurova's voice cut into his awareness. "Jamie, you should take a look at this."

Jamie straightened up, felt his vertebrae pop, and turned toward the comm console, where Stacy was sitting with a headset clipped over her limp sandy-blond pageboy.

"What is it?"

"Latest met forecast from Tarawa."

Jamie saw a polar projection map of Mars' two hemispheres, side by side, on Dezhurova's main screen. Meteorological isobars and symbols for highs and lows were sprinkled across it.

Stacy tapped a fingernail on a red L deep in the southern hemisphere. Jamie noticed that her nails were manicured and lacquered a dark purple.

"That is a dust storm," she said.

Bending over her shoulder to peer at the map, Jamie nodded. And noticed that Stacy was wearing a flowery perfume.

"Way down on the other side of Hellas," he muttered.

"But they're forecasting it to grow." She touched a key and the next day's map appeared on the screen. The storm was bigger, and moving westward.

"Still way below the equator," Jamie said.

"Even so."

"Can you get a real-time view of the area?"

"On two," she replied. The screen immediately to her right brightened to show a satellite view of the region.

"Dust storm, all right," Jamie said. "Big one."

"And growing."

He thought aloud, "Even if it grows to global size, it'll take more than a week to bother us here. Fuchida and Rodriguez will be back well before then."

"But Dex and Possum . . ."

Jamie pictured Dex's reaction to being called back to base because of the possibility of a dust storm engulfing him. I'd have to order him to return, Jamie knew. And he might just ignore the order.

"Tell Tarawa I need to talk to the meteorology people right away," he said to Stacy.

"Right."

"Hey, Mitsuo," Rodriguez called.

Automatically, Fuchida looked up. But the astronaut was beyond his view. Fuchida was alone down on the ledge in the caldera's sloping flank of solid rock. The Buckyball tether that connected him to the winch up above also carried their suit-to-suit radio transmissions.

"What is it?" he replied, grateful to hear Rodriguez's voice.

"How's it going, man?"

"That depends," said Fuchida.

"On what?"

The biologist hesitated. He had been working on this rock ledge for hours, chipping out samples, measuring heat flow, patiently working an auger into the hard basalt to see if there might be water ice trapped in the rock.

He was in shadow now. The sun had moved away. Looking up, he saw with relief that the sky was still a deep blue. It was still daylight up there. Rodriguez would not let him stay down after sunset, he knew, yet he still felt comforted to see that there was still daylight up there.

"It depends," he answered slowly, "on what you are looking for. Whether you are a geologist or a biologist."

"Oh," said Rodriguez.

"A geologist would be very happy here. There is a considerable amount of heat still trapped in these rocks. Much more than can be accounted for by solar warming alone."

"You mean the volcano's still active?"

"No, no, no. It is dead, but the corpse is still warm—a little."

Rodriguez did not reply.

"Do you realize what this means? This volcano must be much younger than was thought. Much younger!"

"How young?"

"Perhaps only a few million years," Fuchida said excitedly. "No more than ten million."

"Sounds pretty damned old to me, amigo."

"But there might be life here! If there is heat, there might be liquid water within the rock."

"I thought water couldn't stay liquid on Mars."

"Not on the surface," Fuchida said, feeling the exhilaration quivering within him. "But deeper down, inside the rock where the pressure is higher . . . maybe . . ."

"Looks pretty dark down there."

"It is," Fuchida answered, peering over the lip of the ledge on which he sat. The suit's heater seemed to be working fine; it might be a hundred below zero in these shadows, but he felt comfortably warm.

"I don't like the idea of your being down there in the dark."

"Neither do I, but that's why we're here, isn't it?"

No answer.

"I mean, we still have several hundred meters of tether to unwind, don't we?"

Rodriguez said, "Eleven hundred and ninety-two, according to the meter."

"So I can go down a long way, then."

"I don't like the dark."

"My helmet lamp is working fine."

"Still . . ."

"Don't worry about it," Fuchida insisted, cutting off the astronaut's worries. It was bad enough to battle his own fears; he wanted no part of Rodriguez's.

"I saw a crevice at the end of this ledge," he told the astronaut. "It looks like the opening of an old lava tube. It probably leads down a considerable distance."

"Do you think that's a good idea?"

"I'll take a look into it."

"Don't take any chances you don't have to."

Fuchida grimaced as he climbed slowly to his feet. His whole body ached from the bruising he'd received in his falls and he felt stiff after sitting on the ledge for so long. Walk carefully, he warned himself. Even though the rock is warmer down here, there could still be patches of ice.

"You hear me?" Rodriguez called.

"If I followed your advice I'd be in my bed in Nagasaki," he said, trying to make it sound light and witty.

"Yeah, sure."

Stiffly he walked toward the fissure he had seen earlier. His helmet lamp threw a glare of light before him, but he had to bend over slightly to make the light reach the ground.

There it is, he saw. A narrow, slightly rounded hole in the basalt face. Like the mouth of a pirate's cave.

Fuchida took a step into the opening and turned from side to side, playing his helmet lamp on the walls of the cave.

It was a lava tube, he was certain of it. Like a tunnel made by some giant extraterrestrial worm, it curved downward. How far down? he wondered.

Stifling a voice in his head that whispered of fear and danger, Fuchida started into the cold, dark lava tube.

SUNDOWN: SOL 49

DEX TRUMBALL FROWNED AS HE LISTENED TO JAMIE ON THE ROVER'S comm link.

"The meteorology people don't expect the storm to get across the equator, but they're keeping an eye on it."

"So what's the problem?" Trumball asked, glancing over at Craig, driving the rover.

The ground they were traversing was rising slightly, and rougher than the earlier going. A range of rugged hills rose on their left, and the last rays of the dying sun threw enormously elongated shadows across their path, turning even the smallest rocks into dark phantoms reaching out to block their way.

"It's a question of timing," Jamie replied. "Each day you get farther from the base. If we wait to recall you until the storm's a real threat, it might be too late."

"But you don't know that the storm's going to be a real threat, do you?"

"The prudent thing to do," Jamie said, "is to turn back and try this excursion again late in the summer, when the threat of storms is practically zero."

"I don't want to turn back because of some theoretical threat that probably won't materialize."

"It's better than getting caught in a dust storm, Dex."

Trumball looked across at Craig again. The older man gave him a sidelong glance, then returned to staring straight ahead.

"You made it through a dust storm, didn't you?" he said.

It took several moments for Jamie to reply, "We had no choice. You do."

"Well, lemme tell you something, Jamie. I choose to keep on going. I'm not going to stop and turn back because of some asshole of a storm that's a couple thousand klicks away."

*　　*　　*

Sitting in front of the comm console, with Stacy beside him and Vijay at his back, Jamie kneaded his fists into his thighs.

If I order him to return and he refuses, then whatever authority I have over these people goes down the drain. But if I let him continue then they'll all know that Dex can do whatever he wants to and I have no way to control him.

He realized that it was Dex who was making the decisions. The idea of putting Craig in charge was a farce from the beginning. Possum was not raising his voice, not saying a word at all.

Which way? Which path? Jamie thought furiously for several silent moments. He drew up in his mind an image of Trumball's route across Lunae Planum and into Xanthe Terra.

"Hold on for a minute, Dex," he said, and cut off the transmission.

Turning to Dezhurova, he ordered, "Let me see their itinerary, Stacy."

She punched up the image on the screen before Jamie's chair. A black line snaked across the map, with pips marking the position expected at the end of each day. Jamie scanned it swiftly, then hit the transmit key again.

"Dex?"

"We're still here, chief."

"If the storm crosses the equator and threatens you, it won't happen for at least four or five more days. By then you'll be much closer to the fuel generator than to the base, here."

"Yeah?" Trumball's voice sounded wary.

"In two days from now you ought to be at the halfway point between here and the generator."

"Right."

"That's going to be our decision point. The point of no return. I'll decide then whether you can keep going or have to turn back."

"In two days."

"Yes. In the meantime we'll keep close track of the storm. Stay in touch with us hourly."

This time it was Trumball who hesitated for several moments before answering, "Okay. Sure."

"Good," said Jamie.

"We'll be bedding down for the night in another hour," Trumball said. "Call you then."

"Good," Jamie repeated.

He cut the transmission and leaned back in the little wheeled chair, feeling as if he had sparred ten rounds with a professional boxer.

Fifteen minutes later, Jamie was in the geology lab, running an analysis of the core samples that Craig's drill had brought up, happy to be dealing with rocks and dirt instead of people. Sedimentary deposits, no doubt about it. This dome is sitting on the floor of an ancient seabed. If we'd been here a few hundred million years ago, he thought, we'd have needed scuba gear.

"Jamie," Stacy Dezhurova called out sharply over the loudspeakers, "we have an emergency message from Rodriguez."

He instantly forgot his musings when Dezhurova's voice rang through the dome. Jamie left the core sample in the electron microscope without turning it off and sprinted across the dome to the comm center.

Dezhurova looked grim as she silently handed Jamie a headset.

Rodriguez's voice was calm but tight with tension. ". . . down there more than two hours now and then radio contact cut off," the astronaut was saying.

Sitting again on the wheeled chair next to Dezhurova as he adjusted the pin microphone, Jamie said, "This is Waterman. What's happening, Tomas?"

"Mitsuo went down into the caldera as scheduled. He found a lava tube about fifty-sixty meters down and went into it. Then his radio transmission was cut off."

"How long—"

"It's more than half an hour now. I've tried yanking on his tether, but I'm getting no response."

"What do you think?"

"Either he's unconscious or his radio's failed. I mean, I really *pulled* on the tether. Nothing."

The astronaut did not mention the third possibility: that Fuchida was dead. But the thought blazed in Jamie's mind.

"You say your radio contact with him cut off while he was still in the lava tube?"

"Yeah, right. That was more'n half an hour ago."

A thousand possibilities spun through Jamie's mind. The tether's too tough to break, he knew. Those Buckyballs can take tons of tension.

"It's going to be dark soon," Rodriguez said.

"You're going to have to go down after him," Jamie said.

"I know."

"Just go down far enough to see what's happened to him. Find out what's happened and call back here."

"Yeah. Right."

"I don't like it, but that's what you're going to have to do."

"I don't like it much, either," said Rodriguez.

Through a haze of pain, Mitsuo Fuchida saw the irony of the situation. He had made a great discovery, but he would probably not live to tell anyone about it.

When he entered the lava tube he felt an unaccustomed sense of dread, like a character in an old horror movie, stepping slowly, fearfully down the narrow corridor of a haunted house, lit only by the flicker of a candle. Except this corridor was a tube melted out of the solid rock by an ancient stream of red-hot lava, and Fuchida's light came from the lamp on his hard suit helmet.

Nonsense! he snapped silently. You are safe in your hard suit, and the tether connects you to Rodriguez, up at the surface. But he called to the astronaut and chatted inanely with him, just to reassure himself that he was not truly cut off from the rest of the universe down in this dark, narrow passageway.

The VR cameras fixed to his helmet were recording everything he saw, but Fuchida thought that only a geologist would be interested in this cramped, claustrophobic tunnel.

The tube slanted downward, its walls fairly smooth, almost glassy in places. The black rock gleamed in the light of his lamp. The tunnel grew narrower in spots, then widened again, although nowhere was it wide enough for him to spread his arms fully.

Perspiration was beading Fuchida's lip and brow, trickling coldly down his ribs. Stop this foolishness, he admonished himself. You've been in tighter caves than this.

He thought of Elizabeth, waiting for him back in Japan, accepting the subtle snubs of deep-seated racism because she loved him and wanted to be with him when he returned. I'll get back to you, he vowed, even if this tunnel leads down to hell itself.

The tether seemed to snag from time to time. He had to stop and tug on it to loosen it again. Or perhaps Rodriguez was fiddling with the tension on the line, he thought.

Deeper into the tunnel he went, stepping cautiously, now and then running his gloved hands over the strangely smooth walls.

Fuchida lost track of time as he chipped at the tunnel walls here and there, filling the sample bags that dangled from his harness belt. The tether made it uncomfortable to push forward, attached to his harness at the chest. It had to pass it over his shoulder or around his waist: clumsy, at best.

Then he noticed that the circle of light cast by his helmet lamp showed an indentation off toward the left, a mini-alcove that seemed lighter in color than the rest of the glossy black tunnel walls. Fuchida edged closer to it, leaning slightly into the niche to examine it.

A bubble of lava did this, he thought. The niche was barely big enough for a man to enter. A man not encumbered with a hard suit and bulky backpack, that is. Fuchida stood at the entrance to the narrow niche, peering inside, wondering.

And then he noticed a streak of red, the color of iron rust. Rust? Why here and not elsewhere?

He pushed in closer, squeezing into the narrow opening to inspect the rust spot. Yes, definitely the color of iron rust.

He took a scraper from the tool kit at his waist, nearly fumbling it in his awkwardly gloved fingers. If I drop it I won't be able to bend down to pick it up, not in this narrow cleft, he realized.

The red stain crumbled at the touch of the scraper. Strange! thought Fuchida. Not like the basalt at all. Could it be . . . wet? No! Liquid water cannot exist at this low air pressure. But what is the pressure inside the rock? Perhaps . . .

The red stuff crumbled easily into the sample bag he held beneath it with trembling fingers. It must be iron oxide that is being eroded by water, somehow. Water and iron. Siderophiles! Bacteria that metabolize iron and water!

Fuchida was as certain of it as he was of his own existence. His heart was racing. A colony of iron-eating bacteria living inside the caldera of Olympus Mons! Who knew what else might be found deeper down?

It was only when he sealed up the sample bag and placed it in the plastic box dangling from his belt that he heard the strange rumbling sound. Through the thickness of his helmet it sounded muted, far-off, but still *any* sound at all this deep in the tunnel was startling.

Fuchida started to back away from the crumbling, rust-red cleft. The rumbling sound seemed to grow louder, like the growl of some prowling beast. It was nonsense, of course, but he thought the tunnel walls were shaking slightly, trembling. It's you who are trembling, foolish man! he admonished himself.

Something in the back of his mind said, Fear is healthy. It is nothing to be ashamed of, if you—

The rusted area of rock dissolved into a burst of exploding steam that lifted Fuchida off his feet and slammed him painfully against the far wall of the lava tube.

EVENING: SOL 49

FUCHIDA NEARLY BLACKED OUT AS HIS HEAD BANGED AGAINST THE BACK of his helmet. He sagged to the floor of the tunnel, his visor completely fogged, jagged flares of stars flashing in his eyes, his skull thundering with pain.

With a teeth-gritting effort of iron will he kept himself from slipping into unconsciousness. Despite the pounding in his head, he forced himself to stay awake, alert. Do not faint! he commanded himself. Do not allow yourself to take the cowardly way. You must remain awake if you hope to remain alive. He felt perspiration beading his forehead, dripping into his eyes, forcing him to blink and squint.

Then a wave of anger swept over him. How stupid you are! he railed at himself. A hydrothermal vent. Water. *Liquid* water, here on Mars. You should have known. You should have guessed. The heat flow, the rusted iron. There must be siderophiles here, bacteria that metabolize iron and water. They weakened the wall and you scraped enough of it away for the pressure to blow through the wall. You caused a geyser to erupt.

Yes, he agreed with himself. Now that you've made the discovery, you must live to report it to the rest of the world.

His visor was still badly fogged. Fuchida groped for the control stud at his wrist that would turn up his suit fans and clear the visor. He thought he found the right keypad and pushed it. Nothing changed. In fact, now that he listened for it, he could not hear the soft buzz of his suit fans at all. Except for his own labored breathing, there was nothing but silence.

Wait. Be calm. Think.

Call Rodriguez. Tell him what's happened.

"Tomas, I've had a little accident."

No response.

"Rodriguez! Can you hear me?"

Silence.

Slowly, carefully, he flexed both his arms, then his legs. His body ached, but there didn't seem to be any broken bones. Still the air fans remained silent, and beads of sweat dripped into his eyes.

Blinking, squinting, he saw that the visor was beginning to clear up on its own. The hydrothermal vent must have been a weak one, he thought thankfully. He could hear no more rumbling; the tunnel did not seem to be shaking now.

Almost reluctantly, he wormed his arm up to eye level and held the wrist keyboard close to his visor. The keyboard was blank. Electrical malfunction! Frantically he tapped at the keyboard: nothing. Heater, heat exchanger, air fans, radio—all gone.

I'm a dead man.

Cold panic hit him like a blow to the heart. That's why you no longer hear the air circulation fans! The suit battery must have been damaged when I slammed against the wall.

Fuchida could hear his pulse thundering in his ears. Calm down! he commanded himself. That's not so bad. The suit has enough air in it for an hour or more. And it's insulated very thoroughly; you won't freeze—not for several hours, at least. You can get by without the cooling fans. For a while.

It was when he tried to stand up that the real fear hit him. His right ankle flared with agony. Broken or badly sprained, Fuchida realized. I can't stand on it. I can't get out of here!

Then the irony really struck him. I might be the first man to die of heat prostration on Mars.

The problem is, Rodriguez said to himself, that we only brought one climbing harness and Mitsuo's wearing it. By the time I go back to the plane, get the other harness and come back here and set it up, he could be dead.

I've got to go down there without a tether, without any of the climbing tools that he's carrying with him.

Shit! Rodriguez shook his head inside his helmet. Can't leave him. It's already getting dark and he'd never survive overnight.

On the other hand, there's a damned good chance that we'll both die down there.

Double shit.

For long, useless moments he stared down into the dark depths of the caldera, in complete shadow now as the sun crept closer to the distant horizon.

Show no fear, Rodriguez repeated to himself. Not even to yourself. He nodded inside his helmet. Yeah, easy to say. Now get the snakes in my guts to believe it.

Still, he started down, walking slowly, deliberately, gripping the tether hand-over-hand as he descended.

It became totally dark within a few steps of leaving the caldera's rim. The only light was the patch of glow cast by his helmet lamp, and the dark rock all around him seemed to swallow that up greedily. He planted his booted feet carefully, deliberately, knowing that carbon dioxide from the air was already starting to freeze out on the bitterly cold rock.

Rodriguez cast a glance up at the dimming sky, like a prisoner taking his last desperate look at freedom before entering his dungeon.

At least I can follow the tether, he thought. He moved with ponderous deliberation, worried about slipping on patches of ice. If I get disabled we're both toast, he told himself. Take it easy. Don't rush it. Don't make any mistakes.

Slowly, slowly he descended. By the time the tether led him to the mouth of the lava tube, he could no longer see the scant slice of sky above; it was completely black. If there were stars winking at him up there he could not see them through the tinted visor of his helmet.

He peered into the tunnel. It was like staring into a well of blackness.

"Hey Mitsuo!" he called. "Can you hear me?"

No response. He's either dead or unconscious, Rodriguez thought.

He's laying deep down that tunnel someplace and I've got to go find him. Or what's left of him.

He took a deep breath. No fear, he reminded himself.

Down the dark tunnel he plodded, ignoring the fluttering of his innards, paying no attention to the voice in his head that told him he'd gone far enough, the guy's dead, no sense getting yourself killed down here too so get the hell out, *now*.

Can't leave him, Rodriguez shouted silently at the voice. Dead or alive, I can't leave him down here.

Your funeral, the voice countered.

Yeah, sure. I get back to the base okay without him. What're they gonna think of me? How'm I—

He saw the slumped form of the biologist, a lump of hard suit and jumbled equipment slumped against one wall of the tunnel.

"Hey, Mitsuo!" he called.

The inert form did not move.

Rodriguez hurried to the biologist and tried to peer into the visor of his helmet. It looked badly fogged.

"Mitsuo," he shouted. "You okay?" It sounded idiotic the moment the words left his lips.

But Fuchida suddenly reached up and gripped his shoulders. "You're alive!"

Still no answer. His radio's out, Rodriguez finally realized. And the air's too thin to carry my voice.

He touched his helmet against Fuchida's. "Hey, man, what happened?"

"Battery," the biologist replied, his voice muffled but understandable. "Battery not working. And my ankle. Can't walk."

"Jesus! Can you stand up if I prop you?"

"I don't know. My air fans are down. I'm afraid to move; I don't want to generate any extra body heat."

Shit, said Rodriguez to himself. Am I gonna have to carry him all the way up to the surface?

Sitting there trapped like a stupid schoolboy on his first exploration of a cave, Fuchida wished he had paid more attention to his Buddhist instructors. This would be a good time to meditate, to reach for inner peace and attain a calm alpha state. Or was it beta state?

With his suit fans inoperative, the circulation of air inside the heavily insulated hard suit was almost nonexistent. Heat generated by his body could not be transferred to the heat exchanger in the backpack; the temperature inside the suit was climbing steadily.

Worse, it was more and more difficult to get the carbon dioxide he exhaled out of the suit and breathable air into it. He could choke to death on his own fumes.

The answer was to be as still as possible, not to move, not even to blink. Be calm. Achieve nothingness. Do not stir. Wait. Wait for help.

Rodriguez will come for me, he told himself. Tomas won't leave me here to die. He'll come for me.

Will he come in time? Fuchida tried to shut the possibility of death out of his thoughts, but he knew that it was the ultimate inevitability.

The hell of it is, I'm certain I have a bag full of siderophiles! I'll be famous. Posthumously.

Then he saw the bobbing light of a helmet lamp approaching. He nearly blubbered with relief. Rodriguez appeared, a lumbering robotlike creature in the bulky hard suit. To Fuchida he looked sweeter than an angel.

Once Rodriguez realized that he had to touch helmets to be heard, he asked, "How in the hell did you get yourself banged up like this?"

"Hydrothermal vent," Fuchida replied. "It knocked me clear across the tunnel."

Rodriguez gave a low whistle. "Old Faithful strikes on Mars."

Fuchida tried to laugh; what came out was a shaky giggle.

"Can you move? Get up?"

"I think so . . . " Slowly, with Rodriguez lifting from beneath his armpits, Fuchida got to his feet. He took a deep breath, then coughed. When he tried to put some weight on his bad ankle he nearly collapsed.

"Take it easy, buddy. Lean on me. We got to get you back to the plane before you choke to death."

Jamie hovered over Trudy Hall, who was sitting at the comm console now. Dezhurova had insisted that she would stay on duty, but Jamie had ordered her to get up and have something to eat.

He was grateful when she obeyed. She was obviously reluctant about it, but she did what Jamie commanded.

"You should take a rest, too, mate," Vijay told him. She had carried a tray of dinner into the comm center for him.

"When they're back safely in the plane," Jamie said. "Then we can all call it a day."

"How long has it been?" Vijay asked.

Glancing at the digital clock above the main comm screen, Jamie said, "More than an hour since Rodriguez started down after him."

Dex Trumball was driving slowly through the inky blackness of the Martian night.

"Supper's on the table," Craig called out. "Come on and eat it or I'll throw it to th' hawgs."

"Why don't we keep on going, Wiley?" Trumball asked over his shoulder.

" 'Cause we don't want to break our cotton-pickin' necks, that's why. Shut 'er down for the night, Dex."

"Aw, come on, Wiley. Just a few klicks more."

"Now," Craig said, with iron in his tone.

With a sigh, Trumball leaned on the brake pedals and brought the rover to a slow, smooth stop.

Once he had shut down the drive motors and come back to the table between the bunks, Dex sank down on the edge of his bunk and stared for a few moments at the tray of prepackaged dinner.

"I know what you're up to, y'know," Craig said, sitting on the edge of his own bunk, on the other side of the folding table.

Dex grinned at the older man. "Yeah? What?"

"You wanta get so close to the generator that when Jamie comes to his decision point we'll be closer to it than to th' base. Right?"

With a nod, Trumball answered, "Why not?"

"You're not scared of a dust storm?"

"Wiley, if Jamie weathered one of those storms during the first expedition, why can't we?"

"Be smarter to be back at the base when a storm hits, nice 'n' cozy."

"*If* a storm hits. How'd you feel if we turned tail and went back to the dome and then no storm materializes?"

"Alive," said Craig.

Trumball considered the older man for a moment. Then, as he dug a plastic fork into the unidentifiable stuff on the tray before him, he asked, "If Jamie orders us back, what'll you do?"

Craig stared back at him, sad, pouchy ice-blue eyes unwavering. "Don't know yet," he answered. "But I'm turnin' over the possibilities in my mind."

Trumball grinned at him. "Yeah? Well, turn this over, too, Wiley. There'll be a finder's fee for picking up the Pathfinder hardware. A nice sizable wad of cash for the guys who bring it back. That'll be you and me, Wiley."

"How much?"

Trumball shrugged. "Six figures, I guess."

"H'mp."

Watching the older man's face carefully, Trumball added, "Of course, I don't need the money. I'd be willing to give my half to you, Wiley. If we keep on going no matter what Jamie says."

Craig's face was impassive. But he said, "Now that sounds purty interesting, ol' pal. Purty damn interesting."

Rodriguez had forgotten about the ice.

He half-dragged Fuchida along the tunnel, the little pools of light made by their helmet lamps the only break in the total, overwhelming darkness around them.

"How you doing, buddy?" he asked the Japanese biologist. "Talk to me."

Leaning his helmet against the astronaut's, Fuchida answered, "I feel hot. Broiling."

"You're lucky. I'm freezing my ass off. I think my suit heater's in refrigeration mode."

"I . . . I don't know how long I can last without the air fans," Fuchida said, his voice trembling slightly. "I feel a little lightheaded."

"No problem," Rodriguez replied, with a false heartiness. "It'll get kinda stuffy inside your suit, but you won't asphyxiate."

The first cosmonaut to do a spacewalk almost died of heat prostration, Rodriguez remembered. Alexei Leonov said his suit was "up to my knees" in sweat before he could get back into his orbiting capsule. The suit sloshed when he moved. The damned suits hold all your body heat inside; that's why they make us wear the watercooled longjohns and put heat exchangers in the suits. But if the fans can't circulate the air, the exchanger's pretty damned useless.

Rodriguez kept one hand on the tether. In the wan light from his helmet lamp he saw that it led upward, out of this abyss.

"We'll be back in the plane in half an hour, maybe less. I can fix your backpack then."

"Good," said Fuchida. Then he coughed again.

It seemed to take hours before they got out of the tunnel, back onto the ledge in the slope of the giant caldera.

"Come on, grab the tether. We're goin' up."

"Right."

But Rodriguez's boot slipped and he fell to his knees with a painful thump.

"Damn," he muttered. "It's slick."

"The ice."

The astronaut rocked back onto his haunches, both knees throbbing painfully.

"It's too slippery to climb?" Fuchida's voice was edging toward panic.

"Yeah. We're gonna have to haul ourselves up with the winch." He got down onto his belly and motioned the biologist to do the same.

"Isn't this dangerous? What if we tear our suits?"

Rodriguez rapped on the shoulder of Fuchida's suit. "Tough as steel, amigo. They won't rip."

"You're certain?"

"You wanna spend the night down here?"

Fuchida grabbed the tether with both his hands.

Grinning to himself, Rodriguez also grasped the tether and told Fuchida to activate the winch.

But within seconds he felt the tether slacken.

"Stop!"

"What's wrong?" Fuchida asked.

Rodriguez gave the tether a few light tugs. It felt loose, its original tension gone.

"Holy shit," he muttered.

"What is it?"

"The weight of both of us on the line is too much for the rig to hold. We're pulling it out of the ground up there."

"You mean we're stuck here?"

NIGHT: SOL 49

"I SEE THAT NONE OF US ARE GOING TO GET ANY SLEEP."

Stacy Dezhurova was smiling as she spoke, but her bright blue eyes were dead serious. Trudy Hall was still on duty at the comm console. Stacy sat beside her while Jamie paced slowly back and forth behind her. Vijay had pulled in another chair and sat by the doorway, watching them all.

The comm center cubicle felt crowded and hot with all four of them jammed in there. Jamie did not answer Dezhurova's remark; he just kept on pacing, five strides from one partition to the other, then back again.

"Tommy must have found him by now," Hall said, swivelling her chair slightly toward Stacy.

"Then why doesn't he call in?" she demanded, almost angrily.

"They must still be down inside the caldera," Jamie said.

"It is night," Stacy pointed out, almost accusingly.

Jamie nodded and kept pacing.

"It's the waiting that's the worst," Vijay offered. "Not knowing what—"

"This is Rodriguez," the radio speaker crackled. "We got a little problem here."

Jamie was at the comm console like a shot, leaning between the two women.

"What's happening, Tomas?"

"Fuchida's alive. But his backpack's banged up and his battery's not functioning. Heater, air fans, nothing in his suit's working." Rodriguez's voice sounded tense but in control, like a pilot whose jet engine had just flamed out: trouble, but nothing that can't be handled. Until you hit the ground.

Then he added, "We're stuck on a ledge about thirty meters down and can't get back up 'cause the rock's coated with dry ice and it's too slippery to climb.''

As the astronaut went on to describe how the tether winch almost pulled out of its supports when the two of them tried to haul themselves up the slope, Jamie tapped Hall on the shoulder and told her to pull up the specs on the hard suit's air circulation system.

"Okay," he said when Rodriguez stopped talking. "Are either of you hurt?"

"I'm bruised a little, Mitsuo's got a bad ankle. He can't stand on it."

One of the screens on the console now showed a diagram of the suit's air circulation system. Hall was scrolling through a long list on the screen next to it.

"Mitsuo, how do you feel?" Jamie asked, stalling for time, time to think, time to get the information he needed.

"His radio's down," Rodriguez said. A hesitation, then, "But he says he's hot. Sweating."

Vijay nodded and murmured, "Hyperthermia."

Strangely, Rodriguez chuckled. "Mitsuo also says he discovered siderophiles, inside the caldera! He wants Trudy to know that."

"I heard it," Hall said, still scrolling down the suit specs. "Did he get samples?"

Again a wait, then Rodriguez replied, "Yep. There's water in the rock. Liquid water. Mitsuo says you've gotta publish . . . get it out on the Net."

"Liquid?" Hall stopped the scrolling. Her eyes went wide. "Are you certain about—"

"Never mind that now," Jamie said, studying the numbers on Hall's screen. "According to the suit specs you can get enough breathable air for two hours, at least, even with the fans off."

"We can't wait down here until daylight, then," Rodriguez said.

Jamie said, "Tomas, is Mitsuo's harness still connected to the winch?"

"Far as I can see, yeah. But if we try to use the winch to haul us up, it's gonna yank the rig right out of the ground."

"Then Mitsuo's got to go up by himself."

"By himself?"

"Right," Jamie said. "Let the winch pull Mitsuo up to the top. Then he takes off the harness and sends it back to you so you can get up. Understand?"

In the pale light of the helmet lamps, Fuchida could not see Rodriguez's face behind his tinted visor. But he knew what the astronaut must be feeling.

Pressing his helmet against Rodriguez's, he said, "I can't leave you down here alone, without even the tether."

Rodriguez's helmet mike must have picked up his voice, because

Waterman replied, iron hard, "No arguments, Mitsuo. You drag your butt up there and send the harness back down. It shouldn't take more than a few minutes to get you both up to the top."

Fuchida started to object, but Rodriguez cut him off. "Okay, Jamie. Sounds good. We'll call you from the top when we get there."

Fuchida heard the connection click off.

"I can't leave you here," he said, feeling almost desperate.

"That's what you've got to do, man. Otherwise neither one of us will make it."

"Then you go first and send the harness back down to me."

"No way," Rodriguez said. "I can't leave you down here with that bad ankle. Besides, I'm trained to deal with dangerous situations."

Fuchida said, "But it's my fault—"

"Bullshit," Rodriguez snapped. Then he added, "I'm bigger and meaner than you, Mitsuo. Now get going and stop wasting time!"

"How will you find the harness in the dark? It could be dangling two meters from your nose and your helmet lamp won't pick it up."

Rodriguez made a huffing sound, almost a snort. "Tie one of the beacons to it and turn on the beacon light."

Fuchida felt mortified. *I should have thought of that. It's so simple. I must be truly rattled; my mind is not functioning as it should.*

"Now go on," Rodriguez said. "Get down on your belly again and start up the winch."

"Wait," Fuchida said. "There is something—"

"What?" Rodriguez demanded impatiently.

Fuchida hesitated, then spoke all in a rush. "If . . . if I don't make it . . . if I die . . . would you contact someone for me when you get back to Earth?"

"You're not gonna die."

"Her name is Elizabeth Vernon," Fuchida went on, afraid that if he stopped he would not be able to resume. "She's a lab assistant in the biology department of the University of Tokyo. Tell her . . . that I love her."

Rodriguez understood the importance of his companion's words. "Your girlfriend's not Japanese?"

"My wife," Fuchida answered.

Rodriguez whistled softly. Then, "Okay, Mitsuo. Sure. I'll tell her. But you can tell her yourself. You're not gonna die."

"Of course. But if . . ."

"Yeah. I know. Now get going!"

Reluctantly, Fuchida did as he was told. He felt terribly afraid of a thousand possibilities, from tearing his suit to leaving his partner in the dark to freeze to death. But he felt more afraid of remaining there and doing nothing.

Worse, he felt hot. Stifling inside the suit. Gritting his teeth, he held on to the tether with all the pressure the servomotors on his gloves could apply. Then he realized that he needed one hand free to work the winch control on his climbing harness.

He fumbled for the control stud, desperately trying to remember which one started the winch. He found it and pressed. For an instant nothing happened.

Then suddenly he was yanked off the ledge and dragged up the hard rock face of the caldera's slope, his suit grinding, grating, screeching against the rough rock.

I'll never make it, Fuchida realized. Even if the suit doesn't break apart, I'll suffocate in here before I reach the top.

NEW YORK

IT WAS A FEW MINUTES AFTER SIX IN THE EVENING IN MANHATTAN, A COLD, gusty, rainy gray autumn day in the Big Apple. Crowds scurried past store windows blazing with lights and elaborate Christmas displays, pushing through the hard slanting rain and down into the dank, noisy subway tunnels, heading for home and family and dinner and the evening's Halloween trick-or-trick jaunts with the kids.

The dark-panelled lounge in the Metropolitan Club was hushed and calm, in contrast. While the wind shook the bare tree limbs of Central Park and rattled the lights on the trees outside the club's awninged entrance, Darryl C. Trumball eased back in his favorite leather armchair to savor his first Old Fashioned of the evening.

Sitting in the next chair, at his elbow, was Walter Laurence, executive director of the International Consortium of Universities. Unlike the "self-made" Trumball, Laurence had been born to great wealth. Unlike the financier, Laurence had spent his adult life in public service, first in the U.S. Department of State, later in the tangled, often troubled world of academia. Very much like Trumball, Walter Laurence enjoyed wielding power, and appreciated the perquisites of high position.

Now he sat sipping delicately at a tall, chilled glass of vodka and tonic, looking very much like the elder statesman: sleek silver hair, a wisp of a gray mustache, impeccably tailored suit of pearl gray.

"What I don't understand," he was saying in his soft, well-mannered voice, "is why you invited that newshound to join us here. He's such a boor."

Trumball smiled knowingly, like the toothy grin of a skeleton. "You remember what Ben Franklin said about making love to older women?"

Laurence allowed a tiny frown to crease the space between his brows. "In the dark, all cats are gray?"

"No, no." Trumball waved a hand impatiently. "He said the main benefit of making love to an older woman is that afterward, they're so damned grateful!"

"H'mm."

Trumball leaned closer and lowered his voice. "I want Newell— and his network—on our side."

"And just which side is that?"

"We've got to get rid of this Indian up there: Waterman."

"Get rid of him? How? The man's on Mars."

"I don't want him directing the expedition. Never did want him, as a matter of fact. I just let the rest of you talk me into it."

Laurence took a longer sip of his tall drink. Then, "I don't see how—"

"He's too much of a dreamer, not the proper man to head the expedition at all," Trumball said. "And he doesn't follow orders. He thinks that just because he's out there on Mars he can do what he wants."

"Ah," said Laurence. "Do you have specific instances? I mean, the team seems to be following the schedule we all agreed upon— except for this extra excursion to pick up the old Pathfinder equipment."

"I specifically gave orders that my son was not to be sent out on that trek!" Trumball hissed, his face paling as he tried to keep his voice down. Still, several people at nearby chairs turned toward him with disapproving frowns.

"Yes, that may be, but there's not much we can do from this distance, is there?"

"Oh, there certainly is," Trumball said. "I want him removed from his position as expedition director. Demoted. Broken."

Laurence sighed. "But don't you see, Darryl, that is merely paperwork. He will still be on Mars and still in command there. From all I've learned, the other team members hold him in extremely high regard. He's their hero, really."

"I want him broken!"

"You'll make a martyr out of him."

Trumball glared at the ICU executive. "That's why I asked Newell to join us. I want to make sure that the news media handle this story the way I want them to."

Laurence sank back in his armchair. "I think you're stirring up a tempest in a teapot."

"Well, I don't."

"It won't make any difference if he's officially expedition director or not."

"Yes it will!" Trumball snapped. "He wants to go out to find some mythical village he claims he saw on the first expedition. As director, he can set up an excursion whenever he wants. With somebody else as director, he'll never get permission to go."

"Do you think the new director would refuse to grant him permission for such an excursion?"

"Damned right I do!"

"But they all admire the man so much. Who would deny him the chance to see if his village actually exists?"

"The new director will."

Comprehension lit in Laurence's mind, but he asked the question anyway, even though he knew what Trumball's answer would be.

"And who might the new director be?"

"My son Dex, of course."

"Of course," Laurence murmured. "Of course."

IN THE PIT

RODRIGUEZ WATCHED FUCHIDA SLITHER UP AND AWAY FROM HIM, A DIM pool of light that receded slowly but steadily. Through the insulation of his helmet he could not hear the noise of the biologist's hard suit grating against the ice-rimed rock; he heard nothing but his own breathing, faster than it should have been. Calm down, he ordered himself. Keep calm and everything'll turn out okay.

Sure, a sardonic voice in his head answered. Nothing to it. Piece of cake.

Then he realized that he was totally, utterly alone in the darkness.

It's okay, he told himself. Mitsuo'll send the harness down and then I can winch myself up.

The light cast by his helmet lamp was only a feeble glow against the dark rough rock face. When Rodriguez turned, the light was swallowed by the emptiness of the caldera's abyss, deep and wide and endless.

The darkness surrounded him. It was as if there was no one else in the whole universe, no universe at all, only the all-engulfing darkness of this cold, black pit.

Unbidden, a line from some play he had read years earlier in school came to his mind:

Why, this is hell, nor am I out of it.

Don't be a goon! he snapped at himself. You'll be okay. Your suit's working fine and Mitsuo's up there by now, taking off the harness and getting ready to send it down to you.

Yeah, sure. He could be unconscious, he could be snagged on a rock or maybe the damned harness broke while the winch was dragging him up the slope. Or the winch pulled loose and he'll come tumbling back down on top of me, winch and all.

The image of the two of them knocked off the ledge and plunging into the black endless pit of hell curdled his blood.

No fear! Rodriguez told himself. No fear. He put a gloved hand against the solid rock to steady himself. You'll be out of this soon, he repeated silently. Then he wondered if his lamp's light was weakening. Are the batteries starting to run down?

Fuchida's head was banging against the inside of his helmet so hard he tasted blood in his mouth. He squeezed his eyes shut and saw his father's stern, uncompromising glare. How disappointed he will be when he learns that I died on Mars, like Cousin Konoye.

And Elizabeth. Perhaps it's better this way. She can go back to Ireland and find a man of her own culture to marry. My death will spare her a lifetime of troubles.

The winch stopped suddenly and Fuchida felt a pang of terror. It's stuck! He realized at that moment that he was not prepared for death. He did not want to die. Not here on Mars. Not at all.

A baleful red eye was staring at him. Fuchida thought for a moment he might be slipping into unconsciousness, then slowly realized that it was the light atop one of the geo/met beacons they had planted at the lip of the caldera.

Straining his eyes in the starlit darkness, he thought he could make out the form of the winch looming above his exhausted body. He reached out and touched it.

Yes! He had reached the top. But he felt faint, giddy. His body was soaked with perspiration. Heat prostration, he thought. How funny to die of heat prostration when the temperature outside my suit is nearly two hundred degrees below zero.

He began to laugh, knowing he was slipping into hysteria and unable to stop himself. Until he began coughing uncontrollably.

Down on the ledge, Rodriguez tried to keep his own terrors at bay. "Mitsuo," he called on the suit-to-suit frequency. "You okay?"

No answer. Of course, dummy! His radio's not working.

The cold seemed to be leaching into his suit. Cold enough to freeze carbon dioxide. Cold enough to overpower the suit's heater. Cold enough to kill.

It was imagination, he knew. You're more likely to broil inside the suit, like Mitsuo, than freeze.

"Get up there, Mitsy," he whispered. "Get up there in one piece and send the damned tether back down to me."

He wouldn't leave me here. Not if he made it to the top. He wouldn't run for the plane and leave me here. He can't run, anyway. Can't even walk. But he could make it to the plane once he's up there. Hobble, jump on one leg. Crawl, even. He wouldn't do that. He wouldn't leave me alone to die down here. Something must've happened to him. He must be hurt or unconscious.

The memory of his big brother's death came flooding back to him. In a sudden rush he saw Luis' bloody mangled body as the rescue workers lifted him out of the wrecked semi. A police chase on the freeway. All those years his brother had been running drugs up from Tijuana in his eighteen-wheeler and Tomas never knew, never even suspected. There was nothing he could do. By the time he saw Luis' rig sprawled along the highway median it was already too late.

He saw himself standing, impotent, inert, as his brother was pronounced dead and then slid into the waiting ambulance and carried away. Just like that. Death can strike like a lightning bolt.

What could I have done to save him? Rodriguez wondered for the thousandth time. I should have done something. But I was too busy being a flyboy, training to be an astronaut. I didn't have time for the family, for my own brother.

He took a deep, sighing breath of canned air. Well, now it's going to even out. I got all the way to Mars, and now I'm gonna die here.

Then he heard his brother's soft, musical voice. "No fear, muchacho. Never show fear. Not even to yourself."

Rodriguez felt no fear. Just a deep sadness that he could not help Luis when his help was needed. And now it was all going to end. All the regrets, all the hopes, everything . . .

For an instant he thought he saw a flash of dim red light against the rock wall. He blinked. Nothing. He looked up, but the top of his helmet cut off his view. Grasping at straws, he told himself. You want to see something bad enough, you'll see it, even if it isn't really there.

But the dim red glow flashed again, and this time when he blinked it didn't go away. Damned helmets! he raged. Can't see anything unless it's in front of your fuckin' face.

He tried to tilt his whole upper body back a little, urgently aware that it wouldn't take much to slip off this ledge and go toppling down into the bottomless caldera.

And there it was! The red glow of the beacon's light swayed far above him, like the unwinking eye of an all-seeing savior.

He leaned against the rock face again. His legs felt weak, rubbery. Shit, man, you were really scared.

He could make out the dangling form of the harness now, with the telescoped pole of the beacon attached to it by duct tape. Where the hell did Mitsuo get duct tape? he wondered. He must've been carrying it with him all along. The universal cure-all. We could do a commercial for the stuff when we get back to Earth. Save your life on Mars with frigging duct tape.

It seemed to take an hour for the tiny red light to get close enough to grab. With hands that trembled only slightly, Rodriguez reached up and grabbed the beacon, ripped it free and worked his arms into the climbing harness. Then he snapped its fasteners shut and gave the tether an experimental tug. It felt strong, good.

He started to reach for the control stud that would activate the winch. Then he caught himself. "Wait one," he whispered in the clipped tone of the professional flier.

He bent down and picked up the beacon. Sliding it open to its full length, he worked its pointed end into a crack in the basalt rock face. It probably won't stay in place for long, he thought, and it won't work at all unless the sun shines on it for a few hours per day. But he felt satisfied that he had left a reminder that men from Earth had been here, had entered the pit and gleaned at least some of its secrets and survived.

"Okay," he said to himself, grasping the tether with one hand. "Here we go."

He pushed on the control stud and was hauled off his feet. Grinding, twisting, grating he felt himself pulled up the rock slope, his head banging inside his helmet, his legs and booted feet bouncing as he was dragged upward.

Worse than any simulator ride he'd ever been through in training. Worse than the high-g centrifuge they'd whirled him in. They'll never put this ride into Disneyland, Rodriguez thought, teeth clacking as he bounced, jounced, jolted up to the lip of the caldera.

At last it was over. Rodriguez lay panting, breathless, aching. Fuchida's hard-suited form lay on the ground next to him, unmoving.

Rodriguez rolled over on one side, as far as his backpack would allow. Beyond Fuchida's dark silhouette the sky was filled with stars. Dazzling bright friendly stars gleaming down at him, like a thousand thousand jewels. Like heaven itself.

I made it, Rodriguez told himself. Then he corrected: Not yet. Can't say that yet.

He touched his helmet to Fuchida's. "Hey, Mitsuo! You okay?"

It was an inane question and he knew it. Fuchida made no response, but Rodriguez could hear the biologist's breathing: panting, really, shallow and fast.

Gotta get him to the plane. Can't do a thing for him out here.

As quickly as he could Rodriguez unbuckled the climbing harness, then tenderly lifted the unconscious Fuchida and struggled to his feet. *Good thing we're on Mars. I could never lift him in his suit in a full g. Now where the hell is the plane?*

In the distance he saw the single red eye of another one of the geo/met beacons they had planted. He headed in that direction, tenderly carrying his companion in his arms.

I couldn't do this for you, Luis, Rodriguez said silently. *I wish I could have, but this is the most I can do.*

MIDNIGHT: SOL 49/50

THE BASE DOME WAS DARK AND SILENT, ITS LIGHTING TURNED DOWN TO sleep shift level, its plastic skin opaqued to prevent heat from leaking out into the Martian night. Stacy Dezhurova was still sitting at the comm console, drowsing despite herself, when Rodriguez's call came through.

"We're back in the plane," the astronaut announced without preamble. "Lemme talk to Vijay."

"Vijay!" Stacy shouted in a voice that shattered the sleepy silence. "Jamie!" she added.

Running footsteps padded through the shadows, bare or stockinged feet against the plastic flooring. Vijay slipped into the chair beside Dezhurova, her jet-black eyes wide open and alert. Jamie and Trudy Hall raced in, bleary-eyed, and stood behind the two women.

"This is Vijay," she said. "What's your condition?"

In the display screen they could see only the two men's helmets and shoulders. Their faces were masked by the heavily tinted visors. But Rodriguez's voice sounded steady, firm.

"I'm okay. Banged up a little, but that's nothing. I purged Mitsuo's suit and plugged him into the plane's emergency air supply. But he's still out of it."

"How long ago did you do that?" Vijay asked, her dark face rigid with tension.

"Fifteen–sixteen minutes ago."

"And you're just calling in now?" Dezhurova demanded.

"I had to fix his battery pack," Rodriguez answered, unruffled by her tone. "It got disconnected when he was knocked down—"

"Knocked down?" Jamie blurted.

"Yeah. That's when he hurt his ankle."

"How badly is he hurt?" Vijay asked.

"It's sprained, at least. Maybe a break."

"He couldn't break a bone inside the suit," Jamie muttered. "Not with all that protection."

"Anyway," Rodriguez resumed, "his suit wasn't getting any power. I figured that getting his suit powered up was the second most important thing to do. Pumping fresh air into him was the first."

"And calling in, the third," Dezhurova said, much more mildly.

"Right," said Rodriguez.

"I'm getting his readouts," Vijay said, studying the medical diagnostic screen.

"Yeah, his suit's okay now that the battery's reconnected."

"Is his L.C.G. working?" Vijay asked.

"Should be," Rodriguez said. "Wait one . . ."

They saw the astronaut lean over and touch his helmet to the unconscious Fuchida's shoulder.

"Yep," he announced, after a moment. "I can hear the pump chugging. Water oughtta be circulating through his longjohns just fine."

"That should bring his temperature down," Vijay muttered, half to herself. "The problem is, he might be in shock from overheating."

"What do I do about that?" Rodriguez asked.

The physician shook her head. "Not much you can do, mate. Especially with the two of you sealed into your suits."

For a long moment they were all silent. Vijay stared at the medical screen. Fuchida's temperature was coming down. Heart rate slowing nicely. Breathing almost normal. He should be—

The biologist coughed and stirred. "What happened?" he asked weakly.

All four of the people at the comm center broke into grins. None of them could see Rodriguez's face behind his visor, but they heard the relief in his voice:

"Naw, Mitsuo; you're supposed to ask, 'Where am I?' "

The biologist sat up straighter. "Is Trudy there?"

"Don't worry about—"

"I'm right here, Mitsuo," said Trudy Hall, leaning in between Dezhurova and Vijay. "What is it?"

"Siderophiles!" Fuchida exclaimed. "Iron-eating bacteria live in the caldera."

"Did you get samples?"

"Yes, of course."

Jamie stepped back as the two biologists chattered together. Fuchida nearly gets himself killed, but what's important to him is finding a new kind of organism. With an inward smile, Jamie admitted, Maybe he's right.

BALLOONS

BEFORE THE EXPLORERS LANDED ON THE SURFACE OF MARS, WHILE THEY were still in orbit, goggling at the rusty worn immensity of the red planet, they released the balloons.

Six winecase-sized capsules retrofired from their orbiting supply vessel and blazed into the thin Martian atmosphere, then released a dozen balloons each. The balloons were brilliantly simple, little more than long narrow tubes of exquisitely thin yet tough Mylar inflated with hydrogen gas automatically when they reached the proper altitude to float across the landscape like improbable giant white cigarettes.

Dangling below each long, thin balloon was a "snake," a flexible slim metal pipe that contained sensing instruments, radio, batteries and a heater to protect the equipment against the frigid weather.

By day the balloons wafted high in the Martian atmosphere, sampling the temperature (low), pressure (lower), humidity (lower still) and chemical composition of the air. The altitude at which any individual balloon flew was governed by the amount of hydrogen filling its slender cigarette shape. The daytime winds carried them across the red landscape like dandelion puffs.

At night, when the temperatures became so frigid that even the hydrogen inside the balloons began to condense, they all sank toward the ground like a chorus of ballerinas tiredly drooping. Often, the "snakes" of instruments actually touched the ground and dutifully transmitted data on the surface conditions each night while the balloons bobbed in the dark winds, still buoyant enough to hover safely above the rock-strewn ground. Barely.

Similar balloons had been a major success during the First Mars Expedition, even though many of them eventually snagged on mountainsides or disappeared for reasons unknown. Most drifted gracefully across the face of Mars for weeks on end, descending slowly each night and rising again when the morning sunlight warmed their hydrogen-filled envelopes, carrying on silently, effortlessly, living with the Martian day/night cycle and faithfully reporting on the environment from pole to pole.

MORNING: SOL 50

JAMIE WAS NOT SURPRISED TO SEE HIS GRANDFATHER WAITING FOR HIM IN the cliff village.

He remembered climbing down from the rim of the Canyon, then slowly and deliberately taking off his hard suit once he had reached the niche in the cliff face. He felt warm and safe walking through the silent ruins in nothing more than his coveralls.

Grandfather Al was sitting on a wooden bench in the bright sunlight, leaning back against the adobe wall of one of the dwellings, his broad-brimmed hat pulled low over his eyes.

"Are you sleeping, Grandfather?" Jamie asked softly. He was nine years old again, and he couldn't tell if he were on Mars or back at the old pueblo where Al bargained for rugs and pottery to sell in his store in Santa Fe.

"Naw, I'm not sleeping, Jamie. I was waiting for you."

"I'm here."

Al looked at his grandson and smiled. "That's good."

Spreading his arms, Jamie asked, "Where is everybody? The village is empty."

"They've all gone."

"Gone where?"

"I don't know. Nobody knows. That's what you've got to find out, Grandson."

"But where could they have gone?"

"To find their destiny," said Al. "To find their own right path."

Jamie sat on the bench beside his grandfather. The sun felt warm and strengthening.

"Tell me about them, Grandfather. Tell me about the people who lived here."

Al laughed, a low, happy chuckle. "Naw. I can't tell you, Jamie boy. You have to tell me."

Jamie felt puzzled. "But I don't know."

"Then you'll have to find out, son."

Jamie's eyes popped open. For once, his dream did not fade from him. It was as vivid as any real memory.

He pushed back the thin sheet that covered him and got to his feet.

After the long night they had all put in, he should have felt tired, drained. Yet he was awake, alert, eager to start the day.

Quickly he stepped to his desk and booted up his laptop, then opened the communications channel to Rodriguez and Fuchida. With a glance at the desktop clock he saw that it was 6:33. He hesitated for only a moment, though, then put through a call to the two men at Olympus Mons.

As he suspected, they were both awake. Jamie's laptop screen showed the two of them side-by-side in the plane's cockpit.

"Good morning," he said. "Did you sleep well?"

"Extremely well," said Fuchida.

"This cockpit looked like the best hotel suite in the world when we got into it last night," Rodriguez said.

Jamie nodded. "Yeah, I guess it did."

Rodriguez gave a crisp, terse morning report. Fuchida happily praised the astronaut for purging his suit of the foul air and fixing the electrical connection that had banged loose in his backpack.

"My suit fans are buzzing faithfully," he said. "But I'm afraid I won't be able to do much useful work on my bad ankle."

They had discussed the ankle injury the previous night, once Fuchida had regained consciousness. Vijay guessed that it was a sprain, but wanted to get the biologist back to the dome as quickly as possible for an X-ray.

Jamie had decided to let Rodriguez carry out as much of their planned work as he could, alone, before returning. Their schedule called for another half day on the mountaintop, then a takeoff in the early afternoon for the flight back to dome. They should land at the base well before sunset.

"I'll be happy to take off this suit," Fuchida confessed.

"We're not gonna smell so good when we do," Rodriguez added.

Jamie found himself peering hard at the small screen of his laptop, trying to see past their visors. Impossible, of course. But they both sounded cheerful enough. The fears and dangers of the previous night were gone; daylight and the relative safety of the plane brightened their outlook.

Rodriguez said, "We've decided that I'm going back down inside the caldera and properly implant the beacon we left on the ledge there."

"So we can get good data from it," Fuchida added, as if he were afraid Jamie would countermand their decision.

Jamie asked, "Do you really think you should try that?"

"Oughtta be simple enough," Rodriguez said easily, "long as I don't go near that damned lava tube again."

"Is there enough sunlight where you want to plant the beacon?" Jamie asked.

He sensed the biologist nodding inside his helmet. "Oh yes, the ledge receives a few hours of sunlight each day."

"So we'll get data from inside the caldera," Rodriguez prompted.

"Not very far inside," Fuchida added, "but it will be better than no data at all."

"You're really set on doing this?"

"Yes," they both said. Jamie could feel their determination. It was their little victory over Olympus Mons, their way of telling themselves that they were not afraid of the giant volcano.

"Okay, then," Jamie said. "But be careful, now."

"We're always careful," said Fuchida.

"Most of the time," Rodriguez added, with a laugh.

"How's the weather report?" Craig asked.

"About the same," Dex Trumball replied, from up in the rover's cockpit. He was driving while Craig cleaned up their breakfast crumbs and folded the table back down into the floor between the bunks.

Craig came up and sat in the right-hand seat. The sun was just clear of the increasingly rugged eastern horizon.

"Want me to drive?" he asked.

"No way, Wiley. I'm going to break the interplanetary speed record today and get this baby up to thirty-five klicks per hour."

Craig made a snorting laugh. "You'll need a helluva tail wind for that, buddy."

"Nope, just some downhill slope."

"Lotsa luck."

"I'm not kidding, Wiley. The plain slopes downhill all the way to Xanthe."

"Shore," said Craig. "And if we had a good breeze behind us we could really make time."

Trumball glanced at him, then said, "Check the incoming messages, huh?"

There were two messages in the file, both from Stacy. The first one told them about Fuchida's accident and Rodriguez's rescue of him. And the biologist's discovery of the siderophiles. The two men listened to Hall's brief summary, then glanced at each other.

Craig let out a low whistle. "I wonder what Mitsuo's Jockey shorts look like."

Trumball laughed and shook his head. "I don't want to know."

Dezhurova's second message was a weather report. The dust storm was spreading, but still confined below the equator.

"As long as it stays in the southern hemisphere we're free and clear," Trumball said happily.

Craig was less cheerful. As he stared at the weather map on their screen he muttered, "It's growin', though. If it crosses the equator we're gonna be in trouble."

"Don't be a dweeb, Wiley. This vehicle's been through a dust storm before, y'know."

"Yeah, and I've jumped off a burning oil platform into th' Gulf of Mexico, too. Doesn't mean I wanna do it again."

Trumball's answer was to lean harder on the accelerator. Craig watched the speedometer edge up past thirty-one kilometers per hour. With a grim smile, he remembered an old prizefighter's maxim: You can run but you can't hide.

TARAWA

PETE CONNORS WAS OFF DUTY, ACTUALLY ENJOYING THE BEACH IN FRONT of the two-story condo where he was living, when the phone call came.

Since he was the chief of mission control for the Mars expedition, Connors carried a cellular phone wherever he went—not that you could get very far from the control center on the narrow islets of the atoll.

He was lying comfortably on an old blanket, his heels wedged into the soft white sand, listening to the rhythmic beat of the surf against the reef, when the little phone beeped. Even from inside the plastic beach bag it managed to sound urgent.

With a sigh of exasperation, Connors pulled himself up to a sitting position and groped in the bag for the phone. He had brought the video attachment, too, but decided not to bother with it unless he had to look at some data.

"Connors," he said crisply, as a gull swooped low across the beach, looking for leftovers.

"Dr. Li Chengdu here," came the Chinese academician's voice, as clear as if he were on the islet with him.

"Dr. Li! How are you?" Connors sat up straighter.

"My health is excellent. And you?"

"Couldn't be better," Connors said, ritually. The truth was he hadn't gotten enough sleep since the explorers had landed on Mars and it made him feel cranky much of the time.

"I want to apprise you of a possible problem," Li's voice said, flat and steady, no emotion in it.

"A problem?"

"Perhaps I am being overly pessimistic, but you were more friendly with Waterman than I was, and—"

"A problem with Jamie?" Connors felt startled.

"Not with him. About him."

"What do you mean?"

Li hesitated only a heartbeat. "As you know, I am on the advisory board of the International Consortium of Universities' committee for the Mars expedition."

"The ICU, yeah."

"I just received a call from the committee chairwoman, Professor Quentin, of Cambridge."

"I know who she is," Connors said, wondering when Li was going to get to the point.

"She, in turn, was called earlier by Mr. Trumball."

Oh, oh, thought Connors. The money man is sore about something.

"Mr. Trumball," Li went on, "is suggesting that Waterman be replaced as mission director."

"Replaced?" Connors snapped. "That's bullshi—er, hogwash."

"Trumball is very insistent, I fear."

"How the hell can they replace Jamie while the team's out there on Mars?"

This time Li's hesitation was more noticeable. "This could affect funding for the next expedition, of course."

"What the hell's Trumball pissed off about?" Connors demanded, forgetting his usual respect for the man who had been the mission director of the first expedition.

"That is not completely clear to me."

"Then what can we do about it?"

"I do not know yet. However, I thought that since you are Waterman's friend, you might want to apprise him of this situation. Prepare him, so to speak."

"Give him the bad news, you mean."

"No, no! His removal is not certain. In fact, I believe that most of the ICU committee favors keeping him in charge. I simply thought he should know what is happening here."

Connors nodded. "Right. I understand."

"Thank you," said Li. Then the connection went dead.

Connors sat there on the sand for a long while, thinking. The committee might want to keep Jamie, but if old Trumball makes enough of a rumpus, they'll dump Jamie just to keep the old bastard happy. If it comes down to a choice between Jamie and the money for the next expedition, they'll go for the money. They'll have to.

AFTERNOON: SOL 50

JAMIE SUITED UP AND WENT OUTSIDE TO WATCH THE SOARPLANE'S RETURN. No problems with the weather, he thought. Despite the dust storm spreading across the southern hemisphere, the sky here was clean and bright, perhaps a shade darker than its usual orange-tan hue, but clear and utterly cloudless. Not even a wisp of cirrus marred the soft tawny bowl overhead.

I should be inside analyzing the data from the beacons that Dex and Possum are setting up along their route, he told himself. Or finishing up the stratigraphy survey of the area around the base. The survey Dex was supposed to do.

A major inconsistency was growing out of their geological data, a problem that increasingly worried and annoyed the planetary scientists back on Earth. They all agreed that at one time Mars had been warmer and wetter than it was today. Once there had been an ocean girdling much of the northern hemisphere, or at least a broad shallow sea. But that had been hundreds of millions years ago, perhaps even billions of years in the past.

Yet the data that the explorers were producing clouded this picture. The geo/met beacons, the core samples that the drills brought up, the data from the drifting balloons all indicated that Mars today was warmer below its bleak surface sands than it had been thought to be. There was more heat flowing from the planet's interior than the geologists had expected. Considerably more.

Mars had been warm less than a hundred million years ago, relatively recently in geological terms. That broad shallow sea had flowed here much longer than anyone had thought possible, if their data were to be believed.

Scientists do not like to change their opinions any more than theologians or truckdrivers do, yet when the facts contradict their convictions they cannot hide from the facts or conveniently ignore them. The facts seemed to be telling them that Mars was warmer and wetter for much longer than they had thought possible. Much longer. It made no sense. It contradicted their carefully constructed theories about the red planet's past. Yet that is what the data from Mars indicated.

When in doubt, when the data and the theories do not agree, search for more data. The planetary scientists on Earth peppered the explorers with requests for more data, more facts, more information about Mars' history. Before they would even think about discarding their cherished theories about the red planet, they wanted, needed, demanded more data.

Jamie knew he should be bending every effort to fulfill the demands from Earth. The inconsistencies in the geological picture disturbed him as much as any scientist back on the blue world. Yet he was doing nothing, standing outside the dome straining his eyes for the first glimpse of the returning soarplane. And thinking about the cliff dwelling. I can't start out for the Canyon until Dex and Possum return, he told himself. I can't leave my responsibilities here and go chasing off on a search that isn't even in the mission schedule.

But he felt the call of that niche high up in the Canyon wall. He felt as if his ancestors were calling to him. Like the first time his grandfather had taken him to the abandoned village of the Old Ones, up at Mesa Verde.

"Your ancestors built their homes here a long time ago, Jamie," Grandfather Al had said.

"They weren't our ancestors," Jamie had replied, with all the righteous certainty of a twelve-year-old. "We're Navaho, they were Anasazi."

"They sure were our ancestors," Al had insisted. "Anasazi means the Old Ones."

Young Jamie had shaken his head stubbornly. "Our people came here after they were gone, Grandpop. I read it in one of the books you gave me."

Al had laughed gently and muttered, "Ahh, book writers. What do they know?"

Maybe Al's right, Jamie thought. Maybe we're all related, all of us, even here on Mars.

Then a flash of movement in the darkening sky caught his eye. A glint of sunlight, nothing more. Jamie searched the coppery bowl overhead, saw nothing.

Another flash, and this time his eye held it. The plane took form as it circled lazily high up in the sky. Jamie did not take his eyes off it, for fear of losing sight of it again. Automatically he touched the keypad on his wrist to tune in on the communications frequency.

"Setting up for the approach leg," Rodriguez's voice was saying, calm, professional.

"Approach leg, copy," said Stacy Dezhurova, equally flat and businesslike.

Jamie listened and watched the plane take shape high in the butterscotch sky while, far off in the back of his mind, he thrilled at the wonder of standing on Mars as two explorers returned to their base after a mission to the tallest mountain in the solar system.

*   *   *

Rodriguez insisted that everyone stay clear of them as he and Fuchida got out of their suits.

"I don't want any stink jokes," the astronaut insisted.

Jamie had allowed them to go directly into the dome without unloading the plane, the biologist leaning heavily on Rodriguez, using him as a crutch. Stacy Dezhurova came out to help Jamie carry Fuchida's sample cases back to the dome's airlock while the two men took off their hard suits and headed straight to the showers. Only afterward would Fuchida permit Vijay to examine his ankle.

The first thing Jamie and Dezhurova did was to tie the plane down properly. Although the Martian atmosphere was so thin that even a stiff breeze would not lift the gossamer sailplane, with a mammoth dust storm growing bigger every day they took no chances and made certain the plane was anchored properly.

After carrying Fuchida's sample cases to the dome's airlock, Stacy said, "I should check out the plane, make certain all its systems are shut down properly."

"Okay," said Jamie. "I'll take Mitsuo's cases inside."

Trudy Hall was waiting eagerly for Fuchida's samples just inside the airlock hatch. She hustled them back to the biology lab while Jamie began to take off his hard suit.

Vijay came to the locker area as Jamie lifted off his helmet.

"How's Mitsuo's ankle?" he asked.

"Badly sprained, but there's no fracture, not even a hairline."

"Good," Jamie said, pulling off his gloves.

She watched him in silence for a moment, then her lips curled into an impish little smile. "Need help undressing?" she asked.

Jamie felt his brows knit. She had a way of embarrassing him that was, well . . . embarrassing.

"I'm not going to attack you, Jamie," she said softly as she helped him lift the hard shell of the suit's torso over his head.

"Too bad," he heard himself mutter.

"You're actually developing a sense of humor!"

"With a little help from my friends."

"There's hope for you yet, mate."

He sat on the bench and leaned over to unfasten his boots. Vijay started to kneel at his feet to help, but he waved her off.

"Too provocative," he said. "I'd never get these leggings off."

Her eyes went wide for a moment, then she burst into laughter. Jamie grinned back at her, then began to laugh himself.

"It's definitely a different species!" Trudy Hall was bubbling with happiness. Even Fuchida had allowed a wide toothy grin to split his usual deadpan.

"*Ares olympicus*," he said. "That's what we've decided to name them."

The six explorers were sitting around the galley table over their dinner trays. As soon as they had come out of the biology lab, Fuchida and Hall had announced that Mitsuo's rock samples from Olympus Mons contained colonies of bacteria similar to, but significantly different from, the bacteria that Craig's deep drill had pulled up from just outside their dome.

"Why not name it after the discoverer?" Stacy Dezhurova asked. "Isn't that the usual thing?"

Fuchida bowed his head slightly. Hall explained, "Brumado and Malater set the precedent with *Ares marineris*, the lichen they discovered at the Canyon floor."

"Yeah, but the Canyon's named after the Mariner spacecraft that discovered it," Rodriguez pointed out.

"Tommy's disappointed that we didn't name the lichen after him," Hall teased.

Rodriguez's swarthy face went a little darker.

"Seriously, though," the English biologist went on, "I think it's a good idea to name the new species we find after the locations where they were discovered, rather than the names of the discoverers."

"Especially since you didn't make the discovery," Vijay teased.

Hall hissed at her.

After dinner Jamie went to his quarters and, as usual, booted up his computer to scan the incoming mail. Mostly the usual stuff, including another query from the chair of the geology committee for the stratigraphy analysis Dex had been scheduled to do. There was also a personal message from Pete Connors.

Wondering what the ex-astronaut wanted, Jamie went through the routine stuff, then pulled up Connors' dark, melancholy face on his laptop screen.

"Got some unsettling news for you, buddy," Connors said, without preamble. "According to Dr. Li, old man Trumball's on the warpath, trying to get rid of you as mission director. Li's afraid the funding for the next expedition will be jeopardized if the ICU doesn't do what he wants. Not much you can do about this, I know, but Li thought you ought to know, and I agree with him. Sorry to lay this load of shit on you, Jamie, but I think it's better that you know about it than have it hit you as a surprise."

Jamie sat back in his squeaking little desk chair and for a long time did nothing but stare at Connors' image, frozen on the laptop screen. *Pete doesn't look worried,* he thought. *More angry than anything else.*

What do I feel? Jamie asked himself. *Numb,* was the answer. *Not angry, not worried, not even resentful. Nothing. No emotional reaction* at all. It was all so far away, a hundred million kilometers from anything he could touch or taste or smell. More than a hundred million kilometers.

So the elder Trumball's dissatisfied with me. Most likely it's over letting Dex go out on his excursion. If they get caught in a dust storm, the old man will go ballistic.

So what? Jamie thought. So he takes my title away from me. What difference will that make? He's thinking like a white man, thinking that my title is what makes me tick. He hasn't the faintest idea of how things work out here. The title isn't important; it means almost nothing. We're working like a family now, a band of brothers and sisters out in the wilderness, depending on each other, not some job description somebody wrote in an office back on Earth.

He shut down the computer, then pulled himself to his feet and headed out toward the galley. A good cup of coffee and then a good night's sleep.

Maybe I should check in with Dex and Possum before I turn in. He decided against it. Their evening report had shown nothing to worry about. The fuel cells were still flat but that was nothing new. The rover was trundling along well enough; they were making good time, in fact.

As long as the storm stays below the equator they'll be okay.

Vijay and Trudy Hall were sitting at the dining table, heads together as if they were sharing some secret—or gossip. Their conversation stopped abruptly when they noticed Jamie approaching.

The coffee urn was almost empty. Jamie got half a cup of lukewarm decaf out of it, then the red warning light started blinking.

"The rule is," Vijay reminded him from her seat at the table, "that whoever gets the last cup has to clean the urn."

"I know," Jamie said ruefully. "I've gotten stuck with it often enough."

Trudy excused herself and left for her quarters. Vijay got up and came alongside Jamie as he rinsed the stainless steel urn in the sink and then opened the dishwasher. It was still filled with the dinnerware.

"I'll empty it," Vijay volunteered. "You drink your java before it cools off."

"It's not all that hot to start with," Jamie muttered.

As she pulled plastic plates from the dishwasher, Vijay asked casually, "So how's it going, mate?"

"Oh, fine. Old man Trumball wants to fire me, but otherwise everything is swell."

"What?"

He told her about the news from Earth. Vijay's usual jaunty expression darkened as he explained what the elder Trumball was doing.

"He can't do that," she said when he finished.

"Maybe he can."

"We won't let him. We won't accept it."

Jamie bent down to scoop the forks and spoons out of their rack. Straightening, he said, "It really doesn't matter."

"Doesn't matter? Don't you want—"

He touched a fingertip to her lips, silencing her. "I don't care what my title is, Vijay. We're here and we're doing what we came for. Old man Trumball can rearrange the organization charts all he wants to, it won't make any difference here."

"But he'll want to put Dex in charge!"

"So what?"

"Don't you care?"

"Not much. In fact, if somebody else takes over the director's responsibilities, it'll free me up to go out to the Canyon and have a good, long look at the village."

"If the new director allows it," she said.

"How's he going to stop me?"

Her eyes went wide. She stared at Jamie for a long moment, then broke into a slow smile. Jamie stood silently before her, basking in the warmth of it.

"That's better," Vijay said at last. "I thought you were just going to lay down and let them walk over you."

"Not very likely," he said. "I'm an alpha male, remember? We alpha males don't let anybody walk over us."

He reached out his hand toward her and she took it in hers and together they walked back to Jamie's quarters.

MORNING: SOL 56

"BY GOLLY, THERE SHE IS!"

Wiley Craig pointed with his right hand while keeping his left on the steering wheel.

Dex Trumball squinted into the bright morning sun. Off on the rough, crimson horizon he saw a tall metal shape, gleaming and alien-looking in the Martian landscape.

The rover was plunging at top speed across a field of rocks, its spindly, springy wheels jouncing and rattling them so hard they had both strapped themselves into the cockpit seats.

"We've drifted too far north, Wiley," said Trumball. "It's going to cost us a half a day to get to her."

Craig's bristly, bearded face was split by a big, gap-toothed grin. "Don't care how far away she is; she shore looks purty, don't she?"

Dex nodded and admitted, "Yeah, she sure does."

The dust storm in the southern hemisphere had petered out at last, according to the previous night's weather report. Craig had expressed great relief. Trumball, equally grateful that the storm would not hit them, played it much cooler.

"Even if it had crossed the equator, we could've ridden it out."

"I don't know, Dex," Craig had said soberly. "Some of those storms last for weeks."

"Not this time of year."

"Uh-huh. And it never rains in California."

Trumball got up and staggered back toward the equipment racks near the airlock, lurching from one handhold to another, while Craig steered the rover through the rock field and onto smoother, slightly higher ground. The generator took shape before his eyes, a tall polished aluminum cylinder catching the glint of the morning sun, resting on three slim-looking metal legs, the nozzles of three rocket engines hanging beneath the vehicle's end skirt.

"Come on," Dex called from the rear of the rover module, "goose her up a little more. Let's make as much time as we can."

"Let's not throw a wheel, either," Craig countered. "Another half-hour ain't gonna kill us."

Trumball grumbled to himself as he checked out the video monitoring equipment. The outside cameras were recording everything; not only would the views be a bonanza for geologists studying Mars, they would be great background material for the virtual reality tours that Dex would beam Earthward.

By the time Craig pulled the rover to a stop next to the generator Dex was suited up and already stepping into the airlock.

"You just wait a minute there, buddy," Craig called to him. "You're not goin' outside without being checked out."

"Aw, come on, Wiley. I went through the checklist myself. Don't chickenshit me."

But Craig would not be put off. He checked Trumball's suit quickly but thoroughly, then pronounced him ready to go outside.

"I'll holler when I'm suited up and you come back in and check me over."

"Yeah, yeah."

The generator was chugging away, sucking up water from the line it had drilled down to the permafrost level under Craig's remote guidance, pulling in the thin Martian air and separating its components automatically.

By the time Craig came through the airlock hatch and stepped onto the rusty ground, Trumball had ascertained that the methane and water tanks were both filled almost to capacity.

"Okay, great," Wiley said. "Now we gotta fill our tanks."

It took more than an hour. While Craig handled the hoses and watched the gauges, Dex beamed a VR session back to Tarawa: the intrepid explorers hacking their way through the Martian wilderness have made their rendezvous with the refueling generator. On to Pathfinder!

Once they climbed back inside the rover, Dex scrambled quickly out of his suit and made his way to the cockpit. A brief scan of the control panel showed everything in the green, except for the glowering red light of the fuel cells. We'll get that into the green, too, he told himself. Soon as Wiley electrolyzes enough of our water to feed 'em.

By sundown they were well on their way toward Ares Vallis, the generator below their horizon and out of sight. Dex was still driving, Craig in back tinkering with the fuel cells.

"How're they holding?" Trumball called over his shoulder.

Craig's exasperated sigh was audible even from the rear of the module. "Leakproof welds my hairy butt," he groused.

"What's the matter?"

"These damn dewars are supposed to hold liquid hydrogen," Craig said, kicking a booted toe on the stainless-steel cylinder on the rover floor.

"Yeah?"

"Well, the damned welds on 'em leak like a sieve that's been shotgunned."

"They're still leaking?"

"Does the pope eat spaghetti?"

"How bad?"

Craig clumped up toward the cockpit and slid into the right-hand seat. "I gotta do some calculations. It ain't good, though, I can tell you that without a computer."

Trumball saw that Craig was more disgruntled than worried. We can get along without the fuel cells, he thought. Hell, we've been getting along without 'em for a week now. Still, it'd be good to get that damned red light off the board.

"The newest fuel cells back on Earth use nanotube filaments to store the hydrogen," Craig was muttering. "Nanotubes *work*, pardner. They soak up molecular hydrogen like a sponge and hold onto it like a vise. But all we got is these leaky damned dewars."

The sun was nearing the horizon, Dex saw. A thin patch of cloud high above was already reflecting brilliant red highlights.

"We're going to have a beautiful sunset, Wiley."

Craig looked up from the panel's computer display. "Yep. A purty one. Reminds me of Houston. We used to get some bee-yootiful sunsets there, thanks to all the industrial waste the refineries poured into the air."

Trumball laughed. "No factories out here."

"No, but . . ." Craig's voice petered off into thoughtful silence.

"What's the matter, Wiley?"

"Those clouds."

At that instant the communications chime sounded. Trumball tapped the ON button and Stacy Dezhurova's somber face appeared on the panel screen.

"Latest weather report," she said, looking worried. "New dust storm has started, this time in the northern hemisphere."

"Where?" Trumball asked.

"Exactly where you are heading," came her reply.

EVENING: SOL 56

JAMIE STARED AT THE WEATHER MAP ON THE SCREEN. HE HAD SUPERIM-posed the position of Trumball and Craig's rover, and the route they had to follow to reach the Pathfinder.

The storm's going to roll right over them, he saw.

"What do you want to do?" Stacy Dezhurova asked from her chair at the comm console.

Jamie looked at her. She looked concerned.

"They're more than halfway to the Pathfinder site," he said, thinking aloud. "If I tell them to turn around and head back to the generator, the storm will overtake them anyway."

"So you think they should just keep on going?"

"The storm's heading east to west; they're going west to east. They could drive through it."

"Assuming they can drive when the storm hits them."

"If not, they'll have to sit still until it passes them."

Dezhurova nodded, her normally gloomy face positively morose.

"If only we could predict how big the storm's going to get," Jamie muttered. "Damn! We've been studying Martian weather for more than twenty years now and we still can't make a decent forecast."

Stacy made a weak grin. "They have been studying terrestrial weather for almost two centuries and the meteorologists still can't make a decent forecast on Earth, Jamie."

"It might not be as bad as it looks," he said, remembering the storm he had endured. "If they button up tight, they'll be all right."

"But what if the storm grows? The big ones take weeks to clear up . . . months."

With a grimace, Jamie said, "This one doesn't look that bad. So far."

Dezhurova countered, "The one in the southern hemisphere hung in for a solid week."

"I know," he admitted, staring again at the weather map, as if he could force it to reveal its secrets if he scowled at it hard enough.

Dezhurova fell silent, letting Jamie work out his thoughts for himself. At last he got to his feet and said, "We'll thrash it out over dinner. Let everybody chip in their ideas."

Their ideas were almost nonexistent. They talked the situation over through dinner, mulling through one possibility after another. It all boiled down to a choice between letting Craig and Trumball continue into the storm or ordering them to turn back to the generator and allowing the storm to catch up with them.

"They're way too far out to get back here before the storm overtakes them," said Rodriguez. "They're gonna get caught in it, one way or the other."

"Dex won't want to turn around," Vijay said, with firm certainty. "He'll want to push ahead, no matter what."

"If only we knew how big the storm will grow," Trudy Hall said. "We're trying to make a decision rather in the blind, aren't we?"

"The storm will grow," Fuchida predicted. "It might even reach us here."

"Here?" Trudy looked suddenly alarmed.

"It's a strong possibility," said Fuchida. He was sitting with his bad leg propped on an empty chair, the ankle wrapped tightly with an elastic bandage.

"Are you a meteorologist, too?" Stacy asked the Japanese biologist, straight-faced.

"Yes, I am," Fuchida replied with dignity. Then he added, "When I call up the meteorology program on my laptop."

Rodriguez pointed out, "The biggest problem is the solar cells. If the dust covers them, the rover loses its primary power source."

"So they go to the batteries," Hall said.

"For how long? Their fuel cells aren't working right, remember? Their backup power system isn't reliable."

Trudy looked surprised. "I had forgotten that."

"They can't sit in the dark for more than forty-eight hours—fifty, tops," Rodriguez said.

"They can stretch it if they power down," said Jamie.

"How far? They got to keep the heaters going, and that's what takes up most of the juice."

Stacy Dezhurova said, "If they go back to the generator they can refill the fuel cells as much as they need to."

"That's right," Jamie said, pushing himself up from the table. "But my instinct is to let them continue ahead; it's the shortest path out of the storm."

"Unless the storm grows much larger and stronger," Hall said.

"If it grows that much they're in trouble no matter what they do."

"And the dust might damage the solar cells," Rodriguez added gloomily. "Degrade them to the point where they can't provide enough power to run the rover even after the storm's over."

"Now that's a cheerful thought," Hall said.

The others nodded glum agreement.

Jamie went to the comm center again and sat at the main console. All the others crowded in behind him. As he called to the rover, Jamie felt the heat and tension in the little cubicle. Too many bodies pressed together. Too many fears building up.

Mars is a gentle world, he reminded himself as he waited for the rover to reply. It doesn't want to harm us.

No, the other side of his mind replied. Not unless you do something stupid, like get caught in a dust storm three thousand klicks from home.

Craig's scruffy face filled the screen. From what Jamie could see, he was still driving the rover through the lengthening shadows of nightfall.

Jamie went through the situation and the two possible courses of action with Craig. Then he asked, "Possum, what do you think? Which way do you want to go?"

Before Craig could answer, Dex Trumball pivoted the camera to himself and said, "We're pushing on! No sense turning tail."

Patiently, Jamie said, "Dex, I asked Possum, not you. He's in charge."

"Wiley and I agree," Trumball insisted. "We want to keep on going and get the hell out of this storm. Turning back would be a waste of time."

"It might be the safer course to take," Jamie said. "You could make it back to the generator before the storm overtook you, and ride it out there, where you're assured of fuel, water and oxygen."

"We're going forward," Trumball snapped.

"Possum, what do you have to say about it?" Jamie asked again.

The camera view swivelled back to Craig's jowly face. "First off, I'd rather be called Wiley than Possum. Second, I agree with Dex: let's push ahead and get through this blow."

Jamie sat digesting that for a few silent moments. He could feel the others stirring nervously behind him.

"You're sure?" he said, stalling for time to think.

"Yep," Craig replied.

It would be safer for them to camp by the generator, Jamie told himself. But if the storm lasts for a week or more they'll run out of food and have to start back. Without getting the Pathfinder hardware. Their whole trek would be for nothing. That's what's eating at Dex. To go all the way out there and return empty-handed. That's what's fueling his fire.

On the other hand, he thought, what if they get killed out there? Is the hardware so important that I should let them risk their lives over it?

Trumball swung the camera back to his own face. His ragged dark beard made him look truculent, belligerent, as if he were daring Jamie to contradict him.

"Well?" he demanded. "What are your orders, chief?" The sarcastic stress he laid on the word *orders* was obvious.

"Keep on going," Jamie heard himself say. "And good luck."

Trumball looked surprised.

Vijay followed Jamie into his cubicle when they all filed out of the comm center. What the hell, Jamie thought. If the others didn't realize we've been sleeping together, they know it now.

Later, cupped against one another in the narrow bunk, she whispered to him, "You did the right thing, Jamie."

"Did I?"

"Dex wouldn't have obeyed an order to turn around. He would have defied you openly."

Jamie sighed in the darkness. "Yes, I suppose he would have."

"It was smart to avoid an open conflict."

"Maybe."

"You don't think so?"

"It's not important," he said.

"But it is!" She propped herself on one elbow and looked down at him. "Your authority shouldn't be challenged."

"That doesn't worry me, Vijay."

"It doesn't? Then what does?"

He gazed up at her lovely face, outlined in the faint glow from the digital clock. So beautiful, so serious, so concerned about him.

"What bothers me is that I *want* Dex to be away from here. Away from you. Away from us."

MORNING: SOL 58

Dex was driving the rover with single-minded concentration through a field of rocks big enough to stop army tanks, steering between the minivan-sized boulders while his geologist's mind begged to go outside and see what they were made of. No time for that, Dex told himself, glancing up at the darkening sky. We'll do the science on the way back.

Craig was peering at the readouts on the display screen. The wind was up to eighty-five knots: hurricane speed on Earth yet only a zephyr in the rarified atmosphere of Mars. But the wind speed was increasing, and off on the horizon before them an ominous dark cloud hung low over the land.

"How're the fuel cells doing?" Dex asked, without taking his eyes from his steering.

Craig tapped a few keys on the control panel. "Down to sixty-three percent."

"Might as well use them as soon as the solar cells crap out," Trumball said, through gritted teeth. "Save the batteries."

"Use 'em or lose 'em," Craig agreed. "Get some work outta them before they fade to zero."

It took a conscious effort for Dex to unlock his jaws. He had clamped his teeth together so hard it was giving him a headache. If it wasn't so scary it'd be funny, he told himself. I'm steering this buggy like a kid in a video game, trying to get through this frigging rock field and out into the open before the storm hits us.

"Any new data on the storm?" he asked.

Craig tapped more keys, stared at the display screen a moment, then sighed mightily. "She's gettin' bigger."

"Great."

We should have gone back to the generator, Dex admitted silently. Jamie should've *ordered* us to go back. Wiley should've insisted on it. This isn't a game; that storm could kill us, for chrissakes.

"Want me to drive?" Craig asked gently.

Dex glanced at the older man. "Wiley, if I wasn't driving I'd be biting my fingernails up to the elbows."

Craig laughed. "Hell, this isn't all that bad, Dex. Lemme tell you about the time a hurricane hit us while we were tryin' to cap a big leak on an oil platform in the Gulf of Mexico. Right near Biloxi it was . . .''

Dex listened with only half his attention, but he was glad that Craig was trying to ease his tension. It wasn't working, of course, but he was grateful that Wiley was at least trying.

"A dust storm, you say?"

Darryl C. Trumball felt a pang of alarm as he glared at the wall screen. Unconsciously he ran a nervous hand over his shaved scalp. It was already dark at four in the afternoon in Boston; out beyond his office windows he could see the Christmas lights strung along the trees of the Common and the Public Garden.

"Yessir," answered Pete Connors' image on the wall screen, his dark face set in an expression that was totally serious, even grim.

"And my son's driving into it?"

"As a matter of fact, Mr. Trumball, your son insisted on driving into it. Jamie suggested that he turn back to . . ."

"Suggested?" Trumball snapped. "By god, he's supposed to be running things up there! What do you mean, suggested? He should've *ordered* Dex to turn back!" He thumped his desktop for emphasis.

Connors seemed to think about that for a moment. "Mr. Trumball," he said at last, "your son doesn't take to following orders very well. Jamie could have stood on his head and I doubt that Dex would have listened to him."

"That's nonsense!" Trumball spluttered. "My son's a team player. He knows how to follow *my* orders, by damn! This redskinned idiot you've got up there just isn't fit to direct a team of prairie dogs, let alone the finest scientists in the world."

"Jamie Waterman is one of the best men I've ever been privileged to meet," Connors rebutted without an eye-blink's hesitation. "You couldn't ask for a better man to run the expedition."

Trumball glowered at the image on the wall screen.

"The storm was totally unexpected," Connors went on, more conciliatory. "It's a big one, but we've seen bigger in the past. We have every confidence that your son and Dr. Craig will be able to ride it out without harm."

"They'd better," Trumball said, reaching for one of the ornate pens he kept on the desk.

"They will, I'm sure. I was in a dust storm with Jamie during the first expedition. We made it through without any real problems."

"If anything happens to my son, I'll hold that man personally responsible. Do you understand? *Personally* responsible. I'll pin his balls to the nearest tree!"

Connors seemed to silently count to ten before he answered, "You'll have to go through me to do that, Mr. Trumball. Me, and a whole lot of other people who have complete confidence in Jamie.''

Exasperated, Trumball banged a fist on his desktop phone console. Connors' smoldering image winked out.

"I'll get you," the old man grumbled aloud. "You and Waterman and anybody else who gets in my way.''

He commanded the phone's voice-recognition system to get Walter Laurence on the line. It's time to pull the plug on this Indian. Don't wait until Dex gets hurt, that'd make it look too personal. Nail his ass to the wall *now*.

"It's definitely going to reach your base camp," said the meteorologist. "At its present rate of growth and forward speed, the storm will overrun your area in two days—er, that's two Martian days, sols.''

Jamie and Stacy Dezhurova watched the report in the comm center. The meteorologist appeared to be in Florida, perhaps Miami. Jamie could see palm trees and high-rise condos through the man's office window, behind his youthful but intently serious face.

The young meteorologist went on to give all the data he could present: maximum wind speeds would be above two hundred knots; the storm's forward progress was a steady thirty-five knots; height of the clouds; dust burden; opacity. Many of the numbers were estimates or averages.

"We must make certain all the planes are tied down really tight," Stacy muttered as the meteorologist droned on.

Jamie nodded. "And the generator, too." He knew, in the calculating side of his brain, that even a two-hundred-knot wind on Mars did not have the momentum to knock down the tall cylinder that housed the fuel and water generator when its tanks were full. The Martian atmosphere was so thin that there was little punch to its winds. Yet the other side of his mind pictured the generator toppling, blown over like a big tree in a hurricane.

Dezhurova nodded. "We must get on it right away.''

"Tomas and I will do the outside work," Jamie said once the meteorologist finished his report. "You see that everything in here is buttoned up and everybody's ready for a blow.''

He slid his wheeled chair to the screen where the meteorologist's frozen image stared out at them, face lined with concern, and punched the transmit key.

"Dr. Kaderly, thanks for your report. It helps a lot. Please keep us updated and let us know immediately if there's any change in the storm's progress.''

Then he turned back to Stacy, sitting beside him. "Send Kaderly's report to Poss . . . I mean, to Wiley Craig and Dex. Then get the others started getting ready for the storm.''

"Right, chief."

Jamie got up and headed for the airlock and the hard suits waiting by the lockers there. Somehow he didn't mind it when Stacy called him chief. There was no mockery in her tone.

As he began pulling on the rust-stained leggings of his hard suit, Jamie thought about Dex and Craig out there between Xanthe and Ares Vallis. They're going to be caught in the storm for two sols, at least. Without a backup electrical system. The batteries ought to see them through okay, if they power down to a minimum. That means they're going to have to stop and sit there until the storm blows past them.

They'll be okay. If they just keep their cool and wait it out, they'll get through the storm all right.

If the dust doesn't damage their solar panels.

AFTERNOON: SOL 58

"WHAT DO YOU THINK, WILEY?" ASKED DEX TRUMBALL AS SOON AS THE meteorologist's detailed report ended.

Craig was driving the rover at a steady thirty klicks per hour. "How the hell fast is one knot? I always get confused."

Sitting in the right seat, staring out at the darkening horizon in front of them, Dex said, "It's one nautical mile per hour."

"What's that in real miles?"

"Does it make that much difference?"

Craig hunched his shoulders. "Naw, I guess not."

"It's about one point fifteen statute miles."

"Fifteen percent longer'n a regular mile?"

"That's right." Trumball was starting to feel exasperated. What difference did fifteen percent make? They were driving straight into a dust storm. A big one.

"So it'll take about two sols for the storm to pass over us."

"If we're sitting still, yes."

Craig glanced over at Dex, then turned back to his driving. "You want to keep mushing ahead?"

"Why not? As long as the solar cells are working, why not push ahead? Get the hell out of this mess as quick as we can."

"H'm." Craig seemed to think it over carefully. "Hell of it is, we got some nice smooth territory here. Pretty easy driving."

The land outside was not entirely free of rocks, but it was much more open and flat than the broken and boulder-strewn region of Xanthe they had been through. The ground was sloping downward gently, generally trending toward the lowlands of the Ares Vallis region.

"We're going to turn this route into a regular excursion for the tourists, Wiley," Dex said, mainly to take his mind off the ominous cloud spreading across the horizon before them.

"Build a road? Out here?"

"Won't need a road. We'll put up a cable-car system, like they're doing on the Moon. Just put up poles every hundred meters or so and string a line between 'em. The cars hang from the line and zip along, whoosh!" Dex made a swooping motion with one hand.

Craig fell into the game. "The cable carries the electrical current to run the cars, huh?"

"Right," Dex said, trying not to look out at the horizon. "Cars can carry a couple dozen people. They're sealed like spacecraft, carry their own air, heat, just like this rover."

"Only they skim over th' ground," Craig said.

"They'll be able to go a lot faster that way. A hundred klicks an hour, maybe."

Without taking his eyes from his driving, Craig said softly, "Wish we had one of 'em now."

Dex stared out the windshield. It was starting to get dark out there. The mammoth cloud of dust was coming toward them like a vast Mongol horde of conquerors. Soon it would engulf them entirely and they would be lost in the dark.

He shivered involuntarily.

Jamie was outside with Rodriguez, adding extra tie-down lines to the planes, when the call from Connors came through.

Inside his hard suit, he could not see the former astronaut, only hear his caramel-rich baritone voice. Connors sounded concerned, worried.

"He's on the warpath, Jamie. I just heard about it from Dr. Li. Old man Trumball called him and raised hell about you. He's calling everybody on the ICU board. God knows who else he's bitching to."

Jamie had asked that Connors' call be put on the personal frequency, so that he could listen to the man in privacy.

"I don't need this," he muttered as he tugged at the line that held the soarplane's wingtip to one of the bolts they had sunk into the ground.

Connors' voice went on, unhearing, more than a hundred million kilometers away. "I've talked to several of the board members myself. None of them really wants to remove you, but they're pretty scared of Trumball. He must be threatening to cut off funding for the next expedition."

Straightening in the hard suit was not an easy task. Jamie found himself puffing with exertion as he looked back toward the dome. Fuchida and Dezhurova were in the garden bubble, carefully checking its plastic skin for pinhole leaks or wrinkles where the wind might grab and tear the fabric apart.

Once the dust starts blowing, will the particles have enough force in them to penetrate the bubble's skin? he wondered. Not likely, but then the odds against the dome being hit by meteoroids were a zillion to one.

Connors was still droning on. "I had a long talk with Father DiNardo about it. He's a damned good politician, that Jesuit, you know that? He says you should sit tight and ignore the whole thing. It'll probably blow over as soon as the storm dissipates and Trumball realizes nothing's happened to his son."

Jamie nodded inside his helmet as he walked over to the soarplane's other wingtip and started tightening the lines already fastened there.

"DiNardo said," Connors continued, "that you shouldn't even think about resigning unless Trumball keeps up the pressure even after the storm blows out and it becomes clear that a majority of the board's going to go along with him."

"Resigning?" Jamie said aloud. "He thinks I should resign?"

Connors went on with his dolorous report, reminding Jamie several times more that he hated to bother him with this political maneuvering, but he thought Jamie ought to know about it.

Finally he said, "Well, that's the whole story, up to now. I'll wait for your answer. Be sure you mark it personal to me; that way nobody else'll look at it. At least, nobody else *should* look at it. I don't know how many people around here are reporting to Trumball on the sly."

Wonderful news, Jamie groaned silently.

"Well, okay, that's it, pal. I'll wait for your answer. 'Bye for now."

Off on the eastern horizon, Jamie saw, the sky was darkening. Or is it just my imagination? he asked himself. I'll check the instrumentation when I get back into the dome. The storm's going to hit here, but it's probably too early to see it yet. And now I've got another storm, a political storm, back on Earth.

The Navaho believe that clouds are the spirits of the dead, Jamie remembered. Will you come to visit me in a cloud, Grandfather? Or will it be the spirits from the Long Walk, come to take their vengeance on the whites who drove them off their land?

He shook his head to clear it of such irrational thoughts, then glanced down at the suit radio's keypad on his wrist. Jamie said carefully, "Personal message to Pete Connors at Tarawa. Pete, I got your message. We're battening down for the storm right now, so I don't have time to reply at length. I want to think about this before I answer you, anyway. Thanks for the news—I guess. I'll get back to you."

Damn, he thought as he stared out at the eastern horizon. It sure looks like it's clouding up out there. Maybe the storm's picked up speed. That'd be good; it'll roll over Dex and Craig and get them out into the clear sooner.

Starting back toward the dome's airlock, Jamie said to himself, Why is Trumball so clanked up? Why is he out to remove me as mission director? Prejudice? Just plain malice? Or is he the type that's not happy unless he's forcing other people to jump through his hoops?

Then Jamie heard his grandfather whisper, Put yourself in his shoes. Find what's bothering him.

Okay, Grandfather, he replied silently. What's bothering the old man?

His son is in danger, came the immediate reply. He's worried about Dex's safety. That's natural. That's good.

But Trumball knew that exploring Mars carried its risks. Maybe he never considered that his own son would have to face those risks, just like the rest of us.

He was all in favor of going after the Pathfinder hardware. But he didn't think his son would go on the excursion and place himself in danger. Now he knows differently and he's scared. He's sitting in an office in Boston and his son is out in the middle of a dust storm a hundred million kilometers away and there's nothing he can do about it.

Except get angry and vent his fury on the most convenient target he can find: the mission director who allowed his son to go out into danger. Me. He's pissed at me because he can't do anything else about the situation. He's scared and frustrated and trying to solve his problem the way he's solved problems before: fire the guy he's mad at.

Jamie took a deep breath and felt a calm warmth flow through him. He heard his grandfather's gentle laughter. "Never lose your temper with a customer," his grandfather had told him years ago, when Jamie had been a little boy angered by the pushy, demanding loud-mouthed tourists who yelled at Al in his shop. "Let 'em whoop and holler, it don't matter. Once they calm down, they're so ashamed of themselves that they buy twice what they started out to buy, just to show they're sorry."

Damn! Jamie said to himself as he trudged back to the airlock. It would be so satisfying to get sore at Trumball, to send him a blistering message telling him to mind his own damned business. So easy to taunt the old man from a hundred million kilometers' distance.

But I can't get angry at him, Jamie realized. I understand what he's going through. I understand him, and you can't hate a man you understand.

As he stepped into the airlock and swung its outer hatch shut, he reminded himself, But just because you understand him doesn't mean he can't hurt you. You understand a rattlesnake, too, but you don't let him bite you. Not if you can avoid it.

* * *

"That's all she wrote," said Craig.

He touched the brakes and brought the rover to a gentle stop.

"It's not even six o'clock yet, Wiley," Dex protested. "We can get in another hour or more."

Craig got up from the driver's seat. "I got an idea."

The sky was a dismal gray above them, getting darker by the minute. Dex could hear the wind now, a thin screeching sound like the wail of a distant banshee.

"I'll drive," he offered.

"Nope," said Craig, heading back toward the bunks. "You gotta know when to hold 'em and know when to fold 'em. We sit still now and get ready for the storm."

"It's not that bad yet," Dex insisted, turning in his seat to watch the older man. "We can push on a little more, at least."

Craig knelt down and pulled open a storage drawer beneath the bottom bunk. "The real danger from the storm's gonna be the damage the sand does to our solar panels, right?"

"Right," Dex answered, wondering what his partner was up to.

Craig pulled a set of sheets from the storage drawer. "So we cover the solar panels."

"Cover them? With bedsheets?"

"And anything else we got," Craig said. "Coveralls, plastic wrap, anything we got."

"But once they're covered, they'll stop producing electricity for us. We'll have to go onto the batteries."

Craig was emptying the drawer beneath the other bunk now. "Take a look at the instruments, buddy. It's gettin' mighty dark mighty quick. Those solar cells are already down to less'n thirty percent nominal, right?"

Dex glanced at the panel instruments. The solar panels' output hovered just above twenty-five percent of their maximum output.

"Right," he replied dismally.

"So don't just sit there," Craig called, almost jovially. "Get up and find the duct tape, for cryin' out loud."

Dex thought, This is just busywork. We won't be able to keep the panels covered once the storm hits. Wind speeds are going to go over two hundred knots, for chrissake. That'll rip off anything we try to cover the panels with.

But he pushed himself out of the chair, wormed his way past Craig, and started searching through the supply lockers, grateful for the chance to be doing something active instead of just sitting and watching the storm come up and smother them.

NIGHT: SOL 58

WILEY CRAIG RAN THE BEAM FROM HIS HAND LAMP ACROSS THE ROVER from nose to tail.

"Well . . . it ain't a thing of beauty," he said, "but it oughtta get the job done."

Standing beside him, Dex thought that the rover's top looked like a Christmas present wrapped by clumsy children. Bedsheets, plastic wrapping, a tarpaulin, even several sets of spare coveralls—sliced apart to cover more area—were spread over the solar panels and taped down heavily.

"Do you think they'll stay put once the wind starts up?" he asked.

Craig was silent for a moment, then said, "Oughtta. Wind must be purty near seventy knots already and they're not flappin'."

Dex could hear the wind keening outside his helmet, softly but steadily, becoming insistent. He thought he also heard something grating across his suit's outer skin, like fine grains of sand peppering him. He almost could feel the dust scratching against him.

It was fully dark now. Dex felt tired, physically weary, yet his insides were jumpy, jittery. In the light from Wiley's lamp he could see that the air was clear; no dust swirling. None that he could see. Yet there was that gritty rasping on the suit's hard shell.

"We could have driven another hour," he said to Craig.

"Maybe."

"Hell, Wiley, I've driven through snowstorms in New England." Despite his words, Dex's voice sounded quavery, even to himself.

"This ain't the Massachusetts Turnpike out here, buddy."

"So what do we do now? Just sit and bite our nails?"

"Nope. We're gonna collect all the data we can. Then we're gonna have dinner. Then we're gonna get a good night's sleep."

Dex stared at Craig's spacesuited figure. He doesn't sound worried at all. The goddamned fuel cells are leaking and the solar panels are shut down and we'll have to live off the batteries for god knows how long and he's as calm and unruffled as a guy riding out a blizzard in a first-class ski lodge.

"Okay, boss," Dex asked, trying to sound nonchalant, "what do you want me to do now?"

"You go inside and check the fuel cells, make sure all the comm systems are workin', and call back to the base, let 'em know we're buttoned up for the night.''

Dex nodded. The commsats in orbit will pinpoint our location. If anything happens to us, he thought, at least they'll know where to find the bodies.

Craig whistled tunelessly as he trudged back to the airlock for a met/geo beacon to plant outside the rover. Dex went back inside and started to take off his hard suit. He knew that he should stay suited up and be prepared to go outside in case Craig got into trouble. But he was too tired, too drained, too plain frightened even to think about that.

His eyes smarted briefly as he painstakingly vacuumed the dust off his suit. Ozone, from the superoxides in the soil, he knew. We could keep ourselves supplied with oxygen just by dumping some of the red dirt in here, he told himself.

Once out of the suit, he went up to the cockpit and stared out at the darkening landscape, feeling his insides fluttering. I'm scared, Dex said to himself. Like a kid afraid of the dark. Scared. Wiley's as calm as can be and I'm falling apart. Shit!

With nothing better to do, he checked the communications file for incoming messages. The usual garbage from the base, plenty of satellite data about the approaching storm. And a message marked personal for him.

Only one person in the solar system would be sending me a personal message, Dex thought. With a mixture of anger and relief he tapped the proper keys and saw his father's glowering skull-like face appear on the rover's control panel screen.

Just what I need, he thought. Comic relief from dear old Dad.

"Well," Jamie said to the five of them, "we're as ready for the storm as we can be."

"So are Possum and Dex," said Stacy Dezhurova.

"He wants to be called Wiley," Jamie reminded her.

Dezhurova sighed dramatically. "The male ego. Perhaps I should change my name, too."

They were sitting around the galley table, picking at their dinner trays. No one seemed to have much of an appetite, despite the hard labor they had put in getting ready for the storm.

Vijay asked lightly, "What name would you choose for yourself, Stacy?"

"Not Anastasia," Dezhurova answered quickly. "And not Nastasia, either. It's too . . . complicated."

"I think Anastasia's a pretty name," Rodriguez said. "I like it."

"Then you can have it," Dezhurova said.

They all laughed. Nervously.

Jamie wondered if he should tell them about Trumball's move to replace him as mission director. It affects them as much as it does me. More, in fact.

Yet he remained silent, unready to burden them with the political maneuverings going on back on Earth. That's a different world, Jamie said to himself. We've got our own problems to face here, our own realities.

It all seemed so unreal to him, so remote and intangible. Like the ghost stories his grandfather would make up for him when he was a child. Like the legends of First Man and First Woman when the world was new.

This is the new world, he realized. Mars. New and clean and full of mysteries. I can't let Dex and his father turn it into a tourist center. I can't let them start to ruin this world the way they destroyed the world of the People. That's why I've got to fight them.

A new understanding flooded through him. It was as if he'd been lost in a trackless wilderness and suddenly a path opened up before his eyes, the path to harmony and beauty and safety.

I can't let them bring tourists here. I can't let them start to tear up the natural environment so they can build cities and colonies. Bring climbers to Olympus Mons. Build ski runs. I've got to fight them. But how?

"Listen to that!"

Jamie's attention snapped back to the galley, the dome, and his five fellow explorers. The wind had keyed up to a higher pitch. He watched their five faces as they stared up into the shadows of the dome. Something creaked ominously.

"The dome is perfectly safe," Fuchida said to no one in particular. "It was designed to withstand the highest winds ever recorded on Mars, with a huge safety factor added in."

"Then what made that noise?" Trudy Hall asked, her voice small and hollow.

"The dome will flex a little," Jamie told them. "Nothing to worry about."

"Really?" Trudy seemed utterly unconvinced.

Jamie made a smile for her. "Really. In fact, if it didn't flex, if it was built to remain totally rigid, it might crack under a high enough wind load."

"Like the mighty oak and the little sapling," Vijay said.

"Oh, yes, I know that one," Hall said, looking slightly relieved. "The oak stands firm against the hurricane and gets knocked down, while the sapling bends with the wind and survives."

"Exactly."

Dezhurova pushed up from the table. "I'm going to check the outside camera views and see if the dust is obscuring them yet."

"Good idea," said Jamie. He got to his feet, too. "I'll put in a call to Wiley and Dex, check on how they're doing."

Vijay turned to Fuchida. "How does your ankle feel?"

"Not bad," the biologist replied. "I can walk on it without much pain."

"Then let's check out the garden one more time before going to bed."

Jamie thought Stacy suppressed a smirk at Vijay's mention of bed.

Rodriguez got up from the table. "Come on, Trudy. I'll play you a round of *Space Battle*."

"Not with you, Tommy. You're a shark. Besides, I won't be able to concentrate on the game with this storm on top of us."

Rodriguez went around to her chair. "Come on, I'll give you ten thousand points handicap. It'll be fun. Take your mind off the storm."

She got up. Reluctantly, Jamie thought.

Jamie felt glad that their electrical power came from the nuclear generator, which would not be affected by the storm. He followed Stacy to the comm center, forcing himself not to turn back to look at Vijay.

As Dex stared at the blank screen on the rover's control panel, he could still see his father's image, like the retinal glow of a flashbulb or the lingering presence of a powerful genie.

He wants to dump Jamie, Dex marvelled to himself. He wants to dump Jamie, but he didn't say a word about who he wants to take Jamie's place.

Dex sank back in the cushioned chair, his mind spinning. Could I do it? The answer came to him immediately. Certainly I could do it. I could head this operation without any trouble. But would the others listen to me? Especially if they think I pulled strings with my father to knock Jamie off.

This is tricky, he realized. The thought of being named mission director filled Dex with a warm flush of pride. They'd listen to me. They'd have to. After all, it won't be just my father who picks me; the whole ICU board would have to vote on it. Probably they'd want a unanimous vote.

But would Dad put me in charge? Does he trust me that much? Or would it be just another one of his ways to keep me under his thumb?

Jesus H. Christ, he swore. I'm on friggin' Mars and he's still got me jumping through his goddamned hoops!

Craig came stomping in through the airlock hatch.

"Gettin' dusty out there," he said, once he lifted the visor of his helmet.

Dex started to get up from his seat, but Craig called back, "I'm okay. It'll just take me a little time to vacuum all this crud off th' suit."

Dex went back anyway and helped him out of the backpack. It too was covered with a thin sheen of pinkish powder. Even Craig's helmet was tainted.

"We're going to get buried in this stuff," he heard himself say. He wished his voice didn't sound so shaky.

"Looks that way," Craig said easily. "Th' covers on the solar panels are holdin' down good, though. Wind might be makin' a lotta noise, but there's not much punch in it."

"That's good."

They were just starting to eat their dinners when the comm unit buzzed. Dex got up and went to the cockpit. He slid into the driver's seat and tapped the ON key.

Jamie Waterman's coppery-red serious face filled the panel screen. The picture was grainy, splotched with electronic snow. "Hello, Dex. How are you two doing?"

"Just having dinner, chief."

Jamie said, "It's starting to blow here. According to the latest met report, you'll be in the storm at least through tomorrow."

Dex nodded. He had seen the meteorology report; studied it hard.

"How are the batteries performing?" Jamie asked.

"We're still on the fuel cells. Wiley decided to run them to exhaustion before we go to the batteries."

"Smart move."

"What's happening there?"

Jamie seemed to think it over for a few moments. "We're in good shape. We've got everything battened down. It's going to be a noisy night, though."

Despite himself, Dex gave a snorting, derisive laugh. "Tell me about it."

"Your telemetry is coming through alright," Jamie said. "We're getting good data from you."

"Fine."

"The transmission will probably degrade as dust piles up on your antennas, though."

"I know." Dex started to feel a tendril of exasperation. Jamie's just talking to hear himself talk, he thought.

"I can't think of anything else we can do for you," he said. "I wish I'd ordered you to stay at the generator."

Dex suppressed an urge to say, *Me too.* Instead, he leaned closer to Jamie's image on the display screen and said as cheerfully as he could, "We're doing fine out here. And when the storm clears up, we'll be that much closer to the Pathfinder site."

Again Jamie was silent for several maddening moments. At last he said, "It's too late to worry about what might have been. Good luck, Dex. Give Wiley my best wishes."

"Right. We'll call you in the morning."

"If the antennas are still functioning," Jamie said.

"We'll clean them off if they're covered with dust," Dex replied, sharply.

"Good. Okay. Goodnight."

"Goodnight." Dex punched the OFF key. Christ, he looks like he doesn't expect to see us again.

Then he thought, Maybe that's what Jamie wants. Get me out of his hair. No, he's not like that. But it's exactly how *I'd* feel if our situations were reversed.

DIARY ENTRY

I hate this storm. The others all pretend they're not afraid
but I know better. They're as scared as I am, but they won't
admit it. They look at me and smile and make brave faces and
they can see how frightened I am. The wind howls out there and
they all pretend they don't hear it. And when I turn my back to
them, when they think I can't see them, they laugh at me. I can
hear them laughing at me even over the noise of the wind.

STORMY NIGHT

TO HIS SURPRISE, IT WAS RODRIGUEZ WHO COULD NOT KEEP HIS MIND ON the *Space Battle* game. Time and again he focused his concentration on the computer screen, but his attention wandered with every shriek of the wind outside. The dome seemed to creak and groan like an old wooden sailing ship in a gale; Rodriguez almost thought he could feel the floor shuddering and pitching.

No fear, he told himself. Yet his insides were shaking.

He and Trudy Hall sat side by side in her bio lab, with two high-speed joysticks plugged into the beeping, chattering computer. The screen showed sleek space battlecraft maneuvering wildly against a background of stars and planets while they zapped at each other with laser beams. Ships exploded with great roars of sound.

Finally, when he had lost the third round of the computer game, Rodriguez pushed his chair back and said, "That's enough. I quit."

"You let me win," Trudy said. There was more delight in her smiling expression than accusation.

He shook his head vehemently. "Naw. I was trying. I just couldn't concentrate."

"Really?"

Rodriguez's shoulders drooped. "Really."

"Worried about the storm?"

He hesitated, then admitted, "It's kinda silly, I know. But yeah, it's got me spooked—a little."

"Me too," Hall admitted.

"You sure don't look it," he said, surprised. "You look calm as a cucumber."

"On the outside. Inside I'm as jumpy as . . . as . . ."

"As a flea on a hot griddle?"

She laughed. "What a ghastly idea."

He got to his feet. "Come on, I'll buy you a cup of coffee. Or maybe you prefer tea."

She stood up beside him, slim and spare next to his solid, chunky build. They were almost the same height, though, and her dark brown hair was only a shade lighter than his.

"Actually, I still have a drop or two of a rather decent sherry in my quarters."

Rodriguez's brows rose. "We're not supposed to take any liquor—"

"It's left over from our landing party. Should have finished it then, I suppose, but I saved a bit for a possible emergency."

"Yeah, but . . ."

"This counts as an emergency, don't you think?"

Inadvertently, Rodriguez glanced up into the shadowy height of the darkened dome. The wind moaned outside.

"There's not enough to make anyone drunk, you realize," Hall said. "Just a bit to take the edge off, you know."

He looked back at her and saw the fear and helplessness in her eyes. She's just as scared as I am, he told himself. She feels just the way I do. But I can't show it, not to her or anybody else.

"Okay," he said.

"Come on, then," Trudy said, holding her hand out to him. "Walk me home."

He took her hand. Then as they walked through the empty shadows of the dome, with the wind howling now and the structure making deeper, stranger noises of its own, he slid his arm around her waist. She leaned her head against his shoulder and they walked together toward her cubicle and a night when neither of them wanted to be alone.

Stacy Dezhurova was staring hard at the display screens, watching how the wind was fluttering the tied-down wings of the soarplanes. The wings of the bigger, heavier rocketplane were also undulating noticeably, straining against the tie-downs fastened to the ground.

"We've done all we can, Stacy," said Jamie, behind her. "You ought to get some sleep now."

"But if one of the planes breaks loose . . ."

"What can we do about it?" he asked gently. "We parked them downwind of the dome. If they break loose, at least they won't come crashing in here."

She nodded, but kept her eyes glued to the screens.

"Stacy, do I have to *order* you to your quarters?"

Dezhurova turned and looked up at him. "Someone ought to stay on duty. Just in case."

"Okay," Jamie said. "I will. Go get some sleep."

"No. I couldn't sleep anyway. I'll stay."

Jamie pulled up the other wheeled chair and sat next to her. "Stacy . . . we're going to need you tomorrow, bright-eyed and bushy-tailed, rested and able to perform at your best."

She looked away from him briefly. Then, jabbing a finger at the digital clock next to the main display screen, she said, "It's twenty-one-fifteen, almost. I'll stay here until oh-two-hundred. Then you can come on until six. That will give each of us four hours' sleep. Okay?"

"One A.M.," Jamie said.

Her serious expression did not change at all as she asked, "Will that give you and Vijay enough time?"

Jamie felt his jaw drop open.

Dezhurova laughed. "Go on. Set your alarm for one. Then you can relieve me."

Jamie got up from the chair thinking, Stacy could take the director's job. She'd be good at it.

Vijay was sitting at the galley table when Jamie left the comm center. He walked straight to her and she looked up at him with her big, soulful eyes filled with—what? he wondered. Anxiety? Loneliness? Fear?

And what's in my eyes, Jamie wondered as he extended his hand toward her. She took it in hers, rose from her chair, and walked wordlessly with him toward his quarters. What am I doing? Jamie asked himself. This isn't love. This isn't the kind of romantic moment that poets write about. It's need; we need each other. We're scared of this storm, of being so far from home, so far from safety. We need the comfort of another person, someone to hold on to, someone to hold me.

They said hardly a word to each other as they stripped and got into Jamie's narrow bunk. Their lovemaking was torrid, as if all the rage and power of the storm had possessed them both. The first time, ten nights ago, they had taken pains to be as quiet as possible. Not this night. Not with the wind wailing outside. Now they lay, languid, spent, thoughts drifting idly, all barriers down, all furies calmed.

Should I tell her about Trumball? he asked himself. There was no urgency in the thought. It simply rose to his consciousness dreamily, like a whisper struggling through a drug-induced haze.

Jamie kissed Vijay's bare shoulder; she muttered something sleepily and snuggled closer to him. As he drifted toward sleep with Vijay's body warm and softly cupped next to him, he knew he would feel empty and alone without her. And afraid.

Sharp, cold reality stabbed through him. You can't talk about love. You can't even think about it. Not here. Not under these conditions. You made that mistake last time and it brought nothing but pain to you and Joanna. You can't expect Vijay to commit her life to you on the basis of what we're doing here.

Which means, he heard himself reason, that you can't burden her with your problem about Trumball. It's your problem, not hers. You've got to find the right path for yourself, alone.

Jamie turned slightly in the bunk and looked over at the glowing red numerals of the digital clock. Get some sleep. It's going to be one A.M. damned soon.

The wind howled louder outside. To Jamie it sounded like the wild laughter of the trickster, Coyote.

*   *   *

It was nearly midnight as Stacy returned to her chair in the comm center and set a plastic cup of hot tea on the console beside the main display screen. The wind was screeching outside, a thin tortured wail like the distant howl of souls in hell. Methodically she started checking all the dome's environmental systems again.

With deliberate calm, Dezhurova tapped into the environmental monitoring display. Everything was normal in the dome, except for one of the air-circulation fans, which had gone off-line earlier in the day. She would attend to that in the morning, she told herself.

She opened the program for the sensors that monitored environmental conditions in the garden dome. Before she could check them, though, the yellow light on the main communications console began blinking and her screen showed: INCOMING MESSAGE.

She grumbled to herself as she tapped at the keyboard. What does Tarawa want now?

To her surprise, it wasn't mission control at Tarawa. Her comm screen showed the scratchy, static-streaked image of a bleary-eyed, tousle-haired Dex Trumball.

Dex could not sleep.

He lay in his bunk listening to the wind shrieking just inches away, hearing the iron-rich sand scratching at the rover's thin metal skin, *feeling* the storm clawing at the rover, trying to find a way inside, a loose latch, a slight seam, the tiniest of openings in the welds that held the rover's skin together.

We could be dead in a minute, he knew. Or worse, buried alive under the sand with the electrical power gone. Strangle to death when the air gives out.

And we can't do anything about it! Just lay here and take it. Let the friggin' storm pound us and batter at us until it finds a way to kill us.

He sat up abruptly, heart racing, chest heaving. He felt sweaty and cold at the same time. He had to urinate again.

Peering through the darkness, he could make out in the faint glow from the instrument panel up in the cockpit the lumpy form of Craig, sleeping in the bunk on the other side of the module. Wiley lay on his back, mouth slightly open, snoring gently.

Christ, he's as relaxed as a baby in its cradle, Trumball thought as he slipped quietly out of his bunk.

He padded barefoot to the lavatory, opposite the racks where the hard suits stood like ghosts in armor. Fear fills the bladder, Dex told himself as he urinated into the stainless steel toilet bowl. This motherfucking storm's scaring the piss out of me. It was his fourth trip to the toilet since he had gone to bed.

"You all right, buddy?" Craig asked softly as he crawled back into his bunk.

"Yeah," Dex snapped. "I'm fine."

"Kinda noisy out there, ain't it?"

"It sure is."

"Don't let it spook you, kid. We're safe as can be inside here."

Dex knew Craig was trying to reassure him, calm him. He knew he should be grateful to Wiley. Instead he felt angry that the older man had called him "kid." And ashamed to be caught in his terror.

The wind quieted a bit. The shrieking softened. Maybe it's over, Dex thought. Maybe it's winding down.

He lay back on his sweat-soaked pillow and closed his eyes again. But the instant he did, the wind gusted again with a furious scream. Dex felt the rover rock.

He bolted up to a sitting position and pounded the mattress with both fists, almost sobbing. Leave me alone! Leave me alone! Go away and leave me alone, please, please, please.

The wind continued to howl, though. If anything, it got louder.

Blearily, he shuffled up to the rover's cockpit and slumped into the right-hand seat. Let's see what's happening at the dome. Talk to somebody. Anybody. Take your mind off this mother-humpin' storm.

Stacy's stolid, fleshy face filled the tiny screen on the control panel. The picture was streaked, grainy, but she looked surprised.

"Dex?"

"Yeah," he said softly, not wanting to wake Craig again. "Too noisy out here to sleep. How's everything there?"

Dezhurova spoke with Dex for a few seconds, then realized that Trumball merely wanted to chat because he could not sleep in the midst of the storm. Reception was weak; his video kept breaking up. Probably dust is piling up on his antennas, she thought. She kept on talking with him, but turned her real attention to the monitoring screens and continued checking the environmental conditions in the garden dome.

Temperature below nominal, she saw. That should not be. Air pressure was falling too.

Her breath caught in her throat. Without even thinking about Dex, still jabbering on the main comm screen, Stacy grabbed the loudspeaker mike and bellowed:

"Emergency! The garden dome is ripping apart!"

Dex gaped at the tiny comm screen.

"Jamie, everyone—the garden dome is ripping apart!" Dezhurova repeated, roaring like the crack of doom. "We need everyone, right now!"

Then the comm screen went dark.

Dex sat in the rover's cockpit, icy sweat trickling down his ribs, staring at the dead comm screen.

My god almighty, he thought, panting with mounting terror as he sat in the shadows. If the garden dome goes, the main dome could go too. Then we'd all be dead.

Mitsuo Fuchida lay in his bunk, staring up into the darkness, listening to the wind and the accompanying creaks and groans of the dome.

It's like being on a ship at sea, he said to himself, except that it doesn't rock.

He had considered taking a tranquilizer before going to bed, but decided that he would not need one. He had looked death in the face, back at the lava tube on Olympus Mons. This wind storm held no more terrors for him. Death will come or not, he thought. What cannot be controlled must be accepted.

Still, he lay awake listening to the storm, thinking about Elizabeth, hoping that Rodriguez would live up to his promise and not reveal that he was a married man. Where is she tonight? he wondered. What is she doing now, at this moment?

He began to build a pleasant fantasy about her.

Until he heard Stacy's shout: "Emergency! The garden dome is ripping apart! We need everyone, right now!"

Automatically he leaped out of bed, a stab of pain from his injured ankle shooting through his leg. Awkward with the bandaged ankle, Fuchida limped to the comm center. Jamie, Vijay, Rodriguez and Trudy Hall were also hurrying there, each of them hastily pulling on rumpled coveralls as they ran.

"The garden dome has been punctured," Stacy said, jabbing a thick finger at the monitor screen.

"Camera view," Jamie snapped, slipping into the wheeled chair beside her.

He peered at the screen. "Can't see anything—wait, the dome fabric is rippling."

"Pressure and temperature both falling rapidly," Dezhurova said, an unaccustomed edge of fear in her voice.

"The plants will die!" Trudy was saying, her voice pitched high, frightened. "The nighttime temperature—"

"I know, I know," Jamie snapped. Turning toward Rodriguez, he said, "We have spare cans of epoxy, don't we? Where are they?"

Rodriguez bent over one of the unused consoles and punched at its keyboard, then started scrolling through a list so fast it looked like a blur.

He saw what he wanted and froze the display. "Repair epoxy," he said, pointing to the screen. "It's stored in locker seventeen, shelf A."

"Go get it," Jamie commanded. "As much as you can carry."

Rodriguez brushed past Fuchida as he raced out of the comm center, staggering the limping biologist. Vijay headed out, too. "I'll help Tommy," she called over her shoulder.

Jamie jumped up from his chair. "Stacy, get suited up. Trudy, you help her. Mitsuo, take over the comm chair."

"Where are you going?" Stacy demanded.

As he rushed out into the dome's dimly-lit central area, Jamie said, "We've got to slap some temporary patches on the holes in the dome, if they're not already too bad."

"You can't go in there!" Trudy yelped.

"Somebody's got to stop the leak before it gets worse."

"Wait for Tomas," Dezhurova said. "The epoxy—"

"No time!" Jamie snapped, sprinting away from them. He headed for the airlock as they yelled after him.

"Get Stacy suited up!" he yelled back. "Mitsuo! Turn on all the lights in there!"

The dome flared into daytime brightness as Jamie reached the airlock that connected to the garden. Not in here, Mitsuo, Jamie corrected silently. In the garden, for the sake of Christ!

The pressure on the other side of the airlock had not fallen so low that the lock automatically sealed, Jamie realized as he pushed through the double hatches. Not yet, he told himself.

It was cold inside the garden. Jamie shivered involuntarily as he stepped in. The wind shrieked louder and the dome fabric was flapping noisily, like a sail luffing in the breeze. At least the overhead lights were on at full intensity. Mitsuo heard me after all.

The emergency patches were stored in a closed box next to the airlock hatch. Tearing it open and grabbing a double handful of the thin plastic sheets, Jamie thought that they should have learned their lesson from the first expedition and scattered the sheets on the floor around the dome's perimeter.

Now he released them and saw them flutter in the air currents, then slap themselves against a pair of puncture holes on the far side of the dome. It's cold in here, Jamie thought. Close to freezing already.

Rodriguez boiled through the hatch, a big spray can of epoxy in each hand. He looked like a two-gun frontier sheriff, grim and determined.

"I'll take them," Jamie said over the shrieking wind. "No sense both of us risking—"

"You're not gonna be the only hero tonight," Rodriguez shouted, pushing past Jamie and heading for the spots where the temporary patches were fluttering against the side of the dome.

Vijay stepped through with more cans. Jamie grabbed one from her and they both ran after Rodriguez.

The plants didn't look too bad, Jamie thought, glancing at the rows of hydroponics trays. But what the hell do I know? Green leaves, mostly curled tight. Are the ones closest to the rips drooping more than the others?

After a furious few minutes of spraying, Rodriguez said, "I think we got it sealed."

Jamie looked around. The dome had stopped flapping. Mitsuo must've pumped up the air pressure, he thought. The wind sounded just as loud, maybe even louder, but now the dome's plastic structure seemed rigid, safe.

"Maybe you're right," he said cautiously.

"It's cold in here," Vijay said, hugging herself.

"Go and tell Mitsuo to goose up the heaters," Jamie instructed. "Tomas, let's spray the whole perimeter of the dome, down here where the fabric joins with the flooring. If there's going to be any more problems, that's where they'll happen."

"Right," said Rodriguez.

Just then Dezhurova clomped in, buttoned up in her hard suit.

"We got it under control," Rodriguez shouted happily at her.

She raised her visor and glowered at him. Rodriguez laughed.

"Stacy," Jamie said, "I want you and Tomas to check the integrity of the dome. Spray anything that looks like a potential leak."

"The epoxy is not transparent. It will cut down on the sunshine the plants receive."

"Can't be helped. The important thing is to ensure the dome's integrity."

Trudy Hall stepped through the airlock hatch. "Oh, my lord! The tomatoes are *ruined*!"

Jamie grabbed her by the arm. "Trudy, you and Mitsuo should check out all the plants, see how much damage has been done. I'll take over at the comm center."

"All right, certainly." She rushed to the trays of plants at the far side of the dome.

MORNING: SOL 59

JAMIE WAS STILL AT THE COMM CONSOLE WHEN THE SUN FINALLY CAME UP and the others began to stir. The wind was still yowling, but with the sunrise the visibility outside improved somewhat. In the screens that showed the outside camera views Jamie could see that the planes were all still there, although one of the soarplane's wings seemed bent oddly. One of the cameras had ceased functioning, but otherwise everything seemed to be in reasonably good shape.

"D'you want some coffee?"

It was Vijay, standing at the comm center doorway with a steaming mug in her hands.

"Good idea," said Jamie, reaching for it.

"How is everything?" she asked, sliding into the chair next to his.

"We're in reasonably good shape."

"How much damage to the garden was there?"

"Trudy was almost in tears over the tomatoes and some of the soybeans. All the strawberries are gone. But most of the plants are all right. We caught the leak in time."

"We won't have to pack up and go home, then?"

He shook his head slowly. "No. We might have to go without soyburgers for a while, but the garden will still feed us."

"That was a very brave thing you did, dashing in there like that."

Jamie felt his brows hike up. He didn't feel very brave. With a shrug he replied, "Seemed like the right thing to do. We had to get those patches in place."

"You could have been killed."

"I never even thought of that," he confessed. "It all happened so fast . . ."

"You're a bloody hero, Jamie." She wasn't joking, he saw. She was in dead earnest.

Feeling suddenly uncomfortable, Jamie changed the subject. "I haven't been able to raise Dex and Wiley yet."

"You expected that, din't you?"

He nodded. "Probably a lot of dust on their antennas by now. We'll just have to be patient."

"You're good at that," she said, with a smile.

He caught her implication. "It's a lot more fun being patient with you than with them," he said, low and swift, afraid of being overheard.

Before she could reply, Rodriguez burst in, white teeth gleaming in a huge grin. "Well, we made it through the night," he said, then burst into a hearty laughter.

Jamie threw a perplexed glance at Vijay, who shrugged her shoulders.

"You were terrific, boss," the astronaut said, beaming at Jamie. "Saved our necks, man."

Jamie shook his head, but Vijay nodded agreement. "If the garden had gone, we'd have to pack up and leave, wouldn't we?"

"Maybe," Jamie conceded. "Anyway, the garden's going to be all right. So let's get on with the program, okay?"

"Right!" Rodriguez said. "You had breakfast yet, boss? I'm hungry enough to eat a Martian buffalo."

From the doorway, Stacy Dezhurova said, "You will have to find one first, Tom."

"Lemme grab some juice," Rodriguez said, still grinning buoyantly, "then I'll spell you at the console while you guys grab breakfast."

"I thought you were starving," Jamie said, getting up from the chair.

"Yeah, I know, but I can wait. You guys go eat. I'll hold the fort here."

Jamie looked to Dezhurova, who said, "I will get your juice, Tom."

"Okay, thanks."

Jamie said. "Well, if you're going to take over, see if you can raise Craig and Dex."

"Right." Rodriguez sat heavily on the little chair, making it roll away from the console a few feet.

As he went to the galley with Vijay and Dezhurova, Jamie wondered aloud, "Tomas sure is chipper this morning. He must have had a good restful sleep."

Dezhurova sputtered into laughter. "Not exactly."

"What do you mean?"

Stacy looked up into Jamie's face. "Didn't you hear them? Him and Trudy? They were at it all damned night long."

Inadvertently, Jamie glanced at Vijay, who was trying to suppress a smirk.

"At least you two are quiet about it," Stacy went on, matter-of-factly. "But my cubicle is next to Trudy's. Tom was snorting all night like Ferdinand the Bull. He drowned out the storm, for god's sake."

Vijay broke out in laughter.

They had just started to eat breakfast when Fuchida limped up to the table, looking distressed.

"What's wrong, Mitsuo?" Jamie asked.

"Am I the only one who wonders why the garden dome began to rip apart?" he asked.

"What do you mean?"

The biologist sat across from Jamie and Vijay and propped his bandaged ankle on an empty chair.

"How can the dust rip the dome fabric?" he asked, like a professor posing a problem for his class.

Dezhurova got up from the table. "I promised Tomas I would bring him juice," she remembered. "He probably needs it."

Fuchida did not catch her insinuation. "The dome's plastic cannot be punctured by sand particles," he said quietly, firmly. "Yet the fabric was punctured."

"I thought it ripped along the base where it connects with the flooring," Jamie said.

"No," Fuchida replied, raising one finger for emphasis. "There are two small punctures. If not repaired so quickly, they would have grown into a rip that would have torn the entire dome off its foundation."

"But we did catch it in time," Vijay said. "Jamie did, that is."

Fuchida acknowledged the fact with a small dip of his chin. "Still, we must ask how the dome was punctured."

Jamie suggested, "Small rocks blown by the wind?"

"I doubt it," the biologist said.

"Then how?"

"I don't know. But it troubles me. The dome should not have failed. That plastic fabric has been tested under much more severe conditions in wind tunnel simulations. It should not have failed."

"Yet it did," Vijay said, almost in a whisper.

"It did indeed." Fuchida looked like a prosecuting attorney to Jamie. Suspicious, almost angry.

"Well," Jamie said, "I don't know how it failed, but we ought to figure out some way of making certain it doesn't happen again."

"Hey, buddy," Craig said cheerfully, "we made it through the night."

From across the narrow table between their bunks, Dex nodded glumly. He felt exhausted, sleepless eyes gummy, coveralls rumpled and stinking of fear.

The wind was still screeching outside. Particles of iron-cored grit were still grinding against the rover's thin skin, like an endless army of soldier ants working tirelessly to break through their defenses and come in and devour them.

"Communications're out, of course," Craig added.

"Of course," said Dex blearily.

"Soon's the wind dies down to less'n a hundred knots, we'll go outside and dust off the antennas. Squirt a signal back to base, let 'em know we're okay."

"If they're okay," Dex replied gloomily.

"They'll be all right," said Craig. "That big dome's built like the Rock of Gibraltar. Been through dust storms before, y'know, over the six years it's been settin' out there."

"I suppose so," Dex admitted.

Unbidden, his mind was cataloguing all the things that might not be okay. If the covers had ripped off during the night, the solar cells could be scratched and pitted so badly they'd be useless. The fuel cells were already down to zero; they were living off the batteries. The gritty dust could have worked its way into the wheel bearings, immobilizing them completely. Then we'll have a choice of starving or suffocating,

Dex thought. Or the dust could have scoured the antennas so badly their comm systems would be completely shot. Then we couldn't navigate, couldn't get positioning data from the satellites, we'd be lost out here forever.

Or the whole frigging base dome might have blown down during the night, he added.

"Hey!" Craig snapped. "You listenin'?"

"Sorry," Dex said, trying to sit up a little straighter.

"I said we'd better stick to a cold breakfast. No sense drainin' the batteries by usin' the microwave."

"I'll get breakfast," Dex said, pushing himself up from his bunk. "You can do the systems check."

"Already did that. After breakfast we power down. Shut off the freezer, let it coast; food'll keep cold inside okay. Air fans on low. Lights to minimum. Until we get the solar panels uncovered and workin' again."

"If they'll work again," Dex muttered as he went back to the compact stand of racks that served as the rover's galley.

"Didn't get much sleep last night, huh?"

"How'd you guess?" Dex pulled out the first two cereal packages he could reach.

"Listen, kid, the worst is over. We made it through the storm. It's peterin' out now. In another couple hours—"

Dex whirled on him. "You listen, pal! You don't like being called Possum? Well I don't like being called kid. Got that?"

"Then stop behavin' like a kid," Craig shot back, scowling.

Dex started to reply, but found he had no answer for the older man.

"You're scared, okay. I am too. What th' hell, we're stranded out here in the middle of downtown Mars. For all I know we're covered with sand twelve feet deep and ever'body in the base is dead. Okay! We'll have to deal with that. You do what you can do. You don't sit around mopin' and grumblin' like some teenager with an acne problem."

Despite himself, Dex laughed. "Is that what I've been doing?"

Still sitting on his bunk, Craig's leathery face rearranged itself into a small smile. He nodded. "Sort of," he said.

"I'm scared, Wiley," he admitted. "I don't want to die out here."

"Shit, buddy, I don't want to die *at all*."

As he put both cereal packages on the table, Dex said, "Maybe we ought to go outside and see how bad the damage is."

"Still blowin' pretty strong out there. Be better to wait a couple hours."

"I'll go nuts sitting in here with nothing to do but listen to that wind."

Craig nodded. "H'm. Yeah, me too."

"So?"

"So let's have us a nice leisurely breakfast and then take our time suitin' up."

"Good," said Dex, feeling some of the fear ease away. Not all of it. But he felt better than he had during the night.

AFTERNOON: SOL 59

"NOT AS BAD AS IT COULD'VE BEEN," CRAIG PRONOUNCED. BUT HIS VOICE sounded heavy, unhappy, in Dex's earphones.

The sky was still gray, sullen. The wind was still keening, although nowhere near as loud as it had been. Dex was surprised that inside the hard suit he felt no push from the wind at all. He had expected to have to lean over hard and force himself forward, like a man struggling through a gale. Instead, the thin Martian air might just as well have been totally calm.

On one side the rover was half buried in rust-red sand. From the nose of the cockpit to the tail of the jointed vehicle's third segment, the sand had piled up as high as the roof on the windward side.

"Good thing the hatch was on the leeward side," Dex said. "We might've had trouble getting it open if it was buried in this stuff."

"Naw, I don't think so," Craig answered, kicking at the pile. Dust flew like ashes, or like dry autumn leaves when a child scuffs at them.

"Maybe."

"Besides," Craig added, "I turned her so the hatch'd be on the sheltered side when we stopped for the night."

Dex blinked inside his helmet, trying to remember if he was driving then or Craig. Wiley's not above taking credit for good luck, he thought.

"Come on, let's see what's happened topside."

As they trudged around the rover, back to the side that was almost free of the dust, Dex could see that at least part of the makeshift coverings they had taped down over the solar panels had been blown loose. One sheet was flapping fitfully in the wind.

As Craig climbed up the ladder next to the airlock hatch to inspect the solar panels, Dex caught sight of the most beautiful apparition he had seen on Mars: the dull gray dust-laden clouds thinned enough, for a few moments, for him to see the bright orange sky overhead. His heart leaped inside him. The storm's breaking up! It's breaking up at last.

"Worse than I hoped for," Craig's voice grated in his earphones, "but better'n I was scared of."

Craig came down from the ladder. "We got some scratches and pittin' up there where the tarp came loose. The rest of the panels look okay, though."

"Good," said Dex, suddenly enthusiastic. "Listen, Wiley, I'm going to duck back inside and put on the VR rig. Nobody's ever recorded a Martian dust storm before. This'll make great viewing back home!"

He heard Craig chuckling inside his helmet. Then the older man said, "Startin' to get some of your spirit back on-line, huh?"

"I . . ." Dex stopped, perplexed for a moment. Then he put a gloved hand on the shoulder of Craig's suit. "Wiley, you really helped me. I was scared shitless back there, and you pulled me through it."

"You did it for yourself," Craig said, "but I'll be glad to take the credit for it."

Dex felt his insides go hollow.

As if he sensed it, Craig said, "Don't worry, son. What happened here is between you and me, nobody else."

"Thanks, Wiley." The words sounded pitifully weak to Dex, compared to the enormous rush of gratitude and respect that he felt.

"Okay," Craig said gruffly. "Now before you start doin' your VR stuff, let's get the antennas cleaned off so we can tell Jamie and the gang that we're okay."

Rodriguez gave a sudden whoop from the comm center.

"Wiley's calling in!"

Jamie bolted up from the galley table while Vijay stayed to help the limping Fuchida. In the comm center Jamie saw Craig's scruffy-bearded face on the main screen.

". . . solar panel output's degraded by four-five percent," Craig was reporting. "Coulda been a lot worse."

"What about the fuel cells?" Rodriguez asked.

"Dex's electrolyzing our extra water; gonna feed the hydrogen and oxy to 'em. That way we can rest the batteries."

Poking his head into the comm camera's view, Jamie asked, "Do you have to dig yourselves out?"

Craig looked very pleased. "Nope. The wheels and drive motors are all okay. We just put 'er in gear and pulled ourselves loose. We're movin' now."

"Wow!" Rodriguez exclaimed.

"That's great," said Jamie, feeling genuinely pleased and relieved. "That's just great, Wiley."

"Oughtta be at Ares Vallis in another three-four days," Craig said. Then he added, "If the weather holds up."

Rodriguez laughed. "There's not another storm in sight."

"Good."

When Craig signed off, Rodriguez began checking the telemetry from the rover and Jamie went back to the inventory list. The wind was still yowling outside like dead spirits begging to come in out of the cold.

The wind was appreciably softer and sunlight actually lanced below the overhanging clouds as the day drew to a close.

Jamie was tired, physically and emotionally drained, as he made his way back to the comm center for what must have been the hundredth time that day.

As the storm wound down, he had spent most of the day in the greenhouse dome, checking and rechecking the area that had been damaged. He had even suited up and gone outside to inspect the damaged areas without the emergency patches and epoxy covering them. It was hard to say, but the areas seemed to have been punctured, not torn. Of course, once punctured the plastic fabric began to rip along the seam where it connected to the foundation of the dome.

What we need here is a forensic structural engineer, Jamie told himself. If there is such a person. Maybe Wiley could make some sense of it.

He took dozens of photographs of the damaged areas and transmitted them back to Tarawa for their analysis. There was nothing more he could think to do, but he kept feeling that he was missing something. Something important.

What is it, Grandfather? he asked silently. What have I overlooked?

Once in the comm center he slumped down on the little chair and put through another message to Tarawa.

"Pete: The greenhouse dome looks okay now, but I'm worried about what might happen in the next storm. Maybe that won't be for another year, but it's a problem we ought to think about now, not when the dust starts blowing again. It's obvious that we overlooked this problem, but with twenty-twenty hindsight I think we ought to pay attention to it.

"Can you get the world's assembled experts to figure out how we can protect the greenhouse dome with the materials we have on hand? That includes native Martian materials, of course. What I'm wondering is, can we make glass bricks out of the Martian sand? Build an igloo that's transparent? Look into it for me, will you?"

The wind died down almost completely after sunset. Jamie was tempted to put on a suit and go out to see if the stars were still in their places, but he felt too tired. The outside cameras showed that the planes were still there, although what condition their solar panels might be in would have to wait for a closer inspection.

The dome was quiet, back to normal, when Jamie finally went to his quarters. Vijay was already there, in the bunk. He blinked with surprise.

"Tomas is bunking with Trudy," she said, matter-of-factly.

Nodding, Jamie muttered, "I wonder if Mitsuo and Stacy are going to get it on?"

Vijay giggled softly. "Not bloody likely."

"Why not?"

"Stacy's gay."

Jamie's eyes popped open. "What?"

"Stacy's a lesbian."

There's nothing wrong with that, Jamie told himself. Still, he felt shocked.

"Poor Mitsuo," he heard himself whisper as he got under the covers beside her.

Vijay moved over to make room for him on the narrow bunk. "I don't know about him. He hasn't come on to any of the women."

"Maybe he's gay, too?"

"I doubt it. I think he's just got more self-control than you Western ape-men."

Jamie wanted to debate the point, but instead he closed his eyes and fell instantly asleep.

GLASS BRICKS

PETE CONNORS STARED GLOOMILY AT THE THICK STACK OF PAPERS ON HIS desk. It's always a mistake asking the experts how to do something, he reminded himself. They snow you under with every detail they've ever come across.

Still, he thought, the NASA guys and the university profs provided the material we asked for damned fast. If only there wasn't so much of it!

He took a deep breath, then booted up his computer and called up the communications program. The tiny red light on the camera atop the display screen winked on.

"Jamie, I'm going to be sending you half a ton of documentation about how to make glass bricks out of in situ materials. It won't be an easy job, but it can be done.

"I'll squirt the technical write-ups to you on the other channel. It's from all sorts of bright thinkers at NASA, MIT, Caltech, places like that. I think maybe some of 'em are Eskimos.

"First thing you'll have to do is build a solar reflector. You can scavenge one of the spare dish antennas from stores and coat it with aluminum spray. The reflector will be the heat source for your furnace; you need to produce temperatures of two thousand degrees Celsius to melt the sand particles from the Martian soil. First you'll have to crush the sand grains down real fine . . . ''

Half an hour later, Connors finished with, '' . . . and then you'll have glass bricks, buddy. Nothing to it.''

Finally, with a weary sigh, Connors turned to the subject he would have preferred to ignore. But he couldn't.

"Jamie, old man Trumball is still pushing to get you out as mission director . . .''

NOON: SOL 63

"I SEE IT!'' DEX YELPED.

They had just topped a low bluff, and the rover was nosing down the steep incline toward the broad low swale where the Pathfinder and its tiny wheeled Sojourner had been waiting silently for nearly thirty years.

Craig was driving. Both men were shaggy, bearded, their coveralls limp and sweat-stained. They were both grinning from ear to ear.

"Look!'' Dex cried, rising halfway out of his seat and pointing at the rocks. "There's the twin peaks! And Yogi! And Barnacle Bill!''

Craig laughed. "You're actin' like you didn't expect they'd be here.''

Dex plopped back in the chair, his insides fluttering. *They're all here. They're really here. After all the years of looking at the pictures and watching the videos, it's all real! It really all happened. They landed the spacecraft here back when they could barely fly a ton of payload to Mars.*

This hardware's worth billions! Dex told himself. *A lot more than it cost in the first place. Like a painting by DaVinci or Van Gogh.*

He wanted to drive the rover, wanted to stomp on the accelerator and race down there in a swirl of dust. But he knew that Wiley wouldn't let him, and he realized it was probably a good thing. *Christ on a crutch,* Dex thought. *I'm wound up like a little kid at Christmas.*

"Maybe you oughtta call back to base and tell 'em we're here," Craig suggested.

"Right," Dex agreed. "And make sure the cameras are getting all this. This is history, y'know!"

Craig chuckled.

They parked a five-minute walk away from the Pathfinder, so they could survey the area carefully and not disturb the site with their rover's cleated wheel tracks.

The old spacecraft sat there, flat and square, with its shrivelled protective shroud pulled up around it like an old lady holding up her skirts. The machine looked strange, alien in the Martian landscape, an angular metal contrivance in the midst of weathered rocks and rust-red sand. Sojourner, so tiny it looked like a wheeled toy some child might have put together from a kit, was still nosed against the rock that had been dubbed Yogi.

Dex was trembling with anticipation as he and Craig got into their hard suits. Once outside, once actually on the ground and standing beside the old hardware, the excitement began to ebb away.

It's all so small, Dex thought. Hell, I had a toy car bigger than Pathfinder when I was ten years old. And I could carry Sojourner under one arm, just about.

He turned a full circle, surveying the area with a geologist's analytical eye. Water rushed through here, all right. A river, or maybe a big flood that broke through an ice dam. You can see the marks of flowing water all over the area.

"Come on," Craig called, "let's get to work."

Carefully they photographed the area for comparison with the catalogue imagery from the Pathfinder itself three decades earlier.

"Water came down from over there," Craig said, pointing. "Busted right along here at a pretty good clip, I'd say."

"Yeah, but where did it go?"

Craig pointed toward the ground. "Let's see how deep it went."

They went back to the rover and broke out the power drill and other tools. While Craig began digging to find the permafrost layer, Dex planted three beacons at the distance of ten-minute walks from the Pathfinder.

The sun was nearing the gently rolling horizon when Craig finally said, "Better roll our buggy up here now. I don't wanta bust a gut carryin' this rig any distance."

"It weighs less than three hundred pounds in this gravity," Dex pointed out.

But Craig was already on his way back to the rover. "And more'n two-fifty," he countered. "The less distance we have to tote it, the better off we'll be. You don't want a hernia out here, do you?"

Dex laughed and started to put the cores that the drill had pulled up into insulated sample boxes. If Wiley had hit a permafrost layer it wasn't obvious; the drilling had gone down to thirty meters without much change in the underlying rock's consistency.

The rover came jinking and squeaking across the red sand like a giant metal caterpillar, its wheels clambering over the rocks scattered across the ground. Craig stopped it when the hatch to the center module was no more than five meters from the silent, squat Pathfinder.

Grunting, straining, together they hoisted the machine up off the ground and, with, "Watch out for the shroud," and "Okay, I've got it," they lugged it to the lip of the hatch and rested it there. Then Craig climbed awkwardly inside the module and, with him pulling and Dex pushing, they shoved it safely inside.

Sweat was stinging Dex's eyes as he sank down to a sitting position and rested the back of his helmet against one of the rover's metal wheels.

"You okay?" Craig asked, hopping down from the hatch. For the first time in weeks, Dex noticed that a man jumps slower in Mars' light gravity than he would on Earth.

"I'm fine," Dex answered. "Wish I could wipe my eyes, though."

"You mean you don't know how to wriggle your arm outta the sleeve and work a hand up past your neck ring?"

Dex blinked sweat away. "You mean you can?"

"Sure."

"You really can?"

"Sure," Craig said. "Only problem is it dislocates your shoulder doin' it." He burst into raucous laughter.

Dex made a sour face but it did no good, since Wiley couldn't see it through the tinted visor.

"C'mon," Craig said, offering a gloved hand to pull Dex up to his feet. "Let's get the little fella and then call it a day."

They trudged slowly over to the tiny Sojourner rover, still sitting faithfully with its proton X-ray spectrometer almost touching the bulbous rock named Yogi. It weighed less than twelve pounds on Mars, so Dex easily lifted it off the ground and turned to head back to the rover.

He saw Craig bend down, a laborious job in the hard suit.

"What're you doing, Wiley?"

"Puttin' a marker down, so's people'll be able to see where she sat."

"Oh. You do that with the Pathfinder, too?"

"Yup."

"What'd you use for a marker?"

"Silver dollars."

Dex felt his eyes go wide. "Silver dollars? What the hell are you doing with silver dollars out here?"

He sensed Wiley trying to shrug inside the suit. "I always carry 'em. For luck. Brought seven of 'em."

They were almost at the rover hatch. Dex looked at the spot where the Pathfinder had sat for nearly three decades. Sure enough, a bright new silver dollar rested there.

"Started carryin' 'em when I was out on the oil rigs," Craig explained. "Guys'd play cards off-shift and they didn't use chips, lemme tell you. Hard cash or nothin'. So I started totin' some silver dollars with me."

Dex just shook his head.

"Jamie, I'm going to be sending you half a ton of documentation about how to make glass bricks out of in situ materials," Pete Connors was saying.

Jamie grinned as he watched Connors' image on his laptop screen. A glass igloo would be the answer they needed for the greenhouse. It didn't even have to be an igloo, he thought as Connors chattered on. We could build a square enclosure around the greenhouse dome, Jamie said to himself, then take the dome down.

Or maybe not, he mused. The plastic dome can be polarized to make it opaque overnight. Keep the heat inside. Can't polarize glass bricks.

He was about to split his screen and check on the technical data when Connors sighed wearily and his voice turned down a pitch.

"Jamie, old man Trumball is still pushing to get you out as mission director. It doesn't matter that Dex and Possum got through the storm okay. He wants your scalp and he's pushing damned hard to get it."

Jamie almost smiled at Connors' choice of words, then wondered in the back of his mind why he didn't mind the black astronaut using Native American similes, but it riled him when Dex Trumball did.

Because you're not competing with Pete, he answered himself. Because you've been through so much with him. Because he's your friend.

Jamie listened to Connors' tale of woe to the end. Trumball had called a special meeting of the ICU board. Li Chengdu had told the astronaut that funding for the next expedition was going to be decided at the meeting. The implication was clear: either they removed Jamie from command, or Trumball would turn off the money flow.

When at last Connors had finished, Jamie transmitted, "Thanks for the information, Pete, both the good news and the bad. I've sent the daily report to you on the data channel; nothing outstanding to report, except that Dex and Craig have picked up the Pathfinder hardware successfully. They'll start on their way back here tomorrow morning.

"Oh, by the way, Craig prefers to be called Wiley instead of Possum. He's a little touchy about that. Otherwise we're all well and healthy here. That's all for now."

*　　*　　*

Jamie was still in the comm center when Fuchida came in, limping slightly, and asked him to come to the biology lab.

"As soon as Stacy comes back," Jamie replied.

Fuchida nodded, almost bowed, and left.

Nearly half an hour later Jamie tapped lightly on the doorframe of the bio lab. Fuchida turned on his swivel stool and swiftly got to his feet.

"Sit, Mitsuo, sit down and take it easy," Jamie said, pulling up the other stool to sit beside the biologist.

Fuchida sat, but his back remained rigid. He glanced at the open doorway, then reached across the lab bench and pulled his laptop computer toward him.

"What did you want to show me?" Jamie asked. "Any new species show up from the core samples?"

"This is not biology," Fuchida said as he booted up the laptop.

"No?"

"No. Detective work."

"Detective?"

Jamie saw on the laptop screen one of the photos he had taken of the damaged garden dome the morning after the storm.

"Do you notice two important things in this image?" Fuchida asked. His voice was low, almost a whisper.

Jamie shook his head.

"Observe," the biologist said, pointing at the screen, "that the dome fabric is puckered outward."

Nodding, Jamie said, "Yeah, it is, isn't it?"

"You took this image from outside the dome," Fuchida said.

"Right."

"What does this outward-facing puckering suggest to you?"

Christ, Jamie thought, Mitsuo's sounding like an imitation Sherlock Holmes.

"You tell me," he said.

"The puncture was made from the inside, not from the outside."

"No," Jamie said slowly. "That can't be. What could puncture the dome from the inside?"

Instead of answering, Fuchida said, "Observe the height of the puncture above the ground."

Jamie peered at the image. "Two and a half, three feet, I'd say."

"Sixty-two centimeters. I have measured it."

"What are you driving at, Mitsuo?"

Lowering his voice until it was almost a hiss, Fuchida answered, "The storm did not damage the dome. The fabric was punctured from the inside. Deliberately!"

Jamie blinked at him. "Deliberately? You're joking!"

"No joke. The puckering shows the puncture was made from inside the dome, not from outside. And the punctures are at the height a man's hand would be if his arm were fully extended downward.''

It took Jamie several moments to realize that Fuchida was completely serious.

"Mitsuo, that can't be. Nobody here would deliberately damage the dome."

Fuchida pointed silently to the display screen.

Jamie said, "For one thing, the puckering makes it look like the damage was done from inside because air from inside the dome blew outward, through the puncture."

The biologist's brows knit. "That is a possibility, I suppose."

"And the height of the punctures is just where the pebbles happened to hit the fabric."

"Both at the same height?"

Jamie shrugged. "A coincidence."

Fuchida looked totally unconvinced.

"Listen, Mitsuo, you can't believe that one of us deliberately punctured the dome during the storm. That kind of behavior would be insane!"

Fuchida nodded. "That is exactly the conclusion I came to."

It was Vijay's turn for the cleanup detail, so while Stacy and Rodriguez went back to the comm center for a final evening's systems check and Fuchida and Trudy went off to the bio lab, Jamie went to his quarters and ran through his incoming messages.

As he scanned the screen his mind wandered to Fuchida's detective work. Mitsuo's overreacting, he told himself. Who the hell would deliberately puncture the garden dome? Why? For what reason? It's all nonsense.

Still, the possibility was there, lurking in his mind like a dark ominous cloud. A madman in our midst? Jamie shook his head, tried to clear his mind of the possibility.

He finished scrolling through his messages, saw that there was nothing that demanded immediate attention, then closed down the computer and went back to the galley.

Vijay was still there. The dome lights were turned down to their overnight level. The dishwasher was humming away; the table was glistening clean. She's waiting for me, Jamie thought happily.

"Everybody else in bed?" he asked.

"Trudy and Rodriguez are," she replied lightly. "Mitsuo's still poking around out in the garden and Stacy hasn't come out of the comm center."

"Oh."

She took a mug and a teabag, then went over to the hot water dispenser. Jamie pulled out a chair and sat in it. He knew it was silly, but he wanted to wait until all the others were in their quarters for the night before he took Vijay to his cubicle.

"Mitsuo thinks somebody deliberately sabotaged the dome," he said, keeping his voice low.

"What?" She turned toward him, her eyes wide with surprise.

"He's got what he thinks is evidence."

"He's daft."

"I hope so," Jamie said.

"I'll talk to him about it," she said, bringing her cup to the table and sitting next to him.

"No, wait. Let me see what else he comes up with first."

Vijay gave him a sideways glance, unconvinced, but then nodded and said, "If that's what you want."

"Dex's father wants to bump me," he heard himself say. The words surprised him. He had convinced himself several times over not to burden her with his problem.

"I was wondering when you'd get around to talking about it," she said.

He felt an instant of shock, then realized that there were no secrets in this hothouse they lived in.

"So everybody knows about it," he said.

"Of course," she said, sitting beside him. "We've been wondering what we can do to help. You know, send a petition to the ICU board, threaten a job action, whatever."

"A job action?"

"Go on strike," she said. "Sit down on our butts until Trumball stops harassing you."

She took a sip of the steaming tea, waiting for him to respond. Looking into her lustrous black eyes Jamie realized again how beautiful she was.

"We've got this whole world to explore," he said to her. "We can't go on strike. That wouldn't help anything."

She replied, "Do you have any better ideas?"

"I've been thinking about it."

"And?"

"Trumball's threatening to hold up the funding for the next expedition."

"Using it as a hostage, I know."

"I can't let him stop the next expedition, Vijay. That would be criminal."

"How can you stop him, then?"

He leaned back and stared up into the darkness. For long moments there was no sound except the soft chugging of the life-support pumps, the faint whispered hum of electrical equipment. And the high, barely audible sighing of the night wind outside, the breath of a world calling to him.

Then he heard Vijay exhale and realized she had been holding her breath, waiting for him to answer.

"I could resign," he said flatly.

"Resign?"

"Step down as mission director. After all, I'm here on Mars; he can't call me back to Earth. I'm here for the duration of the expedition. What difference does it make if my title is mission director or bottle-washer?"

Vijay banged her cup on the table so hard that tea sloshed out of it. "You can't do that, Jamie! You can't!"

"Why not? What does the title mean? It's what we *do* here on Mars that's important."

"But he'll put Dex in charge!"

"I don't think so. I think the rest of you will get a chance to express your opinions. A vote, maybe."

She shook her head vehemently. "That would tear us apart, Jamie. Some would vote for Dex and anyone who didn't would be perceived as a vote against him."

"Yeah," he admitted. "Maybe so."

"You can't step down! That would ruin everything."

"I don't think—"

"You want to go out to the cliff dwelling, don't you? Do you think Dex would approve that?"

"I don't think Dex would be named director," he repeated.

"And who would?"

"Stacy would be my choice."

"She's not a scientist."

"Then Craig."

"Wiley? Do you think he has the respect that you do? Can you see Fuchida following Wiley's orders?"

"It's not a matter of following orders," he said.

"Of course it is! That's what the mission director's position is all about."

Jamie shook his head. "Come on, Vijay, I don't give orders to people. We all work together."

She sat up rigidly and tapped the tabletop with one manicured fin-gernail. "You don't give orders because you don't have to. Everyone here respects you tremendously. Don't you understand that? You lead by example. You're a natural leader."

"So is Dex, according to you."

"Dex wants to be what you already are. He's not there yet."

"And if I give it up, resign," Jamie could barely force the words out, "and Dex is named mission director . . . what will you do?"

She drew in her breath sharply, as if struck by a blow. For long, agonizing moments she was silent.

"What will I do?" Vijay echoed, her voice so low he could barely hear her.

"About us," Jamie whispered.

She stared at him.

"I mean—"

"My god, Jamie," she said, her voice trembling, "if you think I'm sleeping with you just because you're the boss man here . . . if you think I'll prance off to Dex's bed if he's named director . . ."

"I . . . but you said . . ."

"You're an idiot!" she snapped. "A damned fool bloody idiot!"

She stamped off toward her own quarters, leaving the mug sitting on the table in a small puddle of tea. Jamie watched her go, telling himself that she was right: I'm an idiot.

PREDAWN: SOL 64

JAMIE KNEW HE SHOULD HAVE FELT SLEEPY, BUT HE WAS WIDE AWAKE. Grimly awake.

He sat in his coveralls at the desk in his quarters, the glow from his laptop screen etching his face and throwing a dim, lumpy shadow across the back wall. I wonder what time it is in Boston? he asked himself.

The image frozen on his screen showed Darryl C. Trumball at his desk, staring into the camera, his face frozen in an angry scowl, a jewel-tipped pen in one hand. Jamie was studying Trumball's image, trying to find the soul beneath the hard exterior. What does he want? Jamie asked himself. Why does he want to get rid of me?

Jamie had sent a simple message to Trumball more than an hour earlier:

"In the interest of harmony among the ICU board members, I am willing to step down as mission director," he had said, "providing that Stacy Dezhurova is named to the position in my place, and an excursion to the possible cliff dwelling in Tithonium Chasma is inserted into our mission schedule."

The words *harmony among the ICU board* were a code phrase, aimed at assuring funding for the next expedition. Trumball had threatened to hold up the funding unless Jamie was removed from his position. Without putting it in so many words, Jamie was offering his head for an assurance of funds. And a promise to allow him to investigate the cliff dwelling.

Now he sat and waited for Trumball's reply, watching a still image of the old man taken from one of his earlier messages. He opened a window on the screen and checked the current time in Boston. Twelve minutes past two P.M. Trumball should be there; if he wasn't, somebody should have responded with that information by now.

No, he's thinking it over. Or maybe he just wants to let me stew in my own sweat for a while. That would be like his kind of man, the power-trip; all ego and no consideration for anyone else.

Maybe he's trying to talk it over with Dex, Jamie thought. But as he stared at Trumball's image on the little screen he realized that this man doesn't talk things over with anyone. He makes up his own mind for his own reasons and steamrollers anyone who objects. Or tries to.

Jamie had spent a bad hour or so after Vijay stormed out of the galley. He wondered how the others would feel if he resigned, wondered what Dex would do, in particular. I'm not doing Stacy a favor, he told himself, putting her on the hot seat.

But it's got to be done, he realized. Trumball will just make so much trouble that the next expedition will never get off the ground.

That was what had decided him. There has to be a third expedition. And a fourth and a fiftieth and a five hundredth. We have a whole world to explore! I can't let my own ego get in the way. I'd be just as bad as Trumball.

He had paced back and forth in his tiny cubicle for miles, four steps at a time, from the bunk to the accordion-fold door and back again, for hours. Worrying, balancing, tearing himself apart trying to find the right path. At last he realized what it was, what it had to be.

This isn't a contest of wills between Trumball and me. It's not a battle of alpha males between Dex and me. This is about the exploration of Mars, nothing more. And nothing less.

The decision freed him. Calmed him. He sat at his desk, opened the laptop, and sent his message to Trumball.

Now he waited for the old man's response.

And realized, down deep where the hollow tremors of fear begin, that he had lost Vijay. Lost her respect. Lost her love.

The message light on the laptop began to blink, like a yellow eye winking at him.

Jamie touched the key and Trumball's still image seemed to come to life. There he was, behind the same desk, with a different pen in his hand, looking at Jamie with a gruff expression on his cold, grim face.

"I got your message," Trumball said, his voice rough and gravelly. "I'll see to it that the board accepts your resignation. I presume you'll transmit a similar message to each of the individual board members."

Trumball shifted uneasily on his massive, high-backed leather chair, fiddled with his pen, then continued, "About your recommendation of Ms. Dezhurova, I don't know. Will the other scientists up there with you accept her, or will they want another scientist to be named mission director? I'd like to know what they think."

Jamie felt surprised that Trumball was not insisting outright that his son be named director.

"As far as your request to go out and look at your supposed cliff dwelling, it's all right with me if it's all right with the rest of your people. You've got an extra rover vehicle, thanks to my son. Use it to go out there and take a look. If it's real, it'll be the greatest tourist attraction since the Crucifixion."

The picture winked off. Trumball had had his say, he'd gotten his way. Jamie sat there feeling as if a heavyweight boxer had just punched him in the gut.

A tourist attraction. The greatest discovery in the history of the world, of two worlds, and all he can think of is a goddamned tourist attraction!

Jamie wanted to leap to his feet and scream. I'll be working for him! he realized. If the cliff dwellings are real, I'll be leading him to them so he can build a fucking Disneyland around them! I'll be a Judas goat! A traitor to everything and everybody.

He sank his head in his hands. He wanted to cry, but knew that he couldn't.

The sun was already up at Ares Vallis, and Dex was driving the rover while Craig ate breakfast. They had decided to eat in shifts now, rather than stop the rover for meals.

The comm screen flickered, then Jamie's dark, somber face formed on it. With just a glance, Dex saw that Jamie looked terrible, as if he'd been up all night, red-eyed and wrinkled.

"I assume I didn't wake you," Jamie began, his voice tight, almost hoarse.

"No, we've been percolating along for nearly an hour," Dex chirped happily.

Without further preamble, Jamie said, "I've just told your father I'm willing to step down as mission director. I recommended Stacy take over the job."

Dex felt a clutch of surprise, then heard himself ask, "What'd my father say?"

"He said it's okay with him as long as the rest of you agree."

Son of a bitch, Dex thought. Dear old Dad wouldn't recommend me for the job, not him. He doesn't think I could handle it.

He said to Jamie, "What's everybody back there think about this?"

"They don't know about it yet. It's too early for them to be up."

Craig came up to the cockpit, chewing on a piece of precooked omelet, and slipped into the right-hand seat.

"They won't have any objections to Stacy," Dex said, trying to keep his seething anger from showing.

"Do you?" Jamie asked.

"She's not a scientist," Craig said.

Jamie nodded solemnly. "But she knows what she's doing and she understands what we're doing. I think she's the best one for the job."

"Obviously," Dex snapped.

Craig said, "I got no gripes with her. She's got a good head on her shoulders."

"I'd like this to be unanimous, Dex," Jamie said.

"Sure. Why not?"

"You agree?"

"That's what I said, isn't it?"

"Okay, okay. Thanks."

"For nothing."

Once Jamie's image winked out, Craig leaned over and grabbed Dex's shoulder. "You think the job shoulda gone to you?"

Dex grinned at his shaggy-bearded partner. "To tell the truth, Wiley, I think Stacy's better for the job than I'd be."

"Sure you do."

"I do, honest! But that doesn't mean I don't *want* to be the boss."

"You're pissed at Jamie for not namin' you?" Craig probed.

"No," Dex said, shaking his head. And he found that it was the truth. He felt no anger at Jamie. The redskin was only doing what he thought was best for the mission.

But dear old Dad, Dex thought, his insides raging. The old sonofa-bitch wouldn't lift a finger on my behalf. He doesn't think I could handle it. He doesn't trust me with any responsibility at all.

Dex leaned on the accelerator harder. I'll show him. I'll show them all.

How, he did not know. But Dex felt a steel-sharp determination hardening inside him. It doesn't matter if Jamie's in charge or Stacy or the friggin' Man in the Moon. *I'm* going to be the head of this expedition, one way or the other.

Jamie saw the strange, almost feral look on Dex's bearded face before he cut the comm link to the rover. He's angry; pissed as hell. He wanted to be the director and he's furious that he's not getting the job.

He got up from his little desk and stretched, letting tendons crack and vertebrae pop.

I'm free of it now, Jamie thought. Now I can concentrate on getting back to Tithonium and seeing just what that cliff structure really is.

Stacy's going to have a tough time of it, he knew. Dex will be running up her back the minute he gets here.

He shook his head. That's not your problem anymore. Now you're free to do what you came here for. Just one more task, and then you're a free man. All you've got to do now is tell Stacy the joyous news. And the others. They'll all agree that Stacy's right for the job. It'll be unanimous, no sweat.

All you've got to do is tell them about it.

And tell Vijay.

BOOK III:
THE CLIFF DWELLING

   The sky gods placed the red world farther from Father Sun than the blue world, and also much closer to the small worldlets that still swarmed in the darkness of the void, leftover bits and pieces from the time of the beginning. Often they streaked down onto the red world, howling like monsters as they traced their demon's trail of fire across the pale sky.
   Small, cold, bombarded by sky demons, its air and water slowly wasting away, the creatures of the red world had to struggle mightily to keep the spark of existence glowing within them.
   Even so, death struck swiftly, and without remorse.

THE PROCESS OF DECISION: SOL 99

"YOU CAN'T GO ALONE," SAID STACY DEZHUROVA.

"Why not?" Jamie asked.

"It is out of the question, Jamie."

"But there's nobody else who can come with me now that Tomas is hurt."

He and Stacy were in her quarters, which Dezhurova had turned into something of an office since being named mission director. She did most of her work there, summoning people in to see her rather than going out to them, as Jamie had.

He sat on the little wheeled typist's chair that Dezhurova had commandeered for her cubicle, while Stacy sat rigidly in the desk chair facing him.

The responsibility of command has changed her over the past month, Jamie thought, looking over the tight lines around her mouth and eyes. She's doing a good job, but it's taking a lot out of her.

The cubicle was pathologically neat: bunk made up precisely, desktop clear, papers and clothes put away in their proper places. Yet she had stopped wearing the standard-issue coveralls. Instead she had pulled on a heavy khaki loose-fitting shirt with military-style epaulets and a pair of faded jeans from her personal locker. And Stacy had chopped her sandy brown pageboy down to a military buzz cut; Jamie was surprised to see streaks of gray in it.

On the other hand, Jamie felt more relaxed and free than he had ever been. His responsibilities were almost totally gone. He could devote himself completely to planning his trip back to the Grand Canyon and the niche in the cliff face where he had seen the—building. Jamie was certain of that. What he had seen in that cleft in the rock was one or more buildings. Buildings constructed by intelligent Martians.

He was certain of it. But was he right? I'll find out in another few days, he told himself. Once I get past this problem of a partner to go with me.

"Look, Stacy, I'm not trying to give you a hard time," he said, "but I just don't see who you can spare to go on this excursion with me."

"Then you are not going," she answered flatly.

"Now come on . . ."

Dezhurova shook her head stubbornly. "Jamie, you know the safety regulations as well as I do. Nobody is allowed beyond walk-back range alone.''

"But Tomas won't be fit for that kind of work for weeks.''

"Then either you wait, or we pick somebody else to go with you.''

Rodriguez had come close to killing himself in an accident with the solar-heated kiln that made the glass bricks for the greenhouse they were building around the garden dome. He had burned his hand badly, right through the glove of his hard suit. Luckily, Trudy Hall had been working with him. She sealed the pressure cuff at his wrist and helped him back inside the dome, while he groaned with pain.

So now the astronaut's duties were confined to sitting at the comm console and serving as a one-handed mission communicator.

"I can make it by myself,'' Jamie insisted. "We can bend the rules a little, Stacy.''

She gave him a look that was unnervingly like the one his eighth-grade English teacher used to do when he was late with an essay.

"Jamie, you handed me this responsibility, remember?'' she said slowly. "I can't let you go out there by yourself. If you get killed, I would never forgive myself.''

"But there's nobody else available,'' Jamie repeated. "You're needed here. Trudy and Mitsuo have their hands full with the bio work. It wouldn't be fair to ask either one of them to stop what they're doing.''

"Tarawa would not agree to that, in any case.''

"Right.''

"There is Wiley,'' Dezhurova said.

"He and Dex are up to their armpits dating all the samples we've brought in,'' Jamie said. "Besides, he's put in enough time in the rover.''

Stacy shrugged and unconsciously scratched her shoulder. The khaki shirt must itch, Jamie thought.

"There isn't anybody else,'' he said. "Dex is too busy, same as Wiley.''

"Vijay?'' Dezhurova asked.

She had not slept with Jamie since he had told her he would resign his director's position. She was coolly pleasant, but in a brittle, painful way. To the best of Jamie's knowledge, she was not sleeping with Dex, either. He felt glad of that, but it was scant consolation.

"The medic ought to stay here, where most of the team is,'' Jamie said. "Besides, she's still looking after Tomas' hand.''

"She is not qualified for driving the rover, anyway,'' said Dezhurova. She sighed, almost as if she were in pain. "You will have to wait until Tom can work again.''

"I don't want to wait,'' Jamie said firmly. "I'm ready to go now.

I've got no other responsibilities. The extra rover's ready to go and so am I.''

Dezhurova started to say no. Jamie could see her lips forming the word. But she hesitated, took a breath, and said instead, "Let me think about it, Jamie. Let me see if there is something I can work out.''

Jamie understood what she was doing: saying no without using the word.

He got up from the little wheeled chair, making it skitter across the plastic flooring a few inches.

"Stacy, tomorrow is the one hundredth day since we landed. I'm taking the rover out tomorrow, whether you like it or not.''

He turned and left her quarters before she could answer.

As he strode toward his own cubicle he thought, Yeah, go out and take the rover. How can she stop me? Get Dex and the rest of the guys to overpower me?

By the time he had slid shut the door to his quarters and looked at his own messed-up bunk, though, he was saying to himself, Right, steal the rover and leave Stacy looking like an impotent boob. That'd be a great thing to do. Just wonderful. What a fine upstanding example of a jerk you'd be.

But the alternative was to wait a couple of weeks, maybe more. A couple of eternities. Who knew what problems would crop up in a couple of weeks? Something's always getting in the way. We've been here a hundred days tomorrow and I'm no closer to that village than I was the day we landed.

It took three calls for Stacy to locate Vijay. She was not in the infirmary and not in the bio lab. When Dezhurova tried the geology lab, Dex's voice answered brightly, "Yeah, she's right here.''

Ninety seconds later Vijay tapped once on the door to Dezhurova's quarters and slid it back partway.

"Dex said you want to see me.''

Stacy nodded and gestured to the seat that Jamie had been on. Vijay sat down, knees together, hands on thighs. Her coveralls looked slightly faded, but she had tied a bright scarf around her waist and had a smaller one knotted loosely at her throat. Brilliant colors of India, Stacy thought. She makes the rest of us look drab.

"I am having a problem with Jamie," said Dezhurova.

For just an instant Vijay's eyes widened slightly. "What about Jamie?''

"You are the resident psychologist," Dezhurova said, then, with a slight smile curving her lips, "and you know Jamie better than anyone here . . .''

"If this is about our personal relationship—''

"It is not. It is about the work of this expedition. And it is about Jamie and you . . . and Dex."

"Dex?"

"Listen," Stacy said. Then she began to explain.

Vijay listened. Then gave her opinion. Dezhurova thanked her and asked her to send Wiley Craig in. She spoke to Craig for nearly an hour.

When all eight of them were gathered around the dinner table that evening, Dezhurova asked:

"Jamie, what if Dex went with you on your excursion?"

Everyone stopped eating. Plastic forks hung in midair. Drink cups were put back down on the table. Even the chewing stopped.

Startled by the idea, Jamie glanced across the table at Dex and saw that he was just as surprised.

"Wiley says he can handle the geology analyses for a week or so—"

Craig interrupted, "Long as the mapmaker program don't glitch again."

"So Dex can be relieved of his regular duty," Dezhurova finished. "And he is certainly qualified to drive the rover."

"I can make it alone," Jamie said tightly.

"That is out of the question, I told you that," said Dezhurova.

"For what it's worth," Dex said, with his usual impudent grin, "I wouldn't mind going out again. And I can keep on working on the rock dating, as long as Wiley feeds me the data and Jamie doesn't mind doing the driving."

Jamie's mind was racing. I don't want Dex on this trip. He'll spoil it. Ruin it. Somehow he'll make a mess of it.

But he heard his grandfather's voice whisper, Take him with you. That's the only path open to you. Don't fight it. Accept it.

He turned his gaze from Dex's cocky, grinning face to Vijay's. She looked tense, big dark eyes fixed on him as if she were waiting for an explosion. Jamie realized, If Dex comes with me, he won't be here with her while I'm away.

He looked back at Dex. "What do you say, Dex? It might be a wild goose chase."

"Or the greatest tourist attraction of all time," Dex replied easily.

Jamie felt his teeth grind together. This trip might produce the first murder on Mars, he thought.

MORNING: SOL 100

"YOU GOT THE BEST FUEL CELLS," WILEY CRAIG WAS SAYING AS JAMIE and Dex suited up. "Swapped 'em outta rover numero uno."

"There should be no problem of dust storms," Fuchida assured them. "The weather has stabilized. Summer is almost here."

Dex laughed. "Yeah. Maybe we'll get a couple hours above freezing out there."

Vijay hovered to one side as the two men wormed their arms through the sleeves of the hard suit torsos. Craig was assisting Jamie, Fuchida helped Dex.

Boots, leggings, torso. Check the seals at ankles, waist and wrists. Backpack. Check the connections: electrical, air, water.

"Stacy wants to talk to you before you go out," Vijay said.

Reaching for his helmet on the shelf above the suit rack, Jamie said, "You'd better call her, then."

"Yeah," said Dex, pulling his helmet over his head. "We're ready for the big game, coach."

Vijay walked quickly away. Jamie put his helmet on, sealed the neck ring, then he and Dex went through the radio check.

Stacy strode down the corridor formed by the equipment lockers, wearing regulation coveralls. Jamie noticed that with Vijay walking beside her, Stacy looked big, solid, bulky almost. Vijay, also in coveralls, seemed petite yet dark and lush and glowing.

And worried. Jamie looked into Vijay's midnight-black eyes and saw fear.

Before he could say anything to her, Stacy spoke up, "I have carved one full week out of the schedule. I expect you back here in seven days or less."

"Unless we find some Martians," Dex quipped.

Stacy let a tight smile break her stern facade. "Naturally, if you find something startling, we will have to rework the schedule."

Jamie thought that she was turning into a bureaucrat, more worried about the schedule than what they might discover. But she's doing a better job of running the expedition than I did, he admitted to himself.

"The scheduled excursions to the volcanoes and back to the floor of the Canyon are waiting for your return," Stacy reminded them. "All our exploratory work is on hold until you get back."

"I understand," Jamie said softly.

"The soarplanes have mapped your route in detail," Stacy went on.

"We've got the imagery," Dex replied.

"Well . . . good luck, then." She put her hand out to Jamie. It trembled slightly. She's as excited about this as I am! Jamie realized. But she hides it damned well.

Dex shook hands with her, then blew a kiss to Vijay. Jamie wanted to take her in his arms, but he knew that would be awkwardly foolish in the hard suit. She looked into his eyes and he saw fear, anxiety, and something else, something he could not pin down. But she cares, he thought. She cares about me. Or about Dex.

"Good luck," she said, keeping her voice calm, neutral.

"We'll be back in a week or less," Dex assured them.

Jamie ignored the others and stared only at Vijay.

"Come back safe," she said, looking straight at him.

He nodded inside his helmet. I'll come back to you, he wanted to say. But in front of all the others, in front of Dex, he could not speak the words aloud.

Instead, he slammed down the visor of his helmet and started for the airlock hatch.

"Gloves!" Wiley Craig shouted. "Jamie, you gotta put your gloves on."

Jamie stopped in midstride. His gloves, with the power-boosting miniaturized servo motors on their backs, were still on the bench in front of his locker, resting there like a pair of dead lobsters.

"Chrissakes," Craig grumbled, handing the gloves to Jamie, "what-tuvwe got a checklist for if you're just gonna ignore it?"

"Thanks, Wiley," Jamie said, pulling on the stiff gloves and sealing the cuffs around his wrists.

"Jamie wants to Indian wrestle his Martians barehanded," Dex kidded.

Holding up both his gloved hands, Jamie said through his sealed visor, "I won't forget them again."

"Once'll be enough to kill you," Craig grumbled.

Jamie glanced again at Vijay. She looked stricken.

Stacy, ever practical, said firmly, "You two check each other out completely before leaving the rover. Every time. Call in to me whenever you are going outside and we will go down the checklist together. Understood?"

"Yes, Mama," said Dex, with a laugh.

Jamie thought it might be a damned good idea.

Vijay spelled Rodriguez at the communications console until dinner, then the astronaut came back into the comm center.

"Dinnertime," he said, gesturing with his bandaged hand in the general direction of the galley.

"Why don't you eat first," Vijay said. "I'll be okay here until you're finished."

"Already ate," Rodriguez said, easing himself into the chair next to her. "I'm getting the hang of doing it one-handed."

Despite herself, Vijay grinned at him. "You mean you don't need Trudy to spoon-feed you anymore?"

His swarthy cheeks flushed noticeably. "Naw. But don't let her know!"

Vijay laughed.

"Go on and eat," Rodriguez said. "If they call in, I'll give you a yell, okay?"

Reluctantly, Vijay slipped the headset off. "Okay," she said.

Dex put through a routine call when they stopped for the night; strictly business, no personal messages. Vijay picked at her dinner, then headed for her quarters.

Stacy intercepted her. "Come to my office," she said. "We must talk."

Vijay followed Stacy to her cubicle and sat on the stiff little desk chair. Stacy plunked herself down on the edge of the bunk.

"Do you understand why I decided to have Dex go with Jamie?" Stacy asked, with no preamble.

"So that Jamie wouldn't worry about Dex being here with me while he's out on the excursion."

"That is part of it."

Vijay felt her brows rise in a silent question.

"The rest of it is that I didn't want Dex here, where he could—what's the expression?—hit on you."

Vijay scoffed, "I could handle that."

"Perhaps. But this way there is no problem at all; you don't have to worry about handling it."

"Thank you, then."

"I didn't do it for you, Vijay. I did it for Jamie. I didn't want him out there worrying about you. He is too good a man to have to carry that burden."

"I see."

"And also," Dezhurova hunched forward slightly, "I am not so certain how well you would handle Dex. He can be very seductive."

"I had my fling with Dex," Vijay said, feeling a simmering of anger stir within her. "It's over and done with."

"And your fling with Jamie?"

"I don't think that's any of your business, is it?"

Stacy smiled like a patient mother. "No, of course it is not. It's just that . . . I like Jamie. I respect him. I don't want to see him hurt again.''

"Again?"

"His first marriage. It left its marks on him, you know."

Vijay nodded. "Yes."

"Do you love him?"

Startled by the question, Vijay flared, "How should I know? How can any of us know what we're feeling while we're here? This isn't the real world! We're so far away from the real world, so isolated and alone . . .''

Strangely, Dezhurova's smile widened. "Good. That is a good, honest answer. It is what I expected, what I hoped for."

"What are you talking about?"

Stacy got up from the bunk and stood beside Vijay. Bending down to put her face next to Vijay's, she said softly, "There was the chance that you are just a hot-blooded young woman who enjoys sleeping with strong men. Or worse, a fool who thinks it is romantic to go to bed with every man who is attracted to her."

Vijay shot to her feet.

"Don't get angry," Dezhurova said quickly. "I was fairly certain you were not really like that, but I had to find out for myself. A woman like that could wreck this team. Someone could be hurt badly, maybe even killed."

Reining in her resentment, Vijay hissed, "So what have you decided?"

Stacy patted her shoulder. "You are not a safety risk. Not a deliberate one, at least. You have a good head on your shoulders."

The anger drained out of Vijay. She sank back onto the chair and looked up at Dezhurova. "So what should I do about Jamie?"

Stacy shook her head and went back to the bunk. "Don't ask me. All I know about men is that they always end up hurting you."

"Take a look at this," Dex called to Jamie.

He was sitting in the cockpit, a message from his father on the panel's central screen.

The rover was buttoned up for the night. Tomorrow they would reach Tithonium Chasma and Jamie would go down to the cleft in the cliff face and see what was to be seen. Already he felt a tightness in his gut, an anticipatory tingle of excitement and worry.

He made his way past the bunks and ducked into the cockpit, leaning his arms against the back of Dex's seat. The screen showed a list of names, individuals, schools, corporations, with dollar figures to one side of each.

"What is it?" Jamie asked.

"My dear old dad is already lining up backers for the next expedition,'' Dex explained. ''He's raised three bil, just like that.'' He snapped his fingers.

Jamie slid into the driver's seat and stared at the screen. ''Global News . . . Universal Entertainment . . . who's Puget Sound Inc.?''

''Holding company,'' Dex said. ''They own or control half the travel agencies in North America.''

''Travel agencies?''

Dex nodded. ''Don't get worked up. Not yet. We're a long way from bringing tourists up here.''

''Then why would travel agencies want to help fund the next expedition?''

''To get VR tour rights, I guess. Take a trip without leaving the comfort of your living room.''

Jamie looked at Dex. The younger man seemed perfectly serious.

''Look, Jamie, I'd be lying if I said they didn't intend to bring tourist groups to Mars eventually. Hell, they're already packaging trips to the Moon, aren't they?''

''Tourists,'' Jamie muttered darkly.

''Well you don't have to look at me as though I led the massacre at Wounded Knee, for chrissakes,'' Dex said.

''You're the one who wants to do this, Dex, not me.''

''We've got to! How the hell do you expect to raise the money you need to explore this planet otherwise?''

''I'd rather go begging on street corners.''

''And you'd get nickels and dimes,'' Dex snapped. ''Get real!''

Getting up from the chair, Jamie said, ''There's got to be a better way, Dex.''

''Sure. Get the government to do it. It took Brumado twenty years to get the first expedition funded and you didn't see the government rushing to back this one, did you?''

''There's got to be a better way.''

''You find it, let me know about it.''

Starting for the galley, Jamie said, ''You're going to turn Mars into a tourist attraction.''

''How the hell d'you think we got here this time?'' Dex said, with some heat in his voice.

Jamie turned back to face him. ''Because your father ramrodded the funding drive, I know.''

''Because I got him to do it!'' Dex said, jabbing a thumb at his own chest. ''He didn't have the faintest frigging interest in Mars. I got him interested.''

''By telling him he could sell tickets to tourists.''

''By telling him he could make money out of it, yeah. What's wrong with that?''

''We can't do scientific research with tourists crawling over us.''

"Aw, come on, Jamie! We've got a whole *planet* here. We can keep the tourists out of our way."

"Really?" Jamie felt the old seething anger boiling up in him. "They'll want to go to the most interesting places, won't they? Down at the Canyon floor, where we found the lichen, for example. They'll be picking samples and tramping all over the place."

"We won't let that happen."

"How're you going to stop it, Dex? Once we let them start coming here, where do we draw the line? Money talks, doesn't it? The people who pay the money are going to want to do what *they* want to do, won't they?"

Dex strode up the narrow aisle to stand almost touching noses with Jamie. "Christ, you think you're the only scientist in the frigging solar system? I want to do good science, too, y'know."

"If your tourists allow us to."

"Damn!" Dex slammed a fist against the folded upper bunk above his own. "This damned holier-than-thou shit! I've had it up to here!" He pointed his other hand at his Adam's apple.

Jamie felt the heat rising in his own face. "And then you'll want to start building big tourist facilities. Hotels. Parks where they can walk around in their shirtsleeves. You're going to wreck this planet, Dex. A whole world destroyed, and its native life-forms with it."

"That's a hundred years in the future, maybe more."

"It's *now*, Dex. What we do now shapes the future. Every step we take creates our path into tomorrow. What you want to do is going to destroy this world, just as surely as the Europeans destroyed the world of the Native Americans."

"You think I *want* it this way?"

"You talked your father into doing it this way, didn't you?"

"It's the only way we could get here, Jamie! Dammit, the politicians weren't going to back another expedition. Why do you think it took six years to get this one here?"

Jamie glared at him.

"I'm a scientist, too," Dex said. "I talked my father into getting the money for us because *I wanted to go to Mars*! You think you're the only one?"

With a shake of his head, Jamie said, "But the price, Dex. The price. It'd be better if we'd left Mars alone for another hundred years and waited until we could come here purely for the science."

"In a perfect world, maybe," Dex replied, his voice lower. "But then you and I wouldn't be here, would we?"

"No, I guess not."

"Well, I want to be on Mars. Now. Me. Whatever it costs. And you feel the same way, too, or you wouldn't be here."

Jamie looked into the younger man's face. The brash grin was gone, the blue-green eyes were deep and unwavering.

"Maybe you're right," Jamie admitted, heading back toward the galley again. "But I feel like a Judas goat."

"Or Kit Carson, maybe?"

Jamie whirled back and saw that Dex was grinning again. *He knows about the Long Walk, when Carson and the army forced the People off their own land.*

"Right," he said tightly. "Kit Carson. That's me."

AFTERNOON: SOL 101

JAMIE DANGLED HALF A MILE FROM THE CLIFF'S RIM, SWAYING IN THE HAR-ness, the layered reddish rock face a mere arm's length from him. He touched it with one booted foot, then pushed away. It made him tilt back and forth dizzily like a kid on a swing.

"Almost there," he grunted. He realized that he was panting and sweaty, even with the motorized winch doing most of the work.

"Take it easy now." Dex's voice sounded tight, harsh in his earphones. The two men had said almost nothing to one another after their argument the previous night; their only words had been those necessary for their work.

Jamie realized he was trusting his life to Dex, up there with the winch that held his lifeline. He almost laughed to himself. *Our argument is purely philosophical, not physical.* But then he thought of Vijay and realized that it could get physical quickly enough, once they returned to the dome.

Carefully, he touched the power control. The rock face slid past, too fast, almost a blur. He lifted his gloved finger from the control stud and the harness jerked to a stop again, swinging him even more violently than before. He banged against the rock with his shoulder, forcing a grunt from his lungs, then put his legs out again to cushion the next blow.

"You okay?"

"Yeah. Okay," Jamie answered.

"I'm getting seasick watching your imagery," Dex complained.

The balky VR cameras clipped to Jamie's helmet were recording everything, not so much for show business but to maintain a record of the descent. Dex had set up a portable monitor beside the winch, up at the rim of the Canyon.

Reluctantly, Jamie looked down. The cleft in the rock wall was still several hundred meters below. And the bottom of the canyon seemed thousands of kilometers deeper, swaying rhythmically, so far down that it looked like a carpet of red blood waiting for him to fall into it.

How's that look, wiseass? he asked Dex silently.

Then his own stomach heaved. Jamie clutched the thin Buckyball cable with both hands. Closing his eyes, he told himself that the cable could hold more than a ton of weight, that he himself weighed only a third on Mars of his weight on Earth, that the harness held him securely and had never been known to break.

Still, it was a long way down. A *long* way. He leaned back as far as he dared to look up through the visor of his helmet and realized it was a long way back up to the canyon rim, too.

Licking his lips, he said into his helmet microphone, "Okay, one more time ought to do it."

"Be careful," Dex said.

"Right," Jamie said, adding silently, Great advice. Like he gives a damn.

He touched the power stud as lightly as he could, barely kissing it, and the cliff wall slid past more slowly. Maybe I'm getting the hang of it, Jamie told himself. The ride smoothed out as he held his finger frozen on the button and watched the rock face unreel past his staring eyes, layer upon layer, red and brown, pink and bleached pale tan, a streak of yellowish white, a smear of gleaming silver. It looked to him like sedimentary deposits that had been put down billions of years ago, when Mars was young and an ocean covered what was now bleak waterless desert.

And then the land had split apart, ripped open for thousands of kilometers, a jagged wound that left a scar eight kilometers deep; it made the Grand Canyon of Arizona look like a dimple. What broke the ground open like this, what could rip open a canyon so wide you can't even see the other side of it because it's over the horizon?

It couldn't be plate tectonics, like on Earth. Mars' core wasn't hot enough for long enough to cause a rift like this.

A crevice scrolled up before him and Jamie stopped the winch. But it was only a crack in the canyon wall, a long thin cave, dark and empty. No Navahos hiding in it from Carson and his treacherous Ute Indian scouts.

He started down again. No sound except his own breathing; the winch itself was more than a kilometer above him, up on the canyon rim with Trumball.

The rock began to blur again. Too fast. Jamie eased the pressure of his cramped finger and his descent slowed.

He glanced down again and saw, between his dangling boots, the dark edge of the niche. Almost there. Another few meters. Slowly, painfully slowly, he lowered himself.

It was a huge recess in the canyon wall, as big as the hollow at Mesa Verde, maybe bigger. Heavy rock overhang to protect it from the weather, not that there'd been much weather on Mars over the past thousand millennia.

"I'm at the niche," he reported into his helmet mike. "Going to manual."

For a moment there was no reply, then Dex's voice said tightly, "I'm getting your camera view. Looks good."

Jamie nodded. If anything happens to me, they'll have it all on video. Something for the tourists to see.

Swinging in midair, he disengaged the winch's power control and began lowering himself by hand, slowly, carefully, staring into the shadowed recess in the cliff face as he descended.

It was there! Jamie saw a smooth wall of grayish-pink, something like sandstone, rising from the floor of the giant cave. It was laid out so perfectly straight that it couldn't possibly be a natural formation. It had been *built*, constructed by intelligence.

For eternally-long moments he hung there in the harness, swaying slightly back and forth, and merely stared at the wall rising into the shadows of the crevasse, almost as high as the rock ceiling would allow. He could feel his heart thumping against his ribs.

"Are you all right?"

Dex's voice stirred him out of his awestruck daze.

"Do you see it?" Jamie shouted, his voice pitched high with exhilaration.

"Yeah, I've got it on the monitor," he replied. "It really looks like a wall."

"It *is* a wall! A wall that somebody built!"

"Don't go jumping to conclusions," Dex said, his voice strained, harsh.

Slowly, deliberately, Jamie turned his head from one end of the wall to its far corner so that the camera mounted on his helmet, slaved to where his eyes pointed, could record its entire length.

"Nearly a hundred meters long," he reported. "About ten-twelve meters high, I'd estimate."

"Looks like the top edge has crumbled," Dex said. "Hard to tell, though, it's in shadow."

"Crumbled, broken, right," said Jamie. "Must be fairly soft material. Sandstone, or something like it."

"Can you tell how thick it is?"

"Not from here."

No response from above. He knows what comes next, Jamie told himself.

"I'm going in," he said.

Immediately Dex replied, "No! It's too late in the day, the sun'll be going down in another hour or so. It'll still be there tomorrow."

"I can do it," Jamie said. "I've climbed enough mountains on Earth to handle this." Silently he added, The hell with tomorrow. I'm going in there *now*.

He unclipped the spring-loaded tether gun from his equipment belt and held it in both gloved hands, aiming for the niche's rock floor rather than the wall itself. Sandstone might give way, he told himself, but in reality he knew it would be sacrilegious to deface the wall.

Jamie squeezed the trigger and the tether buzzed out, vibrating in his hands as it unreeled. The power spike imbedded itself in the rock floor with a thunk he could hear even in the thin air as he dangled in the harness. When he fastened the gun back on his belt, the tether automatically adjusted its tension to take up the slack. Jamie tested the line; it seemed to be holding fast.

"Dammit, Jamie, if you don't start up I'm going to power up the winch and drag you up! Come on. Now."

Jamie ignored Dex's call. Carefully he pulled himself into the crevice, hand over gloved hand, until his boots touched the stone floor of the niche. The wall loomed above him, pinkish brown, solid, silent.

With trembling hands Jamie bent over to anchor the cable attached to his harness on the spike in the stone floor. He worked with enforced, consciously deliberate motions. He was quivering inside; he wanted to leap out and explore the cliff dwelling, but he knew he had to make certain his lifeline back to the rim of the canyon wall was secure. Like a drunk trying to show he was sober, Jamie tied down the cable with exaggerated exactness.

"Your picture's breaking up." Dex's voice crackled with static in his earphones. "Rock's interfering with the transmission."

"Can't be helped," Jamie said. He started to unclip the harness. His hands were shaking so much it took him three tries to unfasten it completely.

"Jamie, you've got to come up now." Dex's urging voice was weak, distant, scratched with interference.

"Half an hour," he said absently as he finally stepped out of the harness and stood erect and free on the floor of the crevice. His insides were trembling.

"Don't go . . . wait until . . ." Dex's voice fluttered, whined, ". . . Stacy . . . from the dome . . . having a fit . . ."

Jamie ignored him. He looked up at the wall that rose before him, the wall built by Martians. High up, near its top, he saw rectangular openings. A line of them, from one end of the wall to the other.

Windows! They're windows! What had looked like a broken, crumbled roof line from outside was actually a row of windows staring out into the canyon. His knees felt rubbery, his insides fluttered.

They were here, Grandfather, he said in his mind. They really were here. Jamie's eyes blurred, and he realized they were filled with tears.

His earphones were silent now, except for a faint hissing static. The voices from above couldn't reach him here. Jamie was alone with the ghosts of the long-gone past.

The building was *old*. Even encased in the bulky hard suit Jamie could feel the centuries and millennia, the eons that these walls had stood here. The solid, silent stones exuded age, untold spans of years, countless generations of hope and faith and endurance. The burnished dying light from the distant setting sun bathed the walls in a ruddy luster, made them seem to glow from within.

Old, incredibly ancient. Before the cliff dwellings of the Old Ones. Before the Parthenon. Before the Pyramids this building stood here in this niche of rock, waiting, waiting.

Waiting for me. For us. For people of the blue world to find you, Jamie said to himself.

Blinking, forcing his shaking legs to carry him, he paced the length of the stone wall. His geologist's mind was asking: How old? What materials? What purpose? But in his red heart he knew: Intelligent creatures built this community, this village, in this sheltered cove of rock millions of years ago.

Millions of years ago.

They were here! What happened to them? Where did they go?

"Are you getting this imagery?" he asked.

No reply.

Jamie forced himself to walk back to the spike and the tethered cable. He could see that the sky was beginning to darken. What little sunlight left to the day carried no warmth.

"Can you hear me, Dex?"

"Yes! You've got to come up. It's almost sunset."

"Come on down," Jamie said. "I'll send the harness up to you."

"No! I can't."

"Dex, you won't want to miss this. When we report back to Stacy and the others, it ought to be both of us."

A long moment of silence. Then Dex said, "There's only about another half-hour of daylight. Maybe less."

"Enough," Jamie said, unfastening the cable from the spike imbedded in the rock floor. The harness swung free, out beyond the edge of the cleft.

"Take it up," he told Trumball. "Full speed. Don't waste time."

"The safety regulations . . ."

"There were Martians down here, Dex. Living, intelligent, building Martians."

The harness yanked up and out of sight.

While he waited for Dex, Jamie paced deeper into the cleft, along the side wall of the village. He saw low entryways in the wall and, back in the gloomy shadows at the rear of the cave, a circular pit.

A well? he asked himself. Too big for that. A kiva? He laughed nervously. Don't start that. It'd be a kiva back in Mesa Verde, but that doesn't mean the Martians built the same kind of religious centers. Don't jump to conclusions.

But what else could it be? a voice in his head demanded.

Patience, his grandfather whispered. You can't unlock all the doors at once.

"I'm starting down," Dex's voice crackled in his earphones, tense, unhappy.

"Great."

"Nobody's minding the winch, y'know."

"It won't walk away," Jamie said. "We planted it good and firm."

"I hope."

Jamie paced the length of the building, fighting the irrational urge to tear off his hard suit and face these ancient stones unprotected, feel them with his bare hands.

The sky above the far horizon was turning from orange to violet when Dex came into view, dangling in the harness. Jamie wished he could see the man's face, see his eyes pop at his first sight of the dwelling.

He heard Dex's sharp intake of breath. "Christ, how old can this be?"

"That's what we're here to find out," Jamie said.

THE SPEED OF LIGHT

VIJAY FELT THE PRESS OF THEIR BODIES AS ALL SIX OF THE EXPLORERS crowded into the comm center. Rodriguez sat at the console with his bandaged hand tied against his chest by a sling. Stacy Dezhurova sat beside him. No one made a sound, not even a breath, as they stared at the main display screen.

"We've got to get back up to the rover now," Jamie was saying, his voice sounding tired, drained. "I just wanted to make sure that you all saw this. It's a building, for certain. There were intelligent Martians here."

Vijay's throat felt dry, even though she was perspiring in the hot, crowded cubicle.

"I did not think it was real," Dezhurova admitted, her voice low, hollow. "Not until your imagery started to come through did I believe it is real."

"It's real," Jamie said. "Better send the news to Tarawa."

Pete Connors was dozing peacefully in his aluminum-and-plastic beach lounge chair. It was Sunday afternoon. The sun was hot, but the breeze coming in off the reef was brisk and delicious. He had been watching the Kansas City Chiefs playing a night football game against the Philadelphia Eagles on his little portable TV, but had fallen asleep in the middle of a scoreless defensive struggle.

He awoke to his wife rudely shaking his shoulder. "Wha . . . whatsamatter?"

She was frowning. "It's the office. They want you to come over right away. Top priority, they say."

Connors scrambled out of the lounge chair, nearly tripping himself. "What the hell's gone wrong now?" he muttered.

With a peck for his wife's cheek he ran from the lanai around the corner of the tile-roofed house to the garage, hopped on his electric motorbike, and started pedalling furiously down the housing tract street that led to the island's main road.

In less than ten minutes he was gawking at Jamie's footage of the cliff dwelling.

"Oh my good lord," said former astronaut Pete Connors, sinking into a chair in front of the display screen. "This is the big one."

The people crowding around him in the cinderblock-walled comm center were staring too, some grinning, some open-mouthed with awe.

"Feed this to ICU headquarters right away," Connors said.

"It's Saturday evening in New York," one of his assistants reminded him. "They'll be closed."

"Maybe we ought to send it directly to the news media?" someone suggested.

"No!" Connors snapped. "ICU's got to make the announcement, not us. Get the board chairman on the phone, wherever he is. And Li Chengdu, at Princeton."

"What about Mr. Trumball?"

Connors took in a deep breath. "Yeah, Trumball, too. He'd get pretty pissed if we didn't tell him right off."

Walter Laurence was sipping a martini as he supervised the trimming of the family Christmas tree, a chore that he once dreaded, but now that he was a grandfather it was actually enjoyable to watch his grown children struggling to keep their tykes from breaking the ornaments and messing everything up beyond recall.

He sat in his favorite wingchair by the fireplace, wishing it would snow. There hadn't been a white Christmas in simply ages, and Central Park always looked so pretty in the snow. Now it was gray and bare and grimy-looking outside his twentieth-floor window.

The butler brought the phone to him and placed it gently on the sherry table beside the wingchair. "Tarawa, sir." He still pronounced it Ta-RA-wa, instead of properly, Laurence realized with some annoyance.

Wondering what kind of catastrophe would prompt Tarawa to call on the Saturday before Christmas, Laurence touched the keypad.

Pete Connors' dark face appeared on the tiny screen, split from ear to ear by a toothy grin.

"Sorry to disturb you, but I thought you'd want to see this right away."

It took several moments for Laurence to understand what he was looking at. Once he grasped that it was a village built by Martians, he leaped to his feet and gave a war whoop that startled his family so badly they nearly knocked the Christmas tree over.

Dr. Li Chengdu watched his neighbors preparing for Christmas with the cool detached eye of an alien observer. They struggled to string colored lights over their houses, put up elaborate decorations on their lawns, and drove themselves deeper into debt by buying elaborate gifts and throwing too many parties.

Now and then they talked about the religious significance of the holiday, but as far as Li could determine the true purpose of the occasion was to boost retail sales. No matter. He enjoyed the fuss and merriment, even though much of it was underlaid with a kind of desperate determination to do everything right and be happy no matter what the family tensions.

When Connors called from Tarawa, the black former astronaut seemed more excited than the neighborhood children.

"Jamie did it!" Connors blurted. "It's really a village! Built by Martians!"

Li half collapsed into his favorite chair, the comfortable yielding recliner that had been his one luxury on the First Mars Expedition, and stared open-mouthed at the phone screen's display of the Martian building.

His heart thudded beneath his ribs. Intelligent creatures lived on Mars. We are not alone in the universe! Not only life, but *intelligent* life exists elsewhere!

His gaze wandered to his living room window and the twinkling lights on his neighbor's house and lawn, across the suburban street.

What will they feel when the news reaches them? Frightened? Excited? Eager to meet their peers? Or afraid of meeting their superiors?

* * *

Darryl C. Trumball was at home on Saturday evening, struggling with the decision of whether to go downtown to his club for dinner, or tell his wife to have the cook fix something for the two of them.

Connors' phone call ended all thoughts of dinner. Trumball gaped at the views from Mars, then immediately snapped, "Get off this line! I've got six dozen people to call right away!"

Connors said, "The news media—"

"Never mind the stupid media! Let Laurence and his flunkies take care of that. I'm calling money people, man. They'll be *begging* to back the next expedition now!"

"Is this a crank call?" asked the news director.

"Young lady," said Walter Laurence, "I am the executive director of the International Consortium of Universities. My people are phoning all the major networks and print outlets. I chose to call your network personally because your CEO is a close friend of mine."

Then why didn't you call him? the news director wondered. She was a bone-thin, sharp-featured woman of thirty-seven who had seen her share of hoaxes and scams. Intelligent Martians my ass, she thought.

"Look, what you showed me looks like an adobe housing project. You claim it's on Mars?"

It took Laurence fully fifteen minutes and all the patience he could engender to convince her that he was telling the truth. Still, she did not fully believe him until the monitors above her desk—which showed what the other networks were running—all suddenly started showing footage of the Martian cliff dwelling. Even the Saturday night football game was preempted.

That's what finally convinced her.

The President of the United States was startled when his science advisor phoned to tell him the Mars explorers had found intelligent Martians.

"Have you notified DoD?" the president asked immediately.

The science advisor shook her head. She had not had access to the president for weeks, and she was surprised at how much older he looked on her office wall screen without his makeup.

Her office was crowded with grinning, partying young men and women. Champagne corks were popping. People were toasting the Mars explorers. Martian jokes were buzzing through the group: How many Martians does it take to replace a light bulb? Why do Martians have headaches?

"Mr. President, the Martians no longer exist. Their village is empty. They pose no threat to us."

The president blinked his baggy eyes. "Well, this one village may be abandoned, but there might be others, mightn't there?"

The science advisor nodded thoughtfully. He's got a point there. If Waterman and his people have found one village, there must be others, elsewhere on the planet.

The Zieman family sat hunched together on the sofa in their Kansas City living room, staring at the wall screen. It was showing the same view of the Martian dwelling for the twelfth time.

The five-year-old girl said, "How many times are they gonna show that same picture?"

"That's on Mars, stoop-face," her older brother snapped.

"Be quiet," Mrs. Zieman hushed.

Again the screen showed a long, slow panning shot of the wall as the announcer's voice intoned, ". . . built by intelligent creatures who lived on the planet Mars, our next-door neighbor in space. It's night on Mars now, but with tomorrow's dawn, scientists James F. Waterman and C. Dexter Trumball will return to this Martian village to begin the scientific exploration of the first discovery of intelligent life beyond our own world."

It was nearly midnight in Rome. Fr. DiNardo had struggled through the swarming, beeping, lurching preholiday traffic to reach the Vatican, summoned by no less than Cardinal Bryan, reputed to be closer to the pope than anyone else on Earth.

Now he sat in a small office, its walls covered with Renaissance frescoes of saints and martyrs, while Cardinal Bryan paced restlessly back and forth.

"So what does this mean, Father?" the cardinal asked. "What should I tell His Holiness?"

Bryan was an American, in line perhaps to be the first American pope. His Irish ancestry was easy to see in his heavy-jawed, fleshy face.

"It means, apparently," DiNardo answered slowly, "that God was pleased to create intelligent creatures on more worlds than just our own."

"Intelligent, you say."

"They must have been, to build such a village for themselves."

"Intelligent." Cardinal Bryan seemed to muse on the word as he paced.

"Intelligent," Fr. DiNardo repeated firmly.

The cardinal turned toward him. "Intelligent, yes. But did they have souls?"

MORNING: SOL 102

GRANDFATHER AL WAS WAITING FOR HIM WHEN HE RETURNED TO THE VIL-
lage, smiling from beneath his droop-brimmed hat, the black one with
the silver band that he liked to wear when he went out to the pueblos.

"I told you it was here, didn't I?" Al said. He was bundled up in
a fleece-lined leather jacket, hands dug deep into the pockets of his
jeans. It was cold on Mars.

Jamie, still in his hard suit, shook his head inside the helmet. "As
a matter of fact, Al, I don't remember you saying anything about it."

"Aw, I must've," Al said. "Hell, I've been leading you here ever
since you were a kid."

"I know, Grandfather," said Jamie. His hard suit had disappeared.
Like Al, he was in jeans and windbreaker. And a sky-blue baseball
cap. "I'm grateful."

Al laughed delightedly. "Come on, Jamie, let me show you around
the old place."

From somewhere behind him, Jamie could hear water running
freely.

Jamie woke up with a start. He sat up, saw that Dex's bunk was
empty, heard the water recycler running in the lavatory.

The dream dwindled away. Jamie felt disappointed that it had ended
too soon, that Al would never be able to show him the village, that
they would not be able to discover its secrets together.

Dex came out of the lav looking bright and shining. "Hey, y'know
it's going to be Christmas in just two days?"

Jamie grunted as he swung his feet onto the floor. "That's right. I
hadn't thought about it."

"You've given the world a helluva Christmas present, Jamie boy."

He looked at the younger man. "Not me. Us. We. You and the rest
of the team back at the dome."

Dex grinned at him. "You, pal. You drove us here. We wouldn't
be here if you hadn't pushed it."

Standing, wiggling his bare toes on the cold plastic flooring, Jamie
said, "Well, we're here now. Let's get to work."

"Right."

They grabbed a pair of snack bars and drank some juice in lieu of a real breakfast, anxious to get out and down to the village. While Dex started putting on his hard suit, Jamie checked their overnight messages. The list scrolled for what seemed like half an hour.

"Everybody and his uncle has something to say to us," he called back to Dex.

Trumball came clumping up to the cockpit in his hard suit boots and leggings.

"Anything from dear old Dad?" he asked.

Jamie scrolled up and down the list, then shook his head. Connors— or whoever was working the comm console—had starred the messages he considered important. Every news network was starred. Two messages had double stars next to them; Jamie opened them. One was a flowery congratulations from Walter Laurence of the ICU; Jamie suspected it was written more for the media's appreciation than his own. The other was from the chief of the ICU's archeology division, a parched-faced bald middle-aged man with piercing green eyes.

"Do not touch anything," he warned, four times in a row. "Whatever is in or around those structures, *touch nothing*. I want that understood with crystal clarity. Touch nothing. Do not disturb anything."

Trumball laughed. "I think he doesn't want us to touch anything."

Jamie grinned back at him. "Looks that way, doesn't it?"

"Why don't you send him a reply asking if it's okay if we pick up a few souvenirs?"

"And give him apoplexy? No thanks."

Laughing, Trumball headed back for the rear of the module, to finish suiting up. Jamie scrolled through the message list one more time; there was nothing from Dex's father, although he saw personal messages for himself from Li Chengdu and Fr. DiNardo.

They'll have to wait, Jamie thought. We have work to do, even if we're not supposed to touch anything.

The long descent down the cable was like a pilgrimage, Jamie thought. Gives you time to cleanse your mind of everything else and prepare for the experience.

Trumball had insisted on dropping one of the spare video minicams on a separate line, alongside Jamie. He had plugged a palm-sized radio transceiver to it so it could transmit automatically back to the dome. They would mount the pair on a tripod near the edge of the cleft, so they could get a steady view of the village and a communications relay that could pick up their suit radios even when they were inside the building.

Jamie reached the top of the cleft, then slowed his descent manually. The morning sun was streaming into the niche in the cliff face, making the building glow warmly.

It's still here, Jamie thought gratefully. It wasn't a dream. It's real.

He thought he heard his grandfather chuckling at him. Of course it's real, Al said. It's always been real.

He swung himself into the cleft and planted his boots firmly on the rock floor. Then he unclipped the harness and started it back up toward Dex, waiting impatiently up at the Canyon rim.

Jamie walked slowly to the nearest opening in the wall, noticing that he left bootprints on the ground. Dust. It accumulates here from the storms. I wonder if it's worth digging into it to see what might be buried underneath it.

Touch nothing, the cranky old archeologist had said. How can we be here and touch nothing?

The doorway was as wide as a normal human doorway, but only half its height. They weren't very tall, Jamie thought. Or maybe this was an entrance for pets or animals.

He reached out and touched the wall. Hard and smooth. Not like adobe. Some kind of stone. Could it be schist?

"I'm starting down," Dex's voice called.

"Okay," Jamie said absently, wanting to crawl through that doorway and see what was inside the building. But he had promised Dex he would wait so they could go together.

He looked down the length of the wall, down into the shadows deeper in the rock cleft. Two more entrances, both the same size as this one.

On a hunch, he turned back and walked to the edge of the cleft. He paced along the rim while listening to Dex grunting and panting his way down the cable.

There! I knew it'd be along here someplace. Steps, carved into the cliff face. Nothing fancy, just little nicks in the stone, enough to grab with a hand or put a foot into. Jamie got slowly down onto his hands and knees and peered over the edge. The cliff dropped dizzyingly down to the Canyon floor, kilometers below.

He saw a ragged, meandering line of steps carved into the cliff face. They took advantage of all the ledges and every possible resting place. It's a damned long way up here, especially if they were carrying things.

They had hands and feet, he thought. Maybe not exactly like ours, but they had hands and feet that could use those steps to get up here. Maybe they grew their crops down at the Canyon floor.

What made them build their village all the way up here? What *drove* them to hide it up here?

"Where are you?" Dex demanded.

He saw Trumball's spacesuited form hanging in the harness, just below the roof of the cleft, legs dangling, gloved hands gripping the cable tightly.

"Off to your left, along the edge," Jamie said.

"Oh. I thought maybe the temptation got to you," said Trumball.

"No, I waited for you," Jamie said as he looked across at Dex, hanging in the harness, swaying slightly.

"What're you doing? Praying?"

Hauling himself up to his feet, Jamie realized that it must have looked that way. The last time I was in a church was my wedding, he remembered.

"Maybe I'll build a shrine here," he said.

"Not a bad idea," Dex replied.

Jamie strode toward Dex and grabbed him when he swung himself into the cleft. Once the younger man planted his feet on the floor of the crevice, Jamie helped him out of the harness and tied it down on the spike he had left the previous day.

"Okay," Dex said brightly. "Let's go see what they left for us."

Jamie led him to the nearest entrance.

"That's the way in?"

"Either this one or one of the others just like it."

Dex hmphed, then started to bend down.

"Remember the protocol," Jamie said. "Whatever we find inside there, we touch nothing."

"Except for souvenirs," Dex wisecracked.

"Nothing," Jamie repeated flatly.

Dex crawled through the low rectangular opening in the wall, careful not to bang the VR cameras. They had decided to let him wear them today. Bending down to his hands and knees, Jamie crawled through after him, into the Martian dwelling. He got to his feet in a room that was spaciously wide but uncomfortably low; his helmet-mounted video camera scraped the ceiling, forcing Jamie to hunch over slightly.

"We'd beat them at basketball," Dex said, turning slowly as he stepped to the middle of the room.

"The interplanetary Olympics," Jamie mused.

The windowless chamber was surprisingly bright, but utterly empty, its floor thick with reddish dust.

"We ought to take samples of this dust," Dex said.

"Not yet."

"Come on, Jamie! That old fart didn't mean that we couldn't even touch the dust on the floor."

"Let's check with the old fart first," Jamie said. "Or whoever's going to work with us on this."

Dex was silent for a heartbeat, then said, chuckling, "They're probably killing each other back home, fighting to get on the committee that oversees this."

Jamie had seen his share of academic infighting. "You might be right, Dex."

"I can just see the archeologists and paleontologists at each other's throats."

"Science at its finest."

"Well," Dex said, "we'll have to rope these rooms off, so the tourists won't go tramping through them."

Jamie's heart lurched in his chest. "Tourists?"

"Like museums, y'know," Dex went on, "where they show you a room some old king lived in. They rope off the entrance so you can peek in, but you can't touch anything."

"We can't have tourists in here," Jamie said.

"They're probably lining up right now, pal. Paging through their L. L. Bean catalogues to buy hard suits and camping gear for their vacations on Mars."

"That's not funny, Dex."

For several moments Trumball said nothing. Then he answered in a low voice, "Yeah. I know. But it's going to happen, Jamie. There's nothing either one of us can do to stop it."

Jamie had no desire to fight with Dex. Not here, he told himself. Not now.

"Come on," he said. "Let's see what else is here."

"Wait a sec." Dex pulled a digital camera from his belt. "Better take some stills as we go. Old fart-face won't object to a camera flash, d'you think?"

"Go right ahead," said Jamie, thinking, We ought to take scrapings from the walls and try to fix a date for this structure. The dust is probably recent, contemporary. But how old is the building?

Dex popped away with the camera while Jamie turned a slow circle, allowing the video camera fixed to his helmet to take in the full three-hundred-sixty degrees of the chamber.

Then they walked, slightly stooped, from one chamber to another, forced to their hands and knees whenever they crawled through one of the low doorways, shambling like a pair of apes as they prowled through the ancient dwelling, leaving boot prints on the rust-colored Martian dust.

How old is this structure? Jamie kept wondering. How long has it been since anyone lived here?

They entered a bigger, central chamber that had a rectangular opening in its ceiling.

"A light well," Jamie said. "That's how they get light into the rooms inside."

"Like the palace at Knossos," Dex agreed.

Nodding, Jamie murmured, "Minoan. Ancient Crete."

"That's the way upstairs," Dex said, pointing at the square hole.

But there were no stairs, no ladders leading upward to the next floor. The ceilings were so low, however, that Jamie could grip the edge of the opening and lift himself through it. Straining even under the light Martian gravity, he got a knee up on the floor, dragged himself away from the opening, and got to his feet.

"Need a hand?" he offered Dex.

"If you can do it, so can I," the younger man said. Jamie heard him grunt and snort as he climbed up and finally stood beside him.

"Nothing to it," Dex panted.

Inside his helmet, Jamie grinned.

Slowly they made their way to the roof and strode its length with the sturdy sheltering rock hardly a meter above their helmets. It made Jamie feel a tinge of claustrophobia to have the massive, pressing rock looming so close.

"It's all empty," Dex said. "Not a stick of furniture or a basket or a piece of pottery."

"Maybe there's something buried in the dust," Jamie suggested, knowing that he was grasping at straws.

"Nah, the dust isn't thick enough to hide a pottery shard, for chrissakes."

"They must have taken everything with them."

"They sure didn't leave anything here."

The entire building was empty. As if it had been cleaned out, eons ago. Looted? Abandoned by its builders? Jamie wondered. Why? When?

And it struck him all over again, hit him so hard his knees went watery.

Intelligent Martians lived here! They climbed up from the Canyon floor and built this dwelling. When? How long ago? What happened to them? *Where did they go?*

EVENING: SOL 102

JAMIE SHIFTED UNCOMFORTABLY IN THE ROVER'S COCKPIT SEAT AND rubbed his eyes. He'd been reading off the comm screen for hours.

"It's taking more time to answer all these messages than we spent in the village," he complained.

From his bunk, where he sat cross-legged with his laptop screen glowing on his face, Dex said, "Everybody wants to congratulate us— and take some of the credit."

"I suppose."

They had split the task of replying to the calls from Earth. Dex was handling his half from his bunk. Jamie felt his stomach growling; it was long past their normal dinnertime. He had already sent a fifteen-minute report to the news media, to be shared by any station or print outlet that wanted to use it. Jamie could imagine how the video people would edit it down to a sound byte or two.

"Let's take a break and get back to them after we eat," Jamie suggested.

"Good idea—wait a sec! Here's one from Father DiNardo, in Rome." Dex broke into laughter. "Well, whattaya know? Our Jesuit geologist got himself named chairman of the archeology team. How's that for tricky politics?"

"DiNardo? Hold on, I want to see what he's got to say."

Jamie tapped the keyboard between the two cockpit seats and Fr. DiNardo's dark, jowly face came up on the control panel's screen.

". . . congratulations with all my heart," the priest was saying. "God has been very generous to you. And to me, too, I suppose. As I was saying, the ICU has asked me to head the committee that directs your study of the Martian structure."

Dex grinned up the length of the rover module at Jamie and made a slicing motion across his throat with one finger. Jamie understood: there must have been plenty of knives flashing in the dark over the past thirty-six hours or so.

"Apparently the archeologists and paleontologists could not agree on one of their own people to chair the committee, so Dr. Li suggested that I do it, as a sort of neutral entity, not favoring either side."

"God works in mysterious ways," Dex cracked.

"A certain number of anthropologists want to be included, also," DiNardo went on, "but I am not convinced that anthropologists have any special claim to this investigation. Clearly the Martians are not human, by definition. However, the anthropologists insist on being involved."

Knowing that it would take almost half an hour for a reply to reach him from Mars, DiNardo went on without waiting for an answer, without even pausing for a breath, it seemed to Jamie. The man was excited, Jamie realized. Beneath the placid exterior he tried to maintain, DiNardo was just as thrilled as he was himself.

And why not? Jamie asked silently. This is the biggest discovery in the history of the human race. We're not alone! There are—or were—intelligent creatures on Mars.

The priest finally wound down his little speech. "You have already been told to touch nothing in or around the dwelling, I understand. Tomorrow you should set up as many cameras as you can, so we can see as much as possible of the exterior and interior of the building."

"We did a lot of that today," Dex said, more to himself than the image on the screen. Jamie realized that DiNardo had not yet seen the imagery they had sent to Earth.

"The next thing we will want is a tour through the building using the virtual reality system. In that way, our people here can get a better feeling for what you have there."

Jamie nodded. Makes sense, he thought.

DiNardo's image looked up sharply from the screen, at someone or something off-camera. "I must leave you now. We have set up an electronic meeting of the full committee and I must chair it. I will call you again tomorrow. Good-bye, and God be with you."

"Amen," said Dex. "Now let's eat."

Halfway through their prepackaged dinners, Dex looked up from his tray and said, "The virtual reality tour that DiNardo wants . . . it'll make a terrific tourist attraction."

Jamie forced himself to continue chewing.

"I mean, people could buy a trip through the village right in their own homes. Whet their appetites for the real thing."

"I suppose you could make money out of it," Jamie said, trying to keep his voice calm.

"Yeah."

Jamie swallowed carefully, then asked, "Any word from your father yet?"

"No, not yet." Dex took a swig of fruit juice, then planted the plastic cup firmly on the table between them. "Oh, he'll get around to calling. He'll let me wait a day or two and then he'll call. Dear old dad's always worrying about my head getting too big, so he tries to take the air out of my balloon whenever he thinks I need it. Which is always."

Jamie heard more than sarcasm in Dex's tone. He heard pain.

"I'm sure he's very proud of you," Jamie said.

"Yeah," said Dex. "Real proud. Busting his buttons."

Jamie said nothing.

"The thing is, if he really is proud, he's keeping it a deep, dark secret. He's good at that, hiding his pride in his only begotten son."

"I'm sorry I brought it up."

"Ah, never mind, Jamie. It's not your problem." Dex grabbed the juice cup and drained it. As he got up from the narrow table, he asked, "Now, what about moving the dome here? We can't work out of the rover forever."

"I know," Jamie said. "I've been thinking about it."

"And?"

"Moving the dome is a helluva task," Jamie said. "It'll take weeks."

"We can do it between Christmas and New Year's, I bet."

"It would take longer than that."

"So? We've got more than sixteen months to go. You're not going to shuttle back and forth from the present base site to here for all that time, are you?"

"It doesn't sound practical," Jamie admitted.

"So let me work out a plan for moving the dome, the whole base, the L/AVs, the generators, everything."

"Then we'll be ready to receive tourists here with the next mission, is that it?"

Dex looked genuinely surprised, shocked. "Tourists? I'm not talking about tourists. Not yet, anyway. First things first, pal."

"Yes," Jamie replied. "First things first."

MANHATTAN

I SHOULD BE HOME WITH MY FAMILY, THOUGHT ROGER NEWELL. IT'S Christmas Eve, for god's sake. I feel like Bob Cratchit facing old man Scrooge.

Sitting across the tiny round table from him, Darryl C. Trumball seemed to take no notice of the crowds scurrying homeward outside the window of the cocktail lounge. The lounge was half a block from Newell's office in the network headquarters building. He was a frequent customer, immediately recognized by the hostess who sat them by the window. Newell wished for a booth further away but never had the nerve to demand one.

Knowing that it would take a long limo ride from the airport to get to Manhattan, Trumball had taken the jet-speed express train to Grand Central Station specifically to have it out with the news media chiefs. It had been a long and potentially very profitable day for him.

"I've told all the others and I'm telling you, you're free to use any and all of the footage they've taken," Trumball said as he hunched over his scotch on the rocks, "but not the VR stuff."

"But we have our own virtual reality network now," Newell replied, "and we could—"

"No," said Trumball firmly. "We *sell* VR tours of the Martian village to our own customers. We could make five hundred million on the first tour, easy."

"Our audience—"

"Can you put up five hundred mil for the VR material?"

"Five hundred million dollars?" Newell squeaked. "Of course not. Not even close."

"You see?" Trumball leaned back in his chair, smiling coldly.

"We're preparing a prime-time special on the village," said Newell. "Prime time! A science special on prime time. That hasn't been done since—"

"That's all well and good," Trumball interrupted, "but neither you nor any of the other news nets are going to get our VR footage. Not unless you come up with five hundred mil."

Newell shook his head. He had been against the idea of a prime-time special about the Martian village, but the suits upstairs had ignored his advice. Science shows get no audience, Newell knew. Well, maybe this special about the Martian building would do better than most, but still, everybody's seen all the regular footage already. The building doesn't *do* anything, it just sits there, an empty shell. It'll be talking heads, with some of them inside space suit helmets, so we won't even be able to see their faces, for god's sake.

"Of course," Trumball said slowly, reaching for his drink, "once we've shown the VR stuff to our own customers, it might be possible to work out a deal for the first network broadcast of the material."

Newell immediately leaned closer to the older man. "How much?"

Trumball sipped thoughtfully at his scotch, smacked his lips once, and replied, "Global News offered me ninety-five million this afternoon. Can you top it?"

Harry Farber's nose was practically touching his phone screen. He could see his own reflection in the screen, superimposed on the dumb schmuck of a manufacturer's rep from Minneapolis. Harry was sweating, red-faced, grimacing.

"We can't keep 'em in the stores," he was almost screaming. "They're selling 'em so fast we blew out the inventory program this morning!"

"Well that's wonderful, Mr. Farber," said the dumb schmuck. "You know, all our retailers are reporting the same kind of sales. Virtual reality sets are disappearing from the shelves all over the world."

"Yeah, but I need another six gross, and I need 'em *now*!"

The manufacturer's rep seemed only mildly distressed. "Mr. Farber," he said, with a rueful little smile, "if only you knew how many times I've heard that same request over the past few days . . ."

"But I *need* 'em!" Farber insisted. "I got customers waiting in the store right now!" He waved a hand in the general direction of the line of increasingly impatient customers standing by the service desk.

"And you'll get them, Mr. Farber. Just as fast as we can get them to you."

"How soon? When?"

The manufacturer's rep glanced down, probably at some schedule or invoice. "A week to ten days, Mr. Farber."

"A week? Are you nuts? The show from Mars is gonna be aired *tomorrow*! From Mars!"

"It's the best I can do, Mr. Farber," said the rep, with a sad little shake of his head. "Since they discovered that village or whatever it is up there on Mars, everybody wants to buy a virtual reality rig."

THE STUDIOS

IN TELEVISION STUDIOS ALL ACROSS THE WORLD, THE STUNNING NEWS OF the structure on Mars set off a frenzy of talk.

"Tomorrow, definitely," said the sweet-faced gray-haired lady. She was squinting slightly, unaccustomed to the TV lighting.

"Jesus will return to Earth tomorrow?" the interviewer asked, trying to hide his incredulity.

"It's Christmas. His birthday."

The interviewer tried to look sympathetic. He'd seen his share of weirdos and religious fanatics over the years. Inwardly, he sighed. As long as this grandmother stuck to her specific prediction of Christ's return to Earth on Christmas day, she was worth rating points. Today, at least.

In the nearly-invisible receiver lodged in his left ear, he heard the prompt from the show's director, a hard-edged black woman whose job depended on those rating points.

He repeated the question she gave him. "Our Lord left the Earth more than two thousand years ago. Just where has He been all this time?"

"On Mars, of course," said the grandmother, with a beatific smile. "He's been waiting for us to find Him on Mars."

"This is nothing less than mind-blowing!" said the astronomer. He was young, bearded, wearing faded chinos and a red-checkered flannel shirt. It was cold in the unheated observatory, even with the California sun beaming out of a pristine blue sky.

The TV cameraman was shivering noticeably. The interviewer hoped it wouldn't jitter the picture. She was made of sterner stuff; no matter how chilled she felt, she controlled herself absolutely.

"You mean finding the buildings on Mars," she prompted.

"Finding intelligent life!" the young astronomer beamed. "Intelligent! On our next-door neighbor in space!"

"So what does this mean to our viewers?"

The astronomer looked squarely into the camera lens. "It means that not only life, but intelligence, is probably commonplace in the universe. We're not alone. Intelligence may be as common as carbon or water. There are probably zillions of intelligent civilizations out there among the stars."

Now the interviewer shuddered, despite herself.

The president of the Navaho Nation blinked, unaccustomed to the glare of the television lights. Last time he'd been on TV was when the FBI made a drug bust on reservation territory without letting the reservation police force in on it. Claimed the Navaho police might have tipped off the suspects. Hah!

It had taken a lot of lawyers from the People and from Washington to straighten that one out. Now, at least, this story today was a happy one.

The reporter stuck a microphone under the president's chin and asked, "How do you feel about a Navaho discovering this cliff dwelling on Mars?"

The president shrugged and nodded. Then he said, "Pretty good, I guess."

The reporter waited for more. When it didn't come, he scowled slightly and asked, "What can you tell us about Dr. Waterman?"

The president thought about that for a while. The reporter ground his teeth in silent frustration, hoping they'd have time back at the studio to edit these maddening pauses out of the tape.

"I never met Jamie Waterman," the president answered at last. "I knew his grandfather pretty good, though. Al ran a shop over in Sante Fe for many years."

"Yes, so we heard," the reporter sputtered. "But about *Jamie* Waterman, the scientist on Mars—"

"He's only half Navaho, you know," said the president slowly. Then he smiled. "But I guess that's good enough, huh?"

The reporter grimaced. He'd spent half the damned day getting all the way out here for this interview and all he was getting from it was shit.

Hodell Richards smiled with visible self-satisfaction. "Maybe now they'll believe me."

Richards was a lean, almost ascetic-looking man with the kind of perpetually youthful face that made elderly women want to mother him.

Pencil-thin mustache, ash blond hair worn long enough to reach the collar of his tweed jacket.

He sat in a TV studio in England, an expensive leather attaché case resting on his knees, his hands atop it. His interviewer was an intense-looking red-headed woman who specialized in UFO tales of alien abduction and unspeakable medical procedures.

She asked, "Then you firmly believe that the Martians are not extinct? That they still exist?"

"I have proof of it," Richards said, drumming his fingertips on the attaché case.

"And they have visited Earth?" the interviewer asked.

"They have a base here on Earth," Richards replied. "In Tibet."

"But why—"

"They're here to propagate their own species. They impregnate Earth women and force them to bear Martian children."

"Ah-hah," said the interviewer.

In Barcelona, the Swiss-German self-styled space expert cocked a haughty eyebrow at his interviewer, a world-weary overweight Catalan who thought of himself as an investigative reporter. Since the interviewer spoke no German and the interviewee spoke no Spanish, they conducted their show in English. Subtitles on the screen translated instantly, of course.

"Then it is your belief that the Martian village—"

"Is bogus," said the expert flatly.

"You mean it is all a lie?"

"Yes, a lie conducted by the American NASA."

"But why would they lie about this?"

"To get popular support for their space explorations, of course."

The interviewer considered this for a fraction of a second, then asked, "Yet I was under the impression that the expedition to Mars was funded by private sources, not by the NASA."

The expert dismissed that idea with a snort. "That's what they want us to believe. The U.S. government is behind it all."

"But how can they fake a building on Mars? Are you saying that the explorers built it themselves? After all, there are only eight of them on Mars."

"And what makes you think that this fake village is on Mars? They built it in Arizona or Texas or someplace like that."

"Truly?"

"Of course."

"I want to stress," said the professor to the *Tonight Show* host, "that we don't know anything at all about how the Martians looked."

Behind him were lurid paintings of "space aliens."

"Nothing at all?" the host asked, smirking.

"Nothing. They might have had a dozen legs or none. We just don't know."

"So they probably didn't look like this guy, then." The host pointed to an ethereal image with doelike eyes.

"Nope," the professor answered. "Nor like that one either." He jabbed a thumb toward a slimy tentacled monster from *The War of the Worlds*.

The host sighed mightily. "Probably they look like my mother-in-law."

CHRISTMAS EVE

JAMIE AND DEX HAD SPENT AN EXHAUSTING DAY SETTING UP THE FOUR CAMeras they had brought with them at different locations in the cleft, photographing everything in sight and then moving the cameras to another location, time and again.

"I feel like some apprentice flunky to the assistant photographer on a movie set," Dex grumbled.

"You and me both, pal," said Jamie.

After spending all morning photographing, Jamie activated the VR equipment on his helmet and took a long, slow tour through the building, floor by floor, until he was on the roof once again. Dex went with him and stood by the walls and in the centers of the various rooms, to give the watchers an idea of each chamber's scale.

Finally, as the sun neared the southwestern horizon, Jamie turned off the VR rig and they started back down to the ground floor.

"We're assuming this was a dwelling of some sort," Jamie heard himself saying to Dex, thinking out loud. "Maybe it wasn't. Maybe it was a storage area, like a warehouse or a grain storage center."

"Or a religious site," Dex added.

"There doesn't seem to be any evidence of furniture or utensils," Jamie went on. "The kinds of things you would expect to find where people actually lived and worked."

"Maybe it was a fortress," Dex suddenly suggested. "Y'know, like a castle. Maybe they came up here to hide out from enemies."

Jamie had already thought of that possibility. "There would still be some evidence of their living here, some furniture or pottery or something."

"Yeah," Dex agreed as they walked back to the rectangular opening in the roof. "A broken spear or two."

"Arrowheads. Spear points."

"Maybe it was a religious shrine," Dex repeated.

"Maybe," Jamie said, getting down onto his knees so he could lower himself to the next floor.

"Nothing that looks like an altar, though," Dex said.

Hanging by both hands, Jamie lowered himself until he felt his boots touch the floor. Then Dex did the same and they started for the next opening that led to the ground.

"Not even a crumb," Dex grumbled.

"Might be hidden in the dust," Jamie said. "Once we start brushing the dust away, we might find something."

Dex was silent until they got to the ground floor. As they walked slowly, tiredly toward the low doorway that led outside he said, "The thing is, we're thinking of this in human terms. These people weren't humans. They were Martians."

"Alien."

"Right."

"Maybe they didn't have altars or religious shrines," Jamie said. "Maybe they didn't need fortresses and didn't have to make arrowheads or spears."

"Maybe," Dex agreed.

Jamie thought about it as he helped Dex strap into the climbing harness.

"Then we don't even know what we should be looking for, do we?" he mused.

Dex pushed off the rim and dangled in the harness, twisting slowly. "Might be nothing here to find."

"That's hard to believe."

"Unless . . ."

Jamie watched as Dex began to rise slowly out of sight.

"Unless what?" he called.

"Unless this place is so friggin' old that anything less solid than the stone walls has crumbled away."

Jamie stood alone on the rim of the rock cleft and thought about that until Dex finally sent the harness back for him.

"There's a Christmas present on its way to you," Rodriguez said, a lopsided grin on his swarthy, square-jawed face.

Jamie was in the cockpit, checking in with the base, while Dex microwaved their dinner packages.

"What do you mean, a Christmas present?"

"It's Christmas Eve, so Santa's bringing you a present." The astronaut's dark eyes sparkled.

"What?"

"Hold one," said Rodriguez.

His image winked off and the screen showed Stacy Dezhurova instead. The picture was grainy, a little washed out. It looked to Jamie as if Stacy was driving one of the rovers.

"Ho, ho, ho," said Dezhurova, in the deepest tone her voice could reach. "I am your official Father Christmas."

Jamie had to smile at that. "Where's your beard?"

"Never mind trivialities. In all your planning for this excursion you forgot that you would be out there on Christmas day, didn't you?"

"I guess I did," Jamie admitted.

"Our schedule calls for a day of rest, a holiday. No work tomorrow."

With a rueful grin, Jamie asked, "Do DiNardo and his committee know that?"

"DiNardo made a point of emphasizing it," Dezhurova said. "He is a Catholic priest, remember."

"That's right."

"So we are bringing you a present." Stacy allowed a slight smile to curve her lips.

"We?"

"Fuchida and Hall are in this rover with me; we are heading for your site."

"No kidding?" Jamie turned halfway in his seat. "Dex, did you hear that?"

"We're getting company!" Dex hurried up to the cockpit and slid into the other chair.

"Right."

Dezhurova raised her voice to get his attention. "Wait. There's more. We are carrying with us your Christmas dinners."

"Soybean turkey and fake cranberry sauce," Dex groused.

"No, no, no!" Dezhurova cried. "Real turkey and real cranberry sauce! The special dinners were packed aboard by mission control before we left Earth."

"Who the hell did that?" Dex wondered.

"It was a surprise for all of us. The information about the dinners was in today's mission schedule," Dezhurova went on. "I saw it this morning when I went into the daily sked."

"A Christmas surprise," Jamie said.

"For everyone. They didn't know, on Tarawa, that you two would be away from the dome on Christmas day. So we are bringing your dinners to you."

"Company for Christmas." Dex beamed happily. "We'd better clean up the place if company's going to drop in."

*   *   *

Vijay stood behind Rodriguez, watching as Stacy told Dex and Jamie about the Christmas surprise.

She had thought about going out to the Canyon with the others, but that would leave Rodriguez and Craig by themselves for the holiday. Tommy couldn't leave the dome with his hand still on the mend, and Vijay realized that she should stay close to her patient, just in case.

Besides, Rodriguez and Trudy had become a twosome, and now that she had gone to the Canyon to help with exploring the ruins, Tommy had a woeful hangdog look about him. Christmas without his girlfriend was going to be pretty sad for him.

She knew that was a good reason to stay, but not her real reason. She knew that she was afraid to be out there with both Jamie and Dex, afraid of the tensions it would raise, the trouble it could cause. The two alpha males seemed to be getting along fairly well by themselves, no sense stirring up their hormones.

Or mine, she admitted to herself.

Jamie went to sleep that night thinking that tomorrow morning would be Christmas and they were going to have company. Three friendly faces added to their holiday.

It's lonesome out here, he realized, staring at the curving metal overhead. With nobody but Dex, it's like being a cowboy out on the range in the old days. The work is fine and exciting, but at night, when you gather round the old campfire, a few more friends will be welcome.

Hall and Fuchida will stay, according to the plan Dezhurova explained to him. Dex and I will move to their rover and the four of us will work on the village. Stacy will drive the old clunker back to the dome.

Shouldn't call it an old clunker. It's served us very well. It's been great for us.

He closed his eyes and saw Vijay. Naked. Glistening with sweat. Warm and soft and yielding in his arms.

Wish she were coming, too. He turned his head and saw Dex lying on his bunk, hands laced behind his head, staring into the shadows. I'll bet he's thinking about her, too. Good thing she isn't coming. Some Christmas it would be, with the two of us ready to tear out each other's throats over her.

No, she's smart not to come here. Dex and I are just starting to understand one another. If she were here, all that would be wrecked.

Still, he glanced at Dex once again. He's thinking about her, too. I'd bet money on that.

As if he sensed Jamie's thoughts, Dex turned on his bunk toward Jamie.

"How old you think that building is?" he asked.

Jamie propped himself up on one elbow. "I don't know. I get the feeling that it's really old, older than anything on Earth. But that's just a feeling, a hunch. We don't have any evidence yet.''

His fingers still twined behind his head, Dex said, ''There's something screwy here. It just doesn't add up.''

''What doesn't?''

''All our heat flow measurements show that Mars is a lot younger than anybody thought. Geologically, I mean.''

Jamie nodded in the shadows.

''I mean, the Tharsis volcanoes were active until only a few tens of millions of years ago. The planet's interior is a lot hotter than we expected. Right?''

''Right,'' said Jamie.

''But the planet's too frigging small for all that,'' Dex complained. ''It should've cooled off a long time earlier.''

''According to the accepted theories, yes,'' Jamie admitted. ''But when the theories don't match up with the observations . . . ''

''And now this building. You think it's a million years old? Older?''

Shaking his head, Jamie said, ''I don't know. That's what we've got to find out.''

''How does it all fit together? That's the thing of it: How does everything we've found here fit together?''

Jamie almost wanted to laugh. Dex was as perplexed as any child trying to figure out a new puzzle.

''Well, we're not going to get the answers here in our bunks,'' he said. ''Let's get some sleep and tackle it tomorrow.''

He heard Dex chuckle softly. ''Yeah. Right. If we don't go to sleep Santa won't come.''

But Dex couldn't sleep. His curiosity about Mars gave way to thoughts about his father. Good old Dad. I've helped to discover intelligent life on Mars and he hasn't sent a word to me. Not a frigging word. Not even a Christmas greeting. Not him.

He's too busy playing the bigshot financier to say anything to me. Too busy lining up money for the next expedition. And the one after that. He's taking the credit for me, letting them all tell him what a terrific son he's got while he picks their pockets.

Dex turned over to face the curving bulkhead of the rover. Well, when I get back I'm going to take over all that. I'm going to take my fair share of the glory and push dear old Dad out of the picture. Kick him upstairs. Let him be the Old Man while I take the spotlight and set up a regular schedule of expeditions to Mars. All kinds of scientists are going to want to come here: archeologists, paleontologists—hell, they'll open up a new department, a whole new discipline. Alien anthropology. Xenology, that's what they'll call it. Maybe I'll endow a chair of xenology at Yale and take it for myself.

No, he thought. I'm going to take the position Dad has now. *I'm* going to run things. *I'm* going to set up the financing and put the expeditions together. Make a regular corporation: Mars Expeditions, Inc. C. Dexter Trumball, president and chief executive officer.

I'll get contributors to finance individual scientists. The tourists will pay for the scientists! That's the way to do it. Each tourist's fare will pay the way for a scientist to come to Mars. Great!

When I get back to Earth I'll already be famous. That's when I cash in on the fame. I'll fuck every debutante between Boston and Atlanta and screw their fathers out of enough money to send a dozen expeditions to Mars. A hundred. I'll build a tourist facility right here, on the rim of the Canyon, where they can come down and see the village and then go on down to the Canyon floor. Build a regular elevator so they can ride in comfort and safety.

I'm going to make them forget about dear old Dad. When I get back to Earth, *I'm* going to be the star. I'm going to be so frigging important even Dad will have to admit it.

CHRISTMAS

"CERTAINLY WE CELEBRATE CHRISTMAS IN JAPAN," SAID MITSUO FUCHIDA.

He sat on one of the bunks, squeezed between Stacy Dezhurova and Dex Trumball. Jamie sat on the opposite bunk with Trudy Hall beside him. On the narrow table separating them was the remains of their holiday dinners, now little more than crumbs and bones.

The special Christmas dinners had been almost as good as advertised. Real turkey, drumsticks as well as white breast meat, with sweet potatoes, green beans and cranberry sauce. Indestructible fruitcake for dessert. There was even a small ration of white wine in plastic containers for each of them. Dex made extra-strong coffee to soften the fruitcake.

"Is Christianity that big in Japan now?" Trudy asked.

Fuchida shook his head. "Not so much. But we celebrate Christmas exactly the way you do—as a major retail sales event."

Everyone laughed. They were in the rover that Dezhurova had driven. A mangy tree made of aluminum strips stood lopsidedly by the airlock hatch, lit by tiny winking bulbs from the electronics spares supply. They had no gifts to exchange except the warmth of their own company.

It was enough.

Jamie lounged back against the bulkhead as they chattered and bantered back and forth. Tomorrow Dezhurova would drive the old rover back to the dome while the four scientists lived in this one and started the work of thoroughly investigating the dwelling site, under the direction of DiNardo's committee.

It's going to be tedious work, Jamie thought. Painstaking. With a half-hour lag between our asking a question and their answer.

But that's tomorrow, he told himself. Tonight it's Christmas. He felt pleasantly buzzed by the little portion of wine he'd drunk with his dinner. Everyone else seemed to be equally relaxed, equally happy.

Jamie looked across the table at Dex, grinning as he needled Fuchida about the religious significance of a shopping spree. A sudden thought popped into Jamie's mind.

He slid out from behind the table, muttering an "Excuse me," and started toward the cockpit.

"Hey, Jamie!" Dex called. "The pissoir's down the other direction."

He turned and made a smile for them. "I can whiz out the window." Ducking his head, he slipped into the cockpit's right-hand seat.

The four of them were making enough noise, talking, joking, laughing, so that Jamie didn't feel he needed to put on the headset. Still, he plugged it in and held its pin mike close to his lips as he addressed his message to C. Darryl Trumball.

"Mr. Trumball, I don't know where you are and I haven't checked on what the time might be in the Boston area right now, so please excuse me if I'm interrupting your Christmas celebration. I just thought it would be a reasonable present for your son if you called Dex to wish him a merry Christmas."

Glancing at his wristwatch, Jamie continued, "We've got a little less than three hours of Christmas remaining here, so if you're going to call, it ought to be pretty soon. I know Dex would appreciate it. Thanks."

He rejoined the group as they began singing Christmas carols. Trudy had brought a CD with her, and no less than the Westminster Abbey Choir filled the rover with sonorous noels. The five explorers sang along, at the tops of their lungs.

Jamie kept glancing at the control panel up in the cockpit, to see if the message light was blinking. It remained dark. Dex seemed oblivious to what he was trying to do, singing and laughing as hard as any of the others. Harder, perhaps.

By midnight there was still no call from Earth. But if any Martians were roaming across that bitterly cold, almost airless plain by the edge of the Grand Canyon, wafting on the thin night air they would have heard strange, alien voices singing raggedly:

"Deck us all with Boston, Charlie,
Walla Walla, Wash., and Kalamazoo.
Nora's freezin' on the trolley,
Swaller dollar, cauliflower, alley-ga-roo . . ."

EVENING: SOL 111

"MY BACK HURTS."

Jamie looked up to see Fuchida lifting his helmet off. The biologist looked tired; fatigue lines creased his forehead and his eyes were bleary.

Jamie had just finished vacuuming the dust off his hard suit after still another day of sweeping inside the cliff dwelling. Fuchida had been the last of the team to ride up the cable and return to the rover.

For more than a week now the four explorers had been painstakingly, tediously sweeping the dust off the floor and walls of the building. Under the direction of DiNardo's committee of Earthbound archeologists and paleontologists, Jamie, Dex, Trudy and Mitsuo had adapted the brushes originally intended to clean spacesuits and electronic equipment into makeshift brooms and whisks.

Day after day they laboriously cleaned a small patch of one of the rooms, sifting the dust carefully to make certain that they did not miss a shard of pottery or sliver of metal. They found nothing. Night after night they limped back to the rover, backs aching, fingers cramped from hours of gripping the improvised handles of their lowly tools.

"Whoever was here," Dex said tiredly after a week of it, "picked the place clean. There's nothing here. Nothing at all."

Fuchida had already pulled down his upper bunk and climbed into it. "We are wasting our time. Trudy and I should be down on the Canyon floor, where the lichen are."

Jamie, in the galley microwaving his dinner, perked up his ears. If Mitsuo's starting to complain, we've got real trouble here.

"I'll talk it over with DiNardo tonight," he promised. "Maybe Dex and I can finish the sweeping while you and Trudy get back to the lichen."

Hall was sitting on the edge of her bunk, beneath Fuchida's. "His blasted committee takes a week to decide anything."

Dex agreed. "Yeah. I say we check it out with Stacy, and if she doesn't have any problem with the move, we let Trudy and Mitsuo go down to the Canyon floor."

"And DiNardo?" Jamie asked.

"We *tell* him what we're doing, we don't ask him."

Jamie thought it over. The microwave chimed and he pulled his dinner tray out and walked up to the table standing between the two racks of bunks.

Sitting beside Dex, who was already wolfing down his own dinner, Jamie realized that the younger man had matured considerably over the past weeks. He's getting downright likeable, Jamie thought.

"How do you feel about suspending your geology work, Dex?"

The younger man shrugged as he chewed. Then he swallowed and answered, "I sure as hell don't appreciate being turned into a menial laborer. That's grad student's work. But I guess somebody's got to do it."

"I appreciate your help," Jamie said.

Instead of his usual grin, Dex gave him a thoughtful glance. "I just wish we could find something. *Something.* All this damned sweeping and we haven't found a pin."

Nodding, Jamie said, "It's like you said, Dex. Somebody cleaned this place out very thoroughly before they left."

"Who? And where'd they go to?"

"Those are the big questions, aren't they?"

Dex shook his head. "I don't like mysteries. They bother me. I always read the end first."

With a smile, Jamie said, "We don't know what the end is on this one."

"It's enough to drive you nuts!" Dex blurted. "The building is there, but it tells us nothing. Not a goddamned thing!"

"It tells us that there were builders here," Jamie said softly. "Intelligent Martians."

Dex nodded wearily. "Yeah. But that's not enough, is it?"

"Not now," Jamie agreed.

"Anything from the soarplanes?"

"Nothing so far. Nothing that looks like a village or a building. Nothing from the satellite scans, either."

"Nothing *recognizable*."

"Remember that the satellites and soarplanes didn't spot this building," Jamie reminded him.

"Yeah, I know," said Dex. "It took the keen eyes of our Navaho scout."

Jamie smiled. For once, there was no malice in Dex's wisecrack.

The younger man grumbled, "There could be a zillion more buildings like this one scattered across the planet, and we wouldn't know it until we stumbled onto them."

Jamie looked across the table at the two biologists. They both seemed to be asleep already. Mitsuo's right, he said to himself. They should be down studying the lichen, not doing stoop labor here.

He had wondered briefly about Trudy being alone with the three of them, but as far as he could tell there was no sexual tension in the rover. The quarters here are too tight for anything to happen, Jamie thought. Besides, Trudy's made it clear that Rodriguez is her man and Tomas could get very physical with any guy who bothered her. She's well protected, even though he's not here.

Dex intruded on his thoughts. "Well, we might as well go see what the day's soarplane images look like."

"Good idea."

The two men slid out from the table and went up to the cockpit. Jamie spoke briefly with Dezhurova, who swiftly agreed that the biologists should be doing biology, but then added:

"They will need their own rover, to get down to the Canyon floor. I will send Rodriguez with the number two rover."

"His hand's okay?"

"Not good enough to play baseball, but good enough to drive."

"Okay. How soon?"

"A day to stock the rover. Two days to reach you."

"Fine," said Jamie. He thought about asking to speak with Vijay, but with Dex sitting beside him, decided against it. She had not called him, and he had not called her. Probably better to leave it at that, for the time being, he told himself.

"We want to see today's imagery from the soarplane," Dex said.

Dezhurova nodded. "Nothing new, but you should look for yourselves."

She was right, Jamie saw. The imagery showed the rusty, frigid, barren Martian landscape in beautiful detail, down to a one-meter resolution. But no hint of buildings. Not a trace of structure, order. No outlines of ancient foundations. No piles of dressed stones. Nothing but bare, empty wilderness, endlessly. Miles and miles of nothing but miles and miles, Jamie thought. It makes Death Valley look lush and inviting.

"Funny thing," Dex said as they watched the imagery unfold silently on the cockpit screen.

"What?"

"I got a message from my old man. Sort of a belated Christmas card."

"Really?"

"Yeah. Couple days ago. Said he's sorry he couldn't talk to me on Christmas day. He was in Monaco, at an international conference of nonprofit research foundations."

"Raising money?"

"What else?" Dex asked. "Oh, I suppose he chased a few topless bathing beauties. He does that when he's away from home."

"Did your mother call you on Christmas?" Jamie wondered aloud.

Dex snorted. "I got her Christmas greeting two days early. She always sends all her greetings early. Records one message and sends it out to her mailing list. As personal as a department store catalogue, my mom."

Jamie could not think of anything to say.

"The thing is," Dex went on, "Dad said he was proud of the work I'm doing here. He sort of read it, like he was reading it off a tele-prompter. Probably got one of his flunkies to write it out for him."

"I don't think—"

Dex laughed softly. "You don't know the old bird the way I do. But he actually said he was proud of me. I think that's a first."

"Well, I'm glad he did."

Dex looked at Jamie for a long silent moment as they sat side by side in the cockpit. "You didn't have anything to do with it, did you?"

"Me?"

"I mean, the old man never told me was proud of me before. Did you put him onto it?"

Before Jamie could answer, Dex said, "Never mind. Don't tell me. I don't want to know. I'd rather think my dear old dad is getting sentimental in his old age."

Now Jamie chuckled. "He doesn't strike me as the sentimental type."

"No, not hardly," Dex agreed. "Anyway, if you did have a hand in it . . . thanks."

Jamie kept silent, not wanting to strain the slender thread that was slowly strengthening between the two of them.

"Another thing," Dex said, as the barren imagery flowed across the screen. "We've got to move the dome here, sooner or later. I think sooner would be better."

Jamie sighed. "I've been thinking about that."

"And?"

"How about asking Tarawa to send the backup dome here, with cables and equipment to build a better lift?"

Dex's eyes lit up. "That way we wouldn't have to move the base."

"Right," said Jamie.

"The thing is, it'd take five-six months to get it here even if they started on it tomorrow morning."

"True," Jamie admitted. "But trying to move the dome from where it is would take a month to six weeks, wouldn't it?"

"At least."

"And we wouldn't be doing any productive work during that time. The useful work would stop dead."

"Yeah."

"They've got the backup dome just sitting there at Baikonur—"

"And a resupply mission is in the budget," Dex finished for Jamie.

"Right! That's the way to do it."

"Good. I'll tell Stacy and she can relay it to Connors."

"Do you think Tarawa will agree to it?"

"They'll have to," Dex said firmly. "I mean, we can't keep shuttling rovers back and forth. It's wasteful. And we're eating up all our prepackaged food. We'll have no backup food supplies. We're supposed to be living off the garden."

Jamie knew it was true. "We'll have to set up another greenhouse."

Nodding enthusiastically, Dex said, "Why not make it a manned flight? Bring in some of those archeologists who want to get here."

"They'd have to undergo months of training, Dex. You can't just pick a team of people and pop them off to Mars without training them first."

Dex's face fell slightly. "Yeah. Right."

"But it makes sense to pick a few and start training them now," Jamie said.

"I suppose," Dex replied. "The thing is, I was hoping to get some of 'em here soon enough so *they* could do the sweeping work, instead of us."

AFTERNOON: SOL 113

"I'VE GOT SOMETHING HERE."

Jamie looked up from his sweeping. It had been another monotonous, laborious day. They had cleared the entire top floor of the dwelling and found nothing. Not an iota of material of any sort. Nothing but bare walls. Now they were working on the second floor.

Rodriguez had just started his trek in the rover from the dome to them, his departure delayed by a dozen maddeningly tiny but unavoidable holdups, including the fact that he could not squeeze his bandaged hand into his hard suit glove. At the last minute Vijay had to find a larger-sized glove for him. She took one of Craig's from his backup supplies.

Pete Connors had immediately endorsed the idea of sending the spare dome and all its equipment to the Canyon site. He bucked the request to the ICU board, with a personal message to Trumball in Boston about it.

"Mitsuo, was that you?" Jamie asked.

"Yes," the biologist replied. His voice sounded strange, choked, tight with tension. "Come and take a look at this."

Jamie was in the middle of a large room, slowly, carefully sweeping the dust from the floor to the opening that led below. If you pushed the dust too hard it would billow and drift back to the area you had just cleared. And every few minutes they had to sift the dust with screens scavenged from the air duct supplies.

It would be so much easier if they could simply vacuum the dust up off the floors and walls, but the hand vacs that they used to clean their suits could not handle the sheer volume of dust accumulated in the building; it was several centimeters deep in some corners. The hand vacs were running raggedly as it was, working harder than their designers had ever intended each evening when the four of them climbed back into the rover, caked with rust-red dust almost up to their helmets. Rodriguez was bringing a set of backups with him, so that the ones they were using could go back to Stacy and Wiley Craig for some much-needed maintenance.

Besides, the scientists back on Earth had insisted on sifting the dust by hand. The vacuum cleaners might pass or crush some incalculably important shard of pottery or chip of fossilized bone.

Jamie almost had to laugh. They had found nothing. Nada. Zip. Zero. No shards, no chips, no traces of anything but maddeningly endless dust.

Until this moment.

"What is it, Mitsuo?" Jamie asked as he headed for the corner where the biologist had been working. Now he was standing stock-still, facing the wall he had been cleaning.

"You . . . you'd better come and see for yourself."

Dex came striding across the big empty chamber, the royal blue stripes on his hard suit almost indistinguishable beneath a coating of red dust. Trudy Hall was close behind him.

"Whatcha got, pal?" Dex asked. "Find any Martians?"

"I think maybe so." Fuchida's voice was trembling slightly.

Jamie saw he was pointing at the wall he'd been cleaning. It was not a smoothly blank face, as the other walls had been.

There were scratches on the wall. From about halfway down from the ceiling to the level where the uncleared dust still clung, the wall was covered with a fine tracery of curving lines.

"Cracks," said Dex. But his breezy manner was gone.

"Or writing," Jamie said.

"Writing," Fuchida agreed.

In his earphones Jamie could hear all four of them breathing hard, panting, almost.

Trudy said, "Cracks wouldn't be so regular. Look . . ." Her gloved finger traced along the length of the wall. "There's line after line of it."

"Don't touch the wall," Jamie warned.

"I'm not touching it," she said, slightly annoyed.

"Let's get the rest of the wall cleaned off," Dex said.

All four of them fell to it, whisking gently but impatiently. Rust-red dust blew in every direction.

"We'll have to put up plastic tenting or something," Dex was thinking aloud, "to cover the openings, make certain more dust doesn't blow in here."

Jamie nodded inside his helmet. "I wish we could date these walls."

All their attempts to determine the age of the walls had been frustrated. There was no organic material in the pieces of rock that made up the walls. They had been cut and chiselled to fit together like the walls of Machu Picchu, and their interior faces skillfully polished.

"There's going to be a lot of Ph.D.s earned here, trying to figure out a way to get a reliable dating system," Dex said.

"The rock must have come from deeper in the cleft," Fuchida pointed out as they worked.

"D'you think there was ever water flowing in here?" Hall asked.

"Must've been," said Dex.

"No evidence of it," Jamie said.

"We haven't really looked for it," Dex countered.

"It would be very difficult for them to bring water up from the Canyon floor," Fuchida pointed out.

"If there ever was a stream running down there," said Jamie, sweeping carefully, trying to keep control over his growing excitement. More and more lines adorned the rock wall.

"I'll bet we find evidence of a river down there," Dex said.

"But when did it flow?" Jamie asked. "How long ago?"

"Look!" Trudy cried. "It's a picture, I think."

She kept on brushing at her section of the wall, exposing a circle with what appeared to be arrows emanating from it.

"A sun symbol?" Jamie gasped with shock. It looked like the kind of symbol the Navaho and other tribes used to indicate the sun.

"They had eyes like ours," Trudy said, her voice hollow. "They had a sense of vision and they invented writing."

"Writing," Dex breathed. His usual cocky air was gone.

The wall bore a whole row of picturelike symbols. Pictographs, Jamie thought. Like the earliest forms of writing in Egypt.

"What does it mean?" Fuchida asked. "What were they trying to tell us?"

Jamie's throat felt dry. It took him three tries to work up a little saliva and swallow.

"Come on," he said. "Let's clear off the rest of it."

They fell to the work in silence.

Jamie glanced back at the sun symbol. No, it can't be, he told himself. These people can't be our ancestors. They weren't human. They were built differently. They died off . . . they didn't migrate to Earth. That's ridiculous.

"Oh-oh," Dex grunted.

They turned to see what he was doing. Dex had bent down to his knees, to brush away the dust from the bottom of the wall.

The regular lines of well-spaced symbols ended about a meter above the floor. More ragged symbols followed, lopsided and scrawling, compared to the ones above.

"Like children's writing," Hall murmured.

"Or primitive adults," said Fuchida.

"These regular lines up here," Hall said, pointing with her gloved hand, "have been inscribed. They used chisels or some other tools that cut the lines into the rock deeply. See? But these down below . . ."

"They're scratched onto the rock," Dex said. "Like scribbles."

"Graffiti," said Fuchida.

"Children? Vandals?" Hall wondered.

"Tourists," Jamie muttered.

"More drawings down here," Dex said, brushing furiously. The dust billowed all around him.

"Who's got the camera?" Jamie asked.

"I do," said Fuchida.

"Don't take off the lens cap until this dust settles!" Dex warned, wiping at his helmet visor with his free hand. "At least this stuff doesn't cling the way the dust does on the Moon."

"The dust on the Moon is electrostatically charged," Fuchida said. "From the infalling solar wind."

"Tell me about it," Dex groused.

The three of them bent closer as Dex brushed the final section of the wall, down low and at the end where it joined the other wall at a right angle.

"Pictures, all right," Dex said, still kneeling.

Jamie peered through the thinning dust cloud. The pictures at the bottom of the wall seemed crude, hastily drawn.

"What's that?" Hall asked, pointing again.

Jamie saw a lopsided, bulbous figure scratched atop a ragged, sloping line.

"An erection," Dex snickered.

"Don't be an idiot," Trudy snapped.

"Whatever it's supposed to be, it's pretty primitive work," said Dex.

"And this?" Hall asked again. "It looks as if somebody just clawed a half-dozen streaks across the rock."

Fuchida bent so close his visor almost touched the rock. "But look, there are pinpoints here and there . . . this one looks like a cross or an x."

Dex dismissed it with, "Pits in the rock."

"Not this x symbol," Fuchida maintained.

Jamie stared hard at the crude drawings. He knew with all the certainty of ancient wisdom that the primitive artist was trying to tell them something. He didn't just rattle off some graffiti here. These symbols meant something to him. They mean something now. But what? What was he trying to say? What did he want to record in the rock? What is the message he left for us?

"The philologists are going to have a smashing time with this," Hall said.

Straightening up slowly, the joints of his suit grating slightly, Dex agreed, "They'll go nuts, all right."

Jamie felt his spine creak as he stood up, too. "They'll go crazy with frustration. There's no way they can interpret this writing. The pictures, maybe, but not the writing."

"No Rosetta stone," Fuchida said.

"That's right," said Jamie. "The only way they translated languages from antiquity was to find translations into languages they already knew. You need a key."

"And there's no key here," Dex said, recognizing the problem. "It's all Martian."

"No connection to any language on Earth," Fuchida said.

"Maybe the pictures will help," Hall suggested.

"Maybe."

"I wouldn't bet money on it," Jamie said.

Dex laughed. "One thing's for sure."

"What?"

"They'll invent six zillion different explanations for every symbol on this wall."

"And no two of them will agree." Fuchida broke into a giggle.

"But they'll write scads of papers about it," said Hall. She started laughing, too.

Jamie stood silent inside his suit while the three others laughed on the edge of hysteria. Blowing off steam, he realized. They've got to laugh or cry or scream from the rooftops. Can't blame them. It's the greatest discovery of all time. But what does it mean?

What does it goddamn mean?

He stared at the symbols. So neat and orderly at the outset. Professional work. They took pride in it. But down at the bottom, just a scrawl.

What happened here? What happened to these people?

He felt cold and weak, as if his legs were no longer able to support him. The path ends here, Grandfather. They left a message and we have no way of understanding it.

"Jamie? You okay?"

It was Dex's voice. Jamie stirred himself, focused his eyes on the three other humans in their impersonal hard suits.

"Yeah, yes. I'm okay."

Dex said, "I was saying we'll have to report this back to DiNardo and his committee people."

Jamie nodded inside his helmet. "And to the world."

They had recovered from their first reaction. Now they were all business. Fuchida was clicking away with the still camera.

"We should bring the video equipment in here for this," Hall said.

"And the VR rig," said Dex. "Every tourist in the world is going to want to see this!"

Jamie turned and began walking away from the others. For an insane moment he felt it would be better to dynamite the whole dwelling, bury it in tons of rock so that no one could ever find it again, leave it in peace and never let anyone else set foot in it.

DIARY ENTRY

They blame everything on me. I'm their scapegoat. If anything goes wrong, it's my fault. They're much too clever to come right out and say it, but I can tell by the way they talk about me behind my back, by the way they look at me when they think I can't see them. They're so excited about the cliff dwelling and the writing. They'll never want to leave. But I'm going to outsmart them all. I'll fix it so that they'll HAVE TO leave, whether they want to or not.

BOSTON

"WRITING?" DARRYL C. TRUMBALL DEMANDED. "THEY FOUND ACTUAL writing?"

He was in his limousine, crawling through the clotted, beeping traffic along Storrow Drive. A cold winter rain was slanting down, driven by a gusty northeastern gale. The Charles River was overflowing its banks again, snarling traffic even more than usual.

His personal assistant, a bland young man with an MBA from Harvard, seemed excited. His image in the display screen set between the limo's two rearward-facing seats was small and grainy, but the man appeared to be on the verge of breaking into a dance of celebration.

"Writing! Yessir! Martian writing! It's fantastic, the find of a lifetime, the grandest discovery of all time, really!"

Trumball's excitement was more controlled. Stock prices for the top few travel agencies had been climbing nicely; aerospace stocks were doing even better. Each news release about the Mars expedition pushed the prices a little higher.

"Sir," his assistant said, "I believe the time has come to take a much more proactive position on this."

"On what?" Trumball growled, leaning deeper into the limo's plush rear seat. He eyed the bar at his side, but had promised himself he would not start the evening's drinking until he got home.

"On putting together an organization to take tourists to Mars!" his assistant replied eagerly. "The demand is building, and with this discovery of the Martian writing, people are going to want to go see it for themselves! Like the Sistine Chapel or those cave paintings in Spain!"

"You mean there's a measurable demand *now*?"

"There could be, sir, if you take the lead and shape the trend."

"And just what do you suggest?" Trumball asked sourly. He could barely make out the dark silhouettes of the buildings flanking the Drive, the rain was pounding down so hard. A good, warming shot of bourbon was what he needed, but he knew that if his wife smelled liquor on him when he got home she would start another of her tearful lectures about his goddamned blood pressure.

The assistant's answering smile told Trumball that the young man had been figuring this out for days. He wasn't quick enough to come up with a plan on the spur of the moment. Bright, yes. But not fast on his feet.

"I suggest, sir," the assistant said, "that we find a prominent public figure who would be willing to go to Mars on the next expedition. And we send that expedition as soon as we possibly can. We've got to capitalize on the publicity and public enthusiasm while it's still hot."

Trumball said nothing, waiting for more.

The assistant continued, "A well-known public figure, sir. Like a video star, or perhaps even a prominent politician. Perhaps one of the retired presidents!"

"No," Trumball heard himself say. "Not a politician."

He actually smiled at the assistant's eager young image. He knew exactly what he was going to do. And all the credit will come to me, he told himself.

Without disclosing his newly formed plan he clicked off the Picturephone and reached for the bourbon. Let her lecture, he said to himself. Let her whine and wheedle till she gets hoarse.

He laughed so loud that he startled his chauffeur, even through the bulletproof glass partition separating them.

NIGHT: SOL 144

JAMIE WALKED NAKED THROUGH THE VILLAGE ON THE FLOOR OF THE CANyon, the sun hot on his bare, bronzed shoulders. The villagers paid him no attention; they went about their daily business as if he weren't there among them.

They were only shadows, though. Jamie thought he could see right through them, as if they were holograms or ghosts. He tried to speak to them, but no words would come out of his mouth. He tried to touch them, but his outstretched fingers never quite reached them.

"Grandfather," he managed to say, "why won't they talk to me?"

And he realized he was a child, walking alongside his grandfather. Al wore his best suit, the light blue one with the western-cut jacket. His hair was dark and tied in a long single braid that went halfway down his back.

"They can't talk to you, Jamie," said Al. "They're all dead."

"But I can see them."

Al laughed pleasurably. "Sure you can. You can see me, too, and I'm dead."

Jamie realized that his grandfather was right. But when he looked again, the villagers had changed. They were no longer men and women, like the People. They were different creatures. They looked almost like dogs, but they had six legs instead of only four. No, Jamie saw, not six legs. Four legs and a pair of arms that ended in something like hands.

Their eyes were large and sad as Jamie looked down at them. They moved slowly, as if they were very weary.

"They've come a long way to see you," Al explained. "Millions of years."

Six-year-old Jamie wanted to pet them, but his hand went through their shimmering, ethereal images.

"You're all that they've got left, Jamie," Al said, his voice sighing, dwindling into the faint whisper of the breeze. "You're all that they've got left."

And Jamie was in his spacesuit, on the barren empty floor of the Canyon while the meager breeze whispered past his helmet. The village was gone and high up on the face of the cliff he could make out the dark niche in the rock where the Martians had built their temple and gone to die.

"Don't let them die again," his grandfather's voice came through his earphones. "Don't let their spirits be dead forever."

Jamie awoke slowly, fighting his way toward consciousness like a swimmer struggling to return to the surface after being down too deep, too long.

He opened his eyes at last and felt a sudden stab of confusion, almost fear. This isn't the rover!

And then it came back to him. Dezhurova and Rodriguez had flown the backup L/AV to their site on the edge of the Canyon. They were sleeping in its habitation module now, just as they had on the flight from Earth. It was the compromise they had agreed to; the scientists could live in the L/AV much more comfortably than in one of the rovers, while the others stayed at the dome. The two astronauts could shuttle food and supplies to the Canyon site as needed.

Until the backup dome arrived. The ICU board had swiftly agreed to send it, and the Russians were mating it to a rocket booster at their launch center in Kazakhstan. It was scheduled to arrive at the Canyon site on Sol 325—if it was launched on schedule.

Funny, Jamie mused as he got out of his bunk. During the flight I thought this tin can was too small, too confining. Like a jail cell. Now, after weeks of living in the rovers, it feels like a suite at the Waldorf.

It was early, Jamie saw. The module was quiet, except for the inevitable hum of electrical equipment. Nobody else is up yet. He luxuriated in the shower for three full minutes, until the hot water automatically turned needle-cold. Then he shaved quickly, remembering the time in college when he had tried to raise a beard. It came in thin and straight and dark; he looked more like a menacing mandarin out of some old spy movie than a hunky campus stud.

Climbing up the ladder to the galley, Jamie was surprised to see Dex already sitting at the spindly-legged table, grasping a mug of fresh-brewed coffee in both hands.

"You're up early," Jamie said as he went to the freezer.

"Couldn't sleep," said Dex.

Jamie looked at him more closely. Dex's breezy grin was gone. His eyes looked bleary.

"What's the matter?"

"Guess who's coming on the next expedition?"

"DiNardo?"

"I wish."

"Who?"

"My old man."

"Your father?" His voice ran almost a full octave above normal. Dex nodded grimly.

"He's coming here? To Mars?" Jamie slid the freezer door shut and pulled out the chair next to Dex's.

"He's been a busy little beaver. The third expedition is being set up to land here two weeks before we leave. The ICU is recruiting the science team now. Dad's money people are ordering the spacecraft and equipment. Every archeologist and paleontologist on Earth is screaming to come aboard. They might auction off the seats, for chrissakes."

"But *he's* coming along?"

"You bet your sweet ass he is. He'll come and I'll go home. He'll take personal command of the commercial operations here on Mars."

Jamie felt his heart sink. "Commercial operations," he muttered.

"Maybe he'll run the hot dog concession," Dex said humorlessly.

"Isn't he too old? I mean, there are safety regulations and such . . . "

Dex shook his head. "He's healthy as a frigging mule. Hell, they've got feeble old grandmothers traipsing off to the Moon now, with those Clipperships. If you can ride a commercial airliner you can ride into orbit. And if you can get into orbit, you can go to the Moon."

"Or Mars."

"Or Mars," Dex agreed glumly. "He'll be here in a little more than a year."

Jamie looked at the younger man for a long, silent moment. Why is Dex so depressed? he wondered. He's been pushing for tourism and commercial development, and now that his father is coming to move things faster along that line, Dex looks as miserable as I feel.

"Why does he have to come here in person?" Jamie asked. "Can't he do whatever he wants done back on Earth?"

Dex made a sour face. "He wants to show that ordinary people can ride to Mars. He wants to open up the door to tourism. Commercial development. He'll be building a hotel here. A whole tourist center. Disneyland-on-Mars."

"He can't," Jamie groaned.

"He will. He's got to be Mr. Macho. Head man. Show the whole world that *he* can come to Mars and get the show rolling. Make your fortune on the red planet. Invest in Darryl C. Trumball Enterprises."

Jamie said, "You don't seem very happy about it."

"Why the hell should I be? He's coming here to take the glory, to be the important man, to push me aside, out of the spotlight. I'm just the little kid that did some science work, *he's* the big important bull-shit billionaire."

"How on earth can we stop him?"

"We're not on Earth."

"You know what I mean, Dex. This has got to be stopped! Now, before he starts ruining this world. How do we stop him?"

"Put a bullet between his eyes."

"I'm serious."

Dex slammed a fist on the tabletop, sloshing coffee from his mug.

"There isn't any way to stop him! He controls the money, dammit."

"There's got to be a way," Jamie said, feeling desperate. "There's got to be."

Dex shook his head slowly. "It's the golden rule, pal: he who has the gold makes the rules."

Jamie pushed his chair back and got to his feet. "This has got to be stopped, Dex. I'll talk to DiNardo. Li Chengdu. The ICU board."

"Go right ahead. You've got as much of a chance as the Sioux nation did against the U.S. Army."

"They beat Custer," Jamie snapped.

"And got wiped out afterward."

Trudy Hall's head popped up through the floor hatch, dark brown hair bobbing slightly as she climbed the ladder.

"I thought I'd be the early bird this morning," she said, surprised that she was not.

Jamie saw she was in her sweat-stained running suit. She's going to go back to her jogging every morning, he realized. Remembering the noise of her padding around the hab module's outer perimeter, Jamie said to himself, We won't need any alarm clocks.

"No, the worms are all gone, Trudy," said Dex, with a bitter grin.

"Just as well, actually. We have a lot of work to do this morning. DiNardo's people want another set of photomicrographs of all the wall writings."

"Another set? What about the images we sent them last week?" Dex asked.

"Not good enough, I suppose." Trudy went to the freezer, blissfully unaware of the problems that were burning in Jamie's gut.

Now I've got to go out there and do the scientific work I came here to do, Jamie thought. Forget about Trumball and concentrate on the work. That's what's important. Get the work done . . . while you can.

NOON: SOL 147

"NO TROUBLES?" VIJAY ASKED.

Trudy Hall's image on the comm screen looked slightly puzzled by the question. She shook her head. "No, no problem at all."

"That's good," said Vijay.

"It's rather like being the baby sister with three grownup brothers," Hall went on. "Mostly, I'm treated with a certain amount of tolerance, actually."

Vijay was sitting at the tiny desk in her personal quarters. She was recording their conversation, of course; part of her ongoing psychology files.

"And none of them have made any sexual approaches?"

"Not a one." Hall almost pouted. "Perhaps I should be disappointed?" Then she quickly added, "Don't let Tommy know I said that!"

With a laugh, Vijay assured her these psych sessions were strictly private. "Unless you have a complaint to make, naturally."

Hall shook her head again. "Actually, Dex and Jamie are moping around as if the weight of the world is on their shoulders. And Mitsuo . . . well, Mitsuo's always given me the feeling he thinks I'm not entirely human."

A subtle form of racism, Vijay thought. Lord knows you've seen enough of it from the WASPs.

But she kept her thoughts to herself. She ended her session with Hall and signed off, then spent half an hour dictating her own thoughts and impressions for the mission record.

These reports will add up to a series of papers in the psych journals when we get back home, she thought as she dictated. My career will be made; I'll be able to take my pick of tenure-track positions at the best universities on Earth.

Sexual attitudes and behaviors in an isolated environment over an eighteen-month period. That could be the title of the key paper. Might even make a racy book of it: *Sex on Mars.* A bestseller, without a doubt.

But even as she formed the ideas in her mind, she wondered about Jamie. And Dex. And herself. What a mess I've made of everything. What a stupid forlorn mess.

Vijay had spent whole evenings searching through the scientific literature about human relationships on other expeditions, especially the scientific teams that wintered over at Antarctic stations. There had been plenty of information about interpersonal stress and the effects of loneliness and boredom mixed with physical danger, but almost nothing that helped her. Men had attempted murder at Antarctic stations. Men had gone berserk in nuclear submarines during months-long patrols underwater.

But the reports said little about the way relationships between men and women could form and mutate. Nothing about how sex twists everything into different perspectives.

The dome seemed empty with only Craig and the two astronauts in it with her. Sitting in her little cubicle, staring into the now-blank screen of her laptop, Vijay wondered for the thousandth time if she should accompany Rodriguez on his next run out to the Canyon and spend a day or two with the four scientists there.

With Jamie, you mean. Or Dex. Is it Jamie you want? she asked herself. Despite everything, despite his bloody selflessness, is Jamie really the one you care for? You'll have to settle for second-best with him; he's really in love with Mars.

What about Dex? He's . . . powerful. Dynamic. Vijay shook her head. She didn't want to think about Dex. He was a complication. Too upsetting.

She jumped up from her chair and walked swiftly out of her compartment. Get the blood circulating, she told herself, striding hard enough across the plastic flooring to send the staccato of her footsteps echoing across the dome.

Stacy was outside with Rodriguez, loading one of the rovers for the next run to the Canyon. Craig was on duty in the comm center. Glancing at her wristwatch, Vijay saw that it was almost time for her to relieve Craig and let him get back to his geology work.

I could go on the rover with them, Vijay said to herself. They don't need me here; Tommy's hand is healed up nicely and there aren't any medical emergencies to worry about. She realized that her medical work on Mars had been almost entirely pharmaceutical. I've been pushing pills, handing out vitamins and nutritional supplements—and compiling psych profiles.

More psychology than medicine, she told herself. But when it comes to your own emotional problems, you're a hopeless muddle. Physician, heal thyself!

Three of the twelve rooms in the dwelling had writing on their walls: one room on each level. Jamie thought about that as he stared at the latest appraisal of the stone samples they had sent back to the dome. Wiley Craig had worked up a very nice spectrographic analysis of the chips and flakes he and Dex had scraped off the stone walls of the building.

There was enough potassium in the stone to get a reasonably firm date from radioactive decay rates. *If* the decay rates are the same on Mars as they are on Earth, Jamie thought. No reason why they shouldn't be; atoms are atoms, and they behave the same way all over the universe. But there might be other factors at work here, factors we don't recognize, subtle factors that are different from Earth.

We just don't know, Jamie had to admit to himself.

At any rate, the stone was more than a hundred million years old. Same as the stone stratum at the rear of the niche, where the Martians had quarried the blocks that they used to build the dwelling.

And that doesn't tell us much, Jamie thought. The age of the stone isn't what we're after; it's the age of the building. When did the Martians cut those stones and use them to build their . . . temple.

Leaning back in the padded chair of his compartment, Jamie realized that he no longer thought of the building as a dwelling place. They didn't live in it. It was a temple of some sort, a place where they came to perform sacred rites.

Like writing their history on the walls? If that's what the wall markings are, they had a damned short history. Three walls inscribed with elaborate figures, some of them pictographs, most of them looking more like letters or whole words.

And each of them deteriorating into scrawled, scratched messages that looked like the work of children. Or desperate, harried people in a deathly hurry.

A single rap on his compartment door startled Jamie out of his thoughts. Before he could reply, the accordion door slid open and Dex stepped in.

"You've got Wiley's analysis on-screen, too," Dex said, without preamble. "Good."

"It's good work, all right," Jamie agreed, "but it doesn't help us much."

Dex perched himself on the edge of Jamie's unmade bunk. "No, you're right. We've got to come up with some way of dating the building itself."

"Any ideas?"

Dex shook his head. "I've been going through the literature and talking to archeologists back home."

"No joy."

Jumping impulsively to his feet, Dex said, "The thing is, back on Earth we've got the stratigraphy, the radioactive dating, even written records we can decipher. Here, everything's so damned uncertain."

"It's new territory."

"Tell me about it." Dex ran both hands through his dark hair. Jamie noticed it was looser, less curly than it had been when they'd first met. No humidity on Mars, he thought. Bad for your 'do.

"Maybe we should be talking with astronomers instead of archeologists," Jamie suggested.

Dex shot him a puzzled glance.

"The astronomers who date meteorites," Jamie explained. "They deal with rocks that are hundreds of millions of years old. Billions, even."

Sitting back on the edge of the bunk, Dex said slowly, "Yeah, that's right. They can tell when a meteorite was formed and when it was broken apart by collisions with other meteoroids, can't they?"

Jamie nodded. "Maybe they can help us."

"Call DiNardo," Dex said. "He ought to be able to find the right people."

"Or Pete, back at Tarawa. He put in a lot of years with NASA. They should have a lot of background data about meteoroids."

Dex made a huffing sound, halfway between a snort and a laugh. "At least it gives us something to do, a straw to grab for."

"You're not optimistic."

"Not much."

"We've got a mystery on our hands, all right."

"More than one," Dex said fervently. "How old is the building? What happened to the people who built it? What does all that writing mean? Why does it degenerate into those chicken scratches at the end?"

Jamie made a rueful grin back at him. "What was that old line about a mystery inside a riddle wrapped in an enigma?"

"Kennedy, I think. Or maybe Churchill."

"Whoever."

"Where the hell did they go?" Dex growled. "*What happened to them?*"

Jamie spread his arms and tried to look cheerful. "Listen, Dex: you can't do really good science unless you're tackling really tough questions."

Trumball looked at him askance. "We ought to be in line for the fucking Nobel Prize, then," he muttered.

"That would be nice," Jamie said.

"There's got to be an answer!" Dex insisted. "Maybe if we could cut out a few of the characters they inscribed on the wall and test the potassium-argon ratios along the faces of the incisions . . ."

"The archeologists would burn you at the stake if you even touched one of those walls with your gloved fingers."

"We're going to have to touch 'em sooner or later. We can't get any more information out of them by just staring at the damned writing. Or taking pictures of it."

"DiNardo's got the top cryptologists in the world studying the writing," Jamie said.

"Big deal. How're they going to decipher a code when they don't even know what language it's written in?"

Jamie shrugged. "Like you said, it's something to do. It beats sitting around and staring."

"Busywork."

The two men sat in gloomy silence for a few moments. Jamie tried to relax his mind, tried to deliberately not think about the Martians and their temple and the writings on the wall. Neat trick if you can do it, he groused to himself. Try not thinking about an elephant.

Instead, he remembered that there were other things to worry about.

"Dex, we've got another problem to deal with, too," he said.

"My old man."

"Yes. I don't want him here. I don't want him leading the way for shiploads of tourists to come trooping through the temple—"

"Temple? Who says it's a temple?"

With a patient sigh, Jamie answered, "That's the way I think of it."

"A temple."

Waggling one hand in the air, Jamie said, "The Martian equivalent."

Dex grinned at him. "I don't want dear old dad here, either, but how in hell can we stop him? He's got the ICU buffaloed, for chrissakes."

"I've asked both DiNardo and Li to intervene."

"And?"

"No answer yet," Jamie admitted. "From either of them."

"Don't hold your breath."

"He *can't* come here!" Jamie snapped. "We can't allow him to turn this site into a tourist attraction!"

Dex let his head droop between his hands. "When you figure out a way to stop him, pal, let me know. I've been trying to get out from under his thumb all my life, and now he's chasing all the way here to Mars to get his paws back on me."

MORNING: SOL 150

JAMIE SAT ON THE LIP OF THE CLEFT, HIS LEGS DANGLING OVER THE EDGE, morning sunlight flooding over him and washing against the stone wall at his back. The pale, shrunken Sun brought him no warmth. The floor of the Canyon spread far, far below his booted feet, strewn with rocks, but otherwise cold and empty and barren.

He bent forward slightly to peer at the Canyon floor and tried to see it as it once was. A stream must have meandered through it, perhaps a full-sized river, he thought. He pictured the Martians living down there in neat, orderly villages with fields of crops between them. Everything squared off, streets lined up straight, precise rows of the Martian equivalent of corn growing in the sunshine.

Now it was dead, bare, a frozen desert where the air temperature barely rose above zero on the longest day of the summer.

But not quite empty any longer. Hall and Fuchida were riding the cable down to the Canyon floor, ready for a day of working on the sparse few colonies of lichen that clung desperately to life down there.

Suddenly the bulky form of a spacesuited figure came lumbering into view, dangling on the cable and lowering slowly from the overhanging ceiling of rock. Dex, coming down for the day's work. The day's frustration.

"Stacy called from the rover," he said as Jamie pulled himself to his feet.

"I thought Tomas was driving this run."

"Nope. The boss lady decided to do it herself."

Dex planted his boots on the rock floor as Jamie reached him and started to help him out of the climbing harness.

"You bring the day's task list?" Dex asked.

Jamie tapped on the readout screen of the computer on his suit's wrist. "M.O.S.," he said glumly.

"More of the same."

"Right. More photomicrographs. More rock samples to chip out."

"At least we've got all the dust cleared away," Dex said, heading for the cameras and other gear they had left on the ground overnight.

Nodding inside his helmet, Jamie said, "We ought to start putting up plastic sheets to protect the doors and roof openings."

"Why now? No dust storms in sight."

"There's still some wind. A little dust blows in here every day. Sooner or later it'll accumulate enough to be a problem again."

Dex huffed, then admitted, "I guess you're right. I'll tell Wiley to put together a pile of sheeting for the next rover run."

Jamie picked up the set of tools they used for taking samples of the rock and started for the nearest opening in the wall.

"Still no sign of any other buildings anywhere," Dex said. "I spent half the night going over the imagery from the soarplane. Nothing."

"We wouldn't have noticed this site if we hadn't seen it for ourselves," Jamie said. "The planes and the satellites could be overflying a hundred buildings and we'd never realize it."

"Yeah," Dex admitted. "Local rock at ambient temperature. Doesn't give you anything that stands out for the sensors, does it?"

"Not much."

"When's Tarawa going to get the fission-track data to us?" Dex complained. "They ought to have at least a preliminary correlation by now."

Jamie replied, "From what Pete tells me, the archeologists have been arguing with the geologists. I don't know if it's a turf battle or an honest disagreement about the data."

"Flatheads," Dex grumbled.

They crawled through the low doorway and got to their feet again. As they headed for the opening that led to the next level, Dex said, "I got another message from my father, too."

"Oh?"

"He's getting to be real chummy."

"That's good," Jamie said. "I guess."

"Y'know the real reason he's coming out here?"

Walking toward the light well, Jamie answered, "You said he wants to start commercial operations."

"Yeah, but to do that he's got to clear a legal claim to the area."

"Legal claim?"

"Sure. So nobody can set up a competing operation in this area."

"He can't claim ownership of Mars," Jamie said.

"He doesn't have to."

Jamie stopped and turned to face the younger man. All he could see in Dex's visor was the reflection of his own faceless helmet and hard-suit shoulders.

"The thing is," Dex explained, "you can claim priority of *use* for a region. Like the people at Moonbase and the other lunar settlements. They're not allowed to claim ownership of the territory, but they can claim that they're using the area and the International Astronautical Authority gives them the legal right to that use."

Jamie felt confused. "They don't actually own the territory—"

"But they can use it, legally, and keep competitors out."

"That's the law?"

He could sense Dex nodding inside his helmet. "Yep. The Space Utilization Treaty. My father explained it all to me last night."

"It sounds pretty weird," Jamie said.

"Lawyers."

"So your father's coming here to stake a legal claim to using this region of Mars?"

"That's his plan. He wants to claim all the territory we've been working in, which would include this site, the Canyon floor where the lichen are, even Mount Olympus."

Jamie felt his heart sinking. In his mind's eye he saw hotels springing up, tour buses, swimming pools filled with shouting kids. His nightmares come true.

"We've got to stop him, Dex. We can't allow that kind of a precedent to be set here."

"I know."

"I know we've had our differences about this . . ."

Dex said nothing.

"But—" Jamie hesitated, searching for words. "But, Dex, can you see that we can't allow tourists here?"

For long moments Dex remained silent. He turned slowly in a full circle, as if to take in every corner of the ancient empty chamber in which they stood.

"Not here," Dex agreed, his voice low and serious. "They'd wreck this place in a week."

"Not to Mars," Jamie said. "Not to any part of it."

"You don't understand," Dex muttered.

"No, we *can't* allow them to come to Mars," Jamie insisted. "We mustn't permit it. We've got to explore this planet, find the other building sites, find out what happened to the people here—"

"Whoa, whoa!" Dex held up a gloved hand. "I understand how you feel about this, Jamie. I even agree with you. But you've got to understand something: This is all my fault."

"Your fault?"

"My father spearheaded the funding for this expedition because I talked him into it. I told him the expedition could pay for itself, even make a profit."

"By selling tourist tickets?"

Dex said, "Right. By making a commercial operation that would bring high-end tourists here for the trip of a lifetime. The same kind of people who go to that sex palace in orbit. The same kind of people who can afford to go to the Moon and put their footprints where nobody's stepped before."

"But the Moon's dead," Jamie said. "There's no danger of disturbing anything there."

With a bitter laugh, Dex countered, "Tell that to the geophysicists! They go apeshit whenever a busload of tourists churns up the regolith."

"Well, you see what I mean, then," Jamie said. "We have living organisms here, and the ruins of an intelligent civilization. They've got to be protected."

"I know. I understand that now."

They were standing beneath the squared-off opening in the ceiling, the light well that allowed morning sunlight to brighten the windowless chamber.

"So how do we go about protecting it? How do we stop your father?"

"What's this 'we,' red man?"

"He's your father, Dex."

"So?"

"So you've got to stop him."

"Me? Are you kidding? He's never listened to me in his life."

"Then at least you can help me."

"How?"

Jamie had no ready answer. "I don't know," he admitted.

"Well," Dex said, reaching up for the edge of the square opening in the ceiling, "when you figure out what to do, let me know."

He pulled himself up. Jamie followed him, thinking, There must be some way to stop Trumball. Something that can make him see, make him understand. But what?

They spent the morning going through their assigned tasks, carefully chipping still more rock samples from random blocks of stone in the walls on the three different floors. Once they were back on the ground level they went outside again and collected more samples from the outside of the wall.

"How about some samples from the quarry, out back?" Dex asked.

"They haven't asked for that."

"Well, why don't you take this batch up to the rover while I bang out a couple more samples from back there, just for the hell of it."

Jamie knew the samples from the quarry gave them a date for the age of the undisturbed rock. Maybe Dex is onto something, he thought. Maybe the samples from the building will show some difference in the amount of radiation they've absorbed from infalling cosmic particles: a sort of subatomic weathering that might allow us to pin down the age of the building.

But it's the rates of weathering that we don't know, don't even have a feeling for, Jamie knew. All the data we've accumulated don't mean anything because we don't know how fast the weathering action took place.

Not yet, he told himself. The geologists back on Earth have much more sophisticated equipment than we do here. If they can get a fix on the rates, then maybe we can figure out just how old this building really is.

"Okay," he said to Dex. "You take more samples from the quarry. I'll see you in the rover."

"Don't start lunch without me," Dex called as Jamie headed for the climbing harness.

Once in the L/AV's hab module, Jamie checked with Fuchida and Hall down on the Canyon floor, then started testing the morning's rock samples. The sooner our data get to Earth the better, he thought. Give them as much data as we can.

Dezhurova called in; she would be at the site before nightfall, at her present rate of travel. Good.

Jamie was bent over the computer screen in the makeshift lab they had put together when Dex clomped in through the airlock below. Jamie could hear the thin buzz of the hand vac as Dex cleaned the dust off his suit.

He finished the analysis program and sent the data Earthward, then ducked through the hatch into the galley. Dex wasn't there. Jamie found him in the command center, sitting at the comm console, apparently talking with Tarawa. The face on the screen was unfamiliar, but the scenery through the window behind her was unmistakably South Sea island.

"Ready for lunch?" Jamie asked.

Dex quickly signed off and turned in his seat. Jamie saw that the younger man's face was white, his eyes wide and staring.

"What is it?" Jamie asked. "What's happened?"

"They came up with a preliminary date for the building," Dex said, his voice shaking a little.

"Tarawa?"

"The geologists and archeologists weren't fighting about it. They just didn't believe it could be possible, so they checked the work several times before they decided it must be right."

Jamie felt a tendril of anxiety worming through his gut. "They didn't believe the date they got?"

"It's a rough number. Very rough."

"What is it?" Jamie thought he knew what the answer would be.

"Near as they can pin it down, the building was put up about sixty-five million years ago."

"Sixty-five million?" Jamie's voice sounded hollow, far away, even in his own ears.

Dex nodded somberly. "That's it. Sixty-five million years ago."

Jamie's legs felt rubbery. He sat on the chair next to Dex. "The K-T boundary."

"The meteor strike that killed the dinosaurs."

"Something hit here, too," Jamie said. "It killed off the Martians."

"That lopsided sketch on the wall . . . it's a mushroom cloud."

"From the meteor strike."

"They were wiped out the same way the dinosaurs were," Dex said, his voice trembling.

AFTERNOON: SOL 150

"THAT'S WHAT MUST HAVE HAPPENED," JAMIE SAID TO VIJAY.

His image in the display screen looked grave, solemn. Vijay was running the comm center at the dome, Jamie was in his quarters aboard the L/AV out at the Canyon, from the looks of it.

"A meteor?" she asked, feeling the uneasy stir of an old memory, a childhood fear, within her.

"Meteoroid," Dex corrected, leaning over Jamie's shoulder to push his face into the picture.

"Maybe more than one," Jamie said. "The disaster that wiped out the dinosaurs on Earth might've been more than one meteor strike."

Vijay felt the old, old fear clutching at her.

"It must have been a swarm of them," Dex said, his voice strangely flat, drained of emotion. "Big suckers, too."

"On Earth three-quarters of every living species was wiped out, land, sea and air," Jamie said.

"And here on Mars," Dex went on, "nothing survived except the lichen and the bacteria underground."

"Shiva," Vijay whispered.

"What?"

"Shiva, the destroyer," she said, remembering the tales of the ancient gods that her mother had told her.

Jamie's brow furrowed slightly. "Is that—"

"Shiva is a god," Vijay explained. "His dance is the rhythm of the universe. He destroys worlds."

Dex pushed into the picture again. "Shiva is a bunch of big rocks, then."

"His avatar," said Vijay. "His presence among us."

Jamie saw it with his inner Navaho's eyes: The Martians working under a hot sun, their crops waving in the breeze, their villages dotting the fertile land. And then death comes roaring out of the sky. The explosions as the meteoroids impact. The ground quakes. Mushroom clouds billow into the blue sky. The Martians flee to their temples, begging their gods to end this rain of devastation.

The terrible bombardment from the sky goes on and on, without end, without mercy. The planet's air is blown away almost completely, until a mere wisp remains. The seas freeze. The Martians die, every one of them, their crops, their herds, their very memory erased from the planet's surface. Except for a rare temple here and there, in a protected spot, where the last dying members of the race desperately scratch the final chapter of their story into the stones.

Dust covers the frozen seas. Nothing alive remains except the hardy lichen and the bacteria that dwell deep underground. Death reigns over all of Mars.

With a shudder, Jamie forced his attention back to the present, to this moment. He could see on the little laptop screen that Vijay looked somber, almost frightened. Maybe we should all be scared, he thought. Another rock could wipe us out, too.

You don't know that for certain, the rational side of his mind warned him. The data could be off by millions of years. The dating could be just a coincidence. But he could not believe in such a coincidence.

"So that's what happened to the Martians," Vijay said, her voice hardly above a whisper. "Shiva destroyed them. Without mercy. Without warning. They were swept away as if they never existed at all."

Nodding, Jamie said, "But they left this temple. Maybe there are other—"

The yellow priority message icon began blinking on his computer screen.

"Hold on," Jamie said, splitting the screen to see who was calling so urgently.

Dezhurova's dour face appeared. She was obviously in the rover's cockpit, and obviously unhappy.

"Stacy, what's the matter?" Jamie asked.

"I am stopped about fifty kilometers from you," the cosmonaut said.

"Stopped?"

"Wheel malfunction. Must be dust in the bearings. It is overheating badly. If I try to proceed it will probably burn out completely."

"I'll tell the dome," Jamie said. "I'm already talking with Vijay."

"Good. Tell Rodriguez to come in the number two rover with a replacement wheel bearing."

Jamie glanced at the digital clock blinking in the screen's lower right-hand corner. "You'll be stuck there overnight."

"Neh problemeh."

"If we kept a rover here," Dex pointed out, "we could go out and get you before sunset."

"Perhaps," the cosmonaut agreed glumly.

"That might be something to think about," said Jamie. "We have the extra rover . . ."

"Tell Rodriguez to come in the old rover," Dex said, "and then leave it here with us."

"Perhaps a good plan," Dezhurova said slowly. "I will discuss it with Tom."

Close to midnight, as Jamie lay in his bunk, the yellow message light on his laptop began blinking again.

"Now what?" he muttered. It was late, he was tired, emotionally weary from the realization of what had wiped out the Martians. He had spent several hours looking over the archeologists' reports on the age of the building. Then DiNardo had called in, a long, rambling monologue that boiled down to the Jesuit geologist's doubts about associating the demise of the Martians with the extinction of the dinosaurs.

"The error bars on the archeologists' dating for the Martian structure encompass several million years," DiNardo said, his voice almost trembling with emotion. "It is fantastic to believe that the same event that caused the extinctions at the end of the Cretaceous on Earth also caused the extinction of the Martians."

He's frightened, Jamie saw as he studied DiNardo's swarthy, stubble-jawed face. For some reason this idea scares him.

"Father DiNardo," Jamie replied after watching the geologist's message twice, "I have to admit that the data on the age of the building here are pretty shaky. But even if the K/T extinctions on Earth and the end of the Martians happened a few million years apart, they still might have been the result of a single cause. A swarm of big meteoroids could have swung through the inner solar system and collided with the planets over a span of millions of years. We should be looking for evidence of a bombardment around that era on the Moon, don't you think?"

He sent his message to DiNardo, then saw more than a dozen members of the archeologists' committee wanted to talk with him. And the ICU board wanted to discuss the replenishment mission that was going to be launched. And Tarawa was scheduling a media conference for tomorrow.

Jamie had been glad when he attended to the last of his waiting messages and could finally crawl into bed and try to sleep. Then the message light started blinking again.

Who could be calling at this hour? Tarawa wouldn't unless there was some sort of emergency. Nobody at the dome, they're all asleep by now.

Stacy? He sat up on the bunk. Is Stacy having trouble out in the rover?

Jamie reached out and tapped the keyboard. Mitsuo Fuchida's face showed on the screen.

"What's wrong, Mitsuo?" Jamie asked.

The biologist was obviously in his quarters in the L/AV, only a few feet from Jamie's cubicle. Yet he chose to call rather than come over in person. The lighting was dim, but Jamie could see that Fuchida appeared troubled, worried.

"I am convinced we have a saboteur among us," Fuchida said, almost in a whisper.

"What?"

"I have been reviewing the evidence associated with several so-called accidents," Fuchida said, "and I believe they were deliberately caused."

Jamie swung his legs off the bunk and hunched closer to the laptop screen. Great, he thought. Mitsuo's playing Sherlock Holmes.

"What accidents?" he asked wearily.

"The puncturing of the garden dome during the dust storm, for one."

"That was sabotage?"

"Those punctures were made from the inside, not by the storm."

"We've been through all that . . ."

"And Tomas' injury? Do you believe that the tray of molten glass just happened to give way while he was standing beside it?"

Jamie drew a deep breath. "Why are you telling me this? And why in the middle of the night?"

"Because you are the only one I trust," Fuchida answered urgently. "The saboteur might be any of the others!"

"Why would anybody want to sabotage our equipment? Or hurt one of us?"

"I don't know. Maybe he's insane."

There is that, Jamie admitted to himself. According to Vijay we're all a little nuts.

Fuchida added, "And now this bearing malfunction in Stacy's rover. Those bearings are sealed against dust penetration!"

Shaking his head, more in weariness than annoyance, Jamie said, "Okay, Mitsuo, tell you what. You and Wiley check out that faulty bearing when you go back to the dome. If you find any tampering with it, then tell Stacy about it. She's the mission director now, not me."

"But she might be the saboteur!"

"Stacy? That's . . ." Jamie was about to say crazy, then realized that it would fit right in with Fuchida's theory.

"She was on comm duty in the dome the night of the storm, while all the rest of us were sleeping. Remember?" the biologist insisted. "She helped to build the kiln for the glass bricks. She is alone in the rover and it breaks down."

"You think she did it so she could spend the night alone out there?" Jamie asked.

"If she is insane her motives would not be rational," Fuchida replied.

Despite himself, Jamie sighed. "Well, when you and Wiley inspect the bearing—"

"How do we know that Wiley isn't the saboteur?"

How do we know you're not off your tracks? Jamie wondered silently.

"It could be any one of them," Fuchida added.

"All right, Mitsuo, all right. Check out the faulty bearing by your-self, then. If you find any evidence of tampering, tell me about it. Okay?"

Fuchida bobbed his head eagerly. *"Hai!"*

Jamie cut the connection and crawled back into his bunk. Just what I need. Either we have a crazy saboteur among us or Mitsuo's going paranoid. Great.

Jamie did not get much sleep that night.

THE TORRENT OF DEATH

THE COLLOQUIUM HAD BEEN HASTILY THROWN TOGETHER, BUT ALMOST every member of the Institute for Advanced Study's faculty crowded into the auditorium to listen to Li Chengdu.

He felt unworthy of this honor, unprepared for this responsibility, as he slowly climbed the three steps and crossed to the podium standing in the middle of the bare stage. All the buzzing conversations stopped. The auditorium fell absolutely silent as this tall scarecrow of a Chinese sage reached the podium.

Remarkable, thought Li. Nearly two hundred of the most argumenta-tive men and women on Earth, and they all expect me to enlighten them.

For several hushed moments he merely stood there, nearly six and a half feet of lanky scientist, and stared out at the audience. Physicists, mathematicians, historians, biologists, even the economists were well represented. No outsiders, though. No news reporters or photographers.

Good, thought Li.

He began: "As you know, Mars was once inhabited by intelligent species. They were apparently driven to extinction at approximately the same geological time that represents the boundary between Cretaceous period and Tertiary era on Earth, which has been called the Time of Great Dying.

"Three-quarters of all life-forms on land and sea were extinguished on Earth. On Mars, every species above the complexity of lichen was destroyed.

"It would appear, then, that a torrent of death swept through the inner solar system some sixty-five million years ago . . ."

Beverly Urey was only a distant cousin to the Nobel laureate chemist, but she was an astronomer at the Keck telescopes in Hawaii and the news media reporters tracked her down in the vast moonscape of Mauna Kea's ancient caldera.

"We have a report from Princeton that said a torrent of death hit Earth and Mars sixty-five million years ago!" one of the reporters shouted at her.

"Well, yes," she replied, somewhat dazed by their numbers and aggressiveness, "I suppose you might say that."

TORRENT OF DEATH SWEPT EARTH AND MARS

Hilo: ''A 'torrent of death' swept both Earth and Mars sixty-five million years ago, according to a leading astronomer.

Dr. Beverly Urey, of the Keck Telescope Facility on Hawaii, told reporters that the same swarm of meteors that wiped out the dinosaurs on Earth also killed the intelligent race that lived on Mars.

According to Dr. Urey . . .

"But they're not dead," said Hodell Richards, with a thin smile.

The host of the network TV show, a genial intelligent man with a secret passion for astronomy, smiled back skeptically. "The Martians aren't extinct?"

"Not at all." Richards had changed in the seven weeks since the first discovery of the Martian building. His lean, ascetic face had filled out somewhat. His hair was shorter, more in style with the current fashion. He had shaved off his mustache.

"But our scientists on Mars—"

Richards cut the host short. "Do you really think they're telling us the whole story?" he asked archly.

"They're not?"

"Of course not! They couldn't. The government won't let them."

"But the Mars expedition isn't being run by the government."

Ignoring the inconvenient fact, Richards looked straight into the camera. "As I've been saying all along, the Martians have established a secret base for themselves here on Earth, in Tibet. We've got to find it!''

Arching a brow, the host said, "You think, then, that the Martians pose a threat to us?"

"They're here to conquer us through genetic engineering. They want to plant their seed in Earth women and create a new race of Martians here on Earth and take over our planet."

The host kept his quizzical smile in place, but inwardly he was thinking, The things I do just to keep the ratings up.

Pete Connors sat at his desk in Tarawa, surrounded by phone screens that connected him with the Baikonur launch center in Kazakhstan, the office of the chairman of the International Consortium of Universities in New York, the International Space Station in orbit around the Earth, and the office of the woman who headed the expedition's logistics department, thirty meters down the hall from him.

Each of the faces on the screens looked harried, frustrated, almost angry. Each of them was talking—almost hollering—at the same time.

"All right," Connors said firmly, "let's cut the crap."

They all fell silent.

"We've got to set the replenishment mission launch back from our current date, that's clear. All agreed?"

Glumly, one by one, they agreed.

"Okay, it's no gut-buster. Nobody's head is gonna get chopped off and the people on Mars won't be endangered by the delay. Is that clear?"

Nods and mumbles.

"I know you've all been getting a lot of pressure from the media. Just ignore it."

"And just how in hell do we do that?" asked the launch director at Baikonur, a grim-faced Russian.

"Buck any and all media questions to me," Connors said. "I'll handle the news jocks."

"Really?" asked the woman in New York.

With a sweetly reasonable smile, Connors replied, "Yep. I'm setting up a major media conference right here on this balmy tropical isle. Get those suckers out here and off your backs so you can do your work and we can entertain 'em with swaying palm trees and a tour of the mission control facilities."

"I get it," said the engineer in the space station. "It's the slow season for tourists down there."

Connors smiled toothily. "You got it."

Once she got rid of the reporters, Beverly Urey returned to her work.

Hypothesis: A giant swarm of meteoroids swept through the inner solar system roughly sixty-five million years ago.

Evidence: Mega-extinctions on both Earth and Mars caused by the impacts of the meteoroids.

Question 1: Impact craters have been found on Earth and associated with the K/T extinctions. Can we find similar craters on Mars and get accurate dates for them?

Question 2: The Moon would have been hit, too. Can we locate craters of that age on the Moon? And what about the other planets?

Question 3: Can we find the meteoroid swarm?

She sighed as she pondered that last question. Sixty-five million years ago. Whatever's left of the swarm is much too far away for our telescopes to detect.

Then she sat up, eyes suddenly wide with fear. Unless their orbit is bringing them back toward us!

Fr. DiNardo knelt in the small confessional. Usually its dark, cramped confines brought him some measure of comfort, like a return to the womb.

But not today.

His confessor, on the other side of the screen, sat down heavily, making the wooden bench creak. DiNardo smelled the priest's aftershave lotion; it overpowered the distant scent of incense from the altar.

"Bless me, Father, for I have sinned," DiNardo began his confession.

The priest said nothing, waiting.

DiNardo swallowed hard, tasted bile. He took a breath, then whispered urgently, "I have sinned against the first commandment."

"The *first* commandment?"

"I fear that I am losing my faith," DiNardo answered, miserable.

"I don't understand," said the confessor.

"It's the Martians."

"The Martians are causing you to lose your faith?" the priest whispered, clearly puzzled, alarmed.

"Yes."

"How can this be?"

DiNardo hesitated. Then he explained, "How can a just and merciful God create a race of intelligent creatures and then kill them all?"

"How do you know—"

"They were intelligent!" DiNardo hissed. "They constructed buildings. They invented writing. I cannot believe that they did not have souls."

"Yes, perhaps they did."

"Then how could God have destroyed His own handiwork?"

"We cannot fathom the workings of divine purpose," the confessor said.

"It isn't right," DiNardo whispered harshly. "To kill them all . . . all of them . . ."

The confessor was silent for several moments. Then he whispered, "Judgment Day has already come on Mars."

DiNardo gasped at the thought.

"Apparently," the confessor went on, "God decided to bring the trial of tears on Mars to an end. He called the Martians back to him. Their time of testing ended sixty-five million years ago."

"Judgment Day," DiNardo murmured.

"It is not our place to question God's actions. We must accept what He has done."

"Judgment Day," DiNardo repeated.

"It may seem harsh to you, but the Martians are now in their heavenly home, looking upon the face of God. Is that a cruelty?"

DiNardo almost laughed aloud. "No, Father. You're right, of course. I was looking on it from a strictly secular point of view."

"For your penance, I think perhaps a retreat would be in order. Renew your spiritual strength, my friend."

Retreat? DiNardo stiffened at the thought. Spend a week or more in prayer and meditation, cut off from the rest of the world? Miss the news from Mars?

That would be penance indeed, he thought.

IV:
THE DECISION

Listen to the wisdom of the Old Ones. Coyote is
the trickster who brings misery to the People. But
sometimes he helps them. No one can be all bad. Or
all good.

AFTERNOON: SOL 342

"A THING OF BEAUTY IS A JOY FOREVER," SAID WILEY CRAIG, WITH GENU-ine appreciation in his voice.

The garden enclosure by the new dome was finished at last, a squared-off structure of glass bricks built entirely of materials from the Martian sand. Craig and Rodriguez stood by the big parabolic dish of the solar mirror that had provided the heat for their kiln, admiring their handiwork.

Rodriguez nodded inside his helmet. "We finished it in record time, too."

Craig laughed. "Wasn't much of a record we had to beat, Tom. And it helped that nobody got hurt while we were building it."

Flexing his scarred hand inside its glove, Rodriguez murmured, "Yeah, that's right."

The new dome—with its garden greenhouse—sat by the edge of the Canyon cliff. Four Buckyball cables ran down past the niche where the ancient building stood and extended all the way down to the Canyon floor.

Hall and Fuchida were down there, studying the lichen in the rocks, while a new drill chugged away, bringing up deep-dwelling bacteria from below the permafrost level.

The new dome had come on the unmanned resupply mission from Earth with a flexible access tunnel that could be linked to the airlock hatch of a rover by remote control, either from inside the dome itself or from inside the rover. The explorers could now go from the rover to the dome or vice versa in their shirtsleeves.

The replenishment lander had also carried a similar tunnel for the old dome, still sitting at its original site on Lunae Planum. Stacy and Fuchida were attaching it to the airlock hatch.

Over the past six months the explorers had mapped out the extent of the lichen across the entire face of Mars. Fuchida had returned to Olympus Mons to gather more samples of the *Ares olympicus* bacteria, then—with a delight bordering on delirium—discovered similar strains of rock-eating bacteria in two of the other Tharsis shield volcanoes.

Stacy had piloted only one of those flights with Fuchida, despite her ardent desire to fly. The responsibilities of being mission director weighed heavily upon her, but she could not entirely overcome her love of flying. "Rank has *some* privileges," she said firmly when she announced her decision to pilot the rocketplane.

Fuchida handled all the excursions to the volcanoes. Trudy Hall was scheduled for half of them, but the two biologists announced that Trudy would prefer to work on the lichen at the Canyon floor and let Fuchida deal with the volcanoes.

When Dex teased Trudy about being afraid to fly, Rodriguez jumped to her defense. "You think riding that cable up and down four kilometers isn't scary? Man, I feel a lot safer riding in something that's at least got wings on it."

Stacy worked out a meticulous schedule for all eight of them, a schedule that kept Jamie at the new dome by the Canyon while Stacy herself remained most of the time at the old base on Lunae Planum. Jamie marvelled at how she managed to keep Vijay away when he and Dex were both in the same place. He saw Vijay when Dex was gone, and he knew she saw Dex when he wasn't around.

Jamie had not slept with Vijay since he'd stepped down as mission director. He kept telling himself that she wasn't sleeping with Dex, either. He tried hard to believe that, and most of the time he succeeded. But there were moments, when Dex would return from a trip to the old dome with a sly grin on his face that made Jamie's insides burn.

Yet he and Dex were getting along well together. Without Vijay around, they worked and ate side by side. They speculated about the Martian building and the Martians themselves. And they worried about the day when Dex's father would arrive to start his commercial operations.

"Why don't we get the ICU to claim this area?" Dex suggested one night, as the two of them huddled over mugs of coffee in the new dome's galley.

Jamie went through Connors to Dr. Li, and via Li to the chairman of the ICU board.

Walter Laurence's normally imperturbable face looked troubled when he finally replied to Jamie's pleading messages. Jamie waited until late at night to open Laurence's message; the dome was quiet, lights turned down, most of the others already asleep.

Even in the display screen of Jamie's laptop, the executive director of the International Consortium of Universities seemed upset, unhappy.

"Dr. Waterman," he began, stiffly, his earth-brown eyes focused slightly low, at his own display screen instead of the camera atop it, "the entire ICU board of directors has given your request a great deal of thought."

Jamie watched in silence as Laurence wormed through a long, torturous array of excuses. The man constantly ran one hand through his thick mane of silver hair, as though he were in distress.

"So the long and the short of it is," Laurence concluded at last, "that the board feels it would be improper for the ICU to claim utilization of any part of Mars—or any other body in the solar system, for that matter. We are dedicated to scientific research, not real estate development."

When Jamie went over to Dex's cubicle, the younger man was already heading Jamie's way.

"You saw Laurence's answer?" Jamie asked needlessly.

"He's got as much backbone as a slime mold," Dex muttered. "Him and his whole frigging board."

"They're not going to risk getting your father sore at them."

"No," Dex agreed. "Money talks, loud and clear."

"We've only got thirty days before the backup mission launches."

"With dear old Dad aboard."

They walked together through the shadowy dome to the galley. "Your father's really coming?"

"He passed all the physicals. Sent me a video of him in a hard suit, practicing emergency procedures in the big water tank down at Huntsville."

"Money talks, all right," Jamie grumbled.

All through the past six months, Fuchida had been buttonholing Jamie whenever he could to try to convince him that one of the explorers was deliberately sabotaging their equipment.

The burned-out wheel bearing from the rover that Stacy had driven became a bone of contention. Fuchida examined it and claimed he saw evidence of tampering.

"See these scratches, here along the seal that failed?" the biologist pointed out. "Deliberate! Someone purposely pried open the seal enough to allow dust to get in and seize up the bearing."

Jamie looked hard at the bearing in Fuchida's hand. He saw the scratches but had to tell the biologist that there was no way of knowing if they were deliberately made.

"How else?" Fuchida demanded.

"Dust particles," Jamie suggested. "Pebbles kicked up by the wheel, maybe."

The biologist shook his head stubbornly.

"I could ask Wiley to take a look," Jamie said. "Get his opinion."

"Useless, if he is the saboteur," Fuchida replied dejectedly.

Every equipment failure, every minor accident, every time one of the explorers tripped or got nicked in any way, Fuchida added it to the list of "evidence" he was amassing. He called Jamie at least weekly, usually late at night, when everyone else was asleep—and even then Fuchida looked furtive, distrustful, suspicious.

Finally Jamie had to tell him, "Mitsuo, you're getting paranoid about this."

Surprisingly, the biologist agreed. "I know," he said, his voice low and tight. "I am beginning to wonder if I am going mad. Why am I the only one who sees what is happening?"

Jamie tried to make light of it. "Maybe you're brighter than the rest of us."

"Or crazier," Fuchida admitted.

There is that, Jamie thought.

DIARY ENTRY

Nothing works right. Whatever I do, they ignore it. I know they're watching me, but they won't admit it. They won't step up to me, face to face, and have it out. Behind my back, of course, they're talking about me. Whispering, really. I can hear them whispering when they think I'm not listening, not watching. I'm going to have to take drastic steps. The poor deluded fools! Can't they see that I'm trying to save their lives? The longer we stay here on Mars the likelier we'll all be killed. Better to kill one or two of them and save the rest. We've got to get away! Back to Earth, where it's safe. Better to sacrifice a few and save the others.

MORNING: SOL 358

JAMIE WOKE UP SLOWLY, THE REMNANTS OF A DISTURBING DREAM FADING from his consciousness like a mirage dissipating as he tried to reach it. Something about the Martians, he thought, although he vaguely remembered Fuchida in his dream, trying desperately to tell him something but unable to speak a word aloud.

A mini-nightmare, Jamie decided as he quickly showered and shaved. Got to keep up appearances, he told himself while he ran the electric razor across his chin. Its buzzing sounded weak, lower in pitch than normal. The batteries need recharging. Which started him thinking about the nuclear generator buried a full kilometer from the dome. People still freaked out about nuclear power back home. Here we couldn't get along without it.

This is home, Jamie, he heard his grandfather whisper. That other world isn't for you. This one is.

"For a while, Grandfather," Jamie answered in a barely vocal whisper. "Only until Trumball arrives to take it away from us."

He pulled on his coveralls and sat dejectedly at his desk chair. We're just going through the motions, Jamie told himself. The excitement has drained away. Now we're just collecting data bits, like a bunch of graduate students following the drill that the professors back on Earth have set for us.

Nothing new had been discovered in months. The cliff building held its secrets tenaciously, empty and silent, revealing nothing. Except that its very existence told so much.

What do we know? Jamie asked himself for the thousandth time that week.

We know that Mars bears life: lichen in some surface rocks and bacteria deep underground.

We know that once intelligent Martians lived here and they built the structure in the cliff.

We know that they no longer exist.

We're pretty certain they were wiped out by one or more meteor strikes about sixty-five million years ago.

And that's it. They had developed writing. Maybe they even understood what was happening to them.

But we haven't been able to find another building anywhere on the whole planet. We don't understand their writing and probably never will.

So why are we going through the motions of searching the planet and poking around the niche where the building is sited? We don't have the tools or the manpower to find anything more. We don't have the fundamental understanding to figure who or what they were. They could have honeycombed this planet with their cities and farms, but after sixty-five million years they're all lost, gone, covered over by dust or ground into dust themselves.

Jamie admitted to himself, We're wasting our time here. Even the VR shows we beam to Earth have lost their appeal; the audience is down to schools and museums. We might as well pack up and go home.

Then he saw Trumball and his hotel builders and the tourists he wanted to bring to Mars. Bulldozers and buses and shopping malls where you could buy plastic Martian dolls.

Grimly he turned to his laptop and booted it up, ready to review the day's schedule of tasks.

Instead, Pete Connors' chocolate-brown face looked out at him from the display screen, grinning cheerily.

"Congratulations! Today marks the three hundredth and sixty-fifth day since your arrival on Mars. You've put in a full year on the planet's surface. A real milestone, guys."

Jamie blinked at Connors' image. It's only sol three fifty-eight, he saw from the data line at the bottom of the screen.

Then, despite his listless mood, he smiled tightly. Of course, he told himself. Three hundred sixty-five Earth days, not Martian. A full Earth year.

He didn't feel like celebrating.

In the main dome, Vijay was also thinking about the calendar.

"It's a real accomplishment," she said to Stacy, "and we ought to do something to celebrate it."

The two women were in Vijay's phonebooth-sized infirmary. Dezhurova was stripped to her bra and panties, a blood-pressure cuff wrapped around her left arm, six medical sensor patches plastered to her sturdy chest and back.

"What do you have in mind?" she asked warily. As a cosmonaut she distrusted medics, especially doctors who doubled as psychiatrists. It was their job to find reasons to keep fliers on the ground, Dezhurova feared.

"I'm not sure," Vijay replied, seemingly unaware of her patient's latent hostility. "With the group split up like it is between the two domes, it's difficult to bring everyone together for a blast."

"No alcohol," Dezhurova said flatly.

"I didn't mean a booze party," Vijay quickly amended, one eye on the monitor screens. Dezhurova seemed adequately healthy; blood pressure a bit lower than usual, but well within tolerable limits.

"Then what?"

Vijay shrugged and started unwrapping the cuff from the cosmonaut's beefy upper arm. Dezhurova began peeling off the sensors with her free hand.

"We need something," Vijay said. "Morale is sinking quite low. It's been nothing but work, work, work the past several months. No excitement at all. That's not good for our emotional outlook."

"Trudy and Tom seem happy," Dezhurova said as she got down from the examination table and reached for her coveralls.

"When they're together, yes," Vijay agreed. "But he tends to mope when they're apart."

Stacy shook her head. "I can't adjust the work schedule to accommodate their romance."

"No, of course not. And frankly, I think Trudy is grateful for some time away from Tommy."

"You think she does not love Tom?"

"Love's got very little to do with it," Vijay said, her face growing quite serious. "Tommy may be bonkers over her, but she . . ." Vijay's voice trailed off.

"Yes? What?"

"I'm not sure," Vijay said, looking troubled. "Trudy likes Tom, of course. Very much. But I don't think you could call it love, not for either one of them."

"Is that your professional opinion?" Dezhurova asked, sealing the coveralls' Velcro seam.

"Not quite."

Stacy tapped Vijay on the shoulder with a heavy, blunt finger. "Is this what you psychologists call projection?"

"Projection?"

"You can't make a commitment to Jamie, so you believe Trudy has the same problem."

"I can't make . . . ?" Vijay's dark eyes flashed wide, then she looked away from Dezhurova.

With a grim smile, Stacy said, "Dex and Jamie are both in the second dome. I think it's good to keep you away from them. No party."

And with that she walked out of the infirmary.

Instead of a party, Dezhurova linked all eight of the explorers electronically at dinner. She planted a Picturephone unit at one end of the galley table in Dome One and ordered Jamie to do the same at Dome Two.

"We mark this milestone with unity and comradeship," she said, sitting at the head of her table and lifting a glass of grapefruit juice.

"Unity and comradeship," Jamie repeated from the head of his table.

But as he glanced at the three others with him, Jamie knew that the toast was empty. Fuchida suspected that one of their comrades was an insane saboteur. Rodriguez was gloomy because he wanted to be with Trudy, and he knew that when he shuttled back to Dome One, Trudy would be coming here to Dome Two. Tomas probably thinks Stacy is keeping them apart on purpose.

Looking at Dex, Jamie thought that he had changed a good deal over the past year. Especially since we found the building, he told himself. But he's torn up inside over his father. And deep down, where it counts, he still wants to turn Mars into a profit-making venture.

Unity and comradeship, Jamie repeated silently. Not likely.

After dinner Jamie went to the comm center, more to get away from the others than anything else. But it was not to be. Jamie had barely started reviewing the task assignments for the next day when Fuchida stepped in and wordlessly pulled up the second chair.

"What is it, Mitsuo?" he asked, dreading the answer.

Fuchida pulled a minidisk out of the chest pocket of his coveralls.

"I believe I know who our saboteur is," he said, nearly whispering.

Despite himself, Jamie asked, "Who?"

Fuchida proffered the disk. "Take a look at this."

Sliding it into the computer port, Jamie asked, "What is it?"

"I correlated every so-called 'accident' with the job assignments of each one of us," the biologist said.

Jamie saw a bewildering chart on the computer display: eight jagged lines in eight different colors marched across a gridwork background.

"It looks like the Alps," Jamie grumbled.

Hunching closer, Fuchida traced the light blue line across the graph. "Each line represents one of us. This one is me." His finger moved to the red line. "That is you."

"And the axes?"

"Abscissa plots time; ordinate plots the position of each individual. See? Here you are on the first excursion to the Canyon, with Dex, Trudy and Stacy."

Jamie nodded. "Okay."

"Now . . ." Fuchida leaned across and tapped the keyboard. Red arrows began flashing at half a dozen points along the bottom of the graph.

"The arrows represent times when 'accidents' occurred. This one, for example," he touched the screen, "is when the garden dome was punctured."

"Okay," Jamie repeated.

Another few taps on the keyboard, then Fuchida said, "Here all the unnecessary clutter is removed."

Jamie saw that most of the lines had disappeared from the graph. But the red arrows still flashed accusingly.

"Notice that only one individual was present at the time and place of each separate 'accident.' "

"The yellow line," Jamie said.

"Exactly!"

"And who does that represent?"

"Stacy."

"Stacy?" Jamie felt as if the wind had been knocked out of him. "You're saying Stacy is the saboteur?"

Gesturing to the screen, Fuchida said, "The facts show it."

Jamie said nothing, but his mind was racing. It can't be Stacy. Mitsuo's got to be wrong. He's just throwing together some half-assed statistics—

Fuchida interrupted his train of thought. "Stacy was alone in the comm center when the garden dome was punctured. The rest of us were in our quarters, remember?"

"Yes, but—"

"She was alone in the rover when the wheel bearing burned out."

"She wasn't anywhere near the kiln when Tomas burned his hand."

"True, but she had been working on the kiln just before Rodriguez took over."

"It can't be Stacy," Jamie insisted. "Hell, Mitsuo, we don't even know that there is a saboteur. These accidents are probably just that—accidents."

Fuchida shook his head sternly.

"Now wait, Mitsuo," Jamie said. "What about your own accident? Up on Olympus Mons. Did Stacy twist your ankle for you?"

The biologist stared at Jamie like a teacher disappointed in a student's recitation. "Some accidents are truly accidental," he said patiently, his voice low, almost hissing.

"Then why can't the others be accidental?"

"Too many!" Fuchida insisted. "I ran a statistical analysis and compared it against records of other expeditions."

"There's only been one other expedition here."

"No, no, expeditions to Antarctica, deep sea missions, treks across the Sahara, that kind of thing. Our accident rate is twice normal!"

Jamie took a deep, deliberate breath. Stay calm, he told himself. Look at this rationally.

"All right, Mitsuo," he said softly. "I appreciate all the work you've put into this, but I just can't believe that Stacy or anyone else among us is trying to sabotage the equipment."

Fuchida started to reply, but Jamie cut him off. "Why? Why would somebody puncture the garden dome or tamper with the solar kiln? It's not rational."

"That is my point," Fuchida whispered urgently. "This person is not rational. She is insane."

"But wouldn't an insane person show other symptoms?"

Fuchida spread his hands. "I don't know."

"We can't make an accusation without real evidence," Jamie said.

"My statistical analysis is not real evidence?"

"Would it hold up in a court of law?"

"I don't know."

"Neither do I," said Jamie.

"I am scheduled to return to Dome One tomorrow," Fuchida said. "If Stacy realizes that I suspect her, she might try to arrange another 'accident' for me."

"I can't believe that," Jamie said.

"I would prefer to remain here, away from her," he said stiffly.

Jamie thought swiftly. If Mitsuo stays here, then Dex will have to go back to Dome One with Tomas. Trudy and Wiley are coming here. That means Dex will be with Vijay for the next four weeks.

"I'd rather you went as scheduled," Jamie said.

"You could take my place," said Fuchida.

Then I could be with Vijay, he thought. But he heard himself reply, "No, Mitsuo, I can't do that. My place is here."

"I don't want to be in the dome with Stacy," Fuchida said firmly.

Jamie looked at the biologist, studied his face, and saw that Fuchida was neither angry nor agitated. He looked scared.

"All right," Jamie yielded, sighing. "I'll send Dex back."

He wondered if they weren't all going rapidly insane.

NIGHT: SOL 359

STRANGE, JAMIE THOUGHT AS HE STRIPPED OFF HIS COVERALLS, THERE'S just the two of us in this whole dome, yet we hardly said a dozen words to each other all day.

Dex and Rodriguez were trundling back to Dome One, where the astronaut would pick up Trudy Hall and bring her back to the Canyon site. Rodriguez was whistling all the way, grinning like a cat with canaries on its mind.

We're beating a regular road between the two domes, Jamie said to himself. Like the ruts the Conestoga wagons left across the prairies.

He hadn't deliberately avoided Fuchida after the rover departed, and neither of them had suited up to work outside, but somehow he and the biologist seemed to be on opposite ends of the dome most of the day. They had even eaten at different times, each one alone in the galley.

I'm sore at him, Jamie realized. I'm pissed off that he's made me send Dex back to Dome One. Him and his paranoid accusations! Stacy's no saboteur and she's not a neurotic. She's probably saner than all the rest of us put together.

Then who's responsible for these accidents? Jamie asked himself. Nobody, came the immediate reply. They're just accidents.

Still . . . Jamie thought about talking it over with Vijay. She's the psychologist here, she ought to know about this. Yet he hesitated. What Fuchida had told him was in confidence; telling Vijay about it would be a breach of the biologist's trust.

Which is more important? Jamie demanded silently. Keeping Mitsuo's paranoia a secret, or protecting the mental well-being of the whole expedition?

He knew what the answer should be. Yet when he called Vijay it wasn't to protect the expedition and he knew it. He called her because he wanted to see her face, hear her voice. Because for the next four weeks she would be with Dex and he'd be an overnight trip away.

She was awake. Her hair was down, hanging loosely about her shoulders. Which were bare. She was obviously in her own cubicle, preparing for bed. When she saw it was Jamie, she smiled warmly out of his laptop screen.

"Hi, mate," she said cheerfully. "How're the bots biting?"

"Bots?"

"Insects," she said.

"No bites," Jamie answered. "No insects."

"One of the blessings we should be thankful for, eh?"

She seemed genuinely pleased to be talking with him, Jamie thought. Then he realized he must be grinning like a schoolboy at her. But he felt his grin fade as he remembered his reason for calling.

"I think I've got something of a problem here," Jamie said, lowering his voice.

"Oh? Serious?"

"You tell me." He swiftly outlined Fuchida's behavior, leaving the biologist's name out of it.

Vijay listened intently. When Jamie finished, she said, "This isn't Dex you're talking about, is it?"

"No," he admitted, shaking his head slightly.

"And it's certainly not Tommy."

Jamie said nothing.

"So it must be either you or Mitsuo."

"Does it matter who it is?"

"Of course it matters," she said. "And since you're so reluctant to name a name, I've got to assume it's Mitsuo."

"So much for keeping secrets," Jamie muttered.

"How's he performing? In his work, I mean."

"Fine. As good as ever."

"Why din't he come back here this trip? He was scheduled to return here, wasn't he?"

Jamie took a breath. "He didn't want to be with Stacy. He's afraid she'll go off the deep end or something."

"H'm," said Vijay, her brows knitting. "Interesting."

"Well?"

Vijay seemed lost in thought.

"What should I do about him?" Jamie demanded.

Her dark eyes focused on Jamie again. "Nothing much you can do. He's not bonkers. And I doubt that he's dangerous, unless . . ." Her voice trailed off.

"Unless?" Jamie prompted.

Vijay bit her lip momentarily, then replied, "Unless he's been causing these accidents himself and projecting the blame onto Stacy."

Jamie felt stunned.

"I don't think that's the case," Vijay added quickly. "It was just a thought."

"Some thought."

"How do you feel about all this? Are you convinced these accidents are really accidental?"

"I was, but now . . . I just don't know."

"I see."

"I'm getting paranoid, too," Jamie said.

"Not unusual in these circumstances. Everybody gets suspicious of everybody."

"What should I do?" Jamie asked again.

Vijay shrugged her bare shoulders. "Not much you can do, Jamie. Keep an eye on him. Listen to him sympathetically. Humor him. I'll find a reason to come over to your site and talk with him."

"Okay. Good."

" 'Fraid that's all I can offer you right now, mate."

"It's a relief just to talk it over with you."

She smiled again, but now there was a tinge of sadness in it. "Yes, it's good to talk with you, too."

He wanted to tell her that he missed her, he wanted to say that he needed her warmth, her comfort, her presence in his life. But he couldn't form the words. Instead he simply said, "Thanks, Vijay."

She too seemed lost for the proper words. For long moments the two of them simply stared at each other in their screens.

At last Vijay said, "G'night, Jamie."

"Goodnight."

Her image winked off. The screen went dark. Jamie stripped off his underwear and stretched out on his cot. He grinned up into the shadows of the darkened dome.

She's coming here! She's going to find an excuse to come over here. I ought to thank Mitsuo.

His last thought before he fell asleep was about her bare shoulders. Was she wearing anything while they talked? Had she really been naked?

Fuchida seemed to brighten once Trudy joined them. The two biologists started chattering together as soon as she came through the access tunnel. The following morning they rode the Buckyball cables down to the Canyon floor to work on the lichen together.

Rodriguez was obviously happier. He and Trudy bunked together, no pretenses and no questions asked. Jamie had to admit that Trudy made everything brighter. If only she didn't thump around the dome before daybreak every morning with her incessant jogging.

The only sour notes came from Dex. He called Jamie each day to report on the progress of the next expedition's preparations.

"Dear old Dad passed his physicals," Dex said dolorously. "His blood pressure was completely normal. God knows how much medication he took before the test."

The next day Dex reported, "My old man sent me a message about our attempt to get the ICU to claim our territory on Mars. He sat there behind his big fucking desk just as calm and cool as a glacier and told me if I tried another stunt like that he'd disinherit me."

"Oh no," Jamie groaned.

Dex's grin was ferocious. "Like I need his fucking money. I can have my pick of university chairs when I get back home."

Jamie warned gently, "A professor's salary isn't quite the same as the kind of money you're accustomed to, Dex."

With an impatient wave of his hand, Dex said, "I know how to make money, pal. Been watching my father do it all my life. Let him write me out of his will! I don't give a shit! I'll show him I can live damn well without him or his money!"

Sure you will, Jamie answered silently. Aloud, he said to Dex, "Don't cut off your nose—"

"Bullshit!" Dex snapped. "He's trying to chop off my balls. I'll show him."

It wasn't until hours afterward that Jamie realized he was no longer worried that Dex and Vijay might be getting involved with each other. A few months ago such a realization would have made Jamie very happy, but now he was more worried about Dex's father and his coming to claim this part of Mars for his business schemes.

He wondered why he no longer worried about Vijay and Dex. It wasn't because he didn't care about her. He did, more than he could admit to her. But all these personal relationships were tangled here on Mars. She's right to keep it from getting too heavy. We won't get things truly settled between us until we return to Earth, Jamie told himself. If then.

The important thing, the vital thing, is to keep Darryl C. Trumball from doing to Mars what his forefathers did to the Native Americans.

Jamie's grandfather came to him again in a dream.

But not at first. Jamie's dream began in the cliff structure, bare, cold and abandoned. He walked through each of the silent, empty chambers as he had done every day now for many months. He was free of his hard suit, though, striding slowly, purposefully through the rooms in nothing more than his frayed and worn coveralls.

He touched the walls, traced his fingertips along the graceful curved lines of the writing etched into their stones. He could feel the warmth of the sun glowing from the secret symbols.

Alone, he turned and left the abandoned temple, then climbed slowly down the narrow, steep steps carved so painfully into the rugged face of the cliff. The village waited for him down on the Canyon floor, where the river ran peacefully through bountiful fields of crops.

The People were there, alive and vital as he himself, but they paid him no attention. They went about their tasks, men gathering together in the central square and talking together animatedly, pointing off to a distant horizon, a rendezvous with the future. Women sat by their doorways, weaving fine baskets while their children ran and played boisterously. There was laughter and the warmth of life everywhere.

They were real and he was a pale ghost, almost invisible to them. He knew their faces, the sturdy broad-cheeked faces of his own ancestors. Their dark hair and darker eyes. He searched for his grandfather but could not find him.

Then a commotion at the far end of the village. A disturbance. People stopped in their tracks to stare down the long street. Men began running toward the noise, their faces frowning with anger, perhaps fear.

Strangers were there, pale men on snorting, stamping horses. Jamie recognized one of them as Darryl C. Trumball. He was shouting commands, pointing with one hand while he kept his plunging, neighing horse under control with his other.

Then Grandfather Al appeared out of the crowd. He wore his best suit, dark blue, with a turquoise-and-silver bolo at the open collar of his crisp white shirt. Hatless, he strode up to Trumball.

"You can't come here," Grandfather Al said, in a stronger voice than Jamie had ever heard in life. "Go away!"

Trumball blustered. "We're taking over here. You'll be taken care of, don't worry. I'll see to it that you're protected."

"We don't want your protection," Al said. "We don't need it."

"You'll have to go," Trumball insisted.

Grandfather Al turned slightly and beckoned toward Jamie. "No, we're not going. You're the one who'll have to leave. Jamie, show him the paper."

Jamie realized he had a scroll of paper clutched tightly in his right hand. He stepped up to Trumball, still atop his impatient horse.

And woke up.

MORNING: SOL 363

JAMIE SAT UP ON HIS COT, WIDE AWAKE, FEELING STRONG AND REFRESHED. That's it! he told himself. That's what I have to do.

He didn't know whether to offer a prayer of thanks or belt out a wild yell of jubilation. He decided on neither. Instead he booted up his laptop and put in a call to Pete Connors at Tarawa.

It took almost the whole day, but finally Jamie got the correct address and sent his message. Then he had to wait for the reply. Jamie remembered the summers he had spent with his grandfather in New Mexico, the times Al would take him up to the pueblos on the reservation, where he bought blankets and ceramics to sell to the tourists at his shop in Santa Fe.

This might take several days, Jamie realized. They're not going to answer me right away.

To his surprise, the answer was waiting for him when he booted up his computer the following morning. His fingers trembled slightly as he called up the message.

The president of the Navaho Nation smiled from the display screen. "Ya'aa'tey," he said. He was surprisingly plump, his eyes bright and dancing as if it was a pleasure to speak to Jamie, even in the time-delayed manner enforced by the distance between the two worlds.

"I was sure surprised by your message," he went on, "but very pleased about it. I knew your grandfather, and I saw you on the TV that first time you landed on Mars. I hope someday to be able to speak to you in person."

Then he grew more serious. The smile waned but did not disappear altogether. "Your proposal is a real stunner. I like it, but it's not for me alone to decide. I've already called for a council meeting and we'll have to have our lawyers look into it, of course. But I like the idea and I'll do everything I can to push it through.''

He hesitated, then, more serious still, he said, "This is a heavy responsibility you want to give us. I don't know if we're up to it.'' His smile returned, full wattage. "But I'd sure like to try!''

Jamie heard out the rest of his message, then sent an acknowledging, "Mr. President, thanks for your good words. I'll wait for the Nation's official answer. Thanks again.''

Then he put in a call to Dex Trumball.

Dex was at breakfast when Stacy Dezhurova called him to the comm center. He slid into the empty chair beside her and saw Jamie's stolid, earnest face on the message screen. Beside him, Stacy was scrolling through the logistics inventory, checking their supplies.

"What's up, chief?'' Dex asked casually.

Jamie said, "I've offered Mars to the Navaho Nation.''

Dex nearly popped off the chair. "You *what*?''

"I've asked the president of the Navaho Nation if his people will formally claim utilization rights to all the areas of Mars that we've explored so far.''

"But they're in Arizona!''

"I'm here,'' Jamie said firmly. "I represent the Navaho Nation.''

"Holy crap,'' Dex muttered.

Stacy had frozen her screen. She was staring at Dex and Jamie.

"As I understand it,'' Jamie said, "if the Navaho claim use of this land, then your father can't get his hands on it.''

"That's right,'' Dex said, a grin working its way across his face. "He'd have to be here, physically present, to claim utilization rights.''

"And we're already here. So I'm going to file the claim as soon as I get a go-ahead from the Navaho council.''

"Jesus H. Christ on a jet ski,'' Dex said, laughing. "My old man's gonna pop an artery over this! The Indians pull a land steal on the white men! Wow!''

Jamie asked, "Do you think that will really stop your father?''

"It'll keep him away from the cliff building, the main dome, the volcanoes that Mitsuo's explored—yeah, he won't be able to set up for business anyplace we've already been.''

"That still leaves a lot of Mars for him.''

"Yeah, but we've got the good parts! Or, your redskin pals do.''

"Then it can work.''

"Yeah, sure,'' Dex said, sobering. "Only one problem.''

"What's that?''

"There goes the funding for the next expedition.''

*   *   *

Dex was too excited to do any useful work. He went to the geology lab, but spent his time sending frantic messages toward Earth, calling lawyers and professors of international law. Finally, after several hours, Wiley Craig looked up from the heat flow map he was working on and shook his head.

"Hey, buddy, whatever you're doin', it ain't on the work schedule."

Dex looked up from his computer screen. "I'm gathering information, Wiley."

"Not about geology, I bet."

"No, that's damn straight." Dex got up from the stool and headed for the door of the lab. "I've got to get over to the second dome. Got to talk with Jamie, face-to-face."

Wiley merely shook his head and returned to his work, muttering, "Well, *somebody's* got to get the job done."

Stacy was not surprised that Dex wanted to join Jamie at Dome Two. But she was not sympathetic, either.

"You have work to do here," she said sternly, standing in the middle of the comm center like an immovable linebacker. "Task assignments are—"

"You want me to walk to the Canyon?" Dex snapped. "I've got to go there, Stace. The funding for the next expedition is *important,* for chrissake!"

She planted her chunky fists on her hips. "You are going to raise ten billion dollars over at the Canyon?"

Dex gave her a boyish grin. "Maybe, maybe not. But we're sure as hell going to lose ten bil if we can't work out a way to get around my father."

Dezhurova snorted. Before she could reply, though, Vijay stuck her head through the open comm center doorway.

"Did I hear you say you want to take a rover out to Dome Two?" she asked. "I'd like to go there, too."

"What? Why?" Dezhurova demanded.

"I need to run physical exams on the people there," Vijay answered. "And psych profiles."

The cosmonaut raised her eyes to heaven. "Maybe we should all go and abandon this dome completely."

"I've been saying that for months," Dex replied, grinning mischievously.

"Go!" Dezhurova blurted, nearly shouting the word. "Forget about the work, go traipsing around anywhere you like."

"Now don't be sore, Stace," Dex said soothingly. "If it wasn't really important, I wouldn't do it, you know that."

"I know that you always get your way. Go! Take the old rover. At least leave me with one of the new machines."

*   *   *

Night fell before they were even a quarter of the way to Dome Two, but Dex kept driving through the darkness—slowly, but still making progress.

Sitting beside him in the rover's cockpit, Vijay saw that wheel tracks across the dust-covered ground were clearly visible in the rover's headlights.

"You're following the beaten path," she said.

"Yep. Makes it easier. You know you're not going to hit any major rocks or craters."

"Is Jamie's idea really going to work?" Vijay asked, turning slightly in the seat to look squarely at Dex. "Will he be able to keep your father from taking over this region?"

"Looks that way," Dex said, watching his driving. "But the other side of the coin is that we lose my father's drive for funding the next expedition."

Vijay thought about that for a moment, then said, "So you'll have to take his place."

"What?" Dex glanced at her, his eyes wide, startled.

"If your father won't raise the money for the next expedition, then you'll have to do it."

He pressed the brake pedals and brought the rover to a halt. Slowly, methodically, he shut down the drive motors.

"I'll have to do it," he muttered.

"Who else?"

Dex seemed lost in thought as they went back to the galley and microwaved their dinners. They ate in almost total silence. Vijay could see that Dex's mind was a hundred million kilometers away.

"The thing is," he said as they cleaned up the table, "I've never gone against my father. I've always had to do things his way—unless I could wheedle him around to make him think that what I wanted was his idea in the first place."

"Now you're going to have to stand up to him," Vijay said.

Dex nodded slowly. "I don't know if I can."

"Don't you think it's about time you found out?"

They were standing by the galley sink, between the microwave and the racks of hard suits. Dex grasped Vijay's arm just above the elbow and pulled her toward him.

She put the flat of her free hand against his chest. "No, Dex."

"No?"

"There must be several million women waiting for you to return to Earth. You'll have your pick of them."

"That's then," he said. "This is now."

"I'm afraid not."

He let out a breath. "Jamie, huh?"

"Jamie," she admitted.

"He's a lucky guy."

Now she sighed. "I wish he knew that."

Dex looked puzzled.

"He's in love with Mars," Vijay explained. "I've got this whole bloody planet for a rival."

NEWS CONFERENCE

DARRYL C. TRUMBALL WAS NOT ACCUSTOMED TO THE GLARE OF PUBLICITY. He preferred to remain in the background and let his hirelings and puppets face the public.

But as the first "ordinary" person to go to Mars, he had become a celebrity. Now, a scant four days before the backup mission was scheduled to launch from Cape Canaveral, he found himself sharing a long table with four young archeologists and two astronauts, staring out at a sea of reporters and photographers who filled the auditorium to overflowing.

Like his crewmates, Trumball wore coral-red coveralls bearing the stylish logo of the Second Mars Expedition over his heart. He was of course older than any of them, older than any two of them put together, almost. But he was slim and hard and fit. No one knew the fear that chilled his blood; no one could hear how his heart thundered in his chest when he thought of actually climbing into that flying bomb and riding it all the way to distant, freezing, dangerous Mars.

"Why isn't this mission called the Third Expedition?" a reporter was shouting from the floor.

"This is a backup mission for the Second Expedition," explained the senior astronaut, an old hand at fielding inane questions.

"We're going specifically to explore the ancient building that's been discovered in the cliffs of the Grand Canyon of Mars," said the chief archeologist, all of forty years old.

"What about the Third Expedition?" another reporter asked.

"Will there be a Third Expedition?"

Everyone along the table turned to Trumball. "Yes," he assured them all smoothly. "There will be a Third Mars Expedition."

"When?"

"How soon?"

"We are working out the details," Trumball said.

"What about other kinds of flights to Mars?" a woman asked. "When will we be able to take vacations there?"

A slight snickering laugh tittered through the news people.

But Trumball answered the planted question, "That's why I'm going along with the scientists. I want to show the world that ordinary people can go to Mars, can see for themselves the glories of the vanished Martian civilization, walk where the Martians walked, reach the peak of the tallest mountain in the solar system, explore the longest, widest, deepest Grand Canyon of them all."

Several of the archeologists looked dismayed, but no one dared to contradict Trumball.

"Why you, sir?" asked a bald, portly reporter from the last row of the auditorium. "Why do you have to go yourself? Couldn't someone— er, of less prominence, be sent instead?"

Trumball smiled patiently. "You mean why would an old fart like me want to go?"

Everyone laughed.

"I want to show that even someone of my age can make the trip easily, and enjoy it." He paused, made certain the news people were hanging on his next words, then went on, "But remember, older men than I have gone into space, starting with Senator Glenn, nearly forty years ago."

"But, all the way to Mars?"

"Yes," Trumball said, still keeping his smile in place. "All the way to Mars. I'll be the first of millions of ordinary men and women to go there."

Besides, he added silently, there's money to be made up there, and I'm going to make damned certain nobody screws me out of it.

AFTERNOON: SOL 368

JAMIE WAS HANGING IN THE CLIMBING HARNESS, SCRAPING ROCK SAMPLES from the cliff face, when the message came through.

"You did it!" Dex's voice sounded exultant in his helmet earphones. "Listen to this!"

It was the message from the president of the Navaho Nation, the message he'd been waiting for. Jamie wished he could see the man's face, but his words were good enough to make him burn with pride and gratitude.

"The Navaho people accept the responsibility of claiming utilization rights to the areas of Mars explored by the Second Mars Expedition," the president said slowly, as if reading from a prepared script. "We intend to hold it in trust for all the peoples of Earth, and to encourage the careful scientific study of the planet Mars and all its life-forms, past and present.

"We recognize that Dr. James Waterman, whose father was a pure-blood Navaho, will be our people's representative on Mars while this claim is officially filed with the International Astronautical Authority."

There was more, and Jamie listened patiently through it all, dangling two kilometers above the Canyon floor. But he listened with only a fraction of his attention. For a voice in his mind was saying, You've done it. Now Trumball won't be able to claim use of this land. Now we can keep it out of Trumball's hands, out of the greedy paws of the developers and the exploiters. We can keep Mars clean and preserve it for scientific study.

Once the president's message ended, Dex came back on, jabbering, "I just wish I could see my father's face when he hears about this. He'll go ballistic! He's all suited up and ready to come here and now it's gonna be for nothing. He can't touch a thing here! I'll bet—"

Jamie clicked off the suit radio. He hung there in the harness in blessed silence, swaying slightly on the cable, hearing nothing but the soft thudding of his pulse and the faint whir of his suit's fans.

He planted both boots against the cliff face and pushed as hard as he could and let out a wild war whoop of sheer joy as he swung dizzyingly on the cable.

Only four reporters showed up for the Navaho president's news conference, but his announcement that the Navaho Nation, through Jamie Waterman, was claiming usage rights to Mars sizzled through the news media with the speed of light.

By the next morning, the president's office at Window Rock was besieged by an army of TV vans and reporters. Headlines around the world were blaring:

INDIANS CLAIM MARS
NAVAHO NATION TAKES OVER RED PLANET
CUSTER REDUX: INDIANS AMBUSH TRUMBALL ENTERPRISES
NAVAHOS SEIZE E.T. RESERVATION

The chairwoman of the International Astronautical Authority looked distinctly uncomfortable. Darryl C. Trumball had flown her to Boston in his own private jet, put her up in the best hotel on the harborfront, and sent his personal limousine and driver to bring her to his office.

Still, she was obviously nervous and ill at ease as she sat before

Trumball's massive desk, a rail-thin woman with graying hair and the hard-bitten features of someone who had struggled against steep odds to rise to the position she now held.

Jet lag, Trumball said to himself. She's just jet-lagged from her trip here. But he didn't really believe that; she looked displeased, almost angry that she had been summoned to him.

"If you're inquiring about the Navaho request," she said, with no preamble except the coldest of good-mornings, "it seems to be in perfectly legal form and entirely valid."

Trumball sank back in his tall leather desk chair and steepled his fingertips. "I am scheduled to take off with the replenishment mission in two days," he said mildly. "If this Navaho claim is valid, that would seem to be pointless."

"I can find nothing wrong with their claim," the IAA chairwoman replied. Her accent was difficult for Trumball to place. German, perhaps. He had no idea of her background, he had merely told his staff to bring the head of the IAA to his office.

"Then their claim will be accepted?"

She arched a brow. "The full committee must meet and formally approve their request, but I see no problem with that. We are bound by international law and the treaties that the various governments have ratified, going back to 1967."

"I see," said Trumball.

"I would suggest," she said stiffly, "that you cancel your travel plans and allow another archeologist to take your space on the flight to Mars."

Trumball nodded. "That would seem to be the prudent thing to do."

A long silence stretched between them. She's waiting for me to sweeten the pot, Trumball thought. Or to make threats. Pressure her. He studied her thin, sallow face and saw real hostility there. She doesn't like me. She doesn't like American billionaires who throw their weight around. But she likes my money. That's why she agreed to come to see me.

"Mr. Trumball," she said at last, her voice slightly husky.

"Yes?"

"I know that you are disappointed by this turn of events."

He nodded agreement.

"But I hope that this will not affect your contribution to the Third Expedition."

"Why shouldn't it?" he snapped.

"Because the exploration of Mars is more important than . . . than . . . your plans to make money."

There. It was out in the open. She's a damnable socialist, just like the rest of the bureaucrats.

But he kept his voice calm and reasonable as he replied, "More important to you, madam. Not to me."

She looked him squarely in the eye. "Are you telling me that you will not contribute to funding the Third Expedition if we allow the Navahos to claim utilization rights?"

"That is precisely what I am telling you."

"But as I explained to you, we have no choice in the matter. Their claim is legally valid and we must accept it."

"Then you must find your money elsewhere," Trumball said.

The IAA chairwoman shot to her feet. "That is exactly what I expected from someone like you!"

Trumball got up, too. Slowly. "Then I haven't disappointed you. How delightful." He pointed to the door. "Have a pleasant day."

Once she left, Trumball sat down again and swivelled his chair to look out on the city and Boston Harbor, far below him.

I shouldn't blame the Indian for this. Waterman would never have thought of this by himself. Dex did this. Dex has screwed me out of a whole planet. The little sonofabitch has kicked me in the balls.

Strangely, he smiled.

Jamie spent as much time as he could outside, sampling the strata of the cliff face, going all the way down to the Canyon floor to help Trudy and Fuchida, walking alone through the silent and empty Martian building.

But he had to go back to the dome eventually. The cliff face darkened into shadow as the sun sank toward the western horizon. Fuchida and Hall rose past the rock niche on their way to the dome. Vijay, handling the comm console, told him it was almost sundown and he had to come back.

As soon as Jamie stepped through the airlock's inner hatch, he saw that Dex was practically bouncing around the dome floor with delight.

"Half the news media in the world want to talk to you, pal," he exclaimed as soon as Jamie took off his helmet. "They're going nuts back there!"

"Any word from your father?"

"No. But Pete Connors sent word that dear old Dad's cancelled his flight here."

As he wormed his torso out of the suit's upper half, Jamie saw Vijay hurrying toward them.

"That means he's not going to help finance the next expedition, doesn't it?" Jamie said.

"Who cares?" Dex snapped. "I'll take care of that once we get back home."

Vijay looked upset, distressed. "Come to the comm center, quick!" she called, almost breathless. "There's been an accident!"

EVENING: SOL 370

STACY DEZHUROVA'S BEEFY FACE WAS SMUDGED WITH GRIME AND SHEENED with perspiration. She looked grim, angry.

"Complete failure of the main electrical system," she told Jamie. "We are running on the fuel cells now, but even powered down to emergency levels we won't be able to stay through the night."

"What happened?" Jamie asked.

Stacy shook her head. "Everything switched off. The emergency system immediately kicked in, but if we can't get the main system back on-line before nightfall, we'll have to spend—wait. Here's Possum . . . er, Wiley."

Jamie was sitting at the main comm console, Vijay beside him. Trudy, Fuchida, Dex and Rodriguez were crowded in behind them.

Craig's jowly features looked even bleaker than Dezhurova's as he slumped into the chair beside the cosmonaut.

"The nuke's shot to hell," he said. "I think maybe my hard suit's hot from radiation."

"What?"

"Some sumbitch dug a hole down to where the nuclear generator's buried and poured some kinda acid over it," Craig said, looking as if he could scarcely believe his own words.

Fuchida, standing behind Jamie, hissed, "Saboteur."

Jamie's voice sounded hollow as he said, "You mean that one of you two deliberately . . ." The words choked off; he couldn't speak them.

Craig was shaking his head. "Naw, it wasn't one of us. Not necessarily, anyways. Hole musta been dug a week ago or more. Damned acid's been leaching into the generator at least that long. Hadda eat its way through the shielding before it could do any real damage."

The comm center fell absolutely silent. Even the hum of the equipment seemed muted.

"Tell you one thing, though," Craig resumed somberly. "It was sure as hell deliberate."

For long moments no one said a word. Jamie's mind was racing. A saboteur. We have a saboteur among us. A madman. Or a madwoman.

"All right," he said slowly. "Get into the rover and get over here as quickly as you can."

"I must shut down all systems here," Stacy said.

Dex stuck his head in between Jamie and Vijay. "Download all the computers. I think we've got everything up to this afternoon, but download everything, just to be safe."

"Yes. Of course."

Rodriguez leaned over Jamie's shoulder. "We better tell Tarawa we're gonna need a backup nuke."

"We'll fill the dome with nitrogen," Craig said. "No sense risking a fire while we're away."

"Wait on that," said Jamie. "Can't we run the dome on electricity from the L/AV?"

"Yeah, maybe. Use her fuel cells. But it'll take a coupla days to connect her up to the fuel generator and bury the piping."

Dezhurova pointed out, "We should have built a solar energy farm when we first landed. Like they have at Moonbase."

Jamie grimaced. "Should have."

"That's on the schedule for the Third Expedition, isn't it?" Craig asked.

"Right, but it isn't going to do us any good now," Jamie admitted. "Okay, download the computers, purge the oxygen out of the dome, and drive over here. We'll figure out how—"

"What about the garden?" Trudy blurted.

Dezhurova frowned. Craig waved a helpless hand in the air. "Your plants're gonna have to take care of themselves for a while, Trudy."

"Until we go back and rig the L/AV power system to run the dome," Rodriguez said.

Hall seemed close to tears. "What a pity," she murmured. "What a bloody, awful pity."

Dinner was a somber affair. Jamie could feel the suspicion and fear hanging over the galley table, thick enough to smother conversation.

One of us is crazy, he kept thinking. Much as he tried to shut out the thought, the words kept forming in his mind. One of us deliberately sabotaged the nuclear generator back at Dome One.

He looked into the faces of each one around the table as they glumly picked at their meals: Vijay, Dex, Rodriguez, Trudy. Fuchida. The trouble was, he could not picture any of them as a lunatic, a madman deliberately destroying their equipment, a potential killer.

There it was, he realized. Killer. Murderer. Trying to destroy the garden dome, damaging equipment, wiping out the nuke—those could all result in people dying here. We have a would-be murderer among us.

Even though no one ate much, each of them seemed reluctant to be the first one to leave the galley table. They lingered, their conversation desultory, their faces clearly showing their anxiety and the distrust that could destroy this expedition as surely as any murder.

"All right," Jamie said, loudly enough to startle them all. "All right," he repeated, more softly. "One of us knocked out the nuke at Dome One. Anyone feel like admitting to it?"

They all gaped at him, then slowly turned their heads to look at their companions.

Jamie hadn't expected a volunteer. "Whoever it is, it seems pretty certain that he or she is sick. Mentally or emotionally ill—"

"It's happened before," Vijay said, from her seat across the table from Jamie.

"What do you mean?"

"On polar expeditions," she explained. "On nuclear submarines that stayed submerged for months at a time. Someone goes berserk, or—worse—quietly and stealthily cracks up."

"What happens?" Dex asked. He was sitting beside Jamie, with Fuchida on his other side.

Vijay answered, "Most often the individual starts by hurting himself, self-inflicted wounds. Then it escalates into damaging equipment, wrecking things. If it's not stopped in time it can lead to violence, even murder."

"You're the doctor, Vijay," said Jamie. "Has anyone come to you with an injury that could have been self-inflicted?"

She thought about it for a moment, then shook her head. "Just the usual cuts and scrapes. Oh, there was Tommy's burnt hand, but I doubt that that was self-inflicted."

"It sure wasn't!" Rodriguez said, with some heat.

Jamie said, "Without naming names, is there anything in anyone's psych profile that would throw suspicion on him? Or her?"

"No, I can't think of anything. Of course, we're all daft just to be here, but outside of that, nothing."

"What about your psychological profile?" Trudy asked, forcing a smile to show she wasn't being nasty.

"I'm as dotty as any of you." Vijay smiled back. "But that doesn't mean a thing, does it?"

"Who has access to acid strong enough to burn through the nuke's shielding?" Rodriguez asked.

"Any one of us," Dex replied.

For the first time, Fuchida spoke up. "I have detailed photographs of the punctures made in the garden dome during the storm. I could measure their height above the floor of the dome and compare that to the height and arm lengths of each of us."

"That sounds pretty shaky to me," Jamie said.

Fuchida nodded unhappily. "Yes, it would be quite inconclusive. I'm grasping at straws."

"What we need is Sherlock Holmes," Dex quipped. "Or at least Hercule Poirot."

"Miss Marple," Trudy Hall said.

"Ellery Queen."

"Hell," said Rodriguez, "I'd even settle for Inspector Clouseau."

Everyone broke into laughter.

At least the tension's snapped, Jamie thought. A little, anyway.

He made a quieting motion with both hands and said, "All right, we don't have a detective and we don't have a confession. So here's what we're going to do."

They all turned to him, expectantly.

"From here on, nobody goes anywhere alone. We work in teams of at least two. If we can't figure out who's sabotaging us, at least we can stop whoever it is from doing more damage."

"I'll go with Trudy," Rodriguez immediately called out. "I won't let her out of my sight!" He grinned wolfishly.

Jamie hiked his brows, but continued, "That means we keep two people at the comm console all night long. One to man the console itself and the other to watch the dome and make sure nobody's sneaking around when he or she is supposed to be sleeping."

"I'll team with Vijay," Dex volunteered. "We can handle the comm center."

Jamie looked at Vijay and saw that she was staring right back at him. "No, Dex, if you don't mind I'd prefer that you teamed with Mitsuo. The two of you can take the first shift, then Vijay and I will relieve you at two."

Dex hesitated just a fraction of a second, then grinned and shrugged. "Okay, fine."

Vijay continued to look directly at Jamie.

DIARY ENTRY

Nothing I do turns out right. It took more than a week for the nuclear generator to fail. Now, instead of leaving, they're all coming over here. I'll have to do something even worse. Something that will force them to go home, to leave this godforsaken place and go back to where we belong. But what can I do? Perhaps fire. Fire purifies everything. Fire drives out evil. After all, they used fire to drive the evil spirits out of witches, didn't they? Fire is what I need to use now.

TARAWA: SOL 372

"IN THE OLD DAYS," PETE CONNORS WAS SAYING, "EVERY PIECE OF EQUIP-ment was made to order. Every vehicle, every sensor, every nut and bolt was built specially for the project. That's why space exploration cost so much."

The mission controller was strolling along the beach with two reporters, giving them a "background" briefing for the upcoming launch. To their right the surf boomed against the atoll's reef, and beyond that the blue Pacific stretched as far as the eye could see beneath a balmy sky dotted with puffs of white clouds. To their left, the squat conical shape of a Clippership rocket sat on the launch pad, embraced by a steel spiderwork of scaffolding, swarming with busy technicians.

"It's still not cheap," said the woman reporter, raising her voice to be heard over the brisk wind and distant surf. The wind and humidity had tousled her auburn hair. She wore slacks and a long-sleeved blouse, despite the warm sun.

Connors gave her a toothy grin. "No, it's not. But it's a lot better than it used to be. Orders of magnitude cheaper now."

The male reporter, young but already paunchy and balding, had a serious frown on his face. "Yeah, but no matter how you put it, the replenishment mission isn't launching as scheduled. When will you launch?"

Without missing a beat, Connors said, "We're looking at next Monday now. Might be a nighttime launch, we don't know for certain yet."

"But the launch window—"

"We've got a fair amount of flexibility there. With the additional specific impulse that nuclear propulsion gives us, we can widen the launch window considerably."

The woman asked them to stop for a moment. She took off her shoes, shook sand out of them, and stashed them in her copious shoulder bag.

The male reporter asked, "Is a week long enough for you to stock the spacecraft with everything you need?"

"You mean the backup power generator?" Connors nodded vigorously. "That's where our logistics policy pays off. We've kept backup items in inventory since the original launch, back more than a year ago.

The backup nuke is on its way here from the States, and we've ordered a replacement for it, just to keep our spares inventory full.''

"Do you expect another failure of the nuclear generator?'' the woman asked.

Connors smiled his widest. "No. But then we didn't expect the one that did fail to bug out on us.'' Of the several hundred men and women working for the Second Mars Expedition on Tarawa, Connors was one of only five who knew that the nuclear power generator had been sabotaged. He had no intention of letting that number grow to six.

"So you'll be able to launch on Monday?''

"Looks that way,'' he said, nodding. "Even if it's a few days later, that's no sweat.''

"And the flight itself will take five months to reach Mars.''

"Right. They'll land just about three weeks before the original eight are scheduled to leave Mars.''

"What about the scientists?'' the woman asked. "How are they handling this delay?''

"They're impatient to get going, of course,'' Connors admitted. Then he spread his hands out to sweep the beach, the lagoon, the breathtaking sky. "But waiting another week here isn't exactly breaking their hearts.''

Both reporters laughed.

NIGHT: SOL 375

"HI,'' RODRIGUEZ SAID. "THE A TEAM IS READY TO TAKE OVER.''

Without turning to face him, Stacy Dezhurova pointed to the digital clock readout on the main comm screen. "You are early.'' The clock read 01:58.

Trudy Hall said, "I couldn't sleep.''

Dezhurova looked up and cocked an eyebrow at her. "You mean this oversexed oaf would not let you sleep.''

Rodriguez raised his hands. "Hey, don't blame me. It wasn't my fault.''

Wiley Craig got up slowly from the chair next to Stacy's. "Well, I sure as hell can sleep. Hardly keep my eyes open.''

"Go on,'' Rodriguez said. "We'll take over now.''

Jamie's idea that no one work alone had been eagerly endorsed by Dezhurova, once she and Craig arrived at Dome Two. It slowed down everyone's work, but there had been no "accidents" over the past five sols.

Dezhurova got up from her chair. It creaked noticeably.

"Hope that's the chair and not you," Craig wisecracked.

She tried to glare at him, but ended up grinning with the rest of them. She and Craig headed off to their cubicles while Rodriguez sat at the comm console.

"Keep an eye on them," he said softly over his shoulder to Trudy. "Make sure they go to their quarters."

Jamie lay on his bunk, hands clenched behind his head, wide awake. This expedition's turning into a fiasco, he thought. Work's slowed down to a crawl because of this saboteur, whoever he is. Not that we were accomplishing all that much over the past month or two.

He stared up into the dark shadows of the dome. Not even the sighing night wind calmed his troubled spirit.

Well, when the archeologists get here they can poke around the building and let us get back to our original tasks. There's a whole planet to study. God knows how many other cliff dwellings we'll find, once we start actively searching for them.

He heard footsteps padding slowly across the dome. Silently, Jamie got out of his bunk and went to the door of his cubicle. He had left it unlatched: closed almost completely, but unlatched so he could slide it open a crack without any noise.

He saw Wiley Craig shuffling tiredly past, heading for his own cubicle. Stacy must already have turned in, he thought.

Returning to his bunk, Jamie wished for the millionth time that Vijay were here with him. Not now, he commanded himself. This is no time for that kind of thing. I've got to find out who the madman is. He's going to kill somebody if we don't catch him soon!

The digital clock read 03:09 as Rodriguez leaned back in the little wheeled chair and shut down the logistic inventory program.

"We'll be okay until the resupply mission lands," he said, thinking aloud.

"Are they going to land here or at Dome One?" Trudy asked. She had a photomicrograph of one of the deep-dwelling bacteria on the screen in front of her.

"It's gotta be here," he said. "No sense landing at One, nobody's there."

"I wonder how the garden is doing?" Trudy mused, still looking at her screen.

Rodriguez shrugged. "Oughtta be okay for a while. No bugs, no weeds, nothing to bother them. Stacy said she kept the battery power on, so the heaters will keep 'em from freezing at night. If we get back there before the batteries go flat the plants can make it.''

Trudy nodded. She could see the reflection of her own face in the display screen. Pale, drawn, worried.

"And the nutrient pumps, too?'' To herself, her voice sounded small and weak. Frightened.

"Yep, the pumps too. But we gotta get back there and plug in the L/AV power system with the fuel generator.''

She looked over at him and smiled. "Are you volunteering?''

Rodriguez grinned. "Sure, why not? Manual labor is an old family tradition.''

Turning back to the screen, Trudy thought, No, I can't let you do that. It wouldn't be right.

Nearly half an hour later she got to her feet and stretched. "I'm going to get some coffee. Want some?''

"Yeah. It'll help keep me awake.''

Trudy walked swiftly, silently to the galley. She poured two mugs of hot coffee. Into one of them she dropped several of the sleeping pills that Vijay had given her when she complained about difficulty getting to sleep.

"They're very mild,'' Vijay had said. "If they don't do the job, let me know and we'll try something else.''

Trudy had tried the pills and they had worked wonderfully. One little pill and she slept dreamlessly. But how many will it take to make Tommy sleep? Three seemed to be the right amount.

Sure enough, half an hour later, Rodriguez's eyes were glazing over.

"Jeez,'' he muttered thickly, "I can't keep my eyes open.''

"That's all right,'' Trudy said gently. "Take a few minutes' rest. I'll be okay by myself.''

"You sure?''

"Certainly. If anything happens, I'll wake you.''

"Not supposed to . . .'' His words faded into a jaw-stretching yawn.

"Sleep, darling,'' Trudy coaxed softly. "Go to sleep.''

Dex Trumball woke from a troubled dream. He was seven or eight years old again and begging his father to come and see him play a baseball game at the school playground. His father turned into a thunderstorm, terrifying bolts of lightning and sheets of cold, wind-whipped rain that swamped the field and flooded the school and carried all the cars in the parking lot down into a huge swirling whirlpool that dragged Dex himself and all his teammates down, down into cold wet darkness.

He sprang up on his bunk, soaked with cold sweat.

Damn! I'm still scared of the old man.

For long moments he just sat on the bunk, listening to his heart thump inside him, waiting for his panting breath to return to normal.

I'm going to end all that, he told himself. I'm going to stand up to him when I get back. I'm going to beat you at your own game, Pop.

Yeah, he told himself. But first you've got to get through the night without pissing yourself.

He tossed aside the sweaty, roiled sheet and got off the bunk. Pulling on the coveralls that lay draped over the desk chair, Dex padded barefoot out toward the nearer of the dome's two lavatories.

It's not going to be easy, Dex told himself. Dad's going to fight me every inch of the way. He's furious over this Navaho business of Jamie's. Must have half the lawyers in North America trying to break their claim.

As he left the lavatory, Dex saw Trudy Hall stepping out of the comm center.

He put on a grin and waved to her. She seemed startled to see him. They both headed for the galley.

"You're not supposed to be wandering around the dome," Hall scolded, in a sibilant whisper.

"Nature calls," Dex whispered back.

"Well, do your business and get back to your quarters, then."

Surprised at the sharpness in her tone, Dex flipped her a mock salute. "I've done my duty, Captain Bligh, and am now returning to the fo'c'sle."

Trudy did not smile at him. Dex thought she looked more angry than amused.

As he headed back toward his cubicle he glanced through the open doorway of the comm center. Rodriguez seemed to be bent over the console, head resting on his folded arms.

Sonofabitch, Dex thought. Tommy's taking a nap. No wonder Trudy's so stoked. She doesn't want anybody to know that her boyfriend's sleeping on the job.

With her pulse thundering in her ears, Trudy watched Dex walk back to his cubicle and go inside. She stood rooted until she saw his accordion door slide shut and heard the faint click of its latch.

Then she took in a deep, racking breath and headed for the garden.

It would have been so simple if they'd kept the garden covered with a plastic dome, as they had originally. Then all she'd have to do would be to puncture the plastic and let the sub-Arctic Martian night air do its deadly work. But she herself had ruined all that when she punctured the garden's protective dome during the dust storm.

Now the garden was shielded by solid walls of greenhouse glass. She couldn't break them down with anything less than one of the tractors, and even then it would take so long that they'd come out and stop her before she got the job finished.

No, Trudy said to herself, fire is the thing to use. Fire purifies. Fire will force them to see how fragile our existence is here, how close to death we are with every breath we take. Fire will bring us home to safety and warmth and nights where you can walk out and look at the stars and see clouds scudding by and not have to worry that your suit might fail or the dust might get you or the heaters break down and freeze you.

Despite Fuchida's warnings and Jamie's cautions it had been ridiculously easy to get enough methane into the garden to do the job. Just tap some from the fuel generator while you're outside and carry it into the garden in your sample cases. It would remain liquified in the heavily insulated cases, not forever but long enough to get the job done. Two trips was enough, Trudy thought. There's enough there now to get a jolly good fire started. A wonderful, cleansing fire.

Trudy walked calmly, purposively to the comm center and called up the plumbing schematic on the computer next to the snoring Rodriguez. She glanced down at him lovingly as she scrolled through the command list. This is for you, darling, so we can get back to Earth alive, safe, and lead normal lives again.

She found the command sequence that shut off the flow of nutrients to all of the rows of trays that held the plants in the garden. Remembering first to shut down the sound system so that no warning beeps would echo through the silent, sleeping dome, she then cut off all nutrient flow to the plants. She wanted the trays dry when she started her fire.

DAWN: SOL 376

TRUDY WATCHED THE LAUNCH OF THE REPLENISHMENT MISSION ON THE comm center's main screen, using the headset earplug so there would be no noise to wake Rodriguez, still sleeping peacefully next to her. The rocket took off from Tarawa in a roar of flame and thick billows of steam clouds.

Then she turned to the screen that displayed the garden monitoring system. Glaring red lights flashed across its top. The nutrient trays were dry, the sensors warned. IMMEDIATE ACTION REQUIRED flashed in garish Day-Glo letters along the screen's bottom line.

Immediate action, Trudy thought. Yes.

She turned on the greenhouse's overhead lights. The plants already looked wilted. But looks can be deceiving, she knew.

She walked swiftly from the comm center, across the dome floor, to the open hatch of the airlock that connected to the garden greenhouse. Instead of a normal airlock, the dome and the greenhouse were connected by a cermet tunnel that arched overhead. The second hatch was closed, but Trudy easily swung it open manually.

Fifty rows of trays stood before her, lit by the overhead strip lamps, fifty rows of green living things that would soon die.

She began toting her sample cases filled with liquified methane to the nearest of the trays. For several days she had wondered how she would ignite the fire. There wasn't a match or a lighter in the whole inventory of stores. Jamie and all the others thought they had been so clever about it, preventing anyone from producing an open flame inside the dome, but she had been cleverer. A simple electrical spark would do the job. All she had to do was to snip one of the wires that ran the length of the trays and then spark the methane.

It wasn't as easy as she had envisioned it, but at last Trudy had the sample case open and the methane inside it boiling into invisible gas. With hands that trembled only slightly, she brought the two severed ends of the hot wire together. Now don't give yourself an electric shock, she warned herself.

The gas whooshed into a sheet of flame, knocking Trudy back painfully against the tray on the other side of the aisle. The heat singed her face, and she raised her arms protectively. Crawling, she made it to the two other sample cases and began to open the nearer of them. The flames seemed to reach across the ceiling of the greenhouse and dive down toward her. She screamed.

The shrill screech of the smoke alarm yanked Jamie out of sleep. "What the hell . . . ?" He was instantly awake, the alarm's scream freezing him momentarily with fear and confusion.

The only other time the smoke alarm had gone off was when Craig had burnt some chili he had brought along in his personal belongings. They had talked about turning off the detector, but Tarawa had insisted on the safety regulations.

Pulling on his coveralls on the move, Jamie half-hopped, half-ran out onto the dome's open area. Dirty gray smoke was pouring out of the greenhouse hatch. He dashed toward the comm center and bumped into Rodriguez, stumbling out.

The shriek of the alarm roused Rodriguez from his tranquilized sleep. Adrenaline surged through his arteries as he saw the monitor screen's flashing red lights.

"Trudy!" he called. "*Trudy!*"

He pushed himself out of the chair, still slow and stumbling, and staggered for the comm center door.

*   *   *

Grasping Rodriguez by both shoulders, Jamie demanded, "What's happened?"

"Dunno," the astronaut answered thickly. "Trudy . . ."

"Jesus Christ!" Dex's voice yelped behind him. "There's a fire in the greenhouse!"

"Trudy's in there," Rodriguez gulped.

Turning toward the smoky hatchway, Jamie saw that all the others were running across the dome to him.

"Stacy, take the comm center," he shouted, starting for the hatch.

Rodriguez seemed to shake himself and head after him, with Dex close behind. Jamie heard Craig yelling, "Close the goddam hatches and turn off the air in there!"

"No!" Rodriguez bellowed. "Trudy's in there!"

Jamie got as far as the hatch, but the heat and the blinding smoke drove him back, coughing and pawing at his eyes. Rodriguez pushed past him and dived through the hatch.

"Wait!" Jamie yelled, but it was too late. Rodriguez disappeared in the smoke.

"Here, use this." Jamie turned and saw it was Vijay, handing him a breathing mask.

"That was quick thinking," he said, slipping the plastic mask over his mouth and nose.

Vijay slapped the small canister of oxygen against his back and Velcroed it in place.

"All set," she shouted over the crackle of the flames. Jamie felt the cold metallic tang of oxygen in his nostrils.

"Close the hatch behind me," he said.

"No!" Vijay blurted.

"Close it!" he commanded.

"I'll do it," Dex said. "Just rap on it when you want me to open it."

Nodding, Jamie ducked through the hatch. Instantly his eyes began to tear. The tunnel was *hot,* it felt as if he was walking into a furnace.

Blinking, cringing from the flames he could see ahead, Jamie edged forward slowly. Then he felt a shower of water pouring over him from behind.

Dex came even with him, grinning through the plastic mask. He carried a dripping packing case in both hands, water sloshing in it.

"Fuchida's idea," he said.

Jamie nodded. "Soak yourself, too."

Through the open hatch Jamie could see that the greenhouse was a mass of flames and sooty smoke. Nothing can live in there, a voice in his mind howled. There's nothing alive in there.

But Jamie pressed on, feeling the heat of the flames on his face, with Dex beside him, step for step.

At the lip of the second hatch he saw two bodies sprawled: Rodriguez atop Trudy, both of them blackened and blistered.

Dex threw the remainder of his water on them, then tossed the packing case to one side and bent down to help Jamie drag the injured pair clear of the hatch.

"Tell 'em to close the inner hatch," Jamie commanded. Dex turned and headed back up the tunnel. Jamie imagined its walls must be red hot.

The hatch swung shut and the glaring, blistering heat shut off with it. Jamie sank to the floor. The tiles felt warm through the thin fabric of his coveralls. The smoke began to clear away. Dex, Fuchida and Craig appeared.

"Are they dead?"

"I don't know," Jamie answered. "I think Tomas is breathing, at least."

Tenderly they picked up the burned bodies and carried them out into the main dome. Vijay began to cut off their coveralls with a tiny pair of surgical scissors as soon as the men lay the bodies on the floor. Rodriguez groaned, his legs moved slightly.

Stacy came out of the comm center, totally calm, under control. "The fire is out. I pumped the air out of the greenhouse as soon as the inner hatch was closed."

"They're both alive," Vijay announced. "Let's get them to the infirmary. No, there's only one bed in there. Put Trudy in the infirmary, she's worse off. Take Tommy to his quarters."

Jamie, Dex and Fuchida carried the astronaut; his coveralls were burned through over his upper torso, the flesh blackened and oozing. Stacy and Craig took Hall while Vijay ran ahead to the infirmary.

After they lay Rodriguez on his cot Jamie's legs felt rubbery. Dex slid an arm around his shoulders and said softly, "Come on, pal, you've earned a shot of orange juice."

Sitting wearily at the galley table, Jamie saw Fuchida standing near, staring at him solemnly.

"You were right, Mitsuo," he said weakly.

"I wish I weren't," the biologist replied, shaking his head.

"Which one of them was it?" Dex wondered, as he handed Jamie a mug of juice and sat down heavily beside him.

Jamie leaned back and stared up into the shadows of the dome. The place smelled of smoke. And sweat. And fear.

"That's not important," he said.

"Isn't it?"

He shrugged. "No, the important thing is that this expedition has been ruined. We can't stay here any longer. Too much damage has been done. We've got to pack up and go back to Earth."

MORNING: SOL 376

JAMIE HAD NEVER SEEN PETE CONNORS LOOK SO GRAVE. "IT'S A TOTAL mess, all right," the mission controller was saying. "You guys are lucky to be alive. They're calling a special meeting of the ICU committee. I'm sure they'll want to call this an accident and cook up a cover story. Nobody wants to tell the public that one of your people was a psycho."

Jamie nodded as he watched the screen. Outside the comm center the others were going through the motions of breakfast.

"Talk about timing," Connors went on. "The resupply mission went through their transfer orbit insertion burn just eleven minutes before your message came through. They're on their way to Mars. Be there on sol five twenty-two, five months from now. They think they're gonna have a few weeks with you guys to get set up, get oriented. Now they'll have to land and work on their own."

Connors talked on and on, more to have something to say, to feel that he was doing something, than for any other reason, Jamie thought. This disaster's hit him almost as hard as it's hit us.

"You'll have to figure out which one of them did it, which one's the wacko. We'll keep it quiet, don't worry about that. Nobody here wants to admit that one of our own people sabotaged the expedition. But we'll have to know, have to check into the psych profile and background. For future reference, to make certain that type doesn't get included in future missions."

Future missions? Jamie thought. Will there be future missions? They won't be able to keep this out of the news media. Sooner or later somebody will leak the story. He could picture the headlines: Scientist goes crazy on Mars, tries to wipe out expedition.

"For what it's worth," Connors continued, "I think it was Hall. I can't believe an astronaut, a flier, would crack up like that. It wasn't Rodriguez; I'd bet money on it."

Jamie nodded silent agreement.

After Connors signed off, Jamie got up and walked slowly to the greenhouse hatch. If anyone noticed that he had left the comm center unattended, no one said a word.

He pushed the inner hatch open and stepped into the greenhouse. Nothing had changed. The plants were all gone, their trays nothing but twisted, buckled metal frames. The glass bricks of the ceiling and one wall were charred black, the floor littered with burned debris. It smelled acrid, faintly musty, an odor Jamie had not smelled since he'd been a boy, hiding in the unused fireplace of his parents' house. Nothing was wet. Nothing dripped. There was no sound at all inside the greenhouse, it was as silent as death. A mess. A terrible wasteful mess.

When he finally came out of the greenhouse and made his dismal way to the galley, the three other men were still sitting glumly at the table. Jamie still smelled a faint burnt odor in the air. Imagination, he told himself. Maybe not.

"Stacy's in the infirmary, helping Vijay change Trudy's dressings," Dex said, without being asked.

"How're they doing?" Jamie asked.

Craig waggled a hand in the air. "Trudy's got second-degree burns over the upper half of her body. She's a mess."

"Her face, too?"

"Yep."

"And Tomas?"

"Hands and arms, mostly. Shoulders. Looks like he was trying to drag Trudy out of there when the smoke got him."

"Serves him right for sleeping on the job," Dex muttered.

"Tomas? Sleeping?"

"He was snoozing at the console around three this morning," Dex said angrily. "I saw him."

"Not him," Fuchida said, shaking his head.

"I saw him."

"Then she must have drugged him," the biologist insisted. "I know Tom. He would not sleep on duty."

"Then it was Trudy who set the fire?" Jamie asked rhetorically.

"And punctured the garden dome during the storm," Fuchida said firmly. "And the other 'accidents,' too."

Jamie started to go to the food locker for some breakfast, but realized that he had no appetite.

Turning back to the others, he said, "Come on, let's get the video cameras and document the damage. Tarawa's going to need the imagery."

Craig and Fuchida got up from the table and headed off. Dex rose to his feet, too, but remained as the other two left.

"What is it, Dex?" Jamie asked.

"We're packing it in?"

Jamie nodded. "As soon as we do a damage assessment, we'll go back to Dome One and take off for Earth."

"Heading home, with our tails between our legs."

"Not much else we can do," Jamie said. Two people badly injured, one of them a psycho. This expedition is a bust."

Dex looked as grim as Connors had. Grimmer.

"The thing is," he said slowly, "if we leave, that tears up the Navaho claim to this territory."

A flash of fear raced along Jamie's nerves. "What do you mean?"

Very gently, like a doctor breaking the news of a loved one's death, Dex said, "You've got to be on the ground to maintain a legal claim to the utilization rights. Once we leave, anybody can claim this territory."

Jamie felt his insides go hollow. "But we're being forced to leave. An accident—"

"Cuts no ice," Dex said. "I've studied the law, the treaties and all the international agreements. If you abandon this territory, your legal claim goes down the chute."

Jamie sank down onto the nearest chair.

"I'm sorry," Dex said softly.

"But your father won't be," Jamie muttered.

"No, dammit. He'll be overjoyed."

Trudy Hall's hands, arms, face, her entire upper body was wrapped in spray-on antiseptic bandaging. Her eyes were covered, a breathing tube was inserted into her nostrils. There was a small slit where her mouth should be. What was left of her hair looked like the singed pinfeathers of a badly seared chicken.

The medical monitors on one side of the cramped infirmary cubicle were all humming peacefully, however. Blood pressure, heart rate, and most of the other indicators were steady. Her breathing was ragged, but that was to be expected from the fire-heated air she had inhaled.

"Has she regained consciousness at all?" Jamie asked, in a whisper.

Vijay stood on the other side of the bed, replacing a bag of saline solution for the IV drip.

"Only briefly," she answered, her voice somewhat louder than his. "I've been sedating her rather heavily, you know. She'd be in considerable pain otherwise."

"I need to talk to her," he said.

"Not for a while, mate."

"And Tomas?"

"He's in much better shape," Vijay said, allowing herself a tiny smile. "You can talk to him all you want."

Rodriguez lay in his bunk on his stomach, head and shoulders propped up by a small mountain of cushions. Jamie recognized them: they were mattresses from one of the rovers, rolled tightly and strapped with duct tape.

"I just couldn't keep my eyes open," he was telling Jamie, his face showing guilt and puzzlement. "Never happened to me before, I just couldn't keep my eyes open."

"Trudy put sleeping pills in your coffee," Jamie said. He had pulled the cubicle's desk chair up to the edge of the bunk. "Vijay told me she'd been taking pills—"

"I never saw her take any," Rodriguez blurted.

Jamie shrugged. "She must've been saving them to use on you."

"I still can't believe that she'd do that."

"She's emotionally sick," Jamie said. "She must be."

"Yeah, guess so."

"The smoke alarm woke you up?"

Rodriguez nodded, winced. His back must be painful, Jamie realized.

"Yeah. Y'know, I felt like I'd been drugged. Couldn't move fast at first, everything seemed slow, dopey."

"Trudy wasn't in the comm center?"

"No. I saw the smoke coming from the greenhouse hatch. She wasn't anywhere in sight, so I went in to see if she'd been caught inside the greenhouse. And there she was."

There she was, Jamie thought. A poor scared little sparrow who went over the edge. Why? What happened in her mind to make her snap like this?

Another voice in his head sneered, What difference does it make? She's destroyed this expedition and turned Mars over to Trumball and his world-wreckers.

NIGHT: SOL 388

THEY RETURNED TO DOME ONE, DISPIRITED, WEARY, A SAD PROCESSION OF beaten men and women. Hall had to be carried in; Rodriguez could walk shakily, Jamie and Dex supporting him.

After they got the L/AV's fuel cells producing electricity for the dome, Craig and Dezhurova went out to the fuel generator to connect it to the fuel cells.

Fuchida shook his head as he stood in the middle of the dome. "Mars has defeated us," he said quietly.

Jamie suppressed an urge to punch him. "Mars didn't do this," he snapped. "We've defeated ourselves."

Hours later, Jamie was helping Vijay check out the medical stores inventory, comparing what was actually on the shelves of the infirmary against the computer records. The replenishment mission was bringing a fresh cargo of medical supplies, but they had to make certain the computer inventory was correct before they left.

"Remember our first night here?" Jamie asked. "The party?"

"I remember you hiding in your quarters while the rest of us partied," Vijay said.

"I remember other nights, too," Jamie said. He was sitting at her tiny desk, the inventory list on the computer screen in front of him.

She turned from the open cabinet and looked at him. "So do I," she said, her voice low.

"They were good."

Vijay nodded, then turned back to her work.

Jamie found that he couldn't focus his attention on the inventory list. His mind was filled with thoughts of Trumball and the Navaho Nation and how this expedition had been such a disaster even though they had found the Martian building and Mars must be dotted with similar buildings, there must be the remains of cities scattered across the planet, there couldn't be just this one building left on a whole world that was populated by intelligent beings, and how much he wanted Vijay, standing close enough for him to reach out and take in his arms yet miles away, light-years away because he had pushed her out of his life and had no right, no hope, not even a whisper of a chance to bring her back to him.

He heard himself tell her, "I'm not leaving." His voice sounded so damned controlled, not a trace of emotion showing.

Vijay closed the cabinet. When she turned, her luminous midnight eyes were sorrowful. "I know."

That jolted him. "How could you know? I didn't know myself until just now."

She made a rueful smile. "I'm the psychologist, remember? And I know you. As soon as Dex told you that if we all left it would break the Navaho claim, I knew you'd stay."

"You knew it before I did, then."

"No," Vijay said, shaking her head. "You knew it then, too, but you had to go through all the logical steps first. You had to turn it over in your mind and convince yourself you could last here four months or more by yourself."

Reluctantly he nodded agreement. "I guess you're right."

"So you've concluded that you can make it, then?"

"I think so. I don't see why not."

"By yourself?"

He wanted to say, *Not if you'll stay with me,* but knew that he couldn't ask her that. It was one thing to risk his own neck alone on Mars for more than four months, he couldn't ask her to share that risk with him. It meant too much, there were too many complications.

So he merely nodded tightly and said, "By myself, yes."

"Just you and Mars, eh?"

He shrugged. "It shouldn't be that much of a sweat. The garden here is okay. All the equipment is functioning. I won't starve and I won't run out of air."

"But you'll want to run down to the building and poke around some more, won't you?"

"No," Jamie said firmly. "I'm going to stay right here and do some of the geological work we should've done months ago." Then he added, "And I'll try making a few solar cells out of in situ materials. It'd be a big help if we could generate enough electricity out of sunlight to run the entire dome."

"Alone," she repeated.

He hesitated for the barest fraction of a moment, then said, "Alone."

Her face a blank mask, Vijay put her hand out to Jamie and said, "Well, come on then, you'd better tell the others."

The others were gathering in the galley for their last dinner on Mars, all except Trudy, who was still confined to her bunk. The burns on her face would require plastic surgery, and despite all of Rodriguez's assurances that it would all turn out fine, she had sunk into a pit of depression.

Rodriguez tried hard to cheer her, making a show of each time he could get rid of a set of bandages. Stacy, Jamie and even Fuchida had spent hours with Trudy, assuring her that there would be no publicity about her emotional breakdown, no accusations, no blame. Their assurances seemed only to deepen the biologist's depression.

Vijay slapped together a dinner tray for Trudy as the others milled about, making their selections without worrying about the planned menus the nutritionists had worked out for them.

"I'll be happy to see a real steak again," Fuchida said, quite seriously.

"With real beer," Rodriguez quipped.

Without a word to any of them, Vijay started off toward Trudy's quarters with the tray. Behind her, she heard Jamie announce:

"I'm not leaving with you. I'm going to stay here."

She slid Trudy's door open, stepped through, and slammed it shut again.

Trudy was sitting up now, her back healed enough for her to rest it against a water-filled plastic cushion. It had struck Vijay, when she pulled the device out of the medical stores, that they might have adapted it to make waterbeds for themselves. Fine time to think of that, she had huffed at herself.

"How're you feeling?" Vijay asked brightly.

"We're leaving tomorrow?" Trudy asked. The bandages were off her face; her skin was raw and pink. It would be scarred and brittle by the time they reached Earth. She had no eyebrows, no eyelashes. She was lucky that she could still see, Vijay thought, then wondered how lucky it was to be able to look into a mirror when your face is so horribly burned.

"Yes," Vijay replied, keeping her voice light, cheerful. "Tomorrow."

Trudy looked down at the tray Vijay placed on her lap. At last she murmured, "I've made an awful mess of everything, haven't I?"

Vijay answered softly, "I suppose one could say that."

"I could have killed Tommy. I never thought that I'd be placing him in danger."

Vijay wanted to say that she'd placed them all in danger, but she held her tongue. Trudy Hall was going to be a wonderful subject for a psychology research paper, she thought. I'll have five months on the return trip to study her, probe her motivations . . .

"I love him," Trudy said, tears in her eyes. "I wanted to bring him back to Earth where he'd be safe, where we'd all be safe."

"I understand."

Trudy looked up at her angrily. "Do you? How could you? How could you know what it's like to love a man so much you'd be willing to die for him?"

Startled, Vijay had no reply.

"Oh, I'm sorry," Trudy burst. "I'm so, so sorry. I've made such a botch of everything. Tommy won't even want to look at me when we get back home. I love him so much and he won't even want to look at me."

Suddenly Vijay wanted to cry.

"You can't stay here alone," Dezhurova said flatly when Jamie made his announcement to the five of them gathered at the galley table.

"Sure I can," Jamie said, trying to make it sound simple, commonplace.

"Won't be easy," Craig said, "even if you just stay inside here and watch TV for four months."

"There's plenty of work for me to do," Jamie said. "Just sorting out the data you guys amassed during your excursion out to Ares Vallis could keep me busy for four months and more."

"And you're going to try building solar cells?" Dex asked.

"Out of the elements in the ground, yes."

"One of us should remain with you," said Fuchida.

"No," Jamie said. "That's not necessary. I couldn't ask any of you to make that sacrifice. You're going home! I'll be okay here."

"Mitsuo's right," Rodriguez said. "Somebody ought to stay behind with you."

"It's not necessary," Jamie repeated.

"You are not staying for science," Stacy said, almost as an accusation.

"No," Jamie admitted. "I'm not."

Dex looked intrigued, delighted. "You're staying so you can maintain the Navaho claim."

"Right," said Jamie.

"That's what I thought," said Dex.

"It's what I've got to do," Jamie said.

"Uh-huh. Well, I've got a few things to do, too."

"Such as?"

"Now here's my plan," Dex said, with his old cocky grin. "As soon as I get back to Earth I'm going to start a foundation, a not-for-profit organization specifically devoted to the exploration of Mars. Call it the Mars Research Foundation, I guess."

Jamie blinked at him.

"That way we'll be able to raise money all the time, steadily. We won't have to go around with our hat in our hand for each individual expedition. We'll put the exploration of Mars on a solid financial foundation. Get people to contribute all the time, like they buy stocks or bonds."

"But they won't make a profit from it," Fuchida said.

Dex's eyes danced. "Yeah, but they'll be able to deduct their contributions from their taxes. It'll make a neat little tax shelter for them."

Jamie broke into a broad grin. "You've been thinking about this for a long time, haven't you?"

Grinning back at him, Dex said, "About as long as you've been thinking about staying here by yourself."

"Your foundation will work with the Navaho Nation?"

"You betcha. Maybe we'll headquarter it out in Arizona or New Mexico, on the Navaho reservation."

Jamie nodded happily. The thought of Dex on the reservation pleased him.

"Okay, pal," Dex said, sticking out his hand, "you hold the fort here and I'll go out and see the Navaho president as soon as we land."

"Not your father?" Jamie asked, grasping Dex's hand in his own.

Dex laughed. "Yeah, okay, I suppose it'd be better if I face him sooner instead of later."

As they stood facing one another with their hands firmly clasped, Jamie looked into the younger man's eyes. There was no trace of fear there, or hostility. Dex has grown up here on Mars. He's a full-grown man now instead of a spoiled kid.

Suddenly, impulsively, Dex pulled Jamie to him and wrapped his free hand around his shoulders. Jamie did the same, pounding Dex's back as if he were the younger brother he never had.

"Don't worry about it," Dex said, almost in a whisper. "I'll handle my dad and work with your Navaho guys. You're not going to lose Mars."

As they pulled away from their embrace, Dezhurova shook her head stubbornly. "It is dangerous for one man to be here alone. If some emergency comes up—"

"He won't be alone."

Jamie turned to see Vijay striding determinedly toward the galley table.

"I'm staying, too," she said.

"But you can't!" Jamie blurted.

Very sweetly, she replied, "I haven't been asked, that's true. But I'm staying with you, mate."

"What about Trudy? She needs—"

Vijay walked toward him as she answered, "Stacy and Tommy have enough paramedical training to take care of her on the trip back. She's recuperating okay, no worries. If something pops up, they'll be able to get advice from Earth, same as I would."

"You *want* to stay?" Jamie asked, afraid this was all a dream, a hallucination.

She was standing less than an arm's length away from him. Looking squarely into his eyes, she said, "Yes, I want to."

Every other thought flew from Jamie's consciousness. He wrapped his arms around her and kissed her soundly. She did likewise as the others sat there, thunderstruck, until someone let out a low, long appreciative whistle.

NOON: SOL 389

"FIVE SECONDS," DEZHUROVA'S VOICE CRACKLED TENSELY IN JAMIE'S HELmet earphones. "Four . . ."

He and Vijay were standing just outside the dome, gloved hands clasped together, their eyes on the L/AV sitting nearly a full kilometer away.

". . . two . . . one . . ." The top half of the stubby spacecraft leaped up in a sudden crack of thunder that blasted dust and pebbles across the barren red ground. Despite himself, Jamie flinched. He craned his neck as the ascent vehicle rose higher and higher into the cloudless pink sky, the roar of its rocket engines dwindling into a thin, muted rumble and then fading altogether.

"There they go," said Vijay. She sounded almost triumphant.

Jamie followed the bright speck until the top edge of his visor cut off his view. Stacy, Dex and the others were on their way back to Earth, with the Pathfinder hardware and Trudy Hall's problems.

He turned to face Vijay. Before he could say anything, her voice sounded buoyantly in his earphones. "Well, it's just you and me, now, mate."

He felt less than cheerful. I'm responsible for her life now. She trusts me and I've got to live up to her trust.

"We're Martians now, aren't we?" Vijay asked.

"Not yet," he replied. "We're still guests, visitors. We still have to live inside these suits. We still have to respect Mars for what it is."

"Will it always be like this?"

"I don't know," Jamie answered. "Always is a long time. Maybe someday, when we're smarter . . . much wiser than we are now. Maybe our grandchildren will be able to live on Mars, with Mars. Or their grandchildren. I don't know."

As they started back for the dome's airlock, Vijay wondered, "Will we be able to protect Mars the way you want to? I mean, keep people like Dex's father from spoiling it all?"

Even though he knew better, Jamie tried to shrug inside the hard suit. "All we can do is try, Vijay. The ICU is arguing against the Navaho claim, but it looks as if the Astronautical Authority is going to recognize it as legal and binding."

He heard her laughing. "The Navaho reservation is now bigger than the States, isn't it?"

"If you take in all of Mars, yes. But this isn't part of the reservation, it's—"

"Don't take it so seriously!"

"But it is serious," he said. "I'm hoping that this will motivate Navaho kids to get involved in Mars, to study science and astronautics, to—"

"To become Martians?"

He took a breath. "Yeah, maybe. Eventually. Someday."

They stopped at the airlock hatch and, without a word between them, both turned to look over the red, rock-strewn landscape.

"If only we could have met them, talked to them . . ."

"The Martians?"

"Yes. We can't even read the writings they left."

"They've given us their message, Vijay. The important message. They existed. There were intelligent beings on this world. There must be others out there, among the stars. We're not alone."

She sighed heavily. "But it's just you and me here on Mars for the next four months."

"Yes."

"We've got a whole world to ourselves."

"I love it here," Jamie said.

"It's peaceful," she replied. "I'll give you that."

"Dex is going to have his hands full when he gets back. His father's going to fight him every inch of the way."

"Oh, I don't know," Vijay said confidently. "Dex's dad won't cause that much trouble. He'll win the old man over."

"Do you think so?"

"He can charm a snake out of a bush when he wants to."

Jamie said nothing.

"Even if he doesn't," Vijay went on, "Dex'll raise enough money for a fresh expedition with his foundation."

"It won't be profitable," Jamie said.

"You think not? Dex has ideas about virtual reality tours of Mars, y'know. See, feel, hear . . . the complete experience of being on Mars without the expense or inconvenience of leaving home. And selling Mars rocks, that sort of thing."

Despite himself, Jamie gritted his teeth.

"He'll make a profit, one way or the other, don't you worry."

"And pump it into further exploration."

"You'll see."

The sun was high overhead. The soft winds of Mars murmured across the empty, rolling plain. Jamie saw the rocks and the worn rims of ancient craters and the dunes off in the distance, spaced as precisely as soldiers on parade. He looked down for the footprints of the long-extinct Martians and saw instead their own boot prints in the red dust and the cleat tracks of their tractors and rovers.

He looked out toward the horizon again and envisioned his grandfather Al out there, smiling at them. This is where our path has led, Grandfather, Jamie said silently. We're home now.

"Do you love me?" Vijay asked.

A day earlier the question would have startled Jamie. But now he knew. Now there was no doubt in his mind, no conflict.

"Yes," he said, unequivocally. "I love you, Vijay."

Then she asked, "Do you love me more than Mars?"

He heard the smile in her voice. He hesitated, then answered, "That's a completely different thing."

Vijay laughed delightedly. "Good! I wouldn't have believed you if you'd said yes."

She grasped his gloved hand in hers and they turned back to the airlock hatch, ready to begin their first night alone on the planet Mars.

AUTHOR'S AFTERWORD

The story you have read is fiction, based as solidly as possible on the known facts about conditions on Mars. I have extrapolated from those facts, of course; that is the prerogative—and responsibility—of the novelist.

At this moment, no one knows if life once existed on Mars, or if life exists there now. No one knows, and we will not find out for certain until we explore our red-robed neighboring world much more thoroughly.

The idea that Mars once harbored an intelligent civilization may strike the reader as a fanciful speculation. Yet as of this writing, it is a speculation that cannot be disproved.

Not until we travel to Mars to search out its marvels for ourselves will we know for certain. Probably intelligent Martians never existed. Possibly there has never been life of any kind on the red planet. But we will find surprises on Mars, of that you can be sure. An entire world is there to be explored. A new age of discovery is soon to begin.

Mars waits for us.

Ben Bova
Naples, Florida
1998